Merry Christmas Don Camillo

Giovannino Guareschi, known as Giovanni to his millions of English-speaking readers, was born in Italy's Valley of the Po on the 1st of May, 1908. He found his vocation after a package containing cartoons, jokes, prose and proposals was sent to the publisher Angelo Rizzoli, who was planning a new satirical magazine, to be called *Bertoldo*.

For two years during the war, he was incarcerated in one prison-of-war camp after another in Poland and Germany, where he was reduced to a state of despair. Out of it he brought himself to the polemic that would underwrite all his work.

Looking back, he wrote: 'It is not enough to say: "Red is wrong, yellow is wrong, black is wrong." You need a beautiful colour, a colour to harmonise with the world. And you have to be able to say, "*We need this colour*".'

Now, in *Merry Christmas Don Camillo,* his Christmas stories and others written in his quest for harmony in the world appear alongside his wartime experiences, the palette on which he mixed that 'beautiful colour'.

Titles in the Series So Far
An extensive biography of the author is available at the end of the first book in the series.

The Little World of Don Camillo
Book 1, in which Guareschi introduces readers to the Little World of the village priest, Don Camillo, and his adversary, Peppone, the communist mayor – conflict time and again resolved by the gentle humour and shrewd counsel of *Il Cristo* from his place above the altar in the village church. E-book: ASIN: B00HAMIVUC. Paperback ISBN: 9781900064071. Audiobook: ASIN: B07CZPFQDT.

Don Camillo and His Flock
Book 2, in which the people of the Little World again show their passion for politics, culminating in the battling priest's exile to the mountains. E-book: ASIN: B013TFT1YS. Paperback ISBN: 9781900064187.

Don Camillo and Peppone
Book 3, in which politics and prejudice remain to the fore, but the wit and wisdom of *Il Cristo* help bring Don Camillo home. E-book: ASIN: B01CIWE1T8. Paperback ISBN 9781900064262.

Comrade Don Camillo
In Book 4, set against the background of the Cold War, Don Camillo steals a march on Peppone over a matter of conscience and finds himself transported incognito to Khrushchev's Russia. E-book: ASIN: B0722G6GY4. Paperback ISBN 9781900064330.

Don Camillo and Company
Book 5: a unique treasure trove of Guareschi's enchanting, bittersweet stories made available in English for the first time in 2018. E-book: ASIN: B07DKBHFJH. Paperback ISBN 9781900064408.

Don Camillo's Dilemma
Book 6: the local elections are upon us and the village priest discovers that the final straw can break even a Camillo's back. E-book: ASIN: B08KJ6GT7W. Paperback ISBN 9781900064477.

Don Camillo Takes the Devil by the Tail
Book 7. As everyone knows, taking a serpent by the tail is not a good idea, but in the Little World of Don Camillo, hilarious and unearthly things can happen to draw the poison from his bite. E-book: ASIN: B089KLX8KK. Paperback ISBN 9781900064514.

Don Camillo and Don Chichi
Book 8, in which the ageing Don Camillo must come to terms with huge changes in the Little World. E-book: ISBN: 9781900064552. Paperback ISBN 9781900064569.

MERRY CHRISTMAS DON CAMILLO

GIOVANNI GUARESCHI

Edited by
Piers Dudgeon

PILOT PRODUCTIONS

Published by Pilot Productions in 2022
Grove Farm Sawdon, North Yorkshire YO13 9DY

Copyright © Giovanni Guareschi 2022

All illustrations by Giovanni Guareschi unless otherwise stated.

Words by Piers Dudgeon
Copyright © Pilot Promotions 2022

Translation of *La Favola di Natale, 1944*
by Adam Elgar

The right of Giovannino Guareschi to be identified
as the Author of *Merry Christmas Don Camillo*
has been asserted by him in accordance with the
Copyright, Designs and Patents Act 1988.

A catalogue record for this book is available
from the British Library

Paperback ISBN 978-1-900064-59-0

Cover design by BerniStevensdesign.com

E-book production by epubknowhow.co.uk

Typeset in Galliard by Mark Heslington Ltd,
Scarborough, North Yorkshire YO11 3PU

Printed and bound in Great Britain by
Clays Ltd, Elcograf S.p.A.

Contents

Editor's Preface	7
Pre-war	9
New Life	26
War	36
Christmas 1943	49
My Thoughts Turn Inwards	99
Christmas 1944	127
1945 Dreaming True	160
Dopoguerra	175
Christmas 1946: The Birth of Don Camillo	191
Christmas 1947	221
Christmas 1948	230
Christmas 1950	244
Christmas 1952	251
Christmas 1961	263
Piccolo mondo; Piccolo è bello	270

Editor's Preface

Giovannino Olivero Giuseppe Guareschi, known as Giovanni to his legions of English-speaking readers, was born on May Day 1908 at Fontanelle di Roccabianca, a village in the Emilia-Romagna, the Little World of his fictional characters, Don Camillo and Peppone: a microcosm where matters of local interest to a few prove unfailingly to address matters of universal significance to us all.

Giovanni's mother, Lina Maghenzani (known as Mrs Flaminia in his autobiographical stories), was the local primary school teacher; his father, Primo Augusto Teodosio Guareschi (known as Mr Luigi) was the owner of a small shop that sold and repaired bicycles, the principal mode of transport through the country lanes of this flat-bottomed flood-plain, set idyllically between the Apennine mountains to the south and the River Po and further mountains to the north.

In 1914 the family left Fontanelle for the university city of Parma, seventeen or so miles away. Giovanni's mother taught at a school in Marore, a small village a commutable distance from the city, his father became a trader.

In Parma, Giovanni attended the Jacopo Sanvitale primary school (1914–1918), during which time, with his father away in the First War and his mother working in Marore, he was largely looked after by his Grandmamma Giuseppina. In 1921 the family moved from Parma to the school building at Marore and Giovanni joined them at weekends and school holidays.

Later he studied at the Maria Luigia high school and the Regio Ginnasio Romagnosi, where his classical education was masterminded by the Greek and Latin teacher, Ferdinando Bernini, translator of Fra Salimbene de Adam's *Chronicles* and a connoisseur of European humour.

A more immediate influence at this time was Cesare Zavattini, his tutor. Zavattini was only six years older than Giovanni and the regular target of pranks by Giovanni and his mates, who on one legendary occasion pinned his slippers to the floor in the expectation that their tutor would swing his legs out of bed, struggle into them and fall flat on his face on the floor. Master and boy were, however, a natural fit. Both came from the Emilia-Romagna and their fathers were socialists and by one account 'mad as poets'. Giovanni soon began to appreciate that his teacher might direct his particular non-academic talents and energies. A handwritten student newspaper posted on the school bulletin board (and sometimes circulated below desk) and musical and comedy theatre were promising forums. Under Zavattini's influence, even before Giovanni left to take up a place at University he was illustrating posters and contributing amusing sketches, poems and cartoons to a number of publications. It was indeed already clear that this kind of work would soon overtake any academic pretensions, although, quite clearly, he had a sound classical education.

The love of his life, Ennia Pallini, was born in 1906. Giovanni's feelings for her shine through their warmly humorous interplay in his first autobiographical story collection, *La scoperta di Milano* (literally, *The Discovery of Milan*), initially published episodically, then in volume form in 1941. But biographers would be advised to exercise caution in believing everything he writes about Ennia as Margherita (her name in the stories), or indeed all that he writes about himself at this stage in his life. Here, besides Ennia and others, we meet Giovanni's parents, Mr Luigi and Mrs Flaminia, and ... Camillo.

Pre-war

That morning, as it happened, I wanted to walk the 6,000 metres that separate our house from the high school building. Along the way I intended to stop at least a hundred times: gaze at the grass, the ripe wheat, throw some good stones at the insulators on the telephone lines. I am twenty-four tomorrow and I too have the right to live my own life.

Mr Luigi does not understand the fundamental joy of such things: age, business and ill-advised reading have inured him to psychology. Moreover, he has not the slightest trust in his son and this pains me, especially in respect of 'the lock'.

Every morning that is not a holiday, Mr Luigi is ready at eight forty in front of the garden gate and, with a certain whistle of his, calls me to assemble.

It is time to leave for school: I get on my bicycle in front of Mr Luigi. Mr Luigi checks that everything is in order, he checks the tyre pressure, the efficiency of the brakes and the bell, then clicks the lock. And I feel deeply sad. Not because the padlock is large, indeed it is of a pleasing size and not bulky, but because the padlock, when it clicks, fixes the end rings of a steel chain which – passing between the springs of the cycle seat at its lowest position – finds its way to its highest position into a buttonhole made for purpose in the belt of my trousers.

Which means that I am so firmly attached to my velocipede that I can never get away from it. True, I could easily tear the fabric of the buttonhole and free myself: but how to justify the damage at the end of the day? I could jump off my bike, yes, but only in the event of real danger, whereupon I must submit a report with eyewitnesses or some visible damage to my person.

So, Mr Luigi chains me to the bicycle and I take my leave: the time allotted allows me to get to school by pedalling with 'prudent' speed: in case of rain it is increased appropriately. In case of favourable wind, decreased.

So, to get to school on time there can be no stopping, even for a moment. Arriving in front of the high school building, the janitor comes into the picture in possession of a second key to disengage me from the bicycle and promptly to coerce me into the classroom.

Mr Luigi does not trust his son: this sad story of the lock is clear proof of this. And it has been my story for a whole school year now: because Mr Luigi has decided that it is time for me to leave this high school to which I am so attached. According to Mr Luigi, nine years are more than enough to complete three high school years successfully.

Mr Luigi has had some unpleasant things to say on the subject: he even threatened to put me in boarding school if I do not pass the classical high school diploma this year. Okay, I'll take it, but how am I going to tell Margherita?

Margherita will say that I'm doing this because I don't love her anymore, because I'm tired of her, because I want to leave her. I swore to her that I would stay in high school for her all her life: but Mr Luigi doesn't want me to repeat the same class more than three times.

So, anyway, that morning I arrived at school late and without the lock.

Very late because everyone was already leaving school for their midday meal.

Margherita saw me immediately and looked at me very worried.

*

We met in the park that afternoon.

Margherita speaks little: Margherita is a woman of action. She is the woman that Destiny has scattered on my path: she is slender, she has very large black eyes and even blacker hair. She is twenty-four, like me: we were both born in May, the same day. And that day, I believe, the good Lord sent two souls to earth made with the same puff of wind.

We have loved each other for nine years. We met on November 12, 1920: I was fifteen, I had just entered the first class of high school and I had thrown myself on Tacitus and the logarithms with such enthusiasm that Mr Luigi had exclaimed: 'Giovanni, don't overdo it.'

November 12, 1920: I will always remember it. I was the quietest student in the class, the most studious, the most disciplined: who was it then who, at 10:25 am on November 12, 1920, suggested that I throw the first volume of *Georges* towards the south-east corner of the classroom? Confused reminiscences endeavour to explain to me that the matter was caused by Giancarlo who, stationed in the south-east corner, had been bombarding me for half an hour with some chewed paper pallets conveniently dipped in ink. But I don't believe it: Destiny is involved here, the same Destiny that wanted me to come to school this morning on foot and without a lock.

I was asked by the Latin teacher to feel free to get away as often as possible from the school building. The headmaster was of the same opinion and I immediately conformed to their wishes.

I remember: it was a calm and bright November day and the park's leaves were golden; all the benches were empty: only one was occupied – by a girl with black hair.

Destiny wanted me to sit right on the bench occupied by the girl with black hair. The girl was reading a newspaper. I, taking my place a few inches from her, had a Tacitus and a Greek Syntax.

I had read in novels and short stories that it is best, in the exchange of ideas between a man and a woman, to use the second person singular to address your interlocutor. And that is what I did:

'You high school too?'

The girl looked up from her newspaper (eyes to move a university student!).

'Yes, me too,' she confirmed. 'First year high school, section B.'

'Suspended too?'

'Yes, me too. Mathematics: inkwell.'

'I, Latin: vocab,' I said.

We were silent for a long time, then I blushed and informed her that my name was Giovannino.

'Margherita,' replied the dark girl. 'Three days suspension.'

'Three days too,' I murmured.

Then we fell silent because, with all this talk, it was time to go home.

At the park gate we parted:

'Good day.'

'Good day.'

The next morning I returned to the park to watch autumn until midday. At ten, Margherita appeared.

And the next day it was like that too. Always it was like this. We'd be thirty years old by two: in the evening we quickly plotted leaving school:

'Tomorrow?'

'Day after tomorrow.'

And we got suspended. Then we were in the park or on the ramparts and talked about small, innocent things; very often we were silent, sitting a metre from each other, but I felt my heart full of sweetness and I thought of Dido, and the great loves of history.

At the end of the year we both failed.

'Maybe next year they'll put us in the same section,' said Margherita and in my heart I felt happy.

The following year, however, I was moved to section B and Margherita to section A, and, this time by mutual agreement, we failed again.

When I entered the first year of high school for the third time, my heart was bursting with joy: Margherita was in the same section as me!

We decided to go for further promotion: we shouldn't raise people's attention by insisting too much on being in the same class. By the time we reached the second year, Margherita and I were eighteen and one day, in the park, I solemnly swore to her that I would stay all my life in high school, just to have her close to me every day.

Margherita was, as usual, of few words:

'Me too, I swear it.'

We were failed that year again, but entering the second high school for the second time we became aware that we were beginning to raise suspicion in the minds of the evil ones. We realised that for a while at least we needed to separate, at least in the eyes of the world. One of us had to be promoted. I courageously offered myself.

'No,' replied Margherita. 'Love must be a sacrifice especially for women: *I'll* pass.'

I stayed in the second year for the third time, and Margherita moved up to the third year. Then, the following year, Margherita was failed and I passed into the third year. We then both failed, and also failed the following year: we were on top of the world.

The important thing was to stay together, see each other every day, get suspended every week, go to the park to watch spring, autumn and winter. We thought of the holidays with terror.

But then everything had to end: Mr Luigi got it stuck in his mind that I had a duty to graduate and for a year he chained me to my bicycle, as I have described, so that I would not miss any lessons.

How could I tell all this to Margherita?

*

In the afternoon we met in the park. We sat on the bench: Margherita took her box with the needles, thimble, scissors and thread from her purse. How many times, in these eight months, has Margherita patiently remade the buttonhole of my belt, and so well that Mr Luigi never noticed anything?

Margherita has the needle inserted.

'No,' I said to her, 'you don't need to. Fortunately, my bicycle was stolen. But today I have to speak to you seriously.'

Margherita carefully put everything in her purse.

'Margherita,' I stammered, 'only today can I find the courage to tell you how much this has torn at my heart these past eight months.

This year I must pass! My father demands it: he chains me to my bicycle every morning so that I can go to school regularly, and you know how many times I have broken the buttonhole to go with you. Margherita, try to understand me.'

Margherita looked at me with her big deep eyes.

'Do you love another woman?' she asked me in a firm, calm, serene voice.

'No, Margherita!'

'I believe you,' said Margherita. 'I knew that such a beautiful thing could not last forever. It's life, Giovannino. I'll pass too. Will you go to University?'

'No, I'll get work. Mr Luigi spoke to me severely in this regard. He insists that if, after high school, I want to eat on a regular basis, I will have to work. And he seemed to me to be in good faith.'

Margherita approved with a nod of her head.

'My father, on the other hand, says that after high school I will have to think of getting a husband,' she said.

I felt my heart fail:

'And what are you going to do?' I asked, turning pale.

'I will think of getting a husband. There is nothing wrong with thinking about a husband. I thought for ten years that a woman's life consisted of high school. Now I will think that a woman's life consists of marriage. In marriage with you,' she added seeing that I suddenly sat on the bench and looked at her in a singular way.

'But I... I...' I stammered between joy and terror.

'Don't worry,' Margherita reassured me 'we'll repeat the year: five, ten, twenty-five times.'

The sweet young lady who met me at fifteen at high school and who with me, at twenty-four and still at high school, fraternally shares the sad days of school and the happy days of suspensions, smiled. And her big black eyes said to me: 'Oh, Giovannino, Giovannino!...'

*

I am so sad: I will never be able to go back to my dear old high school where for nine years, every day, I could be with Margherita.

I have now left: the exam days disappeared as fast as lightning. At the written tests Margherita and I sat side by side at two tables, separated only by the short space of the aisle. How many times had we looked into each other's eyes! Aesthetic analysis? Déjà vu? Who knew what it was? I continually thought of Margherita and, in the end, the harsh voice of the examiner roused me:

'Deliver, deliver: the time is up.'

I looked around. Everyone was gone, there was only me and the sweet girl who had fraternally shared with me the nine years and three classes of high school.

Without even looking at them, I handed over my exam papers for both Latin and Greek. I had decided I would let myself fail again: Signor Luigi would lose the game again this time; but I would win love.

Instead, Mr Luigi won. I am a victim of my subconscious, of my perverse subconscious. Of my most incorrect subconscious.

We all have a subconscious. Every man carries the spare wheel attached to his back, like cars and automobiles, and, like the famous spare wheel, the subconscious comes into action when a tyre loses its nerve due to some happenstance.

Under normal conditions, the subconscious sleeps when we are awake and is awake when we sleep. You go to sleep and the subconscious begins his work.

But mine is a singular subconscious. He is a subconscious who has taken a different turn: or rather, he follows *my* turn. He watches while I am awake and sleeps while I sleep.

So, when we sleep, I am a man completely left to chance, a defenceless creature, a stone. While when we awake I am a poor man wide-eyed conscious and unconscious at the same time, lest I capitulate to the subconscious fool who, during the nine years of high school, simply cared about what the teachers said. Instead, while thinking about Margherita, my subconscious takes advantage of my distraction and makes me fill sheets and sheets of such valuable literature as to make myself worthy of praise and congratulation.

The wicked subconscious took advantage of me even during the oral exams. Betrayed, I passed with flying colours in everything.

'Explain to me the Lead-chamber Process for the manufacture of sulphuric acid,' the chemistry examiner asked.

'How will I see Margherita every day if we have to drop out of high school?' I was wondering with my eyes fixed on the void.

'Perfect,' I heard the *professore* exclaim. 'You know too much, young man: I congratulate you.'

Perfidious subconscious. Selfish, too: because, having passed with flying colours, today I know not a word of Latin, Greek or algebra and I cannot distinguish a logarithm from a Martialis epigram.

I am so sad: we come together, Margherita and I, in front of the results table. We read slowly all the names, all the results, with only one last hope... Both passed! Both graduates. United in misfortune, I felt Margherita's hand squeeze mine. We went out with our heads bowed, we sat on the bench at the end of the avenue, from which you can see in the distance, framed by green leaves as in a diploma of merit, the high school building.

Goodbye, old high school with all your desks carved from a hundred thousand blades of penknife, with your bell that removes the blue sky from a thousand youngsters every day because the youngsters must learn that perhaps Homer was blind, that Numa Pompilius was succeeded by Tullo Ostilio, that the sulphuric acid formula is so-and-so.

Farewell, *professore* of Latin and Greek who taught us the *consecutio temporum* rules for the agreement of tenses and the aorist tense and stirred the verbal creativity of a hundred generations of schoolchildren with the young poetry of past millennia. For even you, Giovannino, old and boorish as you now are, once thought respectfully of gentlemen in togas who walk under marble arcades, wearing laurel wreaths on their heads.

Farewell, *signor professore di filosofia*: how many times have your youthful feet disrespected the ecclesiastical cloister by attempting to explain to Giovannino what not even Plato could explain? In the end you didn't even raise your head from the register when you heard the clicking of lead shots on your table top.

'Giovannino, out of the classroom,' you said quietly. And I went out in silence. That is, on the occasions when I had been there. Because you said 'Giovannino, out of the classroom' even when I was with Margherita on the distant bench in the park.

Goodbye, old high school: I spent the best part of my Margherita within your walls saturated with Ovid. Mr Luigi is happy and has given me his rifle from before the war: but Mr Luigi has a successful and unhappy son.

Sitting on the bench, Margherita and I waited for the sunset. When the first lights of the evening came upon us, the sweet girl whom the sky scattered in profusion over my high school days, smiled sadly and her big black eyes said to me: 'Oh Giovannino, Giovannino!...'

Giovanni's graduation from high school had been a peppery affair. In 1925 his father had been declared bankrupt, and coping with the practical consequences of it had made studying difficult: 'When returning home for the holidays, I have to sleep on the floor and neglect my studies to build beds, chairs, a table, a sideboard with my own hands, and a desk.' The local parish priest of Marore, Don Lamberto Torricelli, 'a big man, two metres tall with hands as big as shovels' who would 'let fly a smack' when necessary, took him on. In the re-sits,

Giovanni doubled his score in Latin and, in 1929, matriculated in the Faculty of Law at the Università di Parma.

A year earlier, however, he had already begun his career in journalism as a proof-reader for the daily newspaper, *Corriere emiliano*.

Around the year 1440, Mr Gutenberg, having printed the first copy of his first typographical composition, found, in the second line, 'an elephant lady' instead of 'an elegant lady'. Then Mr Gutenberg, having carefully read the whole draft, wrote in pen some of the errors scattered on the sheet, and, finally, cursed harshly his partner Fust who, poor fellow, was not to blame in the slightest.

Thus did he invent the printing error, the proof-reader and the whole proofreading protocol simultaneously. And so, 490 years later, I was able to accept a post as a proof-reader, which was offered to me by the administration of the local newspaper.

I confess that, in the beginning, I was disappointed: the enemy did not engage in battle. He did not show himself. I couldn't find *any* errors. G.T., my predecessor and my teacher, had forgotten to advise me on any strategy whereby I might discover them.

I have tried every system: to read with one eye, to read every other line, to read sideways. I pretend to finish and go out and then come back in a hurry, scrolling through the drafts very quickly.

I have tried to dress up, to mask my face with a moustache and a thin beard... The damn misprints still didn't show. Instead, they treacherously revealed themselves to me the next day, when the newspaper was already printed.

Rereading the sheet, I discovered dozens of them in each section: big, enormous errors, capital letters instead of numbers, inverted lines, sentences that suddenly stopped before resuming halfway down a column on another topic.

I was disappointed, but I was not discouraged. *Errors must be found*. The proof-reader has to find them, these damn mistakes. If Signor Cesare had found the errors in his proofs, today this delightful little city would still have two newspapers. Instead it has only one: the other, the centuries-old one, the national monument, has disappeared, leaving its name, in tiny print, stuck to the masthead of the sister paper that absorbed it.

Signor Cesare was a very smart man, wanted to kick-start his career by correcting proofs. He was hired by the old newspaper and began reviewing the typeset pages. On the sixth day the Editor summoned Signor Cesare to his office. He wore an expression of noble pain.

'My dear Sir,' he said to him, 'a particularly serious matter obliges me to speak to you. May I count on your attention?'

'You may.'

'First of all, I would like us to agree on a principle which I consider fundamental. Do you admit, as I admit, that in order to be able to write, you must at the very least know how to read?'

Signor Cesare admitted this without difficulty.

'Well,' concluded the Editor, 'a singular case has emerged in the printing department of the newspaper that I manage. For three days a man wrote without knowing how to read.'

This interested Signor Cesare, who asked for more details.

'It's that simple,' the Editor explained. 'Three days ago we hired a new compositor and for three days said compositor typeset columns and columns of print – articles, stories and news – even though he was totally illiterate. In other words, he limited himself to tapping the compositor's keyboard with his fingers without having the slightest suspicion that the manuscript sheets that were delivered to him had any connection with the work he output on the machine. He limited himself to doing what he saw his fellow workers do: tapping on certain buttons with his fingers, pressing a certain handle when a certain compartment was full of matrices raining down from the sky.'[1]

'The case is singular indeed and weighted with unbelievable gravity,' observed Signor Cesare. 'Lucky someone has noticed.'

'Yes: someone *has* noticed. The trouble is that *you* didn't notice it when you proofed the articles, and at least a couple of those composed by that errant mechanic were published in full in the newspaper I run.'

Signor Cesare explained to the Editor his inability to remedy the unpleasant matter and the Editor expressed an opinion that Signor Cesare did not have the cerebral configuration required for proofreading.

'I'll try to pass you over to City News,' he concluded. 'You have ingenuity and it shouldn't be difficult for you to write articles about road accidents, thefts, ceremonies...'

Leaving the proof reading department, Signor Cesare devoted himself enthusiastically to City News. The next evening he sent at least ten folders with facts, small misfortunes, a theft of hens, etc into the composing room. The following evening the Editor gave him his

---

[1] In letterpress composition a compositor would cast a solid one-piece line of type, a 'slug', from movable matrices of each letter. The composing room was typically located at the top of the building and had large windows and high ceilings to maximise sunlight, making it easier for compositors to see and pick out the very small individual 'sorts' or letters.

warmest congratulations for the widespread report of a dramatic theft of cheeses, complicated by injury and the onset of flooding.

For ten days things went perfectly: the page of the city news had become the most interesting and adventurous part of the newspaper. On the eleventh, the Editor summoned Cesare to his office.

'Excuse any indiscretion on my part,' he said to him. 'But you must have to work like the devil from morning to night to find so much news material!'

'No: it is actually very easy: a couple of hours at my desk and fifteen folders are full.'

'So, for your city news articles, you don't take your cue from reality...'

'I'm careful not to: only a few writers taking their cue from reality have managed to produce works of any artistic value. I work only in fantasy.'

'I can imagine that,' said the Editor.

Then he explained to Cesare that in City News it was better to follow the traditional system: to describe a theft, an attack, an investment only when these things had actually occurred. Especially if names of real people were inserted into the narrative.

'News isn't right for you,' concluded the editor. 'From now on you will be Managing Editor and you will deal with the political department, the literary department and the news department, but from the point of view of *coordinator*. You will have to make an organic and harmonious whole of the individual initiatives of the editors.'

This immediately interested Signor Cesare: he had four editors under him and about thirty reporters. He harangued them, gave directions. Then he decided to abolish headlines. The newspaper headline was decorative but self-defeating. In News, it summarised the content of the article in two lines, removing the element of surprise and demonstrating that, in a seven word headline, can be said everything in the 200-word article beneath it. In politics, the headline is often a danger and always a gamble. Again, a fact considered important today and therefore highlighted with a heading across six columns, may turn out tomorrow morning to be without any importance, due to incorrect interpretation, or due to the emergence of other facts, etc.

He then gave generic titles to particular pages – 'Up and down the world'; 'Up and down Italy'; 'Up and down the city'; 'Up and down the province'; 'Up and down the world of film'... Then he separated the news articles with simple asterisks.

The next day the Editor called him in and spoke to him sweetly.

'I'm sure you will get something of a shock when you see today's edition of the newspaper,' he said. 'It is organised in a completely different way from how you designed it last night. Fact is, just as the newspaper was about to go to print, I was alerted on the telephone by the printer and the troubled voice of the chief reporter and I thought it appropriate that the newspaper should still come out in line with the now traditional aesthetics common to newspapers around the world.

'May I take the liberty of reminding you, in summary, dear Signor Cesare, that since you didn't hack it as a proof-reader, I passed you over to News; since you didn't hack it as a reporter, I promoted you to Managing Editor. Now, since you can't hack it as Managing Editor either, I find myself in an embarrassing situation: either I sack you, or give you my position as Editor.'

Signor Cesare had a noble and heartfelt exclamation:

'I will never allow it: I will resign!'

But the Editor, who was a person of extraordinary rigour, did not dismiss Signor Cesare, nor even did he give him his position as Editor. Instead, he found a brilliant alternative solution: he sold the newspaper to its competitor in the city and retired to the countryside.

*

I have sworn to flush out the damn printing errors: I don't want to become Managing Editor. I don't want to lead the newspapers to perdition. I made a commitment and yesterday, finally, when I found myself with Margherita, I showed her a copy of the newspaper. '

Margherita,' I said proudly, 'read this word underlined in red!'

'*Bocciofila*,' read Margherita.

'They had written: "*Boccofila*". I found this error!'

The sweet creature, who fraternally shares with me the joys of my half-packet of 'Juba', smiled sweetly and, as her big black eyes flooded with tears, said to me: 'Oh Giovannino, Giovannino!...'

Anyone capable of this sort of article, equal to Dickens or J M Barrie in their earliest days as magazine contributors, can be assured of an interesting future. But there may be more true to life in this particular article than at first meets the eye, for Giovanni did begin as a proof-reader for *Corriere emiliano* and in 1931 entered into a contract with the paper, starting as assistant reporter, then reporter and finally as Editor, moving to an attic room in Parma and later attesting to the role that imagination had played in his meteoric rise, as it had for Signor Cesare:

When I was young I was a reporter for a newspaper and I went around on my bicycle all day long looking for stories worth reporting. Then I got to know a girl, and I began to spend my days in a state of wonder, thinking about what she would do if I became Emperor of Mexico, or if I should die. And in the evenings I began to fill my pages with made-up pieces of news, and people liked these a lot because they were more plausible than the real news. Back then I must have had a vocabulary of more or less 200 words, and I used the same ones to report an old man being knocked over by a cyclist and a housewife losing a fingertip as she peeled potatoes.

So there was none of that literary malarkey, and I am that same reporter today. I still confine myself to reporting items of news, made-up stuff but so realistic that on loads of occasions I've written a story and then seen it happen in real life a couple of months later.

There's nothing extraordinary about this. It stands to reason: you consider the time of day, the time of year, the current fashion and the psychological moment, and conclude that, things being as they are, in Situation X this or that event could actually take place.[2]

Situation X for Giovanni and Ennia meant making their way in fascist Italy. Benito Mussolini, Prime Minister since 1922, had transformed the country into a dictatorship and Italy was caught up in a serious economic depression.

Besides the proof-reading, in 1929 he began to publish articles, poems and drawings in the weekly *La Voce di Parma*. He also worked as an engraver and illustrator of short stories written by his old tutor, Cesare Zavattini, making much needed extra money working summers as a porter at a sugar factory in Parma. But it seems that Giovanni was never alone in facing the many problems that beset him at this time.

It is June 1930, and here I need to explain to you how the so-called Photographic Shooting works. What, pray, *is* a Photographic Shooting Range? It is not a complicated contraption. Whoever, by curious chance, manages to place a bullet in the centre of a certain target, ignites the deflagration of a magnesium cartridge and the release of a lens and is instantly photographed. Photographs taken in this way are always interesting: inevitably one cops a very daring glimpse of the rifle, which is no more nor less than a black circle, but you also get to admire an eye, a cheek, and a little further back, the shoulders and hat of the shooter. Perhaps, too, there is the smiling face of the shooter's girlfriend, wife or companion confidently posing behind him, lending a certain authority to the end result. Then again,

---
[2] *Mondo Piccolo Don Camillo* (1948)

perhaps there is the face of a stranger who, taking advantage of the isolated shooter, obtains a free selfie so to spread his likeness through time and space – a weakness not uncommon among mere mortals.

So yesterday, when I happened to be at the amusement park, I went along to the Photographic Shooting Range, to withdraw from the hurly-burly and set aside my every thought. By a very lucky chance, I hit the bull's-eye almost immediately and had the photograph of the hole of my rifle, cheered up, in its immediate vicinity, by an eye, a cheek, a forehead, a hat and a shoulder belonging to me. I looked carefully at the still wet hypo-sulphate cardboard and I was quite perplexed: I was me and he is fine; but who did the smiling face behind my right shoulder belong to?

It was not the normal sort of stranger to which I alluded above. I was immediately convinced of that through a careful study of certain details revealed in the strange man's clothing (the little that could be seen). Understand me: can anyone walk around the city without being apprehended, wearing a shirt, without a hat, but with great wings on his back? *Vanitas vanitatum* indeed! But it is not my way to tell vacuous stories. The fact is that, in this way, by means of the Photographic Shooting Range I was able to take a photograph of my Guardian Angel. It is now apparent that my every step is supervised. I am followed like a thief. It is sad, but I won't be speaking about the incident to Margherita. Otherwise the sweet girl who, having met me unemployed and happy, is now bent on making me an unhappy salaried man, would smile and, shaking her head, her black eyes would say to me: 'Oh Giovannino, Giovannino!...'

In November 1934, while still employed by *Corriere Emiliano*, National Service called Giovanni to the Secondary Officers School in Potenza. In May 1935 he returned to Parma and published drawings in the *Secolo Illustrato* in *Cinema Illustration*, edited by Zavattini.

Now, Parma is a singular provincial town with yellow houses, many public plane trees, many frescoes painted for a fee – except on Sundays – and many tables in the square. A pretty city ... [but] history repeats itself with great monotony in the newspaper. Said Giovanni one evening:

'Margherita, I'm tired of this monotonous and squalid life, I'm tired of seeing the same people, I'm tired of always knowing, today, what I'm going to do tomorrow. I have been saddened in an office for five years and never a day off: a sense of rebellion shakes my nerves. An internal voice warns me that life is daring, that *we must dare*! Margherita, are we going to Milan on Sunday to see the Trade Fair?'

In Mr Luigi's old house, there hung on a wall for twenty-three years a poster announcing the famous 1906 Fair.[3] It shows a locomotive about to emerge from a tunnel into an immense plain. On the front of the train – taken from a rear point-of-view so that the vaulted tunnel, from which the engine is emerging, frames the boundless plateau – two red figures are seen to crouch: the first wears a winged helmet on its head.

Up to the age of four, thanks to Mrs Flaminia's subtle persuasion, those red men represented for me two devils come from hell to consume bad children. From the age of five to ten, the two men represented for me a lively reason for disappointment because being seen from behind it was impossible for me to draw on their faces the majestic moustaches with which I cheered up other images in the house.

From the age of eleven to fourteen, thanks to the intervention of Mr Luigi, the two red men represented for me Industry and Progress, which, with the building of the new Simplon tunnel, opened up to civilisation a very important new route into the Lombard plain.

Now, though, considering the particular circumstances in which we found ourselves, the two red characters began to represent Margherita and Giovanni who, somehow, had got on a locomotive, left the dark tunnel of their hometown and marched upon Milan which you can glimpse, in the poster, on the horizon line of the boundless plain.

A few days ago I carefully rolled up the poster and took it to Margherita. I explained to her the interpretation I gave it. The sweet companion of my dreams carefully considered the allegory: 'So, I would be this red gentleman on the left, half hidden, and you this red gentleman sitting on the right?'

'Yes, Margherita.'

Margherita shook her head:

'It's not good to travel completely naked,' she remarked. 'And why are you wearing a hat with horns on your head?'

I explained to her that allegories always travel naked and that it was not a hat with horns, but with wings, as befits the figure of Mercury who wore it on his head.

---

[3] The Milan International world's fair, or 'The Great Expo of Work' as it was known, attracted more than four million visitors after it opened in 1906, and in turn marked the opening of the Simplon tunnel, which connects Italy with Switzerland.

The sweet creature, whom Destiny had placed in my life to get me to think of at least something, shook her head:

'Travelling like this, sitting in the front of a locomotive, is dangerous and contrary to regulations. Giovanni, find me an allegory that represents a young man with clothes on who has found a new job and immediately runs to tell the young lady who loves him.'

Giovanni was planning to move to Milan to try his luck 'closer to the sources of livelihood' and Ennia was, in fact, open to anything, even, as Grandmamma Giuseppina suggested, to mount a horse and go to Argentina... Or, yes, to Milan. In Parma, people talked a lot about Milan: they said that Milan is 'something else'.

At this time, following the enforced closure by Mussolini's fascist government of satirical magazines, such as the courageous anti-fascist *Il Becco Giallo* (1924–6), a rapidly rising publisher, Angelo Rizzoli, was bent on founding a magazine in Milan to compete with a ground-breaking satirical bi-weekly, *Marc'Aurelio*, published in Rome and noted for its abstract and surreal humour.

These were provocative times for any satirical journalist. Mussolini, having swept all opposition aside, but retained Victor Emmanuel III as King, had made a powerful friend of Adolf Hitler, who, in 1933, would become German Chancellor and assume the title of 'Führer und Reichskanzler' the following year.

The man commissioned by Rizzoli to map out the editorial strategy and hire key staff for the new magazine was none other than Cesare Zavattini, who had risen fast in magazine publishing. Naturally, he thought of Giovanni. His hiring was not plain sailing, however. Midway through the process, Zavattini and Rizzoli fell out. More or less immediately after his dismissal, Zavattini was signed by the already famous publisher Arnoldo Mondadori as Editorial Director of all his magazines. He would go on to become a notable screenwriter.

Meanwhile, a package containing drawings, jokes, prose and proposals had been sent to Angelo Rizzoli who had entrusted his son, Andrea, with the commissioning of Giovanni as Editor of the new, as yet untitled, Milan-based magazine. Telephone negotiations had dragged on, so Andrea cut to the chase, got in his car and ran Giovanni to ground. Giovanni signed, but in February 1936 he was recalled to the 6th Army Corps Regiment at Modena as an aspiring officer, and only when his national service ended in July of that year was he released by *Corriere Emiliano* to work for Rizzoli.

Bertoldo, as the magazine was named,[4] attracted some of the best young artists and writers, among them the soon to be famous American cartoonist, Saul Steinberg. It had already been out in the market for two weeks when

---

[4] Bertoldo is one of the most famous villains in Italian literature, an amalgam of shrewd intelligence and subtle wit, born out of a literary bed of proverb, riddle, farce, comedy and fairy tale.

Giovanni took the editorial Chair, although he'd had a cartoon on the first page of the first issue, published on 14 July 1936, Saint Bonaventure's day. Rizzoli remains Giovanni's principal publisher to this day.

*

On May 22, 1939, Mussolini signed a defensive alliance (known as the Pact of Steel) with Adolf Hitler. On September 1, Germany invaded neighbouring Poland. Two days later, Britain and France declared war on Germany. At first, Mussolini withheld formal allegiance with either side, but on June 10, 1940, he threw in his lot with Hitler.

Four months earlier, Giovanni had arrived by taxi, with his beloved Ennia, at the church of Santa Francesca Romana in Milan.

We got married in February and the marriage cost me an 'aquilotto' and I had to insist that the parish priest accept my spontaneous offer. A modest but fair offer because the marriage – despite being one of the most solid of the century – was actually not worth more than the five lire.

'Giovannino had no jacket,' recalled the writer and critic Oreste del Buono, 'but, since it was cold, he had an excuse to wear his overcoat instead and, to compensate, he showed off some swanky pinstripe strides borrowed from [writer and illustrator] Carletto Fildiferro. In another taxi followed the witnesses: the writer Carlo Manzoni, his brotherly friend [journalist and caricaturist] Alessandro Minardi, his cousin, a shrewd scholar, Pietrino Bianchi, and Giovanni's co-director at the magazine, Giovanni Mosca.

'Ennia looked very elegant in a black coat. Had the eye of Colonel Efisio Marrasa of the Sixth Artillery of the Army Corps been present,[5] Ennia's wedding coat would have been identified as the dyed former blue cape of his shabby Second Lieutenant Guareschi.'

The sacred rite – if it can be called that – took place in Milan in Santa Francesca Romana, immediately after a very expensive wedding. The church was still full of flowers, the altar glittering with candles and a sumptuous red carpet stretched from the altar to the door. As we entered, there was a scream and swarms of little altar boys were unleashed. And, while a group made the flowers disappear, another put out the candles, a third tore from the altar some big busts of bishops in silver tin and, as Margherita, I and the four witnesses

---

[5] Giovanni's former commander, who, at first glance, had adjudged him to be someone who should be kept away from cannon at all costs.

proceeded towards the altar, a fourth rolled up the carpet so that we didn't even touch it with our hopelessly down-at-heel soles.

It was a flash wedding with peremptory commands: 'Stand up!', 'On your knees!', 'Sit down!', 'On your knees!', 'Yes!', 'Ring!'...

I remember that, at a certain moment, the organist who had remained on the organ stage attacked the wedding march, but a shout from the celebrant immediately silenced him.

Of course, if I had made a film of the ceremony, it would be an anthology piece.[6]

---

[6] *My Home Sweet Home* (1966)

New Life

Here, then, are two creatures walking the path of the good Lord, a young man and a young woman.

One day they decide, 'Let's walk together,' and go forth, arm-in-arm.

They pick up speed, make greater haste: they see that the road ahead is long, difficult, but full of promise. They must surely galvanise themselves: there is no time to lose if they want to reach the mountains of the unknown, glimpsed on the horizon.

Then, all of a sudden, these two creatures of the good Lord are brought abruptly to a standstill. Who is that calling, concealed behind the bush growing out of the middle of that green sward, brimming with yellow and blue flowers?

They leave the main road, run to the middle of the lawn, and behind the bush they find a creature, very small, with two short legs. A screaming baggage of pink!

The two creatures of the good Lord stop. The journey on the main road, leading to the mountains on the horizon, will be resumed later! When that tiny man can walk. They will then make the journey along the main road together. So, they stop in the meadow next to the main road and, little by little, they forget that there *is* a road that leads to the mountains of the unknown. And the meadow, with its yellow and blue flowers, becomes its own destination of choice.

When the screaming little creature has become a big boy, intimations of the main road and the distant mountains will come to him: but, by then, it will be too late for the man and woman to start walking again. Their legs will no longer sustain an expedition to the distant hills. And, in turn, he too will stop and find a small creature that will call to him from behind a bush.

Such is the life of ordinary men: all of a sudden, the ordinary man finds himself sitting next to his companion in a green meadow, watching a little rascal sleeping with one foot in his mouth. And he will say with a smile:

'Margherita, our baby is ten months old today.'

'Just think, in two months he'll be one year old,' Margherita replies.

And Giovanni, faced with that very simple arithmetic operation, is as amazed as Peter at the miracle of the multiplication of fish, caught on the advice of the good Lord after a night of want in the Sea of Galilee.

Everything, if it concerns the little gangster, is of monumental importance.

'Giovanni,' shouts Margherita, 'the child has his eyes open! Giovanni, the child does this with the index finger of his right hand... Giovanni, the child has a nose!...' And Giovanni observes the various extraordinary phenomena and, satisfied, approves.

It is indeed already ten months since I met the sweet creature that God spread with both hands along the main road, and we left to describe a hellish circle around the little screaming bundle, with his eyes open and with the index finger of his right hand indicating the tip of his nose.

How did it happen?

One day, returning home from work – (the secret of success, in this extraordinary city, is to return home from work every day) – I found my bed invaded by a small foreign device. Considering the precedents and hearing the statements of eyewitnesses who had witnessed the arrival of the strange character, I concluded that I was in the presence of a male son. The sweet lady who shares the joys and pains of my salary with me raised her head from a disorderly pile of sheets.

'Well?' she asked. 'Have you nothing to say?'

I asked if she had a stake. Then, having understood from the stern glances gathering nearby, that I had not been as expansive as I might have, I approached my son and slapped him a good slap on his shoulder, exclaiming very jovially:

'Well! How are you, old sport?'

Four or five screams of indignation, disapproval, painful wonder, execration, commented on my gesture. Then two strong hands pushed me vigorously through the door and out of the room.

I went for a walk through the city and, knowing full well that children are particularly fond of candied fruit, crunchy, chocolate, candies, nougat and small liquorice 'beetles', I got myself a nice packet.

...Now, for ten months, we have abandoned the main road that leads to the mountains on the horizon and, standing in the green meadow, we watch the pink two-legged machine. I no longer think of the distant hills. Margherita smiles and her big black eyes say: 'Giovannino, Giovannino!...'

*

Just three months have passed since the evening when our friend Giuseppe entered our rooms, panting. He'd phoned first. He would arrive half an hour before midnight.

'Wait for me: open the doors to the staircase and your study. I have no time to lose.'

We opened the doors wide: Giuseppe's tone of voice had been particularly solemn. The receptionist took up a position in front of the coat rack with her hands stretched out, ready to take his hat. I drew an ideal line passing through the two doors and arranged an armchair, *ultima thule* perpendicular to the extension of said straight line, so that Giuseppe would be seated as quickly as possible.

I arranged myself behind the armchair so that it wouldn't slip. Then Margherita would take her place in the tableau with a glass of fresh orange soda in her hand.

A quarter of an hour later, Giuseppe ran in.

Hat, armchair, orange soda.

A bit of calm restored his respiratory functions. Giuseppe motioned to us to close both doors and windows, then spoke in a low voice, with the utmost circumspection.

'I am just now come by car from the Bibìbi villa, where I'd been all day. An hour ago we heard – by chance, you know! – a foreign radio station. Gigi has a little English – enough to understand everything they said: our intervention in the war is now a sure thing![7] I left the house in a flash: I didn't even stop for a cup of broth. I ran out. I had to warn my firmest friends.'

Giuseppe then left us, after exhorting me to be discreet, and Margherita looked me in the eye, very worried.

'It's a terrible thing, Giovannino!' she exclaimed, her face a picture of the very worst desolation.

'War!'

I spoke to her softly:

'Margherita, try to calm yourself and follow what I have to say you. You, today – June 10, 1940 – sitting here in this armchair, in front of that radio, listened to a historic speech in which Italy's intervention in the war was announced to the world. At the end of it, you were not worried or upset: on the contrary, even as the mother of a small baby boy, you seemed to behave as if you were the mother of the Gracchi brothers.[8] As soon as the girl brought us the special edition of the *Ambrosiano* you wanted to read the speech aloud. And your voice was calm.

---

[7] Mussolini had delayed a Declaration of War until June 10, 1940, after Germany overran Norway, Holland and Belgium and invaded France.
[8] The exemplary mother of the Gracchi brothers, whose careers sparked the revolution that overthrew the Roman Empire.

'Up until ten minutes ago, the war didn't worry you. Giuseppe arrives with one of his wonderful discoveries, tells you what you'd known for almost six hours, and now the war is worrying you.

'Margherita, why? Are there two Margheritas? An official one and an unofficial one? Are you perhaps a creature made up of yes and no at the same time? Or is the war we were talking about a few hours ago not the same as the one that Giuseppe just told us about? Are there perhaps two wars for you? Is one not enough?'

The sweet creature that God scattered on my path slowly shook her head:

'I don't know, but announced on the radio and in the newspapers, war is one thing; shared with us by Giuseppe, it is another. Oh, Giovannino, what will become of us?'

*

June 1930 to December 1940 – exactly ten years and seven months have passed since Giacinto could not resist the temptation to be photographed with me at the Shooting Range. I have already told you about this, but it should be recalled now because it was on account of this episode that, for the first time, I came to meet my Guardian Angel.[9] It was afterwards that he, having seen that he had been discovered, came out of the unknown and could restrain himself no longer in showing himself freely to me.

But now Giacinto has gone too far and any further reserve on my part would be an indication of weakness. Giacinto, let me say, has many flaws. Curious, vain and distracted. Ten years and seven months is too long a period of patient endurance. My patience has reached its limit. It should also be appreciated how serious his recent indiscretions have been. Giacinto, from a professional point of view, may be an excellent Guardian Angel, but as a man he has a lot of flaws. An interesting dichotomy. Meanwhile, it is enough for me, when I am writing a letter, to turn my head suddenly to surprise Giacinto leaning over my shoulder, trying to read the words that flow out of my pen.

Once, when I suddenly turned around while beating on the keys of my portable machine, I found an Angel I had never seen behind me. Giacinto was away pursuing his own affairs and had told the

---

[9] Guardian angels, heavenly intermediaries tasked by God appear to guard and guide us, are present throughout all antiquity and not only in Christianity. A dedicated feast day was first officially observed in the Catholic Church in the 15th century, but even the occultist Aleister Crowley considered the Holy Guardian Angel to be representative of one's truest divine nature, arguably not in the case of Giacinto. How perfect though that 'Camillo' is already a part of the story.

porter's Guardian Angel to 'look after mine too: I'll be right back.' Well, I do not care at all to be protected by the Guardian Angel of a porter: it was a lack of respect on Giacinto's part.

Also, Giacinto is a brawler: I caught him arguing with the publisher's Guardian Angel. And I cannot permit this. Giacinto must not interfere with what I think of my boss when he mistreats me. Moreover, he is impertinent: once I gave him a solemn lecture and told him outright that, if he didn't sort himself out, I would fire him and hire another Guardian Angel.

'It would set a precedent, certainly,' Giacinto replied, smiling. 'It'd be interesting to hear what the Union of Angels thought about it.'

These are not answers worthy of a Guardian Angel. When all's said, Giacinto is *a bad guy*. This is not only my opinion: Camillo and Roberto have said the same thing of him. And they are respectable Guardian Angels.

One night I woke up with a start. Someone next to me was speaking. I squinted one eyelid. And in the pale light of the nightlight I saw, seated at the foot of my bed, three gentlemen in white shirts: one was Giacinto, the other two were Camillo, the Guardian Angel of 'the sweet lady on the fourth floor' [Margherita], and Roberto, the Guardian Angel of our pink rascal [their son, since named Albertino]. They were chatting and Giacinto, of course, was holding court. So, as I listened, I discovered something that I had not known before: the Guardian Angel, when his human dies, does nothing but change affiliation, just as a driver changes a car he owns.

In fact, Giacinto suddenly said with conviction:

'My last one was much better than this one: a more serious guy, a lawyer. I've never had one before that scribbles in magazines. It is not a very decent thing for someone like me, who was with Victor Hugo from 1802 to 1885.'

'So you also worked abroad?' Camillo asked. 'Yes,' Giacinto explained. 'I can speak French, Spanish and Romanian perfectly. Think how funny it is: "heart" in Spanish is "corazón".'

Roberto, my baby's Angel, shook his head:

'Rest assured my brat will not be like his father.'

'And what are you going to make him do?' the Angel of my consort inquired, curious as to how he administered him.

'I don't know,' my baby's Angel replied. 'Anyway, I'd rather let him be a turner than have him work for magazines.'

Giacinto laughed:

'If he has in mind to scribble for the comics, and if he is stubborn as his father, he *will* scribble for the comics, I guarantee it. I wanted mine to be a naval engineer and look where I got with that.'

'What's his mother like? Does she give you a lot to do?' asked Roberto.

'Please! For someone who, like me, has worked with Lucrezia Borgia, Caterina de' Medici and Matilde di Canossa, why would you want to administer to a woman as ministerial as this? The only serious problem is that she is afraid of sirens and I tell you that I have to work like a beaver to make sure she doesn't hit her head against the wall, or fall down the stairs when she goes down to the cellar.'

'I never go down to the cellar when the air raid siren sounds!' Giacinto said boldly.

'You should,' noted the Angel of my consort. 'You mustn't let him go alone: it's okay that he's a man, but four eyes always see better than two.'

'Well what can I do about the bombs?' Giacinto answered shrugging.

'That's not the point,' said my baby's Angel. 'You can always do something. For example, as soon as I accompany my brat to the cellar, I climb up to four or five thousand feet in altitude to monitor the enemy's movements.'

'I don't have a pilot's licence or a hunting licence,' said Giacinto facetiously, 'and anyway I'm generally in bed.'

'Instead of playing the comedian, it'd be better if you took things a little more seriously. If misfortune were to befall your man, the whole thing would rest on your shoulders.

Giacinto started muttering:

'Nice set-up, two against one. Anyway, you didn't understand a damn thing: I don't go down to the cellar when the siren sounds, only when they start shooting.'

'No good at all! You must set off immediately, when we set off!' Camillo screamed threateningly. 'You're so full of yourself because you worked abroad! If I, who worked with Matilde di Canossa, set off at the right moment, you must too, for keep in mind that Matilde di Canossa eats fifteen of your Victor Hugos.'

Giacinto lowered his head, then went to sit with his legs apart on the wardrobe. My baby's Angel went out for a moment then returned:

'Up to 5,000 feet; nothing to report. They'll not come again tonight.'

'Pity!' Giacinto sighed and then Camillo grabbed him by the collar of his shirt:

'You're a bad guy!' he yelled.
'You are worse than a man!' Roberto added.

*

So you see, it's not only me who thinks that Giacinto is a bad guy. He must be slippery because people like Victor Hugo don't trust any old GA. But this scene certainly did not improve the situation.

The real trouble is that Giacinto is also trying to ruin Camillo and Roberto, Guardian Angels that are excellent in every respect. And this, frankly, cannot go on.

Play it cool. Taking advantage of a moment of rest, instead of hitting fingerprints on the typewriter, that evening I sat in the best armchair in the house in order to listen to songs on the radio. The sweet lady, who – thanks to a daring manoeuvre – made a young gentleman her spouse for life, had gone to bed with her screaming rascal. I was alone. Caressing sounds emitted from the radio, while the armchair emitted nothing but was comfortable. It was therefore my precise duty as a citizen and user to fall asleep with a sweet smile on my lips and with a lit cigarette between the middle and index finger of my left hand, arranging things in such a way that, coming into contact with my left trousers, embers could slowly but surely make a hole of respectable diameter in the aforementioned garment.

At the very moment that the embers made direct contact with my skin, I woke with a start. The radio no longer emitted sounds, only strange noises. Not surprising, as two strange guys in white shirts and with blue wings were fumbling around with the knobs of the device.

I recognised them immediately, even though I only saw them from the back: one was Giacinto, my Guardian Angel, and the other was Camillo, Margherita's Guardian Angel. What were the two Guardian Angels doing around my old '5-valve'?

Simple: they were trying to find Radio London. I was very annoyed: I let out a scream and the two Guardian Angels spun around.

'Do you want to compromise me?' I said sternly.

Camillo lowered his head in confusion, while Giacinto began muttering in a bad mood.

'It turns out that I need to find myself a different Guardian Angel,' I exclaimed, and Giacinto just grinned.

The impertinent one takes advantage of the fact that today unemployed Guardian Angels are virtually non-existent. But I am resolute in everything and I told him:

'There is little to grumble about, young man: I can do very well without a Guardian Angel, given what your time as my custodian has served me!'

Giacinto shrugged: at the same time he smiled with irony and this annoyed me.

'I've always managed by myself!' I screamed putting my hands on my hips.

'When you were two years old, if I hadn't been there you would have fallen down the drain in the garden,' replied Giacinto, impertinently. 'I've never seen a less reasonable two-year-old.'

I resentfully pointed out that it's easy to put on airs over a two-year-old.

'Oh, I see,' Giacinto said. 'Listen then: how old were you in 1937? It was thirty-four or am I wrong?' I admitted that in 1937 I was thirty-four. 'And then on August 5, 1937 at five thirty in the morning, who woke you up when you, driving your car like a dog, had fallen asleep and were about to take a dip in the Pavese canal?'

'And who *allowed* me to fall asleep?' I replied. 'Who, instead of watching me while I was piloting, tired after a night of work...'

'After a night of outdoor dancing and alcohol!' Giacinto interrupted.

'Who, instead of watching me while I was driving, fell asleep peacefully, lying like a porter, in the back seat of the car? I don't have a rear-view mirror and two eyes for nothing, dear young man! *I saw you, Mr Giacinto!*'

'I know the rules! *The Guardian Angel must not prevent, he must simply intervene at the last minute*. Article three, second paragraph.'

In my 610 cubic metres of Milan, everything is quiet. The child sleeps and dreams in Technicolor in the room reserved for the rest of the family and her cradle, so small, clinging to one side of the big bed, looks like the lifeboat of a ship sailing in a sea of darkness. Margherita sews something, I watch Margherita sew something.

'Margherita, I think that, after all, the whole thing boils down to one big wheel. Man is born and is found near this huge stationary flywheel. At first he cannot move the heavy mass of iron, but as he grows over the years and in strength, little by little, the flywheel acquires movement under the thrust of his increasingly steady arms.

'The wheel begins to turn, faster and faster, faster and faster. And suddenly, the man realises that he can no longer stop, because now it is the wheel that drags him. You have to turn, turn, as long as the wheel wants. Margherita, I think life boils down to such a thing.'

'You think of strange things, Giovannino,' replies Margherita, without looking up from her canvas. 'You work all day and your brain is tired in the evening; you shouldn't think of cast iron wheels, huge flywheels: it's tiring. Think about lighter things; think of your brand new aluminium alloy bicycle. Ten kilos, 1,300 lire, when you already had a magnificent bicycle in perfect condition!'

'Margherita, seven years have passed since the day we set out to discover Milan. Margherita, doesn't it seem to you that everything is now repeating itself with extreme monotony? Don't you ever think about this?'

'No, Giovanni,' replies Margherita. 'I never think about this, because, if this is a problem, I don't see the solution.'

'We should have the strength to start over, Margherita. Abandon everything, start again as we came, with four suitcases and a few lire in our pockets. Go to another city and start over.'

'Leave the baby too, then,' laughs Margherita without looking up from her work. 'He wasn't there when we came. He could be given to the concierge.'

Everything is quiet in my 610 cubic metres in Milan.

'I think the matter consists mostly of a big wheel,' says Margherita in a low voice. 'When this wheel has started to turn in one direction, it can no longer be stopped to turn it in the opposite direction.'

I open a book and look at the words without taking in what they mean. Margherita finishes what she's doing. She gets up, puts the needles and her hair back in the basket, goes to bed.

'Don't complain, Giovannino,' she says when she arrives at the door. 'Today you have a little world of your own with so many things of your own.

'Good night, Giovannino.'

In those days I lived on art, I lived on love. Indeed I lived on journalism, I lived on marriage. Life was even more about journalism than marriage. Always it was like this, for years: the piece and the columns for *Bertoldo*, the sketches for *La Stampa*, the articles for *Stampa Sera*, the figures for *L'Illustrazione Italiana*, the novellina rosa for *Novella* and *Annabella*, the story for *Corriere della Sera*, the episode of the novel for *L'Illustrazione del Popolo*, etc., etc.

Every night like this – *every* night!...

With the advent of war and the birth of Albertino, Giovanni's thoughts turn to the years of his own early childhood. In 1942 he writes three stories about the spirit of the landscape of his birth, *la Bassa* in the region of Emilia-Romagna, the lowland plain between the River Po to the north and the Apennines to the south, which, four years later, would be the setting for his Don Camillo stories. These initial three stories – 'Plain Madness', 'The Miracle of the Lower Plain' and 'The

Third Telegraph Pole on the Fabbricone Road',[10] celebrate the unremittingly hard and unique otherworldly spirit of the place, a spirit which will become as real for us as it is for its author.

Then, on 8 September 1943, an unsolicited and undeserved rest...

---

[10] See the 2013 Pilot Productions edition of *The Little World of Don Camillo*.

War

Once upon a time there was the Great Reich. And it was originally a triumphant eagle holding a swastika in its talons. A powerful, majestic eagle, which – one day – passing through the blue skies of Italy met a fellow eagle perching on the balcony of Palazzo Venezia, hatching marble eggs and imperial ambitions.

'To whom the riches of pale Albion?' the Nazi eagle asked.

'To us!' the Roman eagle answered confidently.

'To whom the reorganisation of Europe, the inevitable final victory and peace with justice?' the eagle asked again.

'To us!' the eagle answered without hesitation.

'*Gut!*' said the Nazi eagle. 'You are well prepared and we can set out to conquer the world.'

They set out then, but shortly after, the Roman eagle hesitated for a moment: 'And if America intervenes?' she asked haltingly.

'The intervention of America leaves us perfectly indifferent!' the eagle exclaimed contemptuously.

*

Once upon a time there was the Great Reich: and it was a formidable eagle which, together with the Roman eagle of Palazzo Venezia, set out to conquer the world, helped in their noble enterprise by the terrifying yellow dragon, which has its lair on the slopes of Mount Fuji.

And, as fate would have it, the world began to shake. But then, little by little, as the two eagles fluttered and fluttered over the mountains, the seas and the steppes, they began to lose their feathers. And one day, it was discovered that the Palazzo Venezia eagle was a pigeon. And a little later it turned out that the wonderful German eagle was a chicken. Now it is a question of what kind of animal the famous Japanese dragon is. No rush. The important thing is that today we can say: once upon a time there was the Great Reich.[11]

Within months of war being declared it was clear what a mistake Mussolini had made and that Italy was but a dispensable pawn in Germany's grand plan. Giovanni, meanwhile, and despite the Second Paragraph of Article Three in the Guardian Angel's handbook, had, on October 14, 1942, got himself arrested by the political police for howling in the streets at night, defaming Mussolini and his regime.

---

[11] 'Il Grande Reich', Wietzendorf prison camp, 1945

'I got drunk because my brother was missing in Russia and no one had any news of him. That night I shouted a lot and said things which I saw written on two sheets of paper the next morning when I was arrested by the Political Office.'

He was drafted into the army to prevent any more trouble and was assigned to the 11th Artillery of Alessandria, south-west of Milan:

One morning, as I stood in my trim artillery lieutenant's uniform on the barracks parade ground, the bugle called me to attention and something truly extraordinary happened: my heels snapped together with a resounding click.

In order to appreciate the import of this event, we must look back at the long, sad story of my so-called 'unsoldierly attitude'.

One dreary November day, I travelled to the foggiest city of Italy and managed, with some difficulty, to locate the barracks where I was supposed to report.

There, an authoritative-looking individual told me:

'Beginning tomorrow, you'll be in charge of the Sixth Anti-Aircraft Battery, in process of formation.'

I assured him that as a field artillery man, I hadn't even a bowing acquaintance with anti-aircraft weapons.

'No matter,' he answered brusquely, nodding at a non-commissioned officer who proceeded to load me with notebooks and papers. He himself handed me an ordinary pen and said gravely: 'Remember these supplies have got to last you a whole month. Mind you don't bother me with requests for extras!'

As he saw me through the door, he cordially advised me to lose no time in setting up a ledger and roll call.

'They are fundamental,' he assured me.

I thanked him for his advice and asked where I was to find my station.

'In the company office, of course. Every unit has one.'

'And where is it, if you please?'

'You reserve shavetails will drive me crazy!' he shouted. 'How can you even ask? Wander around and question everyone you meet, and you'll find a place to make into a company office.'

'But I –'

'Use your head!' he yelled, slamming the door behind me.

The pen fell on the floor and I inadvertently stepped on it.

'Goodbye to my monthly supplies,' I said, giving it a melancholy salute.

*

I wandered all over the barracks, still staggering under the load of my notebooks and papers, but everyone I questioned about an empty spot suitable for a company office simply shrugged his shoulders in reply. All in vain I slipped twenty lire to the watchman at the supply depot, who was said to be a Very Important Person. And equally in vain I explained to the sergeant in charge of Upkeep and Repairs that the general situation was critical and a new anti-aircraft battery might save the day, but that this battery's formation depended on the setting up of a company office. From purely patriotic motives, he said, he was ready to plaster and paint any place I succeeded in finding. Only I had to find it.

After much wandering, I came upon a young fellow who took it upon himself to claim allegiance to my future anti-aircraft battery and to offer his services as company clerk. I enrolled him on the spot, handed over my load of notebooks and papers, and made him a member of my search party. Eventually, however, I realised that my office staff couldn't be a mobile affair. With my new recruit in tow, I decided to leave the barracks behind me.

'Our office is here,' I announced, when we came to the furnished room I had rented for myself earlier in the day. 'Pick yourself up a subordinate who can, in his turn, take on all the personnel you need, and go quietly to work. I'm moving to a hotel.' And just to make things easier for him, I signed some seventy-five passes.

The goings and comings of large numbers of enlisted men led people to draw entirely mistaken conclusions, and my rooming house proceeded to lose its good name. Aside from this, everything went swimmingly, but the episode was branded 'unsoldierly' and I became an object of suspicion.

There were other little episodes of the a similar kind, which further undermined my reputation, but the last straw was the 'coffee crime.'

One morning my sixty men informed me that, thanks to some sort of confusion in the kitchen, none of them had had a drop of coffee to drink. My answer was to line them up, march them out of the barracks, divide them among the four nearest cafés and treat them, out of my own pocket, to what they needed so badly.

The dim view that my superiors took of this excursion gave rise to the legend of my 'unsoldierly attitude' and indeed so damaged me that I was relieved of the command of the now wholly formed anti-aircraft battery.

If I had been sent to the front I might have had a chance to see some of the famous anti-aircraft weapons. But it was my fate to remain in the rear. As an anti-aircraft man, this is, even today, a sincere regret. But at the time, my attention was distracted by another bit of trouble, connected with the heel-clicking.

*

Do colonels dream?

Yes, colonels do dream, just like everyday human beings and reserve officers. Indeed, their dreams are almost identically the same. Army regulations are not concerned with dreams, and many an old-time colonel dreams about angels. Angels with pale blue wings and golden hair that glide down to earth as gently as those that inhabit the dreams of poets and young girls. Except that when such angels land at a colonel's feet, they draw themselves to attention with a sharp click of their heels.

Now, if any creature, mortal or immortal, in this world or the next, is entitled to go barefoot, surely it is an angel. But colonels are so dead set on heel-clicking that the angels of their dreams never fail to put on a stout pair of army boots, and if the colonels belong to the cavalry the boots have spurs attached.

Well then, beloved kinsman, since your gentle forefather knew how deeply colonels care for clicking heels and he was in daily contact with an old colonel, he couldn't very well overlook this little detail. Indeed, clicking heels were, at this time, one of my chief concerns. I knew that only a succession of successful clicks could destroy the myth of my 'unsoldierly attitude.' But fate was against me. I tried three different pairs of boots and six pairs of spurs, I sought out the expert advice of a blacksmith and a chiropodist, I took private lessons from a retired cavalry sergeant, I made a plaster model of my feet and studied their contour, I practised conscientiously in front of a mirror ... but when it came to the real thing, my heels were like jellied consommé and my spurs like pats of butter.

Plunk! And every plunk brought an expression of acute pain to the colonel's face.

The severest ordeal, and one which I had to face twice a day, was in the mess hall, where the colonel was flanked by a group of high-ranking officers. As soon as they saw me enter the hall, there was a moment of complete silence. Every ear pricked up, and every eye was upon me. I raised my arm in the prescribed salute and desperately drew my heels together.

Plunk! It was like a butter pat falling into a pile of flour. The colonel sorrowfully shook his head and all those present returned to their food. Over every single inclined head I saw a sort of comic-book legend, in letters of fire, reading: 'Unsoldierly!'

Finally I made a deal with a heel-clicking regular army lieutenant, who sat near the door. When I came in and saluted, he was to click his heels under the table. Operation Dubbing, you might have called it, but I tried it twice and no more. The first time, the click came a whole minute after I had come to attention, the second while I was still walking into the room. And so I went back to my plunks, and the colonel continued to look as pained as if I had stuck a pin into his heart. Plunk! Plunk! How many times did I hear that miserable sound?

That, dear descendant, is the whole story. Next time I'll tell you how I came to be in the great central yard of a Polish barracks.[12]

The Armistice

In 1943, with America now also in the war, the Allies landed in the south of Italy and drove the German-Italian alliance back. Dino Grandi and other members of the Fascist Grand Council launched a blistering attack on Mussolini, moving that the King, Victor Emmanuel III, resume full constitutional authority. The motion was passed. Victor Emmanuel had Mussolini arrested the same day. The Armistice between the Allies and Italy was signed on September 3 and publicly declared on September 8. The Italian royal family escaped to Pescara, where a government was set up under the protection of the Allies and declared war on Germany.

Following the decision of the Italian government to negotiate a surrender to the Allies, Nazi Germany declared Italy a puppet State – *The Italian Social Republic*, also known as the Republic of Salò – and took over critical defensive positions, including Italian-occupied south-eastern France and Italian-controlled areas in the Balkans. Horror stories abound of their attempts to disarm Italian soldiers. Giovanni recorded firsthand accounts of many of them in *Il grande diario*, never before published in English. One of them, years later, became the background to Louis de Bernières' novel, *Captain Corelli's Mandolin*, and concerns the fate of thousands of Italian soldiers on the Greek island of Kefalonia.

In the evening of September 21 all Italian resistance is quelled. The Germans advance and as they advance, they capture Italian soldiers and officers and immediately shoot them on the spot. On 22 September they enter Argostoli: the round-up continues and the massacre continues throughout the whole of the 23rd.

---

[12] 'Letter to My Descendant' (extract), *Diario clandestino* 1943–1945

A concentration camp for Italian soldiers is set up in the city, while the officers are gathered in the premises of the old canteen. At 6 am on September 24, the shooting of the officers begins. Some spontaneously present themselves to be shot, others, disguised as soldiers, try to hide among the troops. Soldiers denounce various officers.

The first to be shot is the commander of Italian forces General Gandin, then, four at a time, the others. Before their execution – which is by machine gun – they are systematically stripped of everything. Lieutenant Colonel Fioretti crushes his gold watch between two stones and slams it in the face of a German. Then he falls, mowed down. And like him, 350 officers are murdered. The executions continue from six to thirteen hundred hours: that is, until the German lieutenant who commands the operation yields to the pleas of the chaplain who, kneeling in front of him, begs him sobbing, and allows him to petition his superiors for pardon for the survivors. Which now number only forty-two.

The German command agrees on the condition that the forty-two officers join immediately to fight in the Germanic lines. This is the horrendous story of Kefalonia in which some 4,000 soldiers and 500 officers were massacred.

In Corfu, the 8,000-strong Italian garrison comprised elements of three divisions. All 280 Italian officers on the island were executed during two days. In the aftermath of the Battle of Kos, between 96 and 103 Italian officers were shot along with their commander. In Albania and elsewhere the massacres continued. Short testimonials: In Athens a German is approached by a child selling something. He chases the child away. The child does not go away, the soldier grabs his arm with both hands and breaks it with his knee. In Corfu a child carrying water to Italian prisoners is killed by a German sentry. An open car with an officer and a German soldier passes through a village. In Larissa a six or seven year old boy, in a spontaneous gesture, throws a handful of earth at the car. The officer gets out of the car and approaches the child. He takes his right arm and breaks his wrist against his knee. And so on...

Closer to home, Giovanni was luckier. One day after the Armistice, the Germans entered Alessandria in Piedmont, where he was stationed, and captured the *Cittadella* after a short bombardment. The Italian garrison surrendered. Given the choice to continue to fight with Germany or to surrender, Giovanni chose the latter adopting the slogan:

'I will not die even if they kill me.'

Shortly afterwards he was shipped by train to Poland to begin a lengthy period of imprisonment not as a prisoner-of-war (POW) but as an IMI (*Internati Militari Italiani*), since Italy had not officially declared war on its former ally (a decision of the Badoglio government on October 13), thereby rendering void the rights of these men under the 1929 Geneva Convention. The internationally agreed rules governing imprisonment would not apply.

It was the evening of September 8, 1943, when suddenly the radio broadcasted that it was all over. This was so true that the next morning I woke up in the same barracks, but under the watchful eye of sentries quite different from those that I'd known before, different as regards uniforms, weapons and, alas, nationality as well. The general appearance of the barracks had also undergone a change, thanks to a certain number of artillery pieces, awkwardly inserted among the architectural glories of the *Cittadella*'s façade.

In other words, the Germans had taken over.

One autumn morning, when I was standing in line in the barracks courtyard, and the bugle called me to attention, something miraculous happened. My heels came together with a resounding click. *Tac!*

'At last!' I exclaimed triumphantly.

Then I looked down at my feet and saw the reason why. All my cockiness faded away. I was wearing not my regulation boots, but a pair of wooden clogs the soles of which were three inches above the ground. I was a prisoner.

'And what about the heroic, last-ditch defence?' you may ask.

Just let me tell you one story, my dear fellow, the most dramatic of the lot.

We were under siege, and waiting from one moment to the next for the beginning of the attack. I was in command of twenty-five men, at the truck entrance. The corporal whom I had sent to the supply depot came back and I asked him:

'How many hand grenades did you get us?'

'No hand grenades,' he answered. 'The major told me that without a regular requisition he can't give out so much as a pin. He doesn't want to get into hot water.'

'All right,' I said. 'What about cartridges for our rifles? How many have we on hand?'

'One round per man.'

'Never mind!' I shouted. 'We'll have to be sparing with our shots. Aim at the whites of their eyes!'

'How are we to do that?' one of the soldiers objected. 'They'll be in tanks.'

'Then aim at the tanks! What else can I say?'

*

So much for history. For the purposes of a blow-by-blow account, let us admit that it was all over, but that our troubles had just begun. Towards noon, the rank and file were transferred to the outskirts of the city, while the officers were taken to the 'Gastric Ulcer,' otherwise known as the 'Garrison Mess.' It was a kind thought, when you come down to it, to invite us to lunch. Unfortunately, a big German tank had swept through the mess hall before us, and the follow-up infantry had streamed through the kitchen. So we found it advisable to take refuge, very sleepily, in the clubrooms on the second floor.

That night we managed as best we could. The colonel stretched out on the billiard table, alongside the major. Poor colonel! I remember that he snored in the same key as the march from *Tannhäuser*, and this nocturnal tribute to the musical genius of our great ex-ally was both gallant and pregnant with meaning.

I slept on the grand piano, and dreamed all night long of Heinrich Heine's poem about 'The Two Grenadiers'.

The next day, after a lively discussion with an SS officer, we were moved to the *Cittadella*.

'Citadel?' you may ask. 'What's that?'

'Well, just imagine that an architect of times gone by drew up the plan of a fortified place intended to lodge soldiers and provide storage for their weapons as well. He took pains to make the whole thing highly functional. But then, imagine this: the architect had to go away and in his absence his pet dog, Flick, chewed the blueprint to pieces. And the chambermaid, in order to cover up the disaster, picked up the pieces and glued them together in strictly haphazard fashion. The architect arrived upon the scene, took in at a glance the gravity of what had happened, but simply shrugged his shoulders and said: 'It doesn't really matter!' He sent the blueprint to the war department, where it was enthusiastically approved and forwarded to the contractors, who proceeded to execute it.

That is the Citadel. And now you can see why, in the course of a tour of it, or for that matter of any ordinary military installation, you may come across a room in the shape of a triangular pyramid with the door at the summit, a latrine with the toilet seat stuck onto the ceiling, a balcony opening onto a long hall, a nine-foot door on the third floor connecting with empty space, or a water pipe running into a chimney. In August, 1932, in the Citadel of P, I met a strangely accoutred soldier with a long, white beard.

'In what year were you called to do your military service?' I asked him.

'1899,' he told me.

'And are you still on duty?'

'No, sir,' he replied. 'I got my discharge in 1904, but I couldn't find the way out...'

The Citadel of A was of this same kind, but luckily, after only a few days had gone by, they took us to a prison camp (a *Larger*), where we were considerably better off. Yes, dear Descendant, God preserve you from citadels! For one thing, their walls are horribly hortatory. There isn't an inch of space that doesn't bear some such message as:

> NOTHING VENTURED NOTHING GAINED!
> BELIEVE, OBEY, FIGHT!
> MY COUNTRY RIGHT OR WRONG! EXCELSIOR!

In one picturesque spot, divided into small compartments, I read in huge letters: RUN! Considering the urgency of the emergency, this was really too much to ask.

In the Citadel of A I had occasion to notice various interesting things. For instance, I made my first acquaintance with a German horse. He was a dignified, warlike animal; the look in his eye and his proud demeanour showed that he was conscious of the gravity of the times and the significance of his allotted task, which was no less than the construction of a new pan-European equine society.

He was attached by a formidable complex of harness to a very special kind of small carriage made of iron and cast iron. This carriage was equipped with so many wheels, levers, pedals, hand- and foot-brakes, that one might have supposed it had an accelerator, clutch and gearshift as well. The remarkable thing about the harness was that every one of the holes in the multitude of straps was labelled with a conspicuous, individual number. It looked like a triumphant attempt to mechanise the humble horse. The girth was pulled so tight that his waist was as wasp-like as that of any ballet dancer, whereas the breeching was several inches too long and hung slackly under the tail.

Apparently, German regulations required that this particular type of horse should have its girth fastened at hole number 27, and the breeching at number 12. The good creature was not annoyed by this state of affairs, but rather looked slightly ashamed of the fact that his mother had not shaped him in such a way as to fit the official pattern. If the God of horses had said to him: 'Ask, and it shall be given,' I am quite sure that he would have asked for his waist to be reduced in size and his tail, together with the hindquarters, to be lowered a good six inches.

*

How long did I stay in the Citadel of A? It doesn't in the least matter. The point is that one day I came out and was put on the train to carry us north of the Alps.

On September 13 Giovanni was transported from Alessandria railway station to Bremerwörde, a town 750 miles away in the district of Rotenburg, north-west Germany. The journey took five days, with lengthy stoppages, carriage doors closed.

Carrying our baggage (if we had any) on our backs we went to assemble in the courtyard. My prisoner's knapsack contained not only a miserable miscellany of everything I had been able to gather up from the Citadel of Alessandria, but also a cargo of hopes and illusions.

A German lieutenant circulates a small sheet written in Italian and German: 'I swear to give all my blood for the greatness of the Germanic Reich and for the triumph of the new Europe.' It is simply a matter of signing. Anyone who does not sign in ten minutes leaves. The two trucks are there ready, with their engines running.

A senior from the MVSN[13] arrives, accompanied by an SS officer, who has come to free the officers who belong or have belonged to the Militia. This he says aloud, then under his breath he encourages:

'Come on, come on! Even those who've never been registered. Come! And tonight we all drink.'

We get up on the trucks. Those left on the ground reassure us:

'We are coming on the second journey.'

The trucks unload us at the station and then return to the Citadel, but we don't see any of them again.

On the train I find Rebora (Lieutenant Roberto Rebora)[14] who is very worried because he has a bad tooth. Even for a hermetic poet it must be sad to go into the unknown with a decayed molar. A trickster offers us a Beretta holster for five cigarettes...

At Verona we stop between a freight train overflowing with Italian soldiers and another, whose open cars are packed with Slavs being moved to Germany from an internment camp at Padua. The Italian

---

[13] The Voluntary Militia for National Security, the fascist Blackshirts or *squadristi*.
[14] Roberto Rebora, 'the purest of the poets of this century' (*Corriere della Sera*). 'He followed his inner path without ever getting confused with any group or any school.' Giovanni puts him in the hermetic school: a form of obscure and difficult poetry, which he lampoons in his Christmas Story (1944).

soldiers stare at us without speaking, except for a corporal, by his accent obviously from Rome, who calls out sarcastically:

'You officers, there, all you ever thought about was the shine on your boots...!'

The Slavs hate us just as much, but silently. Upon our solicitation, one of them finally does speak, and then only to give us some purely technical pointers:

'You'll be hungry for the first few months; after that you'll get used to it...'

Trains teeming with humanity arrive, while others leave. In place of the trainload of Italians, there followed a convoy of English prisoners. We had some extra bread and offered it to them, but they wanted only chocolate. After dark they began singing 'Tipperary', and their good cheer may have been quite justified, because the young German sergeant who was in charge of us said that within a few months the war would be over and 'Deutschland kaput.'

*

SEPTEMBER 15, Wednesday: There were people assembled in front of every house close to the railroad tracks and at every crossing. They have come to say goodbye to their deported brothers. Old women dressed in black, whose sons had died in the Julia Division,[15] threw out their arms as we passed by. This gesture and their tearful eyes seemed to reflect endless despair. All the way to the province of Veneto we had met with complete indifference or hatred, but here, in the extreme north-eastern corner of Italy, we breathed a truly Christian and human air. Here we were not 'You officers,' the sons of exploiters and profiteers, but brothers on the way to exile. Train after train of prisoners must have come this way, but still the local population continued to offer some comfort. They insisted upon giving us bread, apples and all they had left of tobacco.

At Basiliano a woman with a tub full of water ran along the platform from one end of the train to the other and if anyone had a handkerchief or an undershirt to be washed, she managed to wash it before the train went on. Her zeal and speed were positively heartbreaking. At Udine a little boy handed me a piece of ice through the window, and in spite of his small size he accompanied it with these unforgettable words:

'We're all the same people.'

---

[15] The 3rd Alpine Division of the Royal Italian Army, a specialist in mountain warfare.

When the train moved, the stationmaster, an old man with a white moustache, drew himself up to attention and raised one hand to his cap in salute…

Marco Moroni, also on his way to Bremerwörde in September 1943, noted: 'During the crossing of Italy many tried to escape, some succeeded thanks to young ladies cunningly playing the Germans, while others were machine-gunned and abandoned along the line…'

SEPTEMBER 16. Thursday. Later on, when we were moved from camp to camp, we travelled for hundreds of miles in sealed freight cars. But for this trip from Alessandria to Bremerwörde we travelled in conventional carriages, which stayed in Germany to work for the greatness of the Reich.

Travelling this way, in an Italian railway carriage, we had no idea of the distance we were covering. Even after we had been through a dozen foreign cities, we should not have been surprised to see the familiar outlines of Milan or Bologna. As we proceeded toward Salzburg, the green fields and flowering gardens of this section of Austria were not too unlike what we were accustomed to at home. Enough of my diary!

SEPTEMBER 17. Friday. After Salzburg, the landscape changes. Behind the bars of a grade crossing, five little boys in brown shirts with a red armband and a swastika watch us go by. All together they make an eloquent gesture signifying that they would just as soon cut our throats.

'We must be in Germany,' said one of my Italian friends.

The prisoners were still almost 600 miles from Bremerwörde, and an eight-mile march from there to Oflag XB, the *Lager* at Sandbostel.[16] Moroni takes up the story:

Exhausted by thirst and hunger we finally arrive in Bremerwörde… We take our backpacks on our shoulders and start the march to our concentration camp… We cross vast deserted countryside, and finally, after about eleven kilometres, we could see a large accommodation surrounded by high fences… In a large square they make us stop and everyone falls to the ground exhausted…

---

[16] Built for 10,000, at one time it housed 70,000 prisoners. Conditions were atrocious; death rate high.

At 7 o'clock they give us stinking boiled water with lime leaves, which they call tea. At 12 o'clock a bowl of water with cabbage leaf, at 2 o'clock five potatoes cooked in water and at 4 o'clock a loaf cut in five, a spoonful of meat and a pound of bad margarine cut in ten... They took us to the sports field of the prison, where 16,000 soldiers were gathered. It seems that someone wants to make a speech. Two fascists, accompanied by Germans, appear in the middle of the field and climb onto a platform. They begin to speak against the King and Badoglio [the war-time Italian Government],[17] trying to intimidate us... They ask us to make the choice between prison and voluntary conscription in the German army.

Nobody answers and our officers make a sign not to yield, but unfortunately among us there were about sixty fascists coming out of the rows. We all looked at them and despised them. At the end, the fascist who made the speech cheered for *Il Duce*, but a bold and fiery voice replied with, 'Long live the King!'

Then we were taken to our barracks. All the prisoners of other nations, witnessing the scene and seeing that no one wanted to fight for the Germans, said that we were good comrades and began throwing us cookies across our fence, cookies and cigarettes that they got through the English Red Cross.

---

[17] In 1943, King Emanuele III appointed Pietro Badoglio as Prime Minister after removing Mussolini.

Christmas 1943

The full itinerary of *Lagers* to which Giovanni was taken after Oflag XB (at Sandbostel near Bremerwörde), was as follows. On the 23rd September 1943 he was taken by rail to Częstochowa in southern Poland, a distance of some 620 miles, arriving on 27th at Nordkaserne Stalag 367, a camp with a horrific history since its inception in 1941. On 8th November he was on the move again, to Stalag 333 in Beniaminów, 160 miles to the north-east, a camp, 25 miles from Warsaw, where, between 1941 and 1944, tens of thousands died from harsh treatment. (From January-February 1944, Stalag 333 became known as Oflag 73.) Then, at the end of March 1944, he was returned to Germany, to Oflag XB at Sandbostel, arriving on the 2nd April. Finally, on 30th January 1945 they took him 80 miles south-east to a camp near the German village of Wietzendorf (*Kriegsgefangenenlager*). The camp had originally been used for 17,000 Russian soldiers who died mainly from the poor sanitary conditions. From January/February 1944 it was known as Oflag 83.

Once upon a time there was a train and it was a wonderful mechanism that smoked and slapped and snorted like a man and, at night, opened two eyes as red as moons that made the iron rails on which it moved sparkle. It was an extraordinary mechanism because it had a locomotive in front and, behind it, a very long queue of wagons, closed with bolts, padlocks, bolts, bolts, railings, makeshift barriers, fences, gratings, and on each wagon was written: 'Horses 8 – Men 40', and within each wagon were Italian internees, numbering 50, 60 or 120 – the equivalent, in fact, of 8 horses or 40 men, as was immediately clear by the quantity of food assigned to them.

Once upon a time there was a train which – loaded with its almost human goods to be transported from one *Lager* to another – set off like lightning, travelled 200, 300 and even 400 metres in a flash, and then stopped in front of some station or other, on which was invariably written in large letters:

ALLE RÄDER MUSSEN ROLLEN FÜR DEN SIEG!

Which meant that all wheels must roll for victory:[18] not including the wheels of the Great Reich's brain, which had already stopped – according to plan – on 1 September 1939, or the wheels of trains loaded with Italian Military Internees [IMI], of course.

So long did the trains stay in the station that when they set off again it was necessary to free the rails from the mushrooms which had sprung up – thanks to the incessant rain that dripped down from the wagons.

These stops were very useful because they allowed us to analyse and understand the sorting system in use on the German railways, a hastily drawn-up system known as 'the push manoeuvre'. The wagons loaded with IMI would come to a standstill in the station and remain there waiting, good as gold, and dripping, until a locomotive with an eagle on its cap came through, snorting to a colleague stationed on the opposite side of the station:

'Hey! Comrade! Do you want these wagons?'

The other locomotive (in homage to the command that all wheels must roll for victory) replied that it should send them over. And the first locomotive, with an energetic kick up the pants, sent over the wagons loaded with IMI.

'What sort of merchandise are these wagons carrying?' the second locomotive asked when he felt the wagons approaching his rear end. 'From the stench they would seem full of manure.'

'Italians,' explained the tender.

'Italians?' the locomotive was indignant. '*Raus!*'

And with a thrust of his kidneys he sent the wagons back to the first locomotive. Which then protested that no return goods were accepted, and kicked them on to another. And so on (from one locomotive to the next and one kick to another) for hours and hours, all night long, and the marvel of the matter – what proved perfect Germanic organisation – lay in the fact that the kick came at the precise instant at which some 'passenger' was dangerously juggling a box in one hand as he made his way among the bodies piled on the floor in an effort to reach the window and pour its foul contents out of the wagon.[19]

---

[18] A propaganda campaign in 1942 to motivate the German population to forgo rail travel that was not absolutely necessary.
[19] Wietzendorf reading, 1945

I changed *Lagers* several times, but the story remained essentially the same... We were loaded onto freight cars and then unloaded from them, stripped of most of our belongings and thrown into the bug-ridden filth of the camp. Buried in communal graves around us were the bodies of thousands of our predecessors. Soon the outside world forgot. The International Red Cross could do nothing for us, because its charter contained no provisions for our status of 'military internees'.

In the beginning was the *Lager*: arid sand, huts in rows and, on the sand and among the huts – like shipwrecked people suddenly thrown on a deserted and inhospitable island – men wandered amazed, strangers to each other, almost enemies.

Once upon a time there was a prisoner. The *Lager* was basically a box of sand surrounded by a barbed wire fence. Tall turrets arose from the four corners of the enclosure, where men with helmets on their heads stood guard, guns always at the ready. They had to be careful, poor fellows, because if they fired at a prisoner and missed they would end up in prison. Waste of a bullet. A consequence of the immutable rationing measures to which the then Great Reich submitted in a spirit of sacrifice in order to achieve inevitable victory and confer justice and a deserved peace upon a battered world.

Once upon a time there was internment. Looked at from the outside, it was a very simple matter, but rather more complicated from within because – in addition to the bedbugs and fleas – there were the non-optional supplements in the deal: runny-slop duty, thick-slop duty, the trading floor, the division of bread ritual and so many other annoying, parasitic undertakings which so greatly saddened our already sad lives.

And besides all this, there was Signora Gestapo, who, to a man, broke into the dormitories, rummaged around everywhere, broke up cigarettes and soap bars for fear that hidden inside were radio transmitters, amphibious tanks, anti-aircraft guns, magnetic mines, Atlantic submarines, four-engine bombers and other stuff prohibited by regulations.

And the prisoners all had the same name, the initials of which they bore on their backs: KGF.[20]

Once upon a time there was a 'castle'. It was an ingenious wooden contrivance, built in such a way as to allow a man to assume the

---

[20] *Kriegsgefangene.*

horizontal position at night without running the risk of falling asleep, an inconvenience endemic to all normal beds.

The castle could accommodate two, four, six, eight, sixteen or up to thirty-two compartments. In the latter case, they were superimposed three storeys high. Occupiers of the mezzanine level had to be slotted into their shelves by specialist personnel, who also took them out in the morning, an operation that was particularly easy during the winter. In fact, the *Lager* – according to the needs of modern comfort and, indeed, International Conventions – was equipped with central heating in the sense that the one stove in the *Lager* was placed in the centre of the hut: a providence that allowed the prisoner to wake up completely stiff from frost. This was both to the advantage of preserving the prisoner himself, and facilitating the morning operation of extracting bodies from the castle, because the workers on duty needed only a large iron grappling hook of the sort for raking ice columns out of refrigerator vans.

Once upon a time there was the castle and every crevice, every little hole, housed a general assembly of fleas or an international congress of bedbugs. And the bugs and fleas were hungry and devoured our very dreams. So, no-one could ever have peace because, in captivity, those who do not dream sleep only with their eyes, while everything else remains awake.

Once upon a time there was a castle and in the morning one would open one's eyes and count one's bones: 'How is it that I had twenty-four ribs last night and now I have thirty-six?' And just as a disease known as the 'washerwoman's knee' exists, so now there was a disease known as 'prisoner's hip', which manifests itself as a large dark-coloured callus on the prisoner's right, or left, hip. If you sleep on your back, belly up, the callus occurs in a more central location of the body, so much so that the disease is then called 'prisoner's coccyx'. And all this occurs because the slats on which we slept were never known for their excessive softness – although the German administration, with touching attention, chose to make them of softwood.

So, during the night, a man often got out of bed and stayed up for a few hours to get a bit of rest. Only after Signora Liberty arrived in 1945 was no one sleepy anymore, because a castle (even if a large British flag flies from its top) can never be as comfortable as a small house with a small Italian flag on the roof...

Once upon a time there was 'l'apèlo', as the Germans called it, but the actual word is 'appppellllllo' with eight 'p's and twelve 'elle's, because the damn thing always started and never ended. Whether it rained, or snowed, or if the wind made the sand swirl, the daily roll call ceremony took place at fixed times and was a highly significant spectacle, particularly in the winter months, because then everyone put on everything they owned: overcoat, fur coat, blankets, camouflage sheets, sleeping bags, straw mattresses, package wrappers and special overcoats made of tarred cardboard, asbestos sheets, corrugated sheet metal and other waterproof fabrics. But the most interesting was the headgear, which ranged from the rigid cap of the Italian army to the out-of-order cap, like the irregular bands aggregated to Chiang-Kai-shek's troops;[21] from a regulation envelope straightened out with a stick of fine wood, to the sad envelope of the last letter received before 8 September.

Once upon a time there was a roll call: and when the cold blew up the pump pipes and peeled off the pieces of cement stuck to their trousers, the prisoners' teeth chattered. But you had to be careful to chatter them in time – *unò, duè*, all together now. Otherwise, Captain P would become angry, and slow down operations by keeping units outdoors for a few additional hours, all to the detriment of final victory and peace with justice.

During roll call it might be necessary to stay outdoors for five hours, even if only four out of the final quintile were left standing.

Once upon a time there was the German ration which included – and in more than enough quantity – all the elements necessary to sustain a man. The only drawback was that it had to serve not one but seven men. This was not very nice because it encouraged doubt among the prisoners as to whether they should continue to breathe or not. However, the considerable upside was that all the microbes and bacilli nestling in the blood died of hunger, which ensured that we would die perfectly healthy. The German ration came with the food table, which was set up every day with admirable regularity, allowing the prisoner to speculate from morning just how many calories he would lack by evening in order to stay alive.

From the point of view of aesthetics and practicality, the German ration was beautiful as it could easily be stored in the wallet without the line of the jacket being disturbed. Out on its own was the soup which, being entrusted to Italian personnel, was affected by a lack of love for precision typical of the Latin temperament, inclining towards the liberal arts rather than towards the exact sciences. So that sometimes, due to the carelessness of the kitchen staff, it happened that a whole pea would be found in a tub of only 80 litres of water. This made the dispensers of the soup very embarrassed due to the

---

[21] Chiang kai-shek, the Chinese Nationalist, revolutionary leader of the Republic of China from 1928.

difficulties they encountered (lacking the appropriate precision instruments) in dividing a pea into eighty-seven equal parts...

It is perfectly useless to try to explain what imprisonment is: those who have suffered it know, those who have not cannot understand it. There are things in the world that cannot be adequately described.

Hunger, for example, is one of these, but imprisonment includes, in addition to hunger, a hundred other things even worse than hunger. To understand imprisonment, you have to live it. And to remember it, you have to relive it. You cannot have the exact feelings simply by trawling through the story. It must be considered step by step. No panoramic views, only details.

Let me take one frame only from the films rolled up inside my memory box, a single frame. Here I am sitting on my sack at the edge of a road. Mud. Shoes busted, feet wet; a large blister under the left heel. Stomach cramps. The sentry leaning against a tree is smoking. I am two months without a cigarette. On the left, a little house with a woman and a child at the window. I am six months without news from home. My companion in front of me has a violet right ear. Detail of the shoe: how am I going to put it back on?

Fix a detail: see yourself in any attitude. Only then can we find all that we thought and felt at that moment; only then do we really relive suffering. It is a ridiculous example, but for all that it is right. When you suffer from an illness you suffer it moment by moment and every moment is a new sensation that has already surpassed the previous one. Fortunately for us, we cannot, finally, sum up the moments of suffering and experience total suffering. Likewise, ultimately, for the purposes of a final exposition on this, after a year of hunger we were hungry for only a moment. However, to communicate the exact value of this moment, we must, as we have said, relive it in *all* its moments and in all our thoughts of the time.

I believe that it is useful to remember the evil of the past, for it helps a lot to bear the evils of the present and allows us to rediscover, among past sufferings, those honest and clean thoughts that can only be given life in suffering.[22]

In the beginning was the *Lager*, where everything seemed temporary, even life itself... The needs of body and spirit forced men to create the essential things of the world from which they'd suddenly been cut off. The most urgent needs were material and the first wave of change was rapidly adopted.

---
[22] *Ritorno alla base*, 2015

In on this rode agents, sub-agents, wholesalers, retailers, advertising. In on this rode *trade*. Everyone discovered in himself unsuspected artisan qualities. Here comes the watchmaker's workshop, the tailor's workshop, the smoker's, the bookbinder's workshop. In came *industry*.

As a first requirement of the spirit, naturally the Church responded: chaplains quickly became parish priests, religious practices became a daily custom. In came *the parish*.

Then *culture* claimed its rights and historical, literary, scientific, artistic conferences, the *lecturae Dantis* [readings of Dante] and modern poetry evenings came in. Language courses, law courses, agricultural courses, engineering courses were established, and a university, with (almost) regular lecturers and teaching programmes. Then, various evenings of music, singing and art were organised and in came the theatre which – when possible – called forth orchestras, and prose and vocal magazine groups.

As if by a miracle, a ball was found, and in came *sport*. In the huts the men divided into teams or small groups of twenty or thirty, representing the various buildings and each building had its own foreman. Various groups of four, five or six people were formed within the teams and small rooms and each of them constituted the family with its head of the family. Groups of huts became districts and the head of a hut was the fiduciary of the district group. The battalions became the various sectors with their department heads, and the Italian commander of the field was the burgomaster of this small city.

A complete little world. With a somewhat fragrant, but covert, market. With an 'almost' sports field. With public offices, clinic, hospital, square, beach, park and pond. With a university, library, art exhibitions and the stock exchange 'noir' [black market], as in the most civilised of cities. And, above all, with that frank, cordial, total lack of solidarity that characterises every human consortium worthy of the name.[23]

La Caterina was most famous of all undertakings – an old wreck of a machine measuring 9 x 10 x 5 cm. She was born in the Bremewörde/Sandbostel concentration camp, Oflag XB. Although the Gestapo knew of her existence and angrily scoured the place for her, they never managed to discover her. Indeed, she even managed to leave that camp and find her way into another and, finally, she made the American commander who arrived with the liberating troops roar with enthusiasm: he wanted her at any price, but had to be content

---

[23] 'Spiegazione del fatto', *Diario clandestino* 1943–1945

with taking an enormous number of photographs, because Caterina was too important to those who had built her and their ultimate weapon of defence.

She was created out of nothing: nothing, that is, in a relative sense, of course. Like the Eternal Father building Eve, who started from a rib of Adam, the builders of Caterina started from a small valve. This small valve 'LQ5', introduced in the *Lager* God knows how, was the only piece in the whole of Caterina not to be man-made. The rest of her was constructed from what was available to a man standing naked in the middle of a clover meadow.

You don't need to be a technician to understand that having a single valve patched with tar (taken from the roof of the hut) and expecting to get a radio receiver from it is like having a distributor and expecting to end up with a perfectly functioning car.

A certain 'variable tuning condenser' was, for example, cut out of a tin can, picked up in the garbage, and with pieces of a celluloid frame cut out of card holders. The other essential, a 'fixed condenser', was built with foil and cigarette papers, while the 'fixed resistance' had, as raw material, the paper in which the rationed margarine was wrapped, treated with pencil graphite.

The group 'coils, antenna, tuning, variometer' found a place for a shaving soap dish, insulated wire from a coil, cardboard rolled into a cylinder and candle wax that worked wonderfully, because everyone referred to it publicly as 'a paraffin firelighter'. Here, however, help from the Great Reich was required. Coil-insulated wire and magnets were needed to build the headset: how can you find these things in a concentration camp?

Our procurer noticed that every day the sergeant at the post office in the camp left his bicycle leaning against the hut for a few hours. He studied the timetables and, one morning, working a few metres from the sentry posted on the watchtower, he removed the dynamo from the bicycle light. Then, having removed the wire and magnets, he screwed it back onto the bicycle.

This was the work of engineer Carlo Martignago. We were very close friends but, these days he no longer talks to me because I have dared to write an article on the 'alfisti' with a certain irreverence, and he is an 'alfista'.[24]

The engineer Olivero, creator of *la Caterina*, established at a certain moment that he needed an anode battery: to build it one had to collect twenty old copper 10-cent coins miraculously from the 6,000 prisoners, then cut out twenty disks from the zinc covering of

---

[24] A collector of Alfa Romeo motorcars.

the wooden sinks and twenty discs of cloth from a blanket. The whole, arranged in the case of an old pocket battery, was placed in a position to supply twenty theoretical volts, for three quarters of an hour of reception, with acetic acid obtained from the lucky few recipients of food parcels from home, from cans of pickles.

With the sergeant's magnets and other little things gleaned God knows how, plus a tin can and a cardboard disk, a headset with a single earphone was made.

The fast-reaction control system, called '*comando della reazione*' – Reaction Command – was found, thank goodness, ready and waiting, and was called 'Olivero'.

Let me explain. The 'Media Centre' was housed in a kind of warehouse, which was, in fact, a hut full of lousy rags and mismatched, muddy clogs. In this hovel was a half-smashed 'castle' – one of those hideous six-seater chicken coops assigned to us as beds. Lieutenant Olivero would perch on a horizontal crossbar of the middle shelf of the Castle, one leg dangling in thin air. With the earphone in one ear, he took control of Caterina with his left hand, while, with his right, he wrote what he was receiving in Italian, German, French and English.

All the while, the leg dangling in the void rose and fell to effect a micrometric regulation of Reaction Command, as it was found that by raising and lowering his foot from the moist clay floor, he could vary the antenna capacity for maximum reception. The antenna was actually his whole body, because Lieutenant Olivero held the wire connected to the 'antenna foot' between his teeth.

This was, in short, the famous Caterina whom the Gestapo angrily searched for with telegoniometers, without ever being able to find her. There was a colossal defence network surrounding Caterina, made up of 12,000 eyes, 12,000 ears and 6,000 brains. As soon as anything unusual was noticed going on, Caterina shut down and off she went on her travels, passing from hand to hand hidden inside an alpine mess tin.

For us, Caterina was a miracle. She represented the victory of intelligence over hunger, cold, anguish, loneliness and abuse. Caterina worked wonderfully well and received all the major European broadcasters. Only on account of her did we know what was happening in the world. She wove for us an invisible, but tenacious, thread that bound thousands of hopeless people to the pillar of Hope.

News picked up was immediately translated and circulated on shreds of paper throughout the camp. Translated into French, it even reached into that part of the camp.

Some men had drawn, partly from memory and partly based on maps torn from some De Agostini cartographic and geographic publications (which had escaped the endless searches), a map of the Theatre of War and, thanks again to Caterina, this map would show the advance of troops that were supposed to come and get us out. And when, in the first days of April 1945, the circle tightened around us, and the war moved close to our camp, and the artillery shells began to whistle over our heads, none of it was a surprise to us – once more, the triumph of Caterina.

That's the sum of it: and let me say that I have not always looked at radio with the distrust and resentment I look at it and its degenerate daughter, TV, today. Sometimes I think that if I had old Caterina here on my desk, perhaps she would bring me, as then, news capable of rekindling the languishing flame of Hope. Then again, perhaps she would only bring me rumours of a world long gone.[25]

*

One day in September 1943, I found myself, along with a group of 109 officers, shipped off to an internment camp in Częstochowa, Poland. This time we travelled with a regular convoy. That is to say closed cattle wagons – in fact, 50 Italian officers to a wagon registered for 8 horses.

SUNDAY 26 SEPTEMBER, 1943 Sad Sunday. We have been locked in the wagons for twenty-three hours and we leave as if from another world. It's raining, the station is deserted, filthy with coal, the Red Cross workers bring us a snort: diuretic tea.

MONDAY 27 SEPTEMBER In Stradom, Polish prisoners who work along the line give us their bread and their cigarettes and welcome us to their battered and generous country. Częstochowa: in German Tschenstochau. The Germans disguised her name by adding many Hs and T's, but Częstochowa remains indelibly Polish.

Thirty thousand Russians passed through Nordkaserne Stalag 367: 10,000 died. They spent their time outdoors. Snow, frost, hunger.

Sofia, Katja, Tamara: three Russian 'comrades' live together with the other Russians. They are very kind to us and offer us bread. All three were taken prisoner in combat. One was a lieutenant in the tank crew. She is currently pregnant.

---

[25] 'Il trionfo della Caterina', *Oggi*, (1966)

*

The captain of the Gestapo discovered that I am a journalist and suggested that he take me to visit the famous Sanctuary of the Black Madonna. What will he want from me in return?

I feel as if I were walking through the streets of a city devastated by the plague. The few people to be seen walk as hurriedly as if someone were following them and cast hasty glances at the ten prisoners of war, preceded by a Gestapo captain and with a suspicious *dolmetscher* (interpreter) bringing up the rear. No matter how fleeting these glances, there is an eloquence in their eyes which only the interpreter is powerless to understand.

Before 1939, Częstochowa was a city of 180,000 inhabitants; a few days after the entrance of the Germans 50,000 of these were gone, transferred to some other locality, in this world or the next.

Many of the captured Russian coats which the Germans distribute to us have a patch on the chest or back, a little, round patch covering the hole where a bullet went in and a soul went out. My coat has such a patch, just over the heart. It is made of stout cloth and carefully sewn, yet a breath of cold air penetrates the patch, even when there is no wind and a warm sun. And my heart aches, when it is pierced by this icy needle.[26]

It seemed as if houses, as well as men, had been deported, taken away from the vast area of wide, empty streets and squares. The surviving buildings were all sad in appearance, as if they had souls and their outward aspect reflected the tragedy which had haunted them for the last four years.

The air was heavy with suspicion; eyes peered out between half-closed shutters, shops were locked and the windows of the few still open displayed the canned and boxed products in which impoverishment tries to conceal itself: dried-egg mixes, fruit and vegetable extracts, soap powder and little bags of desiccated herbs. Every now and then there was a glass jar filled with liquorice sticks or bright-coloured candies, to convince children that something had been spared by the war.

PATRIA BAR ... the Italian word on the sign overhanging the entrance to a deserted café gave the heart a twinge like that provoked by the sight, among a foreign crowd, of a lone familiar face.

The wind swept through the streets and howled in my empty head. I felt like a desperate character who puts on his last good suit and goes to stroll on the main street among the crowd of rich men and

---

[26] *Diario clandestino* 1943–1945

beautiful women, stopping to stare at jewellers windows and to ask for somebody by name in the best café, knowing all the while that this world is no longer his and he has no right to be walking in it. For the moment I had forgotten, but I was sure that as soon as the gate closed behind me I should remember that for a full month I had been hungry.

The Sanctuary is on top of a hill and as soon as we started up the broad approach, the Gestapo captain stopped and spoke to the interpreter, who immediately translated his words for my benefit.

'The captain says the hill you see is more than 400 feet above sea level.'

This was the only thing he found worthy of note. But then altitude is a factual, mathematical sort of thing, as distinct from having artistic and historical properties. A very German point of view...

At the entrance to the Sanctuary we were met by a German-speaking guide. One of the prisoners accompanying me served as his translator.

The Sanctuary is an agglomeration of buildings around a very high bell tower. Originally it was a monastery belonging to the Order of St Anthony Abbot, later incorporated with that of the Dominicans. After the year 1200, when the monastery acquired possession of the famous St Luke Madonna, it was the object of many a pilgrimage, and the chapel grew into the size and importance of a consecrated basilica.[27]

Priors and Polish lords made successive additions to the building, and thus it became a sort of architectural encyclopaedia. Even the lofty, black marble bell tower seems to have been designed by an architect who drew spire after spire and said after every one: 'Let's add something more. We have a long way to go before we touch the feet of St. Peter!'

In short, the effect is that of a jumble, with all around it the world's largest-scale Stations of the Cross, composed of fourteen twice-life-size sculptured figures, dispersed on pedestals fifty yards apart.

Inside, there is such a quantity of marble, both genuine and fake, that when the visitor steps out onto the black and white pebbles of the open piazza, he is tempted to trample them with his heels in order to find out whether they are made of painted wood or real stone.

---

[27] Our Lady of Częstochowa ('the Black Madonna') was recognised as Queen and Protector of Poland by King John II Casimir Vasa, in Lwów Cathedral in 1652.

In certain places, the Sanctuary has something of a citadel about it. High black boots are visible below the white robes of the monks, giving them a disguised soldier's air. (The same thing can be said of many Polish men.) It must, indeed, be a mighty stronghold, in order to have withstood the attacks of Swedes, Hussites, Russians and Saxons.

In 1709, the Swedes stormed and took its impregnable heights, which were manned by only two hundred and twenty monkish and lay defenders. Twelve thousand Swedes were not sufficient, and it took 18,000 to make it fall. The guide pointed out cannon balls imbedded in the walls at this time.

Everywhere, in the piazza, on the steps, the railings, the mural decorations and spires, there is an insignia of a palm tree with two rampant lions and a raven carrying a piece of bread in his beak, which pertain to the legend of St Anthony in the desert. Every day the raven brought him half a loaf of bread and, when once a year St Anthony went to visit him, a whole one. When the saint died, two lions dug his grave with their claws.

In a low voice the guide added a postscript to this story. 'Originally the bird was an eagle. When the Russians came along, they substituted for it a raven. Then came the Germans, and took away the bread.'

From the piazza there is a view over the whole city and the woods, which once belonged to the monastery, stretching all the way to the horizon.

'During the pilgrimages made to honour the feast day of the Black Madonna, there are arrangements in the great courtyard for the confessions and communions of fifty thousand persons a day. And at the altar up there, behind a movable glass door, Mass is said for the hundreds of thousands clustered at the foot of the hill. Naturally, there are loudspeakers...'

The guide continued his humdrum *spiel*, calling attention to the cost of all these installations and the name of the contractor who had built them. I looked down at the foot of the hill, where hundreds of thousands of Poles are wont to gather. The only human soul was a scurrying woman in high boots, whose presence only served to set off the solitude and despair of the empty space all around her.

It was time to attend the daily ceremony held at the basilica. The Black Madonna of Częstochowa is said to be the earliest known portrait of the Blessed Virgin, painted from life by St Luke on a fragment of the board over which she wept during the Crucifixion.

This piece of wood has a most interesting story, having been for 320 years in Jerusalem, 400 in Constantinople, 400 in Hungary and, ever since, 770 years ago here at Częstochowa. In 1430 it was stolen and mutilated by Hussites from Bohemia (it is riddled with Tartar bullet-holes as well). In 1717 it was consecrated by Pope Clement X, and we see it today enshrined in a chapel whose display of gold, silver and precious stones is so rich as to be almost alarming, for after a certain point wealth is divorced from reality and becomes inadmissible.

The image is lodged in a niche above the altar, covered by a massive, solid gold block, weighing 1,600 pounds, which can be raised and lowered like a curtain. Every afternoon, at a quarter to five, there is a brief ceremony, during which the image is exposed to the public view, to the accompaniment of a hymn...

Entering the basilica, we found ourselves among a crowd of women and children gathered in front of a fairytale altar, gleaming with jewels and lights, while an organ played in the background. After a month in surroundings where everything oozed filth and despair, where every spoken word was a cry and every order a threat ... to be suddenly plunged into this atmosphere of calm, this glitter of gold, this warm flow of music I ... I paused at the threshold, then stepped forward, feeling suddenly as buoyant as if I had shed my rag-covered body at the door. The gold block in front of the niche slowly rose, and the miraculous image – pitch-black against the gleaming gold – was, by virtue of the very contrast, utterly mysterious and fascinating.

From the crowd there rose a song which seemed to express the whole soul of Poland, to voice the dignified sorrow of a people accustomed for centuries to oppression and resurrection. When the gold block was lowered, there was a fanfare of trumpets, the notes filled with a desperate and deeply disturbing passion.

'The trumpeters are playing out of tune because some of the best of them are absent,' said the guide. So that was it: those notes of desperate passion were simply out of tune. OK. But I, for one, didn't believe it. Everything in Poland, every gesture and intonation, speaks to me of passion.

Dusk fell over the dark blue-green woods around Częstochowa. From the piazza in front of the Sanctuary we could see a pale moon preparing for the evening spectacle and, on the left, the huge Nordkaserne Stalag 367, with the towers set at intervals around its barbed-wire fencing and its horrific history.

'The carillon in the bell tower is one of the best in the world,' the guide tells us.

'And why doesn't it ever ring?'

'Ever since the first day of the German occupation, all the bells have been silent,' he said under his breath. 'They won't ring again until Poland is free.'

As we filed back down to the city, I thought of the four years that the bells had been mute. Should I hear the bells of Poland peal again?

*

The captain of the Gestapo, who during our visit to the Sanctuary had not divulged the price of his invitation, in the end summons me to his office. He asks if I would like to contribute to an Italian newspaper printed in Germany. I reply that it depends on what newspaper it is. Am I a Republican, in sympathy with the Italian Social Republic?

'No sir.'

'Why?'

'Because I am a soldier of the Royal Italian army.'

He points out to me with a smile that the one to whom I keep faith has not kept his word. I reply with a smile that that's his business.

He dismisses me with courtesy:

'Thanks, that's all I need from you.'

Giovanni never forgot his visit to the Black Madonna and demonstrated her power to defend mankind against totalitarian tyranny in *Comrade Don Camillo*,[28] the collection in which Nazi tyranny of the 1940s is replaced by that of Communist Russia of the 1960s.

On 8 November 1943, Giovanni was on the move again, this time 160 miles to the north-east to Stalag 333 (later known as as Oflag 73) in Beniaminów, a camp 25 miles from Warsaw, where, between 1941 and 1944, tens of thousands died from harsh treatment.

Wherever you look, there, in the background, is the Tower, omnipresent and watchful like the eye of God. Of the God they say is on their side (*mit uns*) so very different from our God, with the harshly sounded name of *Gott*, which they have fastened upon him.

The huts in which we live are like railway cars, buried above the wheels, in sand. One after the other, a whole train of them that has foundered. It seems impossible that they should ever emerge and start moving. And yet that is exactly what, one day, they must do.

Hut No. 18 is one of the myriad examples of wartime architecture: a dark wooden hut with a ditch and a circular hillock around it. A long, low-ceilinged hut, under the infinite sky above the Polish

---

[28] *Comrade Don Camillo* (Pilot, 2017).

plain. A miniature Noah's Ark, drifting over a flood of melancholy. With inside, every conceivable kind of creature, from a louse to a poet, from a rat to a former government employee.

When we entered it for the first time, we huddled near the door, struck dumb by the sight of the three rows of empty bunks, with our eyes wandering over the bare walls, the uneven, dusty floor and the windows that had neither shades nor shutters.

We stood there, with our duffle bags in our arms, like miserable immigrants, penetrating the bowels of the ship that is to carry them away. We remained speechless, and time stamped every passing second on the icy silence, as if it were pitilessly beating it into our heads.

All of a sudden there was an outcry:

'Captain Novello's hammer!'

Here I must recall the world's most accursed tool, a nefarious mixture of monkey wrench, pincers, wire cutter, chisel, file, screwdriver, hatchet and pig's foot. Every cubic inch of this minotaur of the mineral kingdom had a different function from the next, and the whole thing was a hammer worthy of being reviled in some magazine devoted to the defence of the racial purity of its kind.

'Captain Novello's hammer!'

It was the hybrid product of the most detestable American pragmatism and the worst abstract aberrations of the school of Picasso. This damnable gadget had suffered the vicissitudes of a whirlwind adventure in the Steppe, during which its owner had lost everything, but thanks to the miraculous injustice which often regulates human affairs, the hammer was saved.

'Captain Novello's hammer!'

Such was the outcry that broke the icy silence and transformed Hut No. 18 into the eighteenth circle of Dante's Hell. There were eighty of us, and each one had need of hundreds of nails and tacks with which to arrange his personal and public belongings. At all hours of the day, and far into the night, the confounded sound of the hammer could be heard.

How many nails did it drive into the walls? Twenty thousand would be a conservative guess. Italians have an instinctive feeling for nails. Exile an Italian to the shade of the only palm tree in an endless expanse of desert, and the next day you will find his jacket hanging from a nail stuck into the trunk of this solitary piece of vegetation.

Yes, Italians can always put their hands on a nail. When my son was three months old and had never been out of his crib, I found him one day sucking a carpet tack. And in 1912, so the archives of Lomellina tell us, a baby was born with a nail in its hand.

'Captain Novello's hammer!'

How many times did Hut No. 18 echo to that damned cry? Every now and then there were new arrivals from other internment camps. As soon as they entered the hut, they put their baggage down on the floor and without a moment's hesitation asked for Captain Novello's hammer. They were always up-to-date and in possession of the very latest news. Thanks to some mysterious grapevine, every one of seventy different *Lagers*, none of which could possibly communicate with the other, called soup 'hogwash,' cigarettes 'reefers' and the process of toasting bread 'crisping.'

No sooner, then, had our new friends arrived upon the scene than they began to ask around for the confounded hammer. And the hammer went on pounding, bang, bang, bang, like an infernal time-piece, scanning the minutes of our melancholy boredom by knocking us regularly over the head.

As you may have gathered, I hated the thing. The day when the hut was inspected and searched for forbidden tools, I could not resist playing a traitor's role and pushing it into plain sight in the middle of the table. The German soldier saw it, all right, but he only looked at it with a superior air. As a son of the land of pure Aryan tools, he would have been utterly disgusted by the slightest contact with any such bastard Anglo-Jewish contraption.

One day the thing split into two parts, because its pivot screw was gone. Needless to say, I was glad. Although it contained all the accessory tools necessary to make the repairs, it could not very well operate upon itself, any more than a pencil with a lead at one end and a penknife at the other can hope to make itself any sharper. Unfortunately, a six-foot ski trooper found a way to put it right.

'Captain Novello's hammer!'

I hid it among the straw of my pillow stuffing, but that night I dreamed that a nail was piercing my neck, and waking up with a start I found the hammer had emerged from the pillow and was driving the nail into my head. The next night I tucked it away in the mattress, down by my feet. But this time my nightmare was more horrendous than ever. Torquemada himself, with a pair of red-hot pincers, was pulling off my big toe. Awakened by my own shriek of pain, I looked down and saw my toe in the pincers' grasp.

'Captain Novello's hammer!'

One day the hammer disappeared. Some people said that it had cast its vote for a new Republic of Italy, while others insinuated that it had died for love, swallowed up by a hole in the wall. Three weeks later it came back, quite obviously from a round of dissipations, only to be received like a prodigal son, petted, cleaned, polished and fed on fatted calf. At once, it began to hammer again, even more arrogantly than before, and we submitted to its tyranny.

FRIDAY 19 NOVEMBER, 1943
There are people dying of hunger and tuberculosis is making them sick, and people, on the other hand, who feast and get fat. There are people who, during the searches, were stripped of everything and do not have a bar of soap to wash themselves or a shirt to cover themselves with. There are people, however, who have trunks full of stuff. There are people who do not have a thousandth and people, on the other hand, who have water bottles full of pounds of gold.

WEDNESDAY 24 NOVEMBER
People are fabricating shoes to sell to the Russians. I sell my only pyjamas to a Polish worker who is tidying up the roof of our shed. He says he'll bring me some tobacco.

THURSDAY 25 NOVEMBER
The Pole said 'Morgen!' when I sold him the pyjamas for tobacco. Are the Poles learning German already?

Lieutenant Raimondo O. is caught in a hut while stealing a greatcoat. Chased and caught in front of Hut No. 7, he is beaten.

'I'm a Republican!'[29] he shouts suddenly. And they hit him harder.

I hear from a free Polish spirit beyond the fence. The Germans are regaining ground: they are 35 kilometres from Kiev. The Russian action seems to have lost impetus ('progress of the German troops in the Korosten sector'). I lose faith in being home for Christmas. An inspection visit by a German general has been announced.

What was missing for our little world to be perfect? Only newspapers were missing. And so here *the spoken newspaper* was born; here *the spoken literary magazine* blossomed and was shared between hut and hut.

Here, finally, I can resume my old activity: after nine months, here in Beniaminów [Oflag 73] is the first collaboration with a newspaper. *Capanèo*: a name that reminds me of sweet high school days, and the professor who explained to us the Abominable Sands in *Dante's Inferno* and the privilege granted to the damned, who, on that sand, do not collapse as one would expect, but remain upright, finding ever new and growing pride under the burning lash. *Capanèo*, a newspaper so impoverished that it is not even printed, does not pay its

---

[29] Citizen of the wartime Italian Social Republic, puppet State of Nazi Germany.

collaborators, and does not have many contacts, albeit a few subscribers. But if, at this moment, the current director of the *Corriere della Sera* presented himself here and from the height of his 87 centimetres, organised my freedom and return home in June (where it is spring!) and offered me *carte blanche* for the first page of the his big newspaper: 'Mr Ermanno,' I would reply, 'I prefer to collaborate on the last page of *Capanèo*, a weekly of Hut 21 B!' It is a much more serious thing.[30]

*

Extraordinary gathering, during which Colonel Billia talks to us about lice and remembers the 30,000 Russians and 10,000 Jews who died of petechial typhus in this camp. He says we have to be careful. Anyone who has lice should report them immediately. As dirty and filthy as we are, I think lice should rather be reporting *us* to avoid getting infected.[31]

... To my *Lager* comrades I was no more nor less than a single unit and to them will always remain No. 6865. There, in that sand and in that melancholy, everyone was stripped of his clothes and his crust and was left naked, and he showed himself what he really was. The big name that so-and-so had in the outside world, or his high rank in the army, didn't matter; everyone counted only as much as he was worth intrinsically. Every one of us was a single unit, and he was judged solely by performance.

...We didn't live like brutes; we didn't shut ourselves up in our selfishness. Hunger, dirt, cold, illness, the desperate longing for our homes and families and the dark sorrow we felt for the misfortunes of our country were not sufficient to dampen our spirits. We never forgot that we were civilized men, heirs to a past and possessors of a future.

...We were worse than abandoned, and yet we did not turn into brutes. Out of nothing we rebuilt our civilisation. We organised spot news talks, lectures, church services, university courses, plays, concerts, art exhibitions, sports, crafts, a library, regional assemblies, a radio listening centre, a commodity exchange, want-ad publications and manufacturing and trade enterprises.

I spent a good part of my time going from hut to hut and reading aloud ... pieces which were intended at the time only for camp consumption and not at all for publication in the world outside. And

---

[30] Spoken newspaper, *Capanèo*. Beniaminów (1944)
[31] *Diario clandestino* 1943–1945

yet, now that years have gone by, these pieces are the only ones that seem to me to have some validity.[32]

Giovanni Mosca: 'Guareschi sang. I don't mean that he really sang, but it is not wrong to say that he was the star of the concentration camp. Every evening, to his fellow prisoners, he read the things he had written during the day, and since nostalgia is the sweetest of evils and also slakes one's hunger, he added to the few potatoes that were the main dish of the daily meal the re-enactment not only of the big things, but above all of the small things we'd left behind.

'He called them, these re-enactments, *fairy tales*, they were so far away in time and space, so as to seem unreal or 'lived' in another life. Once upon a time... Once upon a time there was Mum, once upon a time there was the tablecloth, once upon a time there was baking, once upon a time there was the cinema...

'Guareschi read, and was almost always accompanied by an accordion. Not that he sang then, but his words followed the rhythm of the music that was the background, and behold! at the end, we cried in the hut, we cried for the tablecloth, for the inkwell, for the matches: yes, because once upon a time, in that far away country which was perhaps now gone, which was called Italy, there were also matches. And those who cry are not hungry. Not even those who laugh are hungry. Guareschi also managed to make his comrades laugh at their misfortunes. Carrying them into the future, he embellished the horrible present in a fairy tale.'

Vikto Frankl: 'We who lived in the concentration camps can remember the men who walked through the huts comforting others, giving away their last piece of bread. They may have been few in number, but they offer sufficient proof that everything can be taken from a man but one thing: the last of human freedoms — to choose one's attitude in any given circumstances, to choose one's own way.'[33]

SUNDAY 14 NOVEMBER, 1943 In Hut 9, used as a theatre, there is a piano. And there too is invariably Lieutenant Coppola, who plays the piano beautifully. I force him to play for a few hours. I realise that every act of my life is linked to a little bit of melody. From '*Tripoli, bel suol d'amore*' to 'St Louis Blues', from '*No, cara piccina, no*' to 'And the Angels Sing', I leaf through the whole book of my life. Then, having reached the last page, I find myself outside Hut 9, in the mud of Stalag 333, but it is no longer the same as it was yesterday, when I

---

[32] *Diario clandestino* 1943–1945
[33] H Viktor Frankl's words in *Man's Search for Meaning* (1962)

Christmas 1943

thought I only had four rags inside a backpack, and now, instead, I realise that I have everything.'

A creative gang is forming – the characters of the little world of the *Lager*: the artist Giuseppe Novello, the existentialist philosopher Enzo Paci, the hermetic poet Roberto Rebora, the actor Gianrico Tedeschi and the musician, Arturo Coppola, along with the writer's fictional characters. Vittorio Vialli, who had smuggled in a camera, took a photo of Giovanni (left) and Novello (right).

FRIDAY 19 NOVEMBER Now, we wander cautiously around the last castle of Hut 18. I live on the ground floor, and this is not dangerous; but in the upper bunk lives Giuseppe Novello, and Novello has started drawing from life. I return to the hut with a bucket of water that threatens to tear off my arm.

'Stop, please!' says Novello,' and I have to stay there for ten minutes with my left foot still raised, becoming the figurine.

Another poor soul is eating his ration with such a hunger that he can no longer see.

'One moment, please!' the voice yells at him. And here is this unfortunate man stuck with his spoon in mid-air and his mouth open, until the voice we know so well gives him the 'green light'.

Even if you are falling off the roof and Novello says to you: 'One moment, please!' You must stop in mid-air and wait for the OK: 'Thank you, please continue to fall.' Because you cannot refuse Novello anything.

From Radio London it seems that Zitomir has been re-taken by the Germans (the Soviets had evacuated Zitomir to avoid being surrounded). Are we swimming against the current?

THURSDAY 30 NOVEMBER I did not believe in the existence of hermeticism. Tonight, however, Enzo Paci came to the hut, who, together with Rebora, expounded ideas on modern poetry and now I believe in the existence of a hermetic literature and a hermetic poetry which speak a language *incomprensibile*.

WEDNESDAY 1 DECEMBER First session of the spoken newspaper *Domani*: Pratellesi, Paci, Rebora, Novello, Bernabei, Garaguso, Sassi, Vialli.

By order of the German command, Colonel Billia announces the first proposal of voluntary work. By accepting the offer we will no longer be seen as military. By signing the contract, officers will become common civilian workers.

'The Geneva Convention,' Colonel Billia continued, 'allows that a captive officer, in order to improve his conditions, can accept non-war work offered to him by the detaining nation. I, on my own, accept.'

I am amazed by the reasoning of a man like Colonel Billia, who has always behaved very proudly with the Germans and who, on November 9, in the presence of the Gestapo interpreters, had the courage to start the daily chat to his 3,000 officers with these words:

'First of all, I would like to inform you that tomorrow, or later, a commission will come here to propose that you join the RSI.[34] And now, to talk about cleaner things, I warn you that the latrines...'

But what of the Geneva Convention, Colonel? Here we are dealing with making an agreement with one's own conscience. I do not consider myself a prisoner, I consider myself a fighter and therefore I cannot pass over to the enemy in any way. I am a fighter without weapons, and I fight without weapons.

The battle is hard because the thought of my distant and defenceless family, hunger, cold, tuberculosis, dirt, fleas, lice, discomforts are no less deadly than bullets. Everyone dies as his conscience allows. Among so much nonsense, Mussolini said one thing incontestable: 'You serve your country even if you're simply guarding a petrol can.' I serve my country by guarding my dignity as an Italian and if, by doing this, I die of pneumonia, or of hunger or typhus, I am no less dead than he who dies from a stroke.

It's something that makes less noise, that's all.

The fleas that are here cannot be Polish fleas. They must be German fleas. They are too big, annoying and stupid.

SUNDAY 5 DECEMBER It is very cold, but the big problem is that Novello continues to sing from dawn to dusk. Opera: he knows all of them and also does duets.

---

[34] *The Repubblica Sociale Italiana*, Nazi sponsored Italian Social Republic.

From 'Caterina' (the secret radio) we know of the Tehran conference[35] and that everything is ready on the Allied side and that 'they only have to press a button'.

The number of officers who have signed up for voluntary work is 800.

A captain of Hut 6 takes the button pressing literally and bets 30,000 lire (to be paid at home) that everything will be over on Wednesday.

MONDAY 6 DECEMBER They have stepped up control of the black market. I want to quit smoking and stop being a slave to the habit. I buy twenty-five grams of tobacco for 250 lire! It is the last of my money.

Everything seems to have stopped: I lose any belief that the war will end within the year. Bolivia declares war on Germany. Well, that changes everything: we *will* meet again before summer!

*

TUESDAY 7 DECEMBER, 1943 Magnificent sunny day. The statement from Tehran claims that everything is ready: the month, day and time of the attack from the South-West has been set. The Turkish ambassador is said to have met with Churchill in Tehran. Radio London reports that a French saint, who died in 1870, had predicted a great war in the first half of the twentieth century, which war would end when the tips of the moon touched the cross (the Turkish crescent and the English cross of St Andrew). Do the Saints also get to work for propaganda?

FRIDAY 10 DECEMBER Snow, preparation for Christmas! I am thirty-five years old but I remember that one day I was eight and, tucked up in my moustache, I built a small cardboard crib. I made it again but portable so that it could be disassembled: you never know...'[36]

Above the crib Giovanni drew the Marore school, barely visible in the picture today, to which his family had moved to escape the bombing.

---

[35] The first conference to feature the Big Three leaders of the Allies: Stalin, Roosevelt and Churchill.
[36] *Diario clandestino* 1943–1945, Beniaminów (1943)

SATURDAY 11 DECEMBER 1943 Perplexed, I look at the footprints imprinted on the white carpet which the night has laid between our shack and the latrine shack. Doubts and concerns of the walkers. Here one advanced up to a metre from the door of the latrine, turned left, at a right angle and, after twenty steps, came back making a wide curve and, turning all around the hut, before finally entering by the door.

Why did he do this? Based on what reasoning? These slopes through the snow are a graphic part of the madness that is slowly becoming epidemic.

Lean day of events. We will talk about it again next autumn. The Geneva Red Cross refused to accept our protection. The case of the Italian military internees is not covered by the conventions. We inaugurated it. Only God protects our interests: but that is better than Geneva.

At 10.30 pm a warehouse burns. The snow falls in veils of pink and the sky looks like a Christmas card.

SUNDAY 12 DECEMBER 1943. First performance of my magazine. The story that I recount – the crowd didn't like it. They said that 'the feminine element is missing'.

The sailor Moroni and the *carabiniere* Ernesto, attendants of the theatre, made some gnocchi and invite me to lunch. They liked the magazine very much, so I'm happy after all.

Today is Saint Lucia! Polish girls approach the fence on the side of the appeal camp and throw packets of fruit, *focaccia* and bread with jam. The sentry lets them do it and hands us the packages.

Under my bowl I found this letter...
I read, then the paper goes blank.
I put out a shoe for Santa Lucia.

It is a tradition in Italy for children to write letters at Christmas to tell their parents how much they love them. The letter is placed secretly under the father's plate, to be discovered and read after Christmas Eve dinner. In 1952, by which time Stalin had replaced Hitler as the totalitarian threat, Giovanni would write 'The Missing Gift', celebrating the festival of Santa Lucia, the great precursor to Christmas. With a candle-lit wreath on her head to light her way, the 3rd-century martyr took food to Christians in the catacombs during their last and worst persecution by the Roman Empire.

Christmas was approaching with the speed of a horse spurred headlong to the gallop and as usual Tarocci's wife was preparing to lend a hand at her brother's pastry shop in the city. Before leaving, she said to her husband: 'Remember tomorrow night.'

'Tomorrow night?' asked Tarocci. 'What's happening tomorrow night?'

'Santa Lucia!' the woman exclaimed. 'I must have told you fifty times and still you don't take it on board.'

'I remember only too well: it's a nonsense we would do well to forget. Why do you insist rooting such confusion in the boy's head?'

'Gigino is barely six years old and for the moment he must be allowed a little wonder in his life. Everything in its own time. Don't take this precious time away from him – I would never forgive you!'

Tarocci shrugged:

'Just as you like. Take it easy. I'll sort him out in due course.'

The woman went away reassured, but the following morning Tarocci had forgotten all about their conversation. Had the opportunity arisen to pass by toy stalls and shops selling gifts for Santa Lucia, then for sure he would have remembered. But it was a particularly hardworking Friday for Peppone's general staff and Tarocci had to keep at it until late in the evening at the People's Palace, a place where nothing to do with saints in general, let alone Santa Lucia in particular, are given time of day.

As for Gigino, Tarocci had no worries: old Rosa, who came to do the housework when his wife was away, would keep a firm hand on all that went on at home.

After leaving the People's Palace that evening Tarocci went with Peppone and the rest of the gang for a bite to eat at the inn at Molinetto and remained there until midnight.

When he got home he was dead tired and fell asleep as soon as his head hit the pillow.

Next morning he awoke at eight, dressed hurriedly and left the house immediately. It was a Saturday and woe betide anyone who is not in the piazza early on market days if they're looking to buy fresh food. He barely caught a glimpse of Gigino, who was getting ready for school, and old Rosa, who was helping him, paused only to shout: 'What a good boy he's been!' as Tarocci left by the door. Neither she nor Tarocci had an inkling that there was anything different about him...

In point of fact, that morning the boy had woken much earlier than usual. He'd jumped out of bed at five o'clock and made straight for the kitchen window that overlooked the garden, which he then opened to collect a pair of shoes from the windowsill. Gigino had placed them there before going to bed the previous evening, after having cleaned them with great care. To his surprise the shoes were empty, and a little bag of croutons and bran, which he'd taken care to place close by for Santa Lucia's donkey, remained unopened.

What this meant was that Santa Lucia had forgotten him.

Old Rosa, a little lost to the passing years, had long since given up keeping a calendar and as Gigino hadn't spoken to her of Santa Lucia, the boy's great sorrow was reserved for himself alone. When he arrived at school he found the kids in full swing recounting their very different experience: everyone spoke of what Santa Lucia had brought them, making a show of the advance allowed them by their parents from the gifts of sweets, mints or chocolate left in their shoes by the saint.

Gigino bottled up his feelings for as long as he could, but at last collapsed in class and began to sob.

His teacher, a young woman, approached the sad little figure and asked him what was wrong. Gigino just shook his head as if to say that nothing was wrong, then someone took it upon himself to explain the mystery for all to hear:

'He's crying because Santa Lucia didn't bring him anything.'

Gigino was the quietest and most diligent child in the school. He kept his own counsel and said little. Normally, the teacher only had to look at him and he would freeze like a plaster statue, even holding his breath. And now, seeing him sobbing because Santa Lucia had brought him nothing, she felt a crazy desire to start crying too.

She didn't know what to say to console him, so she let him be, waiting until the lesson ended, at which point she instructed him to remain at his desk until the others had left. Then she called the boy to her and gave him a bag of chocolates.

Gigino shook his head.

'Why?' The teacher asked him gently.

'I wanted mine,' he answered softly.

Presented with a child of little more than six refusing a gift of chocolates on a matter of principle, there is little to discuss. The young teacher felt completely nonplussed and put the chocolates back in the drawer of her desk.

On the way home Gigino saw that a group of children had stopped a little way ahead to chat, so he took the path across the fields, walking slowly. It was cold and the earth was hard from the frost: he continued walking for a long time until, coming upon a shed of maize silage, he sat down on the damp straw to think.

*

At about half past one that same Saturday afternoon Tarocci had returned home from market, and old Rosa had explained that the child hadn't yet returned from school, although all the others were already back.

This was unusual.

Tarocci took his bicycle and set off to the school, but found everything closed up. Eventually his knocking raised the caretaker.

'Have you seen my Gigino?'

'He left with the others,' the woman explained. 'But he turned onto the dirt track before the bridge and took the shortcut across the fields.'

Tarocci left his bicycle with the caretaker and took the shortcut too, but he didn't find Gigino. He arrived home expecting to see that he had in the meantime returned – but no Gigino.

Retracing his steps, he called out to the child, but again to no avail. Finally, as the Almighty would have it, Tarocci found the boy asleep on the damp straw inside the hut of maize silage.

Tarocci was furious and woke the still sleeping child with two slaps. Then, as the boy looked up at him trembling with cold and fear, he grabbed him by an ear and dragged him out after him.

After about twenty steps, Tarocci let him go and left him in peace until they got home.

'You made me search for two hours!' he reproached him harshly. 'Why, instead of coming straight home did you go and lose yourself in the fields? Why didn't you come back with the others?'

'The others got all had stuff and I didn't,' the boy whispered.

'What stuff?'

'Santa Lucia's stuff,' the boy explained.

Tarocci sat at the kitchen table stunned: Santa Lucia! His wife's instruction...! But then to appease that thought a furious anger seized him:

'Santa Lucia!' he shouted. 'It's a load of nonsense. There isn't such a person as Santa Lucia.'

'There is,' replied Gigino. 'Everyone else found gifts from her in their shoes.'

'Rubbish!' shouted Tarocci.

'It's true,' said Gigino. 'I saw what they got.'

For a child of six years, nothing can serve to demolish the iron construction of simple perceptual logic.

'It's all your mother's idiot-fault!' Tarocci seethed. 'Anyway, make this the first and last time you go off on your own instead of coming home straight away.'

Gigino sighed:

'I'm always good, so why didn't Santa Lucia bring me anything? She brought everyone else a gift. Everyone except me. What did I do wrong?'

Tarocci shrugged: 'Who knows? We must see how you behaved at school!'

'The young teacher, when she learned that Santa Lucia had brought me nothing, wanted to give me her chocolates. That shows that I behave well.'

'If the teacher wanted to give you chocolates, you should have taken them!' said Tarocci.

'No: I want my own stuff,' the boy explained. 'The stuff from inside my shoe.'

Tarocci stopped eating his tea:

'What is it about fairytales like this? Aren't sweets the same inside and outside a shoe?'

'No. I have always been good and Santa Lucia has to bring me a gift in the shoe.'

Tarocci thought for a moment and realised that to sway a child of six, a tactical shift was in order.

'You are right,' he replied calmly. 'What's for sure is that you have been good, but Santa Lucia has brought you nothing, not even chocolates. This means that Santa Lucia has it in for you, and only you.'

It was now the child who looked stunned:

'For me? Why?'

'She can see that you don't like her. Or – maybe, what everyone says is true: Santa Lucia does not exist.'

'And the children who got the presents?'

'They believe it was Santa Lucia, but who knows who it was that left the gifts. And then you don't have to look at what others do and think: only look to yourself. Have you been good?'

'Yes.'

'Have you asked Santa Lucia to bring you a gift?'

'Yes, every night.'

'Did she bring you one?'

'No.'

'There is little to say, my dear boy: facts are facts. Santa Lucia does not exist for you.'

Gigino could find nothing in his small brain to object to this logic. He was sorry that Santa Lucia didn't exist for him, and didn't know how to remedy the disaster.

'So then – to get the gift, who should we pray to?' he asked in a voice full of anxiety.

A certain story that Tarocci had read or heard somewhere came to him and needed minimal adjustment to draw the child into a trap.

'I think we should pray to Stalin,' he replied.

'Stalin?' The child inquired. 'Is he a saint?'

'He's someone who does extraordinary things,' conceded Tarocci. 'Tonight you must pray to Stalin to bring you a gift because you've been good. If Stalin brings you a gift it means that he exists for you, while Santa Lucia, who has not brought you anything, does not exist for you.'

The child brightened up.

'Should I put a bag of bran for his donkey near the shoe?'

'No,' Tarocci replied rashly. 'Stalin comes from a place where donkeys eat well and there is no need for them to depend on charity.'

He realised he had said something stupid, but Gigino was as yet unaware of involuntary paternal deviationism.

'How do you pray to Stalin?' Gigino asked. 'Should we kneel and then make the sign of the Cross?'

'Not necessary,' Tarocci explained embarrassed. 'Just say three times: 'Stalin, I was good, bring me a present.' And Stalin will bring you the gift you want.'

But the child objected: 'When we pray to God or the saints we must make the sign of the Cross and kneel.'

'Do as you want,' concluded Tarocci. 'The important thing is that you don't tell anyone about this.'

'I'll also put out the bran,' Gigino said. 'Maybe the donkey is hungry even if he ate at his house.'

Tarocci left the child and went about his business. Towards evening, a few minutes before the shops closed, he bought a wind-up train, a packet of sweets, one of them chocolates, and a box of coloured pencils. He stuffed everything in his jacket pockets and, instead of going home, stopped to eat at Molinetto's.

When he'd finished, he played cards with Peppone and his associates until midnight.

Leaving with the Mayor, he said:

'Boss, I'm dead tired. I had to stay out late tonight to find my boy...'

On the way, he gave Peppone the whole story, along with the trick he'd devised to democratise Santa Lucia.

'Good idea, eh Boss?' he concluded.

'Sure,' muttered Peppone.

'We must act without sentimentality,' Tarocci continued. 'You can listen to women up to a certain point beyond which decisive action has to be taken. We begin to free up our brains bit by bit. We begin to dislodge the saints from the soul of our children by putting something more substantial in their place. It's time to debunk the fairytales. Don't you think?'

Peppone shook his big head seriously:

'As a concept, sure. But you doing what you did tonight, while you may have destroyed the legend of Santa Lucia, you have created another. In my opinion you should have explained to your child that instead of praying to the saints, who do not exist, just write to Stalin who does exist, and Stalin will send the gift by post. That way you transfer the whole affair from the supernatural plane to that of reality.'

'Okay, sure,' Tarocci replied, 'but we have to do things step-by-step. A child cannot write letters denouncing the charm of fairytales. Until he can, let us be satisfied with a first step. In the boy's mind the symbolic significance of the shoes has passed from Santa Lucia to Stalin. And the child has learned that praying to Santa Lucia gets you nowhere, while if you pray to Stalin you get what you want. Am I not right? '

'You are right,' Peppone acknowledged frankly.

They had now arrived at Tarocci's house.

'Stay here for a moment while I go into the garden and put the stuff in the shoes on the kitchen windowsill,' said Tarocci in a low voice.

Peppone took up his post and before long Tarocci was back.

'Done?'

'All okay. Santa Lucia finito! '

Peppone left and Tarocci cautiously entered the house. The child was asleep in his room with a sweet smile on his lips.

Tarocci undressed quickly and slipped into bed in the knowledge that he had done a good day's work.

But sleep did not come.

'It always happens that way when you're over-tired,' he thought. Inevitably, the Santa Lucia business came to mind. From the propaganda point of view it was a magnificent blow for the Party. And it had no doubt relieved him of the grief he would have suffered at the hands of his wife. Although, with wives, if you pick the right moment, you could generally force through an agenda. In the end, the deal worked best for their son. Children must not have their brains cluttered with such nonsense. Whichever way you looked at it, the business was concluded and he didn't have to think about it again.

He turned over in bed. True, he had given two slaps to a child of six, and then almost torn off his ear. But the fault was that of his wife who had set the whole thing in motion. From now on the child would be educated by him and him alone.

He wanted to get up to check on the child.

'I need to see if I hurt him. I have to get up, though for sure the child will wake up early in his desire to look at the shoes.'

He couldn't make up his mind to get up. A little because of the cold. A little because for some reason he was wary of the dark.

It was ridiculous, but darkness did seem to have its own agenda that night.

Perhaps he had eaten too much at the Molinetto.

Suddenly he made the decision to get out of bed: his legs didn't want to move and he was struggling in some crazy way to walk. As if he had bones made of lead. Slowly he made his way across the room, reached the corridor and opened the door of the child's small room: but the bed was empty, and the window open wide.

Tarocci jumped painfully over the windowsill and found himself in the garden. He passed the hedge and dragged himself along, panting through the fields. He arrived at the little hut of maize silage and there was Gigino, asleep on the wet straw.

He pulled him up again and began to slap him. And he continued to slap him even when his hand began to hurt. He wanted to stop beating him, but he couldn't.

Then he found himself lying in his bed with his right arm badly bent under his body and with his forehead dripping with sweat.

The hours sounded in the bell tower and he counted four!

He jumped out of bed in despair: he had to reach the kitchen windowsill before Gigino woke up. He knew he must remove the train and all the stuff he had put in the shoes. He struggled to get there and when he did it was too late: he met Gigino in the small corridor on his way back from the kitchen.

Tarocci felt full of despair, but his heart immediately rose again:

'Not even Stalin brought me anything!' Gigino exclaimed, bursting into tears. 'Nothing: not even sweets!'

Tarocci grabbed him and put him into the big bed.

'Now sleep and then tomorrow we'll put everything right.'

He fell asleep and really needed it.

*

It was a dark Sunday in December, full of cold mist. Tarocci woke up around seven and found Gigino already dressed.

Tarocci did not listen to him until he was ready. Then he gave his full attention to the child.

'So? Did you find anything in the shoes?' he inquired.

'Nothing,' the child replied with tears in his eyes.

'This means that to pray to Stalin you get nothing,' explained Tarocci.

'Nor even to pray to Santa Lucia!' Gigino complained. 'So how do you do it?'

Tarocci put the little coat, the scarf and cap on the boy's head. Then he got himself together and went out.

'Come, let's fix everything,' he said, taking the child by the hand.

The country was still deserted and silent, immersed in that rotten fog.

At a certain point Tarocci stopped:

'Gigino, I'll wait for you here; you go to church and tell baby Jesus: "I have to report that Santa Lucia has forgotten me, but I have always been good."'

'Do I have to talk about that other one? ...What is he called?'

'Nothing, just talk about Santa Lucia. Everything will be okay. In these cases the infant Jesus personally organises stuff at Christmas.'

The child ran off and Tarocci waited for him, leaning against a pillar on the porch.

Gigino emerged from the fog after about ten minutes.

'Did you do as I instructed you?' Tarocci inquired.

'Yes, Dad.'

'What did he say?'

'He'll take care of it.'

'Good,' Tarocci muttered quietly, taking the child by the hand and towing him home.

And it all seemed very natural; it did not even cross the threshold of Tarocci's brain that it was at least curious, if not strange, that the child Jesus should answer Gigino: 'I'll take care of it.'

Nor did he wonder why, when with his own hands, Tarocci himself had filled Gigino's shoes with the gifts from Stalin, Gigino had found the shoes completely empty.

Nor even did he wonder what had become of the train and the other things. All that mattered was that Gigino had found the shoes empty and that Christmas was just around the corner.

That the Christ child would put everything back in its proper place, Tarocci knew instinctively.

To tell the truth there was nothing miraculous about the disappearance of Stalin's gifts because Peppone, after getting them out of Gigino's shoes, went and threw them into the river, muttering:

'This is really not a good service that I do to Comrade Stalin.'

But then, when the water of the Great River had swallowed up all the gifts, he took comfort by saying to himself:

'God sees you; Stalin doesn't.'

Too late did he realise that with such a slogan he'd fallen like a fish into the net of American-style capitalist propaganda, at its most lucid come Christmastime.

And he was sorry about that.

But only up to a point.[37]

*

The Gestapo clamours, builds new fences, unleashes its spies, threatens, punishes, but the soldiers, snuffers and German officers who guard the camp all continue their trade with the Italians, and the sentries always let themselves be bought to turn a blind eye to the bread with which the Poles, who come to work in the field, pay for the goods.

The Prince of the Black Market is head of the enterprise, the Polish Sereneck, who, among other things, is a very important head of the underground organisation of Polish patriots and uses the enormous sums he earns to arm his men and prepare the insurrection. The Germans don't know this, but the Poles trust us.

The Poles love Italy: I believe they are the only ones in the world. Nobody loves Italy like the Poles. Not even the Italians.

---

[37] 'Il dono mancato' (aka 'Il dono di Stalin').

TUESDAY, 14 DECEMBER, 1943 I need more... I have exhaustion. It is clear that I need more nourishment. My head is empty. Inside I feel ashamed that I am hungry, but I have to take a sad step: I will sell my overcoat.

Eden says everything is ready. It seems that Turkey has declared war on Germany... I don't believe it anymore.

At the shop, a pocket comb costs 16 zlotys (80 lire) and a shaving soap 40 zlotys (200 lire).

Petruzzelli lends me a typewriter.

WEDNESDAY 15 DECEMBER Boredom increases. The usual vague and bizarre news circulates. Goodbye old *zimarra*: I sell the overcoat for 22 kilos of bread and two and a half kilos of jam. Difficulty in hiding twenty-two loaves.

I am selling a pencil for some *zampironi*.[38] The issue of the Russian winter army is back. Helped by Captain Malavasi, who speaks Russian very well, I made a deal with the Russian Ivan and threw my overcoat over the fence. In fact, I had Second Lieutenant Pedrotti throw it because I couldn't manage it. Ivan promised me twenty-two loaves and two and a half kilos of jam.

THURSDAY 16 DECEMBER Cloudy day. Tonight I talked about newspapers and printers and the damage of Croce's chatter.[39] While Italy is divided and torn apart, philosophers chat.

By October, Giovanni could note: The lectures, which started out in such a praiseworthy fashion, have turned into oratorical orgies. There are five or ten of them every evening. In whatever hut you choose to visit after 8 pm you are sure to find someone standing on a table haranguing his fellows. Music, poetry, science, political economy, history, philosophy, drama, films, vaudeville, literature, chemistry, religion, high finance.

Before saying too much let us go inside. We too are Italy.

The Black Market exchange and trading centre is in Hut 12. Second lieutenant N, Captain, a former officer of the PNF,[40] favour themselves by ignoring the prisoners.

Ivan threw the loaves at me tonight. I sleep with 22 kilos of bread on me: two in my stomach and 20 on my feet and perhaps Albertino is dying of hunger. What will become of us?

---

[38] Insect repellant.
[39] Benedetto Croce was a famous Italian philosopher.
[40] The National Fascist Party.

Caterina reports that Churchill is seriously ill. It doesn't worry us. There's a guy who, if he doesn't win the war, won't die even if they slaughter him.

FRIDAY 17 DECEMBER In the kitchen there are men in cahoots with the Krauts who peel the potatoes coarsely and then sell the skins to the Italian officers.

SATURDAY 18 DECEMBER I dream of a visit by Albertino.

WEDNESDAY 22 DECEMBER I worked on my Christmas reading: '*Favola di Natale*', *1943*. It gives me joy because it serves me to fill the void that impending Christmas puts in my soul. While I was reading the manuscript to Massimi, Coppola, Guelfi, Tedeschi, Talotti, in the theatre at 9 pm, the interpreter Kladocek came and took it out of my hand: it is an intimate offence. Poor us prisoners!

There is talk of a Russian winter offensive in the Nevel area with eighty kilometres breakthrough. Maybe, but it's already December 22nd and I'm starting to lose hope of being home for Christmas.

Fleas devour me.

THURSDAY 23 DECEMBER Snow and fog. I like to walk on the virgin snow because I don't want to walk on other people's thoughts. Each step is a thought.

Albertino calls me in the night from beyond the fence. I walk on one side of the fence. On the other, the sentry and between the two fences the images of our thoughts meet. Snow and Christmas air.

Captain Novello has painted and cut out of cardboard a large Nativity scene with angels and bells and, in the background, our homeland and, among the adoring shepherds, a group of internees.

Almost everyone grinds, or kneads, or cooks something.

Those who had stuff to sell sold it to get a handful of flour, a piece of lard, a bag of beans. Those who had nothing, for ten days made savage savings on the ration, and now, with that poverty of ingredients, they make very sorry cakes or pastries. Gastronomic fervor, an air of family and ... little women. Poor Italy! But maybe it's a sentimental need. At 10 pm the German inspection lieutenant wishes us happy holidays.

Massimi dreams that his little girl is coming to visit him.

Malavasi gives Rebora and me some beans to celebrate Christmas. Everyone prepares cakes and tortellini.

There is a rumour that bad news will be ours after the holiday. A new German wickedness to poison the Christmas holiday?

I have nothing for Christmas, only my memories: I had staked everything on the jam that Ivan owed me, but Ivan turns out to be a cheating Russian.

Earlier, Giovanni had drafted a letter to Ennia on an official form, beginning with a request for a food parcel and a warning to be careful to keep to what is allowed:

I went away from the group and began to fill up the twenty-four lines allotted to me with tiny print. I wrote clearly, with a pencil, above the dotted lines, as the international conventions that protect the rights of prisoners of every nationality require.

'Signora: Robust 5-kilo *pacco* with 1/2-coupon omitting medicines and inflammables. Include cigarette tobacco ... and dried chestnuts. But if you think the chestnuts would do more good to our little boy, please keep them for him. I don't really need anything. All I have to ask is this: that on Christmas Eve you set the table as gaily as you can. Get out the best silver and glasses, spread the embroidered tablecloth and light all the lamps. Set up a big Christmas tree, with as many candles as possible, and put a crib near the window, just as you did last year.

'Signora, you must do all these things for me. Every night my thoughts leap over the barbed-wire fence. I know it is difficult for you to picture this exactly, for thoughts have no faces; they are no more than gusts of air. So picture me, myself, leaping over the barbed-wire fence. Picture a Giovannino as light as a dream and as transparent as the wind on a quiet, cold winter night.

'Every night, when the others are sleeping, I fly away, over the boundless silence of foreign lands and cities. Below me, everything is dark and sad, and I am in search of light and peace. I see the statue of the Madonna atop our Milan cathedral, but the streets and squares are no longer the same as they were before, and I have a hard time locating our floor.

'Signora, don't call me reckless if I come in through the roof; you ought to approve of my prudence in shunning the battered stair. Besides, there's a hole in the roof, and I can get in all the more quickly. I recognise the arrangement of our rooms and look for memories under the dust of the crumbled walls. But here, too, everything is dark and cold and sad. Only with the help of the moon can I hope to make out the pattern of the tapestries still hanging on the walls and the layout of the furniture, once known so well.

'No one walks in the deserted streets, except Fear disguised as the moon. On a shred of wallpaper from what used to be our front hall, I can make out a strange five-petal flower. Do you remember when Albertino decorated the apartment with tiny hands dipped in indelible ink? I have searched in vain in my old office building for reminiscences of days gone by; the building simply isn't there, and in its place is a grim pile of smoke-blackened rubble.

'Now, leaving the darkened city behind me, I am revisiting the spots where you and I were boy and girl together. Again, nothing but melancholy greets my eye. And so I come, at length, to the rude cottage where what's left of my belongings and my earliest longings have come to rest. You are asleep, Albertino is asleep, my mother and father are asleep. Perhaps, in your sleep, all of you are searching for my unknown abode. Our city furniture is heaped up in disorder in the small, shadowy rooms, while up in the attic there are cases of my books, with the words frozen on the pages.

'Signora, in pursuit of light and warmth and peace I have found only cold and darkness; I cannot see my son's face, and even the lake shore is empty and unlit. Ruefully I fly back to the barbed-wire enclosure. Down on the hard bunk flop the congealed bones of No. 6865.

'Signora, on Christmas Eve, when my thoughts leap over the barbed-wire fence, they must find some bright, warm corner. I want to be dazzled with bright lights, I want to look upon your face and recover the peace I once knew. Otherwise, what fun is there in being a prisoner of war?'

...At this point I broke off, with a distinct feeling that I had run through the twenty-four allotted lines. As a matter of fact, I had spread myself over the twenty-four lines on my side of the form letter, the twenty-four lines on the blank reply page and the better part of five other forms that happened to be lying around. Conscientiously, I scratched out the 150-odd lines that I had written and began all over again.

FRIDAY 24 DECEMBER, 1943 Christmas Eve. We made the Christmas tree. I finished writing my 'Christmas Tale, 1943' with a desperate heart. I drew 'The Father's Letter' on a panel of Novello's Nativity scene, as he finished it.

'In this "Father's Letter" written and illustrated by Giovanni in Beniaminów on 24 December 1943,' writes his son, 'a double meaning was intended: one written for the Gestapo, the other integrated with drawings exhorting his companions in misfortune to keep alive the hope of returning to their families.'

> The Motta panettone[41] means 'home' to all Italians at Christmas. To preserve the prisoners' love for their distant homeland the intricate Milan Cathedral spires trace a decorative *emme* similar to the neon sign of the original Motta café, both being central to the city. To remain faithful to the oath of allegiance made to the King, and refuse to collaborate with the Third Reich and join the Italian Social Republic, all should resist changing the *emme* to another.'

Once upon a time there was the Motta panettoni which infused and encoded all the houses in the city and round about in the countryside with its red *emme* [M]. On all the roofs were nocturnal promises of sweetness; sweet neon promises.

In August, February, November and September, the great red emme reminded us that Christmas was coming once again.

Once upon a time there was Panettone Motta, and Milan Cathedral had come into being precisely and only to serve as a backdrop for Panettone Motta.

And the great *emme* had embroidered her sweet, red and peaceful figure on the walls of all the houses.

Then the *emme* was changed to another.

At 16.30 Colonel Billia came and Captain Salvadori made a speech, we were all belted up and dressed as men. The colonel thanked us with tears in his voice. A big flag lay before the Nativity scene. Some people had fasted for three days to make Christmas lunch. It's like a return to civilisation.

I remember we wrote the names of presents on bits of paper, which we put on the tree. I touched one marked A KILO OF NOUGAT, which made me very happy, because nougat has always been my passion.

After that, Lieutenant Roberto Rebora read one of his own poems. I remember exactly how it went.

---

[41] Angelo Motta perfected what became known as Motta's panettoni, a Christmas cake made with butter, raisins and spices, a tradition that dates back to 1599. From where Motta's panettoni were produced in Milan emanated a perfume which infused the dwellings of all those who lived nearby.

'Toward Christmas, 1943'

From the motionless vigil of houses
in well-remembered streets
the bleak winter morning is born.
Over numb roof-tops
an icy moon lingers
and flies over chimerical walls,
as memories of fabulous gorges in the heart
of gardens ache with loving pity.

In the still dreamy streets
hesitant human emotion tries
the truth in barely spoke syllables.
High heaven intercedes
Deafly: a mute violence in the tangle
of lost images.

Space alerts awakened eyes
long fearing a word of praise.
Cautiously the earth works its beginning
Again: as names of nights apply
mistily, wandering the streets
touched by a desert Christmas.[42]

Next I read some of my melancholy prose and Coppola played his own delicate compositions on the accordion.

Fellow IMI inmate Mario Moretti designed a symbolic picture, 'Holy Night, 1943', showing the camp fence breached, queues filing towards the chapel hut, unimpeded, while in the sky, Madonna and child enact the Nativity attended by swallows, which become crows as they reach the camp. Giovanni's '*Natale, 1943*' was read that evening at Hut 18; also on Christmas Day and Boxing Day at Hut 9 (known as 'the theatre'); and in the afternoon on 27 December at the Infirmary and again in 'the theatre'.

Once upon a time there was a soldier with an iron helmet on his head and many belts about him hung with rifles, pistols, bullets, bombs, binoculars, compasses and other terrible devices of death. At that time the machines had taken over and were making war against

---
[42] Beniaminów (1943)

mankind by spewing fire and iron upon villages and cities, and no one could stop the infernal automatons anymore.

Every evening, the soldier with the iron helmet on his head and the rifle in his hand climbed up a wooden watchtower and stood guard, rummaging through the darkness with a large dazzling searchlight.

From his perch he could see a piece of the world and in its midst a flock of wooden huts, hedged in by a high barbed wire fence. Men who lived in the huts were forbidden to cross the line of the fence even as distant voices borne on the wind would incite them to breach it. Such was law and the reason why the soldier with the iron helmet stood guard and scanned the darkness with his lighthouse eye.

It was a winter night: to the vacant stare of the hut windows the December wind polished icicles and stretched out a lacework of frost under the eaves. The eye of the soldier's light made a circle of yellow sand sparkle, and a green grove green, and as it panned across the roof of a hut, the fretwork of the fence became a silver spider's web.

It was a winter night: the soldier with the iron helmet, alive to every palpitation in his darkened world, stamped his feet on the wooden floor of his turret and suddenly heard the pawing of hooves on the ground, hardened by the frost. Directing his searchlight towards the source of the sound, he looked out, raising his rifle to his shoulder. An old man appeared in the circle of light holding a donkey by its bridle, on which was a beautiful young woman.

'Who goes there! To approach the line is forbidden!'

'Forgive us, soldier,' said the old man. 'We didn't know. We've come a long way.' The beautiful young woman moaned.

'Get away!' the soldier repeated, brandishing his rifle.

'She is sick,' the old man said. 'We've tried villages, towns, but everything is in darkness, everything is closed, everything is deserted, everything is abandoned, inhospitable and she is sick. The night is cold: please sir, let us in. Give us shelter in one of your little sheds.'

'Be off with you!' shouted the soldier, fumbling with his rifle bolt.

The young woman moaned again, and again the old man pleaded.

'Away!' repeated the soldier. 'It's forbidden... The colonel would lock me up.'

But the cold beam of the searchlight struck the already pale face of the young woman and the soldier saw her eyes were full of tears.

'A corner in the smallest hut,' whispered the old man.

'And how do you plan to get in?' the soldier asked.

The old man plunged into the shadows, and reappeared shortly afterwards inside the fence.

The soldier turned off the searchlight and climbed down from his watchtower.

'First time I've made such a serious breach of regulations,' he muttered. 'You'll have me thrown in jail. Follow me and don't make a fuss.'

Off he set and the old man, donkey and young woman in pain followed, the sand melting under the donkey's hooves as if it walked on velvet. They came to a halt before a shack with broken glass in the windows. The soldier took out a key and removed the padlock from the door of a storeroom piled to the rafters with bedding boards, stools and smashed barrels. In one corner was a coarsely constructed bunk-bed and the soldier removed the scraps of wood piled up around it.

'You can sleep there,' he whispered, 'there's a pile of wood shavings over there. I'll pick you up at dawn.'

He also let the donkey in, bolted the door and returned to his watchtower. He couldn't shake the thought of the terrible risk he'd exposed himself to, but then he saw in his mind's eye that pale face and those tearful eyes and shrugged:

'May whatever God wants to happen, happen!'

Hours passed by slowly in darkness and silence, the camp asleep under that immense sky, which seemed to crush the low huts and make them seem yet more miserable. Midnight came and with it, suddenly, a vivid glow broke through the darkness. The soldier gasped.

'They've set light to the store! He's set the shavings alight with his damned pipe!'

The windows of the hut looked like the open doors of an incandescent stove. The soldier fled his turret and ran to the hut, releasing the bolt and throwing open the door. But there was no fire: the beautiful woman and the old man were kneeling at the foot of the bunk and on a loose mattress of shavings on the lower bed a pink baby was moving. There was no fire, no light burned, but the hut was full of radiant light with no clear source. Voices rang out in the camp square.

The soldier pushed the woman and the old man behind a pile of boards and even managed to conceal the donkey, but could not cover the baby even with his scarf. In marched his colonel.

'What's burning?' he demanded.

And the soldier could not answer. Then the colonel saw the baby and stopped.

'This is outrageous!' The colonel was indignant: 'This is the most serious breach of regulations I have ever seen!'

Men appeared and the colonel barred their way at the door.

'Let no one in!' he ordered. 'Everyone back to your huts. The bucket brigade, too: leave! There was a fire and it's already extinguished.'

The soldier was barring the windows with canvas and boards so that no more light leaked outside, while the colonel considered the little baby with serious intensity.

'Outrageous!' he repeated several times. 'How dare you come here to be born!'

'We could regularise his position by registering him and providing him with a number,' suggested the soldier, coming to attention.

A crackle of machine guns rang out and the colonel left the storeroom. From the top of the watchtower, machine gunners were firing at something shiny swooping down from the sky. Then it became plain that it was no aircraft but a huge star with a long silver tail: and when it reached the hut, the star remained motionless, only its long silver tail fluttered gently in the night wind.

The colonel went inside and frowned at the little boy.

'This is all down to you!' he said very sternly. 'You may also like to know that light signals of any kind are prohibited here.'

But by this time the child had fallen asleep and the colonel merely shook his head, mumbling: 'It's unheard of!' as he left, ordering the soldier to stand guard outside the hut and not let anyone approach.

'Tomorrow we will ask for instructions from high command,' he concluded.

And off he went, illuminated by the star, his shadow stretching ever longer on the sand, while, perched above the hut, the long silver tail of the star was waved by the wind of the night.

Later, the light went out and, returning to the darkened hut, the soldier found it empty. He went to the colonel to make his report and the colonel shrugged:

'There's no point in filing reports. High command does not understand such things. Good night.'

'Merry Christmas, Colonel.'

Once upon a time there was a soldier with an iron helmet...

*

At 2 am we are still up and the German lieutenant in charge of inspections came, but said nothing untoward. Indeed, he wished us a happy holiday.

SATURDAY 25 DECEMBER, Christmas Day. Last night Albertino came to see me with a little sister,[43] and the good Lord, so as not to show them to me, covered the high wire fence with white flowers of frost. Gift of the Child Jesus: given the times, he couldn't have done more.

The child Jesus was added to the Nativity scene...

Since 9 September Rebora and I have shared our hunger as brothers and today we celebrate Christmas with the wider family because Captain Malavasi and Captain Rizzardi gave us some beans and a piece of lard to contribute.

I remember that long Christmas lunch.

I did not find a letter under my bowl, as I found under my plate last night. And no one found one.

But lunch prevailed and was full of joy because there is nothing better than a happiness that serves to make one feel deeply sad. It was an extraordinary lunch. Captain Jacobacci worked on the stove all day and in vain did Captain Rizzardi try to bring it on.

Captain Jacobacci was the witty alchemist of the food ration: everything miraculously transformed in his hands: the most squalid soup became flan, pie, flan, pudding, *focaccia* at will.

He carefully studied what had been passed to us from the kitchen and worked on the stove all day. The pasta and the potato stew were broken down into their constituent elements.

---

[43] Ennia was already pregnant when Giovanni was arrested in September. Unbeknown to him his daughter, who features in this dream, had already been born.

'I will make an excellent macaroni pie with the pasta, raw bread and potato mash made from the stew,' Captain Jacobacci explained. 'With the canned meat, the pasta sauce and toasted and pulverized bread, I will make some excellent meatballs. With the remaining canned meat, margarine from the ration and the potatoes left over from the stew, I will finally make a delicious meat flan.'

It was a very promising menu and the captain worked on three pots at the same time.

After some time the pots were reduced to two.

'I've decided to agitate matters,' the captain explained. 'After all, meatballs and meat flan are the same thing. In addition, the bread has reused to bind the meatballs. So, I put it all together and make a large meat flan.'

Then the two pots became one. The pasta, cooked and re-cooked, had lost its substance, the potatoes had disintegrated, the canned meat had become sauce. So, it was more convenient to put everything together in a large composite soup. Just add a little tea and a pinch of salt...

With Massimi, Libotte, Coppola, Schneider and Cagna for lunch at Hut 5 with cappelletti [stuffed pasta]. We found a piece of lard in the mess tin, together with the beans. Malavasi says that he put it there, along with his beans: truth is that Albertino brought it to us. Rizzardi also gave me a small piece of lard.

Captain Jacobacci, on the other hand, thanks to his witty effort, ate borrowed bread and jam.

Later, there were those who tried to saw the large composite soup but, as it was too hard, burned it whole.

When, after a long time, we saw our homeland again and parted, we divided the pieces of Novella's Nativity scene into five: to Novello the background, to Rebora the group of internees, to Malarini the ranks of shepherds, to Malavasi the roof of the hut with the angels and bells, to me the group with the Bambinello and the rest of the hut.

Every year, at Epiphany, we would gather at an agreed location and each would bring his piece, and the Nativity scene would be reassembled. (Novello considered the idea too romantic and the project was not followed up.)

But, the first year, the crib lacked the roof with the superstructures of the angels and bells: and instead of the roof and the angels we put Malavasi's telegram.

The second year the Bambinello was missing, in addition to the shelter of the roof (and this time the telegram did not even arrive) the earthly homage of the shepherds. Malarini was on his honeymoon and the Bambinello, instead of sheep, had to be satisfied with a few white sugared almonds.

The third year the group of internees deserted. Neither the roof returned nor the shepherds showed up: the poet Rebora (Roberto), having abandoned hermeticism, had composed verses for Campari and turned to film directing, settling in Rome and producing large-scale films.

The following year the landscape in the background of the scene moved to Africa together with its owner Novello; the old, worn colours of Europe were no longer enough for our painter, and only the charm of the impossible colours of those extraordinary lands could attract him.

The old Beniaminów Nativity scene is reborn again every year, and the Bambinello from his squalid roofless hut, devoid of angels and bells and no longer weathered as well as it was, searches in vain for the hosts of sometime worshipers.

The fact is, we all think of Christmas as a day off the calendar.

Like a day out of time. Christmas is a point of arrival for us all. And our dream is to trudge through the year and then stop for a while. As if, for that day, time were to stop.

And instead we can never stop, because time does not stop.

A single minute's rest would be enough: but this is not granted to either the living or the dead because eternity is a closed circle that always begins and never ends. And something that continues without ever having begun and without ever being able to finish.

And unconsciously we think about this when Christmas arrives: and we try to explain our immense anguish with trivial reasons. But the fact is that we, on that day, look out for an instant on the abyss of infinity and admiration for the greatness of God is not enough for us men of insufficient faith to make us forget our infinite smallness.[44]

SUNDAY 26 DECEMBER, Boxing Day. In the evening, in the 'theatre' hut: '*Natale, 1943*', with Coppola at the piano. I was moved. Warm applause at every part. The German assistant came to congratulate me, shake my hand and wish us happy holidays. Tripodi gives Novello and me five Papiroski [Russian cigarettes] to thank us for having made the Nativity scene and for the reading.

Another in the audience sent Giovanni a hand-written note:

---

[44] Considerations by Mr Morlai in *Il tentimo clandestino*.

'Just now I came back from the theatre, where I listened to you with my eyes closed! Don't be surprised by this letter, as enthusiastic as that of a little girl. And you will certainly not be surprised when I tell you that the two "little, simple words" and your "little, simple things" have brought me back for an hour to my little house in Rome, where I live every hour in my imagination, in the subtle, aching nostalgia of every day.'[45]

I received two letters of thanks for yesterday's reading: it is a demonstration of a revived sense of civilisation.

Spiritual habits are reborn that seemed stemmed by elementary material needs. The huts become houses for the birth of intimacy, the bonds that once existed between house and house are being reconnected between hut and hut.

Second reading in the theatre: a great warmth and a packed room.

MONDAY 27 DECEMBER I repeat *Natale 1943* in the infirmary [and] in the theatre.

TUESDAY 28 DECEMBER My tobacco has been stolen: sad surprise...

The camp is flooded with chatter. 'Let's escape!' people say. And a new illusion is added to the long series.

The journalist De Bernardis who attacked me for 'Cuore' (*Bertoldo* column) comes personally to accuse me of being, with my readings, the cause of future disaster in Italy. Reminding people of family values, these family people, prisoners in their houses, will continue to enslave themselves. The bourgeoisie will shut themselves up again at home and so on.

With spirits high following the readings of '*Natale, 1943*', De Bernardis throws a political hand grenade into what he sees as a bourgeois sell-out. To De Bernardis, a passionate, politicised journalist, nostalgia is sentimentality, and sentimentality the enemy of post-war progress. He gets through to Giovanni, even affects his dreams.

THURSDAY 30 DECEMBER *Carabiniere* Ernesto gives me a large potato. In the hut all the tobacco that Massimi had given me is stolen from my backpack.

Last night I dreamed that I was returning home and immediately quarrelling with Ennia. When I left the house, my bicycle and

---

[45] Vietri n.p., Professor Alan Perry.

raincoat had been stolen. I can only think that De Bernardis has got to me: he wants controversy!

Not only here! He will also haunt me at home!

I make a drawing of a Christmas present: Albertino comes to visit me, here in the hut, and with him a very small girl.

FRIDAY 31 DECEMBER This disastrous year is finally over and it seems as long as a century... Only one auspicious event (I hope): in November another Albertino was born. I don't know anything about what happened at home. God grant that everything has been done in the best way. And God grant that I can greet Advent of 1945 in my home and beside all of my family.

At 2.30 pm I received my first letter from Italy! All good. Signorina Carlotta Guareschi was born. Last night, while I was doing that drawing, I felt it.

Tonight everyone (having semi-fasted for a few days) is having a feast. I am hungry, but I pretend not to see what's going on. I think about what Carlotta will be doing right now.

I get the feeling that at home they think we are on vacation. Maybe they expect us to bring home some nice gifts.

Forty-five new Italian prisoners arrived today from Tarnopol.

In the theatre, Captain Labignan meets Captain Sorrentini, Gold Medal decorated on the Atlantic. They hug each other, crying. A German soldier who sees them starts to cry too. Novello and I are invited to Hut 4 in the old camp by Captain Pertile and friends.

Thus began the year.

To my mother, my father, my wife, Albertino and Signorina Carlotta, my best wishes!

*

While I'm working curled up in front of this kind of desk that my industrious little hands and my Leonardesque flair have created in the very interior of my 'castle', at the foot of the bunk, Coppola – who lives upstairs together with his accordion – makes the notes of his admirable composition rain upon my curly little head (together with the usual shavings and random debris). Quick, then! To me an almost clean sheet and we immediately write the words to that music!

The poet Rebora (Hut 65) eats his hands for envy in front of my wonderful verses. The actual philosopher Paci (also hut 65) rages with envy for the depth of the concepts contained in my composition. But there is nothing to be done, hermetic gentlemen and existentialist gentlemen: the song was born and now I could sing it to

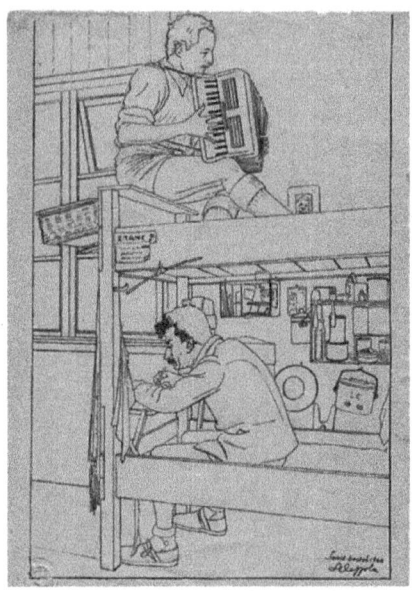

you full throated. But in order not to aggravate your suffering, and out of consideration for any feeble persons present, I will entrust the task to my friend, Gatti.

The song is about a certain Signora Carlotta who was born while her father was in a distant *Lager*, and who spends her time on the balcony waiting for her much vaunted dad to return. The naive song is, therefore, dedicated to those who – like me – have children whose names are all that they know of them.

'Carlotta'

*... Carlotta is sitting on the balcony
and she is waiting for her papa
whom she has never seen...*

*... Who knows, who knows how it will be
this oh so famous mama's beau
maybe he will have a moustache
a beard and tummy
pipe and stick
and glasses on a string
(who knows, who knows ... maybe papa's in a bad way!)...*

*... Now behold, a splendid warrior appears around the corner
with stars upon his helmet,
with silver breastplate;
blue jerkin and buttons all in gold:
It is The Father! And he almost looks a hero!...*

Carlotta Guareschi: I write your name to summon a physical reality out of its very existence.

I think of the day when I will leave my house leading an almost new Albertino by the hand and carrying a brand new young lady in my arms. I often think about it, but it is one day 1,200 kilometres away from the world at war and it seems almost impossible to get there. And then I ask myself: will I see you, Miss Carlotta? What if I can't? It doesn't matter, Miss Carlotta. It doesn't matter why – despite my old physics professor trying to confuse my ideas – I know the whole business of words perfectly. Words are born but do not die. Nothing dies in this world. Words are born and then, being lighter than air, they rise up and reach the point where the sky ends and eternity begins. And there they stay. As if a hundred balloons were released in a room: when they reached the ceiling they would stop. So, the words in the sky... Up there are all the words in the world: from the threatening cry of Cain, to Farinacci's last speech,[46] from the chant of the ragman, to the song of the lover. *Verba volant*. Words fly, they do not evaporate. This is important, Signora Carlotta: because, if the good Lord puts wings on my shoulders before I see you, I will go and sit on the star that is right above our house and, as your short words rise to the

---

[46] Roberto Farinacci was a leading fascist politician.

sky, short as semiquavers, I will seize them on the fly and make them all fast in a silk bag. Then, every so often, I'll take a pinch out of them and shake them like a bunch of little bells and enjoy hearing them jingle. Thus: do, re, mi, fa, sol, la, si...[47]

---

[47] 'Oh Miss Carlotta'

My Thoughts Turn Inwards

For present purposes, the main thing of interest is that, even in prison, I remained a stubborn native of the province of Emilia, of the lower reaches of the Po Valley; I gritted my teeth and said to myself: 'I won't die, even if they kill me!'

And I didn't die, either, probably only because they didn't kill me, but at any rate I didn't die. I stayed alive in spirit as well as in body, and kept right on working.

THURSDAY 9 MARCH, 1944 Six months, boredom alters the scale of things. Minutes are no longer fractions of an hour, but elements of eternity.

Once upon a time there was the clock and it was a very ingenious thing that was used to divide time into many small pieces. This was very useful, because it allowed the hours of pain to be divided and the moments of joy to be multiplied; and very harmful because, in this way, an hour of pain was transformed into sixty eternal minutes, and an hour of joy was reduced to a flash of seconds

Kneeling on the sand, I wash the soup buckets and look at my hands. Where are the hands of the past? Livid and gaunt, they discover an angry play of swollen and twisted tendons and veins. A tiny greasy cobweb has stuck on the skin, and the thumb and index finger of the left have black tips, toasted by desperate butts.

While Giovanni was scouring the pots with sand IMI Vittorio Vialli took a photograph. Giovanni later wrote: 'This was me in May of '44. Now I have long trousers and a jacket and, if someone takes a surprise photograph of me, I don't feel like throwing the mess tin at his head, as I did then.'

I go to pump water, and the two buckets tear my arms, and it seems to me that, dragged down by that enormous weight, they will soon bury me in the sand up to my knees.

I wash myself, and my hands describe an unknown architecture of bones that seem to me to belong to a stranger.

I catch sight of myself in a puddle and see clouds floating over my head so distant and indifferent that they seem to belong to another world. To a world in which men have now resumed their usual life, while up here forgotten men continue a useless and cursed effort.

I sit at the table to write, and my back breaks: the words weigh on my shoulders like sandbags.

Six months, some 4,000 hours.

In my calendar the dead days line up far into the future: I cross every day that passes with a pencil cross, and I think back to the desperate years of college, to the dark months of military school. Even then, I would check each day that passed. But then I knew it had to be five long years, and then six eternal months.

Here, I don't know anything.

Bones in the sun. Hollow bellies, protruding ribs, knotty joints, collarbones that look as if they were coming through the skin. All these are reminiscent of pictures in old medical books or the captions under photographs in the French magazine, *L'Illustration*: 'Victims of the plague in Kuantung... Aspects of the famine in India...'

Back then my weight was 46 kilograms: gross weight, including my rags, my lice, my fleas, my wooden clogs – a big fat man like that.

WEDNESDAY 15 MARCH, 1944 A hand has taken hold of my stomach and is trying to wrench it out of my body. For a moment it loosens its grip, only to tighten it again a moment later.

Two soldiers arrive at noon with a great steaming bucket; they slide it off the pole on which they carried it and which they deposit on the floor. There are men that shout for joy at the arrival of the soup and eagerly watch over the filling of the aluminium bowls lined up on the table. As for me, I might as well swallow cement, and there is nothing that I can do but take refuge on my bunk.

Once more I am crying. My thirty-five years stare at me in amazement and I feel as if I were looking on at the tears of a child.

I see a man walking down a familiar, dusty country road with a knapsack over his shoulder. The ditch running alongside the road is filled with bracken water. The echo of a church bell still floats in the air and a rooster is crowing. There, as here, it is high noon.

The man stops in front of a closed gate. Who will be the first to appear in the dark rectangle of the doorway? He stands motionless. The shadow of the closed gate falls upon the white, dusty road, but the figure of the man casts no shadow.

Crying again. I feel as if I were abandoned by everyone, including myself, since my body seems to me to belong to times long since gone by. I wait in vain for someone to appear at the door. Between myself and the people of this house, between my host and life, there is a veil of tears, and everything seems written on tremulous water.

I pace up and down, from one side of the fence to another; I move quickly, but hunger stalks me. Every mark on the sand is the trace left by a man's footstep or a man's thought. My footsteps and thoughts are superimposed upon a thud of others.

I fly over the nearby fence and over faraway mountains until desperate desire brings me down in familiar ground. The central square of my native city is golden with sunshine, and umbrellas are raised over the café tables. There sit my friends, watching the pretty girls go by. Warmth fills the air. The happy memories of bygone days look out at me from the faces and walls that meet my eye. But hunger impinges upon my thoughts and drives me away from the square and down a side street nearby.

'Bread! Bread!' it cries. 'You want white bread fragrant from the oven, so fresh that it crumbles between your fingers.'

I come across one bakery after another, even in localities where I have never seen them before. Bread! Bread! The slicer screwed onto the heavy beech-wood table moves up and down, cutting loaf after loaf, which delivery boys carry away in baskets balanced on their shoulders.

As I pace from one side of the fence to another, my feet trample crisp loaves of bread instead of yielding sand. Stalking hunger kneads my stomach and steam from the oven beclouds my eyes. I regularise my step, attempting to lose myself in the byways of memory. I want to cry out that I am hungry, but I am afraid to hear my own voice, and I start running. But hunger is right at my heels.

Bread, milk and cheese. Hunger restores a taste for simple foods, just as distance creates a desire for all that is pure and eternal. Hunger and sorrow cleanse both soul and palate; they deliver a man's life back to its default position.

*

At the end of March 1944 Giovanni and his fellow prisoners were returned to Germany – back to Oflag XB, Sandbostel, near Bremerwörde, which they had left in September 1943.

Albertino wakes up, and his eyes – two tiny black suns – peer over the edge of the pale blue crib alongside our bed. (Now, beyond the barbed-wire fence, amid a field of green barley, a lark rises – singing – vertically into the air, then stops flapping his wings and glides against the wind, without a pause in his song. He is like a jet of sparkling water, fanning out at the summit of its upward spurt like a crystal flower. The trills of the motionless bird are like clear water drops, which fall, like flower petals, laden with sun and song, to the ground below.)

The trill comes from the pink crib on the other side of the bed, where Carlotta has opened her eyes to greet the new day.

Women pass among the farmhouses, carrying baskets of fragrant white bread; men pour buckets of creamy, foaming milk into the heavy zinc cans in which they will travel to market. Nearby, one fellow is beating butter, still not fully clotted as it comes out of the churn.

A boy walks toward the fields, eating a slice of buttered bread and a handful of nuts.

Hungry! Yes, hungry, that's what I am! To the matutinal longings of my heart are added the matutinal rumblings of my stomach. I pace up and down, but hunger still breathes down my neck. I swallow a mixture of air and saliva, while my hands vainly search my pockets.

Not a grain of tobacco, not for days. A good smoke might drive hunger away, but cigarettes are only to be obtained by bartering bread. It's an infernal, vicious circle.

The sentry gazes indifferently out of his watchtower, the lark sings on in the sky, and the sky is filled with wind and sun. It's quite useless for me to tell my sorrow to the soldier, the bird, the sun, the wind, the sky, for they are German, all of them. Everything around me is alien and inimical.

Back in the hut, I throw myself down on the blankets piled up on my bunk and whisper my shame to my neighbour.

'I'm hungry,' I gasp.

Without a word, he hands me a clipping from an Italian newspaper, which served to stuff a recently received food parcel.

'When will interned Italian officers weary of eating buttered rolls at the expense of our German allies?'

MONDAY 1 MAY, 1944 [Giovanni's birthday] Out of the crowd swarming in the vicinity of the barbed-wire fence in expectation of roll call, there emerges the yellowish wind jacket of Rebora. From the worn collar of Rebora's jacket emerges Rebora's head, which looks unusually large because it is balanced atop such a thin neck. And from one jacket sleeve, I can see the tips of Rebora's fingers, close around a little pink package. These days, Rebora resents the universe's indifference toward him, and there is an aggressive tone in his voice.

'I have an idea it's your birthday,' he mutters, passing the pink package to me. 'Here.'

The package contains cigarettes, rationed cigarettes.

On this wind-beaten, sandy shot, buffeted by the dark waves of boredom, there is the flotsam and jetsam cast up by the terrible storm that has broken the lives of so many men. And all of a sudden, quite miraculously, out of this shapeless, dirty mass of humanity, there emerges something clean and pure, something that is a sign of civilisation. Someone has remembered a friend and the ways of friendship. And he has infused a note of poetry into an overpowering quantity of sordid prose.

But then, after all, Rebora is a poet.

THURSDAY 4 MAY Without overcoat, without bed, without soap, without mail, without cigarettes! Has Divine Providence forsaken me?

SUNDAY 14 May Albertino's Birthday. Today is my son's fourth birthday. In him I relived my childhood, but now this is taken away. I count his days rather than my own, and even though I am a prisoner I wish that I could stay time for a moment.

'The Chicken'

...It came about that last night I saw Albertino. I was dozing in the upper chamber of my 'castle', with my fellow prisoners sleeping soundly around me, when suddenly, in the ray of light streaming through a crack in the paper over the window, I saw a tiny figure, apparently made of moonstuff. He was standing, clad in a long nightshirt, where my potbelly used to be; he had curly hair and a piratical expression. Albertino had come to look for his father, for the man that had made him a son.

He stared at me, and I asked him where he was going. He said he was searching for his father, and I said that I was he, at the same time moving my face into a ray of light. He gazed at me gravely and ran his fingers over my hollow cheeks. I inquired discreetly about the other members of the family, and he gave me all sorts of interesting news, His grandfather made a face like a lion, his grandmother told the story about the three little pigs and his mother threatened him all the time with the most dreadful punishments.

'What does she say?'

She says that if I am a bad boy, the Germans will come and eat me up.'

'Quietly there, Albertino! The enemy is listening.'

I pulled him underneath the blanket. The ray of light fell on one corner, where there was stamped an imperial German eagle, with its wings outspread, ready to fly.

'Chicken?' he checked.

'Here's hoping, Albertino!'

For a long time we whispered to each other. He told me about a bunch of flowers that bloomed afresh every day in a glass set before an ancient and unspeakably benign face of the Redeemer. Then he searched the pocket of his nightshirt and pulled out a green rubber ball, a gold button and a key from my old typewriter.

'I have a gun, too,' he told me.

'I only wish I could say the same!'

I pushed up the paper that served as a blind over the window and saw the first signs of dawn in the sky.

'Go home, Albertino,' I said. 'Mother's waiting.'

'What about you?' he asked.

'I'll be coming along,' I said. 'Tomorrow. Morgen.'

He emerged from under the blanket, shaking his head, and waved bye-bye with his transparent hand. I raised the blind and saw that it was nearly light outside.

Albertino fluttered in the air overhead, then set his course due southwest. He hovered a moment above the Sanctuary.

'What are you up to, silly?' I wondered.

Cautiously I opened the window. Then I saw ten, a hundred, a thousand other Albertinos fly out of the camp windows and gather together over the bell-tower before, like an army of doves, they winged their way toward the sunlit south. Suddenly a big tri-motor plane descended upon them out of the upper regions of the sky. I choked down an anguished cry. But the army of doves remained unbroken.

No one can intercept a prisoner's dreams. The doves flew on, the sky took on a pale blue colour and I rejoiced in my heart. There was going to be another beautiful day come autumn.

THURSDAY 25 MAY, 1944 In the bright stillness of noon, under a colourless sky, among the inflexible, geometrical outlines of the camp buildings and the desolation of the sand, *despair* is no longer of the earth but hangs, suspended in the air, penetrating the emptiness of our abandoned existence. Every man in the camp breathes it in; what started as an individual ill is soon a general obsession. It is not sorrow or anxiety, but despair.

Captain X has just had news that his only daughter, fourteen years old, died in Florence forty days ago. *Despair.* His friends took him by the arms and shoulders to prevent him from dashing at the fence and tempting the sentry to shoot him down. They are still holding him, but it is no longer necessary, for now his gesture of rebellion is to stand, with taut nerves, immovable as a stone. He does not tremble but seems to vibrate all over, as if he were made out of glass, like the wide-open eyes out of which he stares into space. Surely, at any moment, he may crack or shatter.

Despair, that is to say, the oppressive, unbearable feeling of total *impotence.*

Men have become so used to the monotony of their days that they imagine life outside has come to the same halt. That fate has suspended its laws, and nothing will happen before they go home. Then, all of a sudden, this illusion is violently broken.

In the outside world, life and death go on as usual.

The prisoners feel as if they were left by the roadside while others continue their way, moving so far ahead that there is no way to overtake them.

SATURDAY 3 JUNE The German June begins with a cold, rainy, autumnal day. The sky seems to be aware of the gravity of the times in which we are living; it is surly as the race of northern men, whom from birth to death it oppresses.

The university courses, which were to have begun yesterday, have been postponed until the return of good weather. The university has a well-ordered schedule and a top-notch faculty, but no roof over its head. A little group of men seated on the ground behind hut No 3 is the Law School; behind No 7, Humanities; behind No 10, Engineering, then Agriculture, Accounting and the rest.

In the watchtower across from Humanities, a sentry listens indifferently to a passage from Dante, every word of which is unintelligible to him.

Some there I mark'd, as high as to their brow
Immersed, of whom the mighty Centaur thus:
'These are the souls of tyrants, who were given
To blood and rapine. Here they wail aloud
Their merciless wrongs...'

THURSDAY 20 JULY Ghosts lurk, by night, at every corner of the huts.

In the darkening room an accordion is playing: we lie in our bunks, one beside, one over the other. The ghosts, summoned by the music, come and sit down around the table.

The big huts, those where 280 men sleep in bunks at different levels, their ragged clothes and things hanging from the ceiling, huts where, by day, noisy individuals mill about the stoves and tables, they are like those Gold Rush cabins, which served as stores, taverns, bars and dancehalls as well. At any moment I expect a dancer to jump on a table and do her stuff, or gunshots to sound or arrows hiss in the ear and go plant themselves on the cabin's wooden walls. But of course none of this happens: the men around the tables are weighing potato rations as they would gold nuggets.

A blast of the bugle, and here are 6,000 men, standing mute and motionless before the silence of the empty huts. When I am standing in line and the bugle calls me to attention, my personality is completely lost and I am only an infinitesimal part of collective impotency, like one brick in a high wall. Amid this deathly immobility something dreadful is about to happen.

My little boy runs out from behind one of the huts, and a man runs after him with intent to kill. He catches sight of me and calls for help. But I am a brick in the wall, and my heart is a live insect shut up in a diamond. The 'at ease' signal has been given. I am surprised to find that I can still move and talk.

'How shall we sing the Lord's song in a strange land?'[48]

*

---
[48] Psalm 137, v.4.

Here, in Oflag XB, some men throw themselves into historical, political, philosophical, artistic and literary discussions; they argue about Proust, Croce, Marx, Cezanne and Leopardi. This is the instinct of self-preservation; it reflects the necessity of injecting oxygen into the *Lager*'s dank, stuffy air.

Following two spoken newspapers, a spoken magazine is born: *Orientation* – a cultural and moral magazine of the Betta brothers (philosophers & literary types).

Even the editors of *Orientation*, like those of the spoken newspaper *Capanèo*, and like the hundreds of lecturers here, arrive at the conclusion that Benedetto Croce is a great thinker who has thought about everything concerning aesthetics, philosophy, morality, life.

Giovannino, on the other hand ... well, it is clear that he has not arrived. While he too has to set up a newspaper, he makes it a 'special edition of *Bertoldo* for Italians abroad, humorous, chatty, accompanied by music'.

Giovanni had always disassociated himself from the ego-emotions of the politically and intellectually opinionated around him, and, still exercised by the personal attack on him by De Bernardis, was reminded of this as he resurrected *Bertoldo*.

When the magazine first appeared in print in 1943, Existentialism, with its hostility to just the kind of 'bourgeois sentiment' that stuck in the craw of De Bernardis about Giovanni's readings, was beginning to become fashionable among the intellectual elite. Many attached to its masthead the ideologue Antoine Roquentin of Jean-Paul Sartre's novel, *Nausea,* in which the character is definitively 'existentialist': detached, alienated, nauseous of his own humanity and of the absurdity and meaninglessness of the bourgeois world.

Now, in Oflag XB, Giovanni remembered the day the movement dawned in *Bertoldo's* offices, and the editorial team's response to it:

There were three of us (Giovanni Mosca, Carletto Manzoni and myself) sitting at our table and we were grinding out lines to show the designers.

The editorial secretary arrived and handed us a typewritten piece of paper with a trembling hand.

It was a morning in June 1943, serious events had occurred in Africa and we felt that it was necessary to do something strong to revitalise us physically and morally.

'Direct order from the Directorate-General for the Press!' announced the secretary.

We read it with considerable agitation, considering that the piece of paper would surely impinge on important future events.

'Attack the existentialists.'

This was how the order read, and after reading it we looked at each other a little perplexed.

'So, let's get stuck into the existentialists!' one of us said. And all three of us grabbed our pencils ready to go on an assault of our blank white sheets.

Then a pause. And confusion returned to our eyes.

'What the heck are existentialists?'

We consulted the *Encyclopaedia Italiana*, asked colleagues from nearby editorial offices, quizzed the administration and the chief archivist.

No one had ever heard of existentialism.

Eventually someone remembered a book by Enzo Paci[49] and it was our salvation. The libretto was bought quickly and after a few hours we knew that existentialism is a newly made philosophical system. Nothing else.

It would be interesting to look at the humorous newspapers of the months June-July of '43 (should the possibility ever be offered). In all of them you will find cartoons or small articles against existentialism and you will then have a lot of fun looking at the results of the useful and spirited initiative.

I will limit myself to reporting the result achieved by me personally with a cartoon.

The drawing depicts a fat gentleman turning a fat ham in his hands, standing upright in front of a shelf full of cured meats.

The dialogue between two characters who look upon this important ceremony through the opening of a door is highly significant:

INTELLETTUALOIDI

---

[49] Enzo Paci, *Existentialism*, 1943.

'Who is it?'

The caption read: 'He is not a vulgar hoarder, but a disciple of the new philosophic theory of existentialism which he is studying on a large volume in his library.'

The joke was Carletto Manzoni's and when asked with disgust what existentialism has to do with the ham business, the wretch replied:

'Maybe existentialists don't like ham?'

Thus spake the author of *Il signor Veneranda*, and we bowed our heads, crushed by that Venerandian logic, and set about attacking existentialism.[50]

WEDNESDAY 30 AUGUST, 1944 Giovannino is sitting on the ground, on barren sand. He is alone, but he is not alone. Life dealt him three children, but gave nothing to the second – neither crumb of light, nor breath of air, nor name. Because death had already frozen him in time at birth.

So Giovannino gave sound to Ci's muted mouth with a hiss of his own breath; lit up his dark eyes with a little light from his own, and gave him a name from a little piece of his heart: Ci [pronounced Chee]. So – though unborn – he lives and remains always with his father. Even now he is here, with Giovannino, albeit nobody else knows it.

Time passes for other children; minute by minute they grow older: but for Ci time does not exist; he will never grow old. Giovannino has three children: two are a link to him in life; one is a link to him in death. Two make life sweet; Ci makes death sweet.

*

Cruel men have separated Giovannino from his other children, but Ci is with him always; no one, not even Death, can take Ci away. Even when Giovannino fragments into a bundle of bones, Ci will still be there at his side. And he will take him by the hand, and together they will walk on the dark clouds and stormy seas of Eternity.

A little bird has made a nest in Giovannino's heart: taken up residence there. For three years Giovannino has been warming Ci with his love for him, and his pale flesh has turned pink, and his eyes shine like two black beads, and his dry hair covers his little head with miniscule curls.

---

[50] Częstochowa, 1943

Now Giovannino has made Ci a long white shirt down to his feet. So dressed, although no actual height or weight, he looks like a little angel off a Christmas card. He cannot speak, Ci, but he understands his father because he lives in his heart, draws life from the very beat of his heart.

*

Sitting on the lifeless sand, at the edge of the camp, Giovannino seems alone. But Ci is there with him, sitting on his right shoulder, with his face resting on his gaunt cheek. And together they look beyond the hedge and beyond life, waiting for ... something.[51]

Ironically exhibiting characteristics of the existentialist, Giovanni is at a crossroads, but in a receptive state of mind. He is 'waiting ... for something'. As in Beckett's *Waiting for Godot*, nothing – and everything – is happening. Months earlier he wrote in his diary that boredom had set in. But the state of withdrawal he is in now is different. He is detached from family by being imprisoned, but now he is deliberately trying not to think of his wife for fear that it will get him down. Increasingly alienated, he is seeking his own company more and more. Intrusion upon his state of mind at this point would be anathema.

In *Il prenotiere*, a piece written for the spoken edition of *Bertoldo*, he imagines withdrawing completely, hiding under a covering of branches in an out of the way corner of the prison camp, wary of intrusion from outside, which he raises to absurdist levels (ever his way of making sense of life).

Il prenotiere is a hoarder. Gathering up whatever you can and thinking about how to preserve it appears essential when you're facing a survival crisis. Immediately after he is shipwrecked, Robinson Crusoe begins to make an inventory, taking pains to furnish himself 'with many things I foresaw would be

---

[51] 'Ci', *Diario clandestino* 1943–1945

very necessary to me.' Giovanni had written a piece comparing his situation to a shipwreck the previous April: 'Snatches of song, remembered names of men and institutions, inconclusive greetings from one prisoner to another, these things float upon the sea of sand and tar by which we languish like the spars of some enormous shipwreck.'

The *prenotiere* is someone who keeps his eye on every last thing of use, someone bent on amassing stuff for his own survival, an accumulator or hoarder certainly, but hoarding is a disorder of the mind. Reasons for someone becoming a hoarder include stress, OCD, and altered levels of serotonin. The *Lager*, where there is little of anything to accumulate, would be a special hell for the hoarder and for those around him and, to Giovanni's frustration, he is intruding himself upon his mind to facilitate his crazy purpose:

I am telling you about my wife today, because this very day someone came to remind me that my wife still exists. I pretended to myself to have forgotten about her and this was very convenient and made my solitude less burdensome. But now a damned individual has broken the spell.

The first time I saw our guy was towards the beginning of last October and I managed to hide in the most remote corner of the Campo and, in order not to attract attention, I camouflaged myself with tent cloth and a load of branches.

After furiously rummaging through all my pockets and throwing away all my luggage, I had managed to find a cigarette butt and wanted to enjoy it quietly until the last puff, even if it stank of bad lavender like a whole hairdressing syndicate.

Suddenly a voice behind me made me start:

'Sorry: can you reserve me that butt?'

'But it's a cigarette that I'm smoking,' I replied dryly.

'No problem,' the other said. 'Can you reserve me the butt of the butt?'

So I met *il prenotiere*. And, from that day on, I always had him on my back. Was I planning on splitting the margarine cube for the hut?

Behold *il prenotiere*:

'Can I reserve the wax paper?'

Was I peeling my potatoes? Yes.

Behold *il prenotiere*:

'Can you keep me back me some of those skins?'

I get some jam from home and spread myself a slice.

Behold *il prenotiere*:

'Can you keep me a lick of the knife?'

I get hold of the *Voce della Patria*[52] and jump into my bunk to read those pleasant articles in peace.

Behold *il prenotiere*:

'Can I bag a small piece for toilet paper?'

Was I sunbathing, sitting on one of the five tufts of grass scattered around the *Lager*?

Behold *il prenotiere*:

'Can I book a seat next to you for ten minutes?'

Was I returning from the parcel office with my bundle in my arms?

Behold *il prenotiere*:

'Can I put my name down for a name card? Can I reserve six nails, how about an empty box?'

Was I picking up my mail and throwing myself headlong into reading a letter?

Behold *il prenotiere*:

'Can I book up for any interesting news from Italy? '

I remember one evening. With my thoughts alone I wandered around the silent and deserted field. Suddenly I stopped to contemplate the marvellous celestial firmament and fixed my gaze on the seven twinkling stars of the Big Dipper. When there is a voice in the darkness:

'Can I take a look at the Ursa Maggiore?'

When we changed camp the booker was assigned to another hut and I only saw him a few times and from afar.

But this morning he came to seek me out and it was, as I said, he who reminded me that my wife exists.

I was in bed with the fever that for some days had made me sick and wasted, and I was thinking of the beach of Viareggio and Lake Garda when the booker appeared in front of me.

'You're sick?'

'Yup.'

'Much?'

'Quite.'

'So, if nothing else, can I book myself in for your widow?...'

Being increasingly detached, watching, listening and examining things and himself objectively, from a distance, Giovanni is granting his own consciousness a remarkable independence and, like Antoine Roquentin, giving reality the full weight of its sense – but all this with a difference that will redefine him as anything but existentialist.

---

[52] A German sponsored propagandist newspaper.

THURSDAY 7 SEPTEMBER, 1944. 'New Worlds'
Here everything on which the eye falls is examined for possible significance, be it a blade of grass, a hair, a speck of dust. An immense world has suddenly been closed to these men, and they feel the need to create another in the few handfuls of sand granted to them, populating their tiny enclosures with a thousand little things that they are discovering each day. Every minute thing acquires significance for men who no longer have anything, just as every smallest action acquires value for men condemned to inaction.

Their minds – now mortified by the sterile, vain and painful game of nostalgia and regrets belonging to the dead past – try desperately to cling to the slightest thing that might bode well for the future. A Russian, a cloud, a lark, a ray of sunshine, the stamp on a postcard, the colour of the sentry box: everything here suggests a thought to someone, everything serves to convince these men that they are still part of 'a living world'. And they think they are discovering it, this world, when in fact they are creating it from elements they brought with them from outside. It's no new world that they're discovering, but an old world, theirs: they are discovering themselves.

'Autumn Evening'
I look at my dried hands and bony wrists and feel very sorry for myself. Under the sixty pounds of weight I have lost there was something I considered long since dead. My spirit was submerged in fat, but now it is so crystal clear that I can mirror myself in it and rediscover an image of my distant youth. When I look at my small bones, I feel the same consuming anxiety as I feel for the frailty of my son. In short, I begin to regard myself with love.

Just now I'm hungry to the point of weakness. My illness prevents me from eating any of the camp rations, except the slippery, tasteless potatoes. I am alone in the hut, and there is a knapsack full of food at my feet, brought by some new arrival. In the sultry air of the August evening I am so completely lost in my thoughts that I hardly see a gaunt hand searching the knapsack. I say and do nothing; I allow the thin fingers to grasp a piece of white bread.

Then I mingle with the hundreds of men walking up and down the length of the barbed-wire fence, and munch the bread along the way. The searchlights which circle around from the tower and periodically fall upon me seem to be ferreting out my guilt. My heart skips a beat, but I am not too deeply upset; in fact I am happy. My son was hungry and I let him steal a piece of bread.

'I'm my own son, really,' I reflect. And I feel as if I were under my own protection.

'Finally Free'
Somebody was a prisoner within me. He was oppressed by my flesh and my fleshly habits. Confined as if in a pressurised, deep-sea diving suit, he looked out from his prison darkness, his eyes sharp, but the crystal of mine, through which he drilled his gaze, was clouded with the greasy vapours of conventional living.

His heart was locked in mine, he had to adjust the beat of his heart to match the heavy throb of my heart. His voice was clear and sweet, but overwhelmed by the hard, clumsy timbre of mine.

Someone was a prisoner of my self, and my thick rind oppressed him: but now he has escaped from his prison.

One day I was walking on this God-forsaken sand, and I was tired and I dragged my bones, heavy with nostalgia, when suddenly my steps felt miraculously light, and the sky appeared to me unusually deep as if, as I watched the world from behind the dirty glass of a window, that window – yes! – suddenly opened wide. And I saw the smallest details and the smallest things never seen before, like a new world, and everything was complete in all its details. And I could hear even the slightest rustling as if my ears were uncorked, and I heard voices, unknown words, and it seemed to me that it was the voice of things, but it was my voice: the voice of my prisoner.

I turned and saw that I had come out of myself, I had pushed myself out of my fleshly shell. I was free. I saw my other self move off, and with him all my affections drifted away; and of them only the essence remained. As if a flower had been taken from me, and only the perfume in my nostrils and the colour in my eyes were left of it.

Will I meet my other self again? Is he waiting for me beyond the prison fence to take hold of me once more? Will I always return to be oppressed again by my fleshly shell and habits?

If this is to be the case, my imprisonment will be prolonged indefinitely.

Dear God, don't take my freedom from me.[53]

There is heightened awareness of something: 'Everything on which the eye falls is examined for possible significance, be it a blade of grass, a hair, a speck of dust.' But, while other 'minds – now mortified by the sterile, vain and painful game of nostalgia and regrets – try desperately to cling to the slightest thing that might bode well for the future,' Giovanni is turning his back on the 'dead past'. Interventions and nostalgic distractions are resisted, like he resists hunger. And he is waking up to a transcendental dimension 'long since dead', 'an image of my distant youth' rediscovered, a 'self' imprisoned all this time in

---

[53] 'Finalmente libero', *Diario clandestino* 1943–1945

his outward-looking fleshly frame, 'clouded with the greasy vapours of conventional living'.

A verse from the gospels comes to mind. 'Anyone who wishes to be a follower of mine, must leave self behind' (Mark 9.34–36). Cut off from family and all that conditioned his old self, his narrow limited ego, all the petty concerns and ambitions, trivia and distractions, he is even trying to forget Ennia, and his preoccupation with his son is now a search for the child within, the boy Giovanni once was. He may not have been looking for God, but it seems that God was going to work in him.

'Someone was a prisoner of my self, and my thick rind oppressed him: but now he has escaped from his prison.' It is nothing less than a spiritual awakening – Giovanni has turned inward, no longer are his senses running out into the world of his old self, but all unturned and collected, he is reaching into the ground of his soul.

Giovanni's pronouncement upon his imprisonment – 'I will not die even if they kill me' – is no longer the paradox it once seemed, and the irony of a prison-house being a place of freedom wasn't lost on him. Here, in Oflag XB, he taunted the Nazis with the thought:

Signora Germania, you have fenced me in and made sure that I do not get out.

But it's no good, Signora Germania: I can't get out, but whoever wants to come in is welcome. My loved ones come in, and my memories.

And that's not all, Signora Germania, because the good Lord also enters in and teaches me all kinds of stuff forbidden by your regulations.

Signora Germania, you rummage in my knapsack and rummage through the shavings of my bedroll. But it's no good, Signora Germania, you can't find anything, yet documents of essential importance are hidden here: the plan of my house, a thousand images of my past, what I plan for the future...

And that's still not all, Signora Germania. Because there is also a large topographical map at a scale of 25,000 to 1 in which the exact point where I will be able to find faith in Divine Justice is marked with extreme precision.

Signora Germania, you dominate me, but it is no good. Because the day when, gripped by anger, you make a racket with one of your thousands of weapons and lay me down upon the ground, you will see that from my motionless body another self will rise, more beautiful than the first. And you will not be able to put a dog-tag around his neck because he will fly away over the fence, and that will be that.

Man is like that, Signora Germania: his outward self is a very easy matter to dominate, but inside there is another, whom only the Eternal Father commands.

And there's the catch, Signora.[54]

A sculptor hammering and chiselling away at a block of stone gradually releases from it a figure more beautiful than the dense column with which he started. Here the sculptor is Giovanni and he is working on himself and 'the figure more beautiful' is released from its prison within.

That the real possession of God is to be achieved within would soon become the principal theme of the Don Camillo stories, where it will always be the child that instinctively and unquestioningly understands matters of the spirit, the child being closest to the ever-diminishing echo of the heavenly source:

...Heaven lies about us in our infancy!
Shades of the prison-house begin to close
Upon the growing Boy,
But he beholds the light, and whence it flows,
He sees it in his joy;
The Youth, who daily farther from the east
Must travel, still is Nature's Priest,
And by the vision splendid
Is on his way attended;
At length the Man perceives it die away,
And fade into the light of common day.[55]

What was revealed to Giovanni in the *Lager* was 'something that I considered was long since dead', his inner child. And Don Camillo first hears the inner voice of God as a boy, as Giovanni described in 'The Apple Tree'.[56]

Don Camillo was celebrating Mass and all the while a criminal gang were hatching a dastardly plan.

---

[54] Reading of 'Signora Germania', Hut 18, Beniaminów (1944)
[55] 'Ode: Intimations of Immortality from Recollections of Early Childhood' by William Wordsworth.
[56] *Don Camillo Takes the Devil by the Tail* (Pilot, 2020).

The gang had made their way surreptitiously under the hedgerows to the side of the fields and having reached the hedge that bordered the presbytery garden, had attached grappling hooks to the base of it in order to clear a way through the blackthorn and red *cagapoi*.

Six jailbird *manqués* were led by a bullyboy wearing a red-and-white striped hooligan's shirt and with a large tuft of curly hair dangling over his left eye. His legs were covered with scratches, and a rip in the seat of his pants exposed enough of his backside to convince anyone that he must surely be a seasoned raider.

Inside the church, in the hollow of the apse, flanked by the choir stalls, two large, yellow and blue windows were putting the gang's exploits at risk. For these windows were wide open and through them, from where he stood at the altar, Don Camillo could, by turning one eye to the right, observe what they were up to. There could be only one objective, as the apples that weighed down its branches were just aching to be snitched.

Having opened a way through the hedge, at a sign from the gang leader one of the bullyboy's six co-conspirators slipped into the vegetable garden and, crawling through the Savoy cabbage patch, reached the apple tree and climbed it as quick as a monkey. Reaching inside the canopy of the tree, where the trunk was divided into four large branches, he began to explore the possibilities, before speedily descending to report to his accomplices, who remained on the far side of the hedge.

'Nothing doing,' he explained. 'Up to the fork it's fine, because you can use the trunk as cover, but then you have to work in the open and the priest can see.'

The bullyboy boss spat out a blackthorn that appeared to have stuck in his craw: 'Let him see that *macaque* then!' he said in a voice full of contempt. 'I'll go up the tree and knock down. You stay on the ground and catch as the apples fall. No noise: not one apple must fall to the ground. Listen good: if one of you messes up, I will see to him personally.'

All of them went into the vegetable garden except the 'stake', and the boss spread his men out beneath the apple tree.

'At the first sound of alarm,' he said, concluding his briefing, 'you lot scatter – everyone travels on his own and we'll meet up at the Old Mill. I'll take care of myself.'

'If the priest sees you,' one of the gang objected, 'he'll recognise you and even if you manage to get away from him, it'll mean trouble for you later.'

'The boss chuckled and, taking out his handkerchief, spread it out over his face like a bandana, knotting it behind his head. Essentially, given the tufts of hair dangling over his left eye, only the right eye remained uncovered, and the bullyboy whispered:

'Recognise me, now, if you can.'

*

Don Camillo, who was still celebrating Mass, suddenly heard the voice of Christ saying softly:

'Don Camillo, you seem to have gone wrong. You are not on the right page.'

'Excuse me, Lord,' answered Don Camillo, busily flicking through the pages of the Missal.

'That is not the right page either,' said Christ again.

'Forgive me,' said Don Camillo. 'I don't know what's happening to me.'

'Maybe it's something to do with your looking out of that window as you turn the pages of the Missal, instead of looking *at* the Missal.'

The masked bullyboy, who had reached that part of the tree where the bigger and prettier apples grew, settled astride a branch and worked quietly away as if he were on the balcony of his house. He twisted the apples off their stalks and threw them to his accomplices quickly, confidently, without a shade of concern for what he was about.

'Don Camillo,' Christ warned the archpriest once again, 'why do you keep looking out of the window?'

'Lord,' moaned Don Camillo, 'there is someone on the apple tree in the presbytery garden.'

'Don Camillo,' Christ whispered sternly, 'do four apples make you forget your God?'

'Not four, Lord,' gasped Don Camillo. 'But 400 or even 4,000! It seems that the little devil has a hundred hands.'

'I understand, Don Camillo,' sighed Christ. 'This is so serious that you just have to stop the Mass and run to defend your apples.'

Don Camillo objected:

'Lord,' he said 'I didn't stop the Holy Mass when the river broke through its banks and water flooded the church.[57] Nothing and nobody in the world could make me halt Mass. I don't care about my apples. The cheek of that little bandit offended me, that's all.'

'"Little", did you say?'

'"Little", so to speak: he'll be eight or nine years old.'

---

[57] See 'When the Rains Came', *Don Camillo and Peppone* (Pilot Productions, 2016).

'Then I wouldn't call him a bandit, Don Camillo. I once met someone else who, as a child, picked apples from that tree and later...'

'*Orate fratres*,'[58] Don Camillo cut Christ short, suddenly no longer interested in what was happening on the apple tree.

*

The apple tree that opened its large umbrella over the presbytery garden was as old as the cuckoo. An almost miraculous apple tree because, forty years earlier, it gave three large baskets of fragrant apples every autumn and now it gave four, and was as healthy as it was then.

Even when the parish priest's apple tree was young, marauding bands were going around the countryside, leaving in the morning with a pieces of bread in their pockets and returning in the evening with their shirts stuffed with fruit to split amongst them.

Indeed, in those days, the gangs that went around raiding fruit trees were far more numerous than today and on several occasions they even cut down trees and took them away along with all their fruits. Come late summer, dozens and dozens of gangs from the bigger villages deployed themselves around the countryside and, where they passed, they didn't even leave the leaves on the trees.

One of the most feared gangs was the Chiavicone, so-called because it had its headquarters at the Stivone barrage gate over the old sewer: they were then a dozen assorted would-be jailbirds, about nine or ten years old, but as dangerous as any eighteen-year-olds.

Sure, the fruit was of interest to them, but even more than the fruit, the 'work' itself is what seduced them. They did their stuff wherever there was a favourable opportunity and in open competition with other gangs, but what they were most passionate about was working their own territory. In other words, a gang had its own Section, onto which no other gang dared trespass.

The Chiavicone gang knew how to gain respect, and it came to be respected above all because included within its territory were the ten most dangerous targets in the entire region. This made the whole business a matter of prestige, even of honour, and the more the unfortunate orchard owners became angry and tried to increase surveillance and defences, the more the boys of Chiavicone got a taste for what they were up to.

Among these ten targets was the parish priest's apple tree. A very risky one because it was located in a built-up area and it was guarded

---

[58] Brethren, let us pray...

by a sexton who thought nothing of peppering a thief caught in the act with shot, and, finally, because when the apple tree was stripped, the old parish priest used his sermon to complain and instil an ardent desire in parents to knock some sense into their children.

The Chiavicone gang was a limited number organisation and worked better than all the others because it had only one commander, and the rest of the gang never questioned his authority.

However, after three years of activity, they suddenly lost one of their men. He just disappeared and nobody knew where he had gone or why he had left.

It happened when the little gadabouts were seven years old and, for the next three years the missing member never showed.

In fact, he didn't bob to the surface again until the summer of the third year, and they could hardly recognise him. For, if the face was still the same as before, nothing else fitted the fellow they once knew.

In point of fact, the young chap came back dressed in a cassock, like a priest. They had put him in the seminary, and now after three years they had allowed him to spend his summer holidays back home.

Everyone in Chiavicone agreed with the gang leader when he told them that this fellow wouldn't have the courage to meet them face to face. They'd waited for him for three years. He'd come back dressed as a priest and now they considered him worse than dead. They would take the Rossetto boy from Casa Bruciata instead.

When the cherry season began, the gang went to work. Eleven o'clock, one morning, they met by the acacia grove at the Stivone barrage gate to plan the first enterprise of the new season, and had been arguing for a quarter of an hour, when the man on guard sounded the alarm:

'Enemy in sight.'

*

They lurked behind the acacia bushes and before long the priestling appeared on the embankment road.

At a whistle, the gang surrounded him and dragged him to the old sewer.

'What are you doing around here?' asked the boss in threatening manner. 'Are you here to spy on us?'

'No,' said the young boy, 'they told me you'd taken the Rossetto boy from Bruciata in my place. That's not fair: as long as I'm alive, that place is mine.'

They laughed at him. 'Go say your Rosary to the parish priest,' the gang leader replied. 'We don't need priests. Priests are enemies of the people.'

They were big words for a ten-year-old brat, but the boy had heard them a million times in his house, or in the meetings of the Reds, and so up to a certain point they counted.

'Priests are ministers of the Lord and therefore especially friends of the poor,' replied the priestling.

They covered him with an avalanche of foul words and when the boss gave them a sign, they jumped on him and pinned him down.

'Now,' explained the leader, 'go back home and if you see one of us cast your eyes down. But, you know, we need your priest-dress. So, without making a fuss, you will undress down to your shirt.'

This idea thrilled the members of the gang, but the priestling did not take to it. Shaking like a tiger caught in a net, he managed to slip away from the clutches of his attackers and cut loose.

He lifted his cassock with both hands and ran like one cursed by the Devil. Unfortunately, he ran towards the river and the others, chasing him, fanned out to block him along the shoreline. They stitched him up good and proper and the priestling no longer had a chance, because already his feet were in the water.

The gang boss ordered the others to stand still and advanced towards his victim.

'I'll cook his goose myself,' he crowed fiercely. 'We will send him to the village naked and, if he wants to get there, he will have to swim.'

But the Great River took pity on the priestling and sent him a staff of black locust wood a metre long and a couple of inches thick, washing it up close to the shore.

The gang boss had got priests all wrong and couldn't have imagined what would then happen by the water's edge. In fact, the priestling, to deceive his opponent, made an even more frightened face than he felt and then, as soon as the gangster nosed his pumpkin up to his, he bent down, fished the wood out of the water and stung him with a blow to the head.

The gang leader collapsed, but the priestling didn't lose sight of the other ten scallywags and, before they even realised what was happening, they saw themselves bowled over by a crazed person with a deadly stave making breathtaking reels at them. They dispersed among the poplars, disappearing into the surrounding area, while the gang boss found himself with a champion bump on his head and at the mercy of the priestling, who seemed very willing to continue the dance.

'Truce,' muttered the gang leader, pulling himself up.

'*Pace*,' replied the priestling. By and by, the others floated back, one at a time, and when they were all present, they agreed with the boss: the vacancy in the gang was to be filled by the priestling. They left immediately for the intended target and the little priest followed them, still trailing his black locust wood behind him.

In view of the cherry trees they intended to 'work', the chief turned to the priestling and muttered: 'How are you going to climb trees? Your cassock is going to get in the way.'

'I'm not climbing anywhere,' explained the priestling. 'I belong to the gang, but I don't participate. While you do your job, I will pray.'

The gang swarmed all over the cherry trees while, kneeling on the other side of the hedge, the priestling prayed.

They returned to base in no particular order for the proper division of the loot.

'*He*,' said one of the gang pointing to the priestling, 'did nothing and has no right to any of it.'

'I don't want any,' replied the priestling. 'I cannot transgress the Seventh Commandment: "Thou shall not steal."'

'Then what are you doing with us?'

'I pray God to forgive you.'

The gang boss made eleven piles and finally mumbled, 'But it's not fair that he has nothing at all.'

'I'm not entitled to anything,' insisted the priestling. 'Of course, if someone makes an offer unasked, I can't refuse.'

Everyone gave a handful of cherries to the priestling. And everything fell into place.

*

The Chiavicone gang conducted a brilliant campaign that year and the parish priest's apple tree was sacked in the final, most prestigious operation of all.

'I can't go with you this time,' said the priestling. 'I will pray in the church.'

Punctually, at half past one in the afternoon, while the band raided the apple tree in the presbytery garden, the priestling knelt in front of the high altar.

All of a sudden, he heard a distant voice:

'What are you doing?'

The priestling understood instinctively that this was the voice of the crucified Christ above the high altar, and humbly bowed his head:

'Lord,' he replied, 'I beseech you.'

'On whose behalf?'

'Of boys who don't understand the importance of the Commandments and steal fruit.'

'For *all* boys who steal fruit?'

'Yes, Signore. But especially for my friends who are stealing it right now. Jesus, they have a poor education and cannot reason properly. They are not bad. Forgive them!'

'If your friends have a bad habit of stealing fruit, why do you not persuade them to break it? Do they not want to listen to you, perhaps?'

'No, Lord: they listen to me. But if I were to convince them not to steal fruit, how can they give me my share?'

Christ smiled: 'I appreciate your honesty and your innocence, but I cannot approve your conduct. This is not how sinners are turned.'

Tears came to the priestling's eyes: 'I know, Lord, but I like fruit a lot and in the seminary they give us so little...'

'The way you have chosen is hard and full of sacrifice...'

In the vegetable garden, there was uproar and the priestling jumped on a choir stall to look through one of the windows in the apse: the sexton had caught the gang red-handed and was running towards them, screaming. The boys of the gang jumped quickly from the apple tree and cut loose. The gang boss, who'd been working the top of the tree, was not so fast, as up there the branches were slender and fragile. Unfortunately, panic seized him and a branch did break beneath his feet. He didn't fall because he was able to grab a larger branch on the way down, but it left him dangling in the void, and even the branch that saved him threatened to break at any moment.

'Lord,' exclaimed the priestling. 'While we were talking, I stopped praying and see what's happened to that poor fellow. Forgive me, but when one is praying, one must not be distracted!'

The branch creaked and the priestling, hoisting himself onto the windowsill, made it into the garden in one leap. What he had in mind was nothing short of madness, but if Christ had distracted him while praying, then that would make him feel responsible for what happened next and surely he would help. The priestling arrived under the apple tree just as the weakening branch broke and the boy fell. He grabbed him in flight before he hit the ground and both boys ended up in the middle of the cabbage patch.

The priestling had to stay in bed fifteen days because everything was dented and a lot of bones were out of place. But God only knows how he got by without breaking both arms, or his neck or spine.

When he was able to get back on his feet, he went to kneel before Christ at the high altar.

'Jesus,' he said, 'thank you for saving my friend and me. As for fruit, I understand...'

'Don't worry,' Christ interrupted him. 'We will return to the subject of fruit later. There is time...'

*

Don Camillo continued to celebrate Mass and made tremendous efforts not to take account of the fact that a bandit was stripping his apple tree, right there in front of his nose, while he was looking on.

It is not known what actually happened, but those who attended Mass that morning never forgot what they then saw. Suddenly, Don Camillo span away from the altar as if he'd been sucked up by a whirlwind: in a flash he was in the vegetable garden under the apple tree, and the wretched gang leader was hanging onto a branch bent to breaking point, like the gang leader of old. And then he fell into Don Camillo's arms.

The priest put him on the ground and tore the handkerchief from his face.

'If nothing else, you're lighter than your father,' he roared, letting loose an atomic boot on the boy.

Then Don Camillo went back to church and finished Mass.

He did not point out to the crucified Christ that Peppone's son, by raining down on him from the tree, had popped one of his ribs.

But of course Christ knew that only too well.

That the voice of *il Cristo* is available to all, the world over, is suggested in stories such as 'Conscience',[59] where it is identified as the faculty of knowing within oneself what is right, what is true, a faculty inborn but too often clouded over by the ego-emotions, which may range from pride, power, our need to be right all the time, to feel important, to win, to dominate and control others (never more obvious than in Hitler's Germany, Mussolini's Italy and in Russia today), and at the fundamental level to our *insecurity*, which is what obscures the light for young Magrino in 'Conscience':

'Don Camillo,' said Jesus, 'how do minnows learn to swim? It is instinct. Conscience is not taught; conscience is instinctual. We are born with it. It is not given to some who do not possess it. It is not

---
[59] *Don Camillo's Dilemma* (Pilot, 2019).

like a lamp brought from outside into a dark room. This light is burning all the time. Only in Magrino's case the room was dark because the light was covered with a thick veil. Remove the veil, and his world lights up.'

Don Camillo spread his arms.

'But who unveiled the light in that boy's soul?'

'Don Camillo, when the darkness of death descends, everyone instinctively searches within for the light. For now, do not ask how; just thank God that the little boy found the light that burned under the veil.'

The voice within, the faculty of knowing within oneself what is right, what is true, may be all that we can know of God in this world, but the means to hear it is innate. When the sensory powers have been completely withdrawn from their preoccupations with the outside world and are turned inward, then in the silence and the darkness is the veil lifted and the word spoken. So it was for Giovanni in the prison camps of Germany and Poland. Giovanni's spiritual enlightenment revealed a deeper reality within, one where neither space nor time exists, one therefore that only God can know, but which he used his imagination and high sense of humour to create the magical illusion of knowing and shared with us from above the high altar in Don Camillo's village church.

For conflict resolution the voice of *il Cristo Crosifisso* has no peer. It counsels Don Camillo with wisdom, compassion and gentle humour in 154 of the 346 stories, exposing and undermining the stubborn priest's politics and prejudices (as no doubt Giovanni would have liked to have done for De Bernardis in 1944), suggesting solutions and alternatives so simple that they are beyond the reach of political minds clouded with ideology and the need to win. Neither victory nor supremacy is sought, only harmony and equanimity within Don Camillo's Little World, achieved through an understanding and acceptance of what being human means.

Intervention from on high does not presume a controlled or deterministic Little World. For there would be no need for such a power if free-will were not a feature of life. Don Camillo remains free to choose whether to follow *il Cristo's* advice and often proves himself all too human in electing not to do so (as, in turn, God knows that he will).

We generally understand freedom as our right to conduct ourselves in whatever way we choose (freedom of speech, etc). But fundamental to the Don Camillo stories is that true freedom is not licence. Rather, it is a will freed from all preoccupations in the material world, all that usually conditions our responses, our thinking – born of our personal history, social and cultural conditioning, our politics, desires, ambitions and passions – acres of potential prejudice which mark out our conduct, speech and thought as anything but free.

In 'Comrade 'Penèlopo'[60] Don Camillo says to Peppone, 'I don't yearn for the sort of freedom you go on about,' because being a communist the mayor can never truly break free to follow his 'inner voice'.

These days, young people searching for Truth are mixed up. They are full of good will, but are seeking someone to teach it to them, to start them out along the right way. 'We've plenty of time, and among us there are some very good scholars. We ought to have courses in it.'

They would have Reconstruction courses, courses in the Future, politics courses, freedom courses. It's a polemical disease in the blood.

The truth cannot be taught; you have to discover it, conquer it. Think, get a conscience. Don't look for someone who thinks for you, who teaches you how to be free.

What you have before you [the war] are effects, now trace back to their causes; identify the evil.

Break away from the crowd, from collective thought. Resist being like a cobbled stone set rigidly in sand, bound together to the masses. Discover the individual, the *personal* conscience, within yourself. Articulate the moral issue.

Tomorrow, as soon as you step onto your native soil, you will find one who will teach you the truth, then two, then four and five. They will all want to teach you the truth in different, often conflicting, terms.

We must prepare ourselves here, in captivity, 'free ourselves' here in captivity, so as not to become prisoners to the first person waiting for us at the station, or the second or third. Instead, scrutinise every word they utter with your conscience and, having identified the falsehoods of each, discover the real truth.[61]

So effective was the author in persuading Don Camillo and Peppone of this in the last collection of stories he prepared before he died that the two colossi looked into the future with a certain sadness:

'You and I continue to fight a war that has in fact been over for a long time,' Don Camillo observed. 'Before long, we will be kicked out of office – me by my people and you by yours – and we will find ourselves miserable and broken and having to sleep under a bridge.'

'So what?' Mayor Peppone replied. 'We will continue to fight under the bridge.'[62]

---

[60] *Don Camillo and Company* (Pilot, 2018).

[61] 'The Search', *Diario clandestino* 1943–1945

[62] 'Young People Today Are Complicated', *Don Camillo and Don Chichi* (Pilot, 2021).

Christmas 1944

In the *Lagers*, towards the end of 1944, Giovanni awakened from the depths of despair not in a state of existential aloneness nor to a detached aloofness as an island unto himself, but to an ever-closer fellowship with his fellow prisoners, the Little World which he now refused to leave, even after the Germans offered him an assured route home.

> Never have I had such a sense of belonging as I've had since being in prison... Once upon a time there were my thoughts and they were all mine because they were born in my brain from my joy or my pain. But one day the joy disappeared, and the pain became of a thousand, ten thousand, a hundred thousand people. It became everyone's pain and my thoughts became everyone's thoughts. Once upon a time there were my thoughts, but I don't regret not having them anymore. In fact, joy will return, and it will be a colossal, immense, boundless, infinite joy because it will be *the joy of all*. And I will feel then forty million times happier than if the joy were mine alone.[63]

Such an awakening as Giovanni experienced in the *Lagers* so flooded his soul that it ran over into the outer world, which seized as a unity all that earlier he had regarded as threatening. *Resistance* was the glue that bound Giovanni closer to his comrades. Resistance meant writing for, and reading to, his fellow prisoners, but now allegory took a more prominent role in his repertoire: he began to enjoy aiming satirical swipes at his German captors, while at the same time managing to see out the war without hating them.

---

[63] Bremervörde reading, 1944

I did the anti-German propaganda: but at the right time. That is to say *there*, in the *Lager*, when it was a question of resisting pressures, threats, enticements... when the Germans were strong and could destroy us... Now, no. Now I work for a free Europe that can never exist without the Germans.

The key binding element in Giovanni's circle in the camp was an unshakeable refusal to fight or even to work for the Germans in exchange for privileges. It may well have been his vocal resistance on this issue that encouraged his captors to send him home.

...Everyone could have gone out, simply by agreeing to collaborate... Twice I was offered the chance to leave: first, to leave and be a journalist in Berlin; second, to go back home and be a journalist in Milan. I said: 'I will go out when and if my companions go out.'

[To] a young man today [who] has never known hunger or appetite... it may be impossible to believe that someone can refuse to leave a concentration camp. How he would laugh if I told him about a humble friar, Father Crosara, a chaplain in the Alpine regiment, who, having returned from the Russian front to his monastery, learned that his Alpini had been captured and imprisoned by the Germans, put his Alpine uniform back on and presented himself to the German command to insist on the right to follow the fate of his flock. He was interned and spent nineteen months in the *Lager*.[64]

Odoardo Ascari, a fellow inmate, remembered well Giovanni's attitude to collaboration: 'In the *Lagers* there were three types of refusenik. To begin with, "*the ideological No*" of the communist Alessandro Natta, who was my neighbour in our bunk-bed. Then came "*the most widespread No*", that of the officers and *carabinieri* who had sworn allegiance to the King, and this was the only No that the Germans understood. Finally, there was "*the No of Don Quixote's children*", like me, like the painter Giuseppe Novello, like Giovannino Guareschi, like Enrico Allorio, later a great jurist. It was the No of those who said to the Nazis: "I'm not going along with you, even if you kill me!"'

One hundred and nine officers go out to pick cherries for the Great Reich. They say that dignity can only be maintained on a full stomach. In amongst the trees their bellies will swell with cherries and when their bellies are swollen enough to die, they will find that it was not a dignified exercise after all. But (with their bellies full or empty) they will never discover that this is not about dignity, but about

---
[64] 'La Coda di Riccardo', *Oggi (1966)*

something more important... There are some things, thank God, that cannot be explained.[65]

As he pronounced in the 'spoken' *Bertoldo*, collaboration was an indelible stain on a prisoner's conscience.

'Macchie indelibili'[66]

Scene: The scene opens in the boarding house, after the prisoner's return. The former inmate is lying thoughtfully in an armchair, while his wife is cleaning up her grey-green uniform.
She: It is useless to insist, this stain does not want to go away. What is it?
He: (sighing painfully) It's a cherry stain.

The French Resistance recognised the significance of the Armistice refuseniks, writing to Italian officers of Fallingbostel prison camp: 'We French, appreciated the courage shown by the Italian people in overthrowing Mussolini and abandoning Germany in the middle of the war. As for you officers who refused to take up arms on behalf of Germany despite the advantages which were offered to you, you showed by these sacrifices, your agreement with the spirit of all the movements of Resistance of Europe. The French Resistance assures you of its sympathy and hopes to see, after the signing of peace, normal relations be established between our two countries.'

It would henceforth always be Giovanni's way to tilt at windmills. With the child in him leading the way, and the satirist following hard on its heels, Giovanni started thinking about celebrating this new sense of fellowship with his comrades by using the allegorical potential of a fairytale to deliver a blow to their captors.

The project he had in mind was bigger than anything he had attempted before, a children's story, one that is still today being read over a handful of nights to Italian children in the build-up to Christmas and is published here in English for the first time. *La Favola di Natale, 1944* returns him to the landscape of his imagination as a child, to a place where 'the sparks sailed in the dark night towards the woods populated by gnomes and witches, towards the turreted abodes of princes and princesses. "It's time! It's time!" the sparks cried. Warriors, ogres, cats in boots, little girls with little red riding hoods, fairies with blue hair woke up and – galloping on winged horses – quickly arrived at the chimney where the wind was waiting for them.' Giovanni had set the child

---
[65] *Ibid*.
[66] 'Indellible Stains'.

within himself free, 'something I considered long since dead... I'm my own son, really.'

The fun in it, for his fellow prisoners, came from its allegorical elements, the fact that the Germans failed to recognise themselves 'in character' as crows, poisonous mushrooms, etc. The encounter of the crows with the sparrows is central to the tale. Just as the sparrows refuse to fall for the crows' offer for a toasty time on their skewers, so Giovanni and his comrades refused to fall for the obviously deceitful blandishments of the Germans to work for them.

The Germans attending the performance didn't realise that they were eating only into 'the crust' of the theatrical meal Giovanni was serving up. They were laughing, but were unaware they were laughing at themselves, while the uproar from the prisoner audience egged the hilarity in the prison huts to ever higher levels.

The *Lager* is the reference point of the piece. At time of writing, returning home was still only a dream and the tale is what it is, a transition piece inspired by his awakening to 'the figure more beautiful' within, but not yet coloured by it, as his future work will be. 'You need a beautiful colour, a colour to harmonise with the world. And you have to be able to say: "*We need this colour*". And I, today, I don't know precisely what that colour is.' There is, however, meaningful reference to the despair into which Giovanni fell and his subsequent spiritual awakening in the haunting 'Song of Melancholy' and the 'clandestine light here which illuminates the days without sun and nights without stars'.

After the war, there would be a book, for which Giovanni supplied the accompanying illustrations, and in 1945, in Milan, the first of many public performances of the production. How one would have loved to compare this and subsequent performances with the original 'in the squalid hovel that was our theatre, stuffed with miserable people', who nevertheless proved the point that all theatre is at its very best when the audience adds something of its own to it.

One night, by dint of thinking about home and that very fancy teenage son of mine, Albertino, I found the brat at the bedside of my kennel again, come in a dream to find his faraway father.

The next morning I told my friend about this episode and he advised me: 'Christmas is coming: why don't you write a beautiful story for these beggars, devoured like you by hunger, love and nostalgia? There is no better way to bring them back to their homeland pastures, to reconnect them to life.'

...I liked the idea and wrote the story on crumpled and greasy pieces of paper... and on his accordion my friend Arturo Coppola accompanied the songs, the text for which I had written. And they were performed by a group of beggars like me, full of cold, of hunger and nostalgia, delivered to a squalid shack-full of other beggars also like us...

Among the six or seven thousand officers imprisoned in the *Lager*, there were professional and amateur musicians and singers. One of them had managed to hold on to his instrument, and the French prisoners from the neighbouring camp lent others. Coppola arranged the music and rehearsed the orchestra, chorus, and soloists. The violinists were unable to move their fingers because of the extreme cold: the damp put the violins out of tune and made them lose their fingerboards. Voices were barely audible because of that hunger, clothed in rags and cold. But on that Christmas Eve, in the squalid hovel that was our theatre, stuffed with miserable people, I read the story and the orchestra, chorus, and soloists commented on it magnificently, and the 'sound effects' brought the most animated episodes to life...

I will grace you with the symbolism of the fairy tale. I don't mean to give the idea of wanting to transform this very humble story into the Divine Comedy. At the most it's a simple curiosity, but I will tell you that the story had a polemical content (a controversial content that the illustrations made later make evident today). Each figure is real: each character, each action has a precise reference to someone or something in reality.

In short, it is a fable that plays a double game: under the species of the nostalgic and fantastic tale, a devious action of sabotage is directed against *the enemy*, who were trying by all means to lure us into their ranks...

'I'll tell you a story, and you will tell it to the wind this evening, and the wind will tell it to your children. And also to your children's mothers and grandmothers, because it's our story: the miserable story of each one of us.'

On Christmas Eve 1944 I ended the introduction with these words: but will the wind have heard? And, if it heard, will it have been able to get past the ramparts of the censor? Will it have lost some sentences along the way? Can the wind be trusted with so delicate a business?

'A Christmas Fable', 1944

Once upon a time there was a prisoner... No, once upon a time there was a little boy... Or better still, once upon a time there was a *poem*...

Or let's say this instead: once upon a time there was a little boy whose Papà was a prisoner.

And you'll say, 'What about the poem? Where does the poem come into it?'

The poem comes into it because the little boy had learned it by heart so that he could share it with his Papà on Christmas Day. But, as we have explained, the little boy's father was a prisoner in a country far, far away.

A curious country where summer only lasted for a day, and even on that day it often rained or snowed. An extraordinary country where everything was made out of coal: sugar, butter, petrol, rubber. Even honey, because the bees didn't suck the blossoms of flowers, only bits of anthracite.

A country like no other, where everything that is necessary for existence was calculated with such wonderful exactness in milligrams, calories, ergs, and amperes that one small mistake in adding up – during a meal – was enough to leave you stone dead from hunger.

This was how things were when Christmas Eve came and the little family was gathered around the dinner table, but one chair remained empty. And they were all looking thoughtfully at that empty place, and everything was still and silent in the room because even the clock had stopped ticking and the flame wasn't moving, as if it had frozen in the hearth.

Well, the little boy – who knows why? – stood up on his stool opposite the empty chair and recited his Christmas Poem:

Ding dang dong, the little bell
is going to ring tonight,
and in the sky one silver star
is going to shine so bright.

The little boy recited his poem in front of his Papà's empty chair and, when he finished, the window opened and a breath of wind blew into the room. And the poem spread its wings and flew away on the stream of it.

'*The poem spread its wings?*' you say. 'And how does it do that? Is it a butterfly then?'

No, Poesy is a little bird. A little bird made of blue sky infused with a moonbeam. A little bird burgeoning (as a flower blooms) in the

Christmas 1944

warm heart of a poet to split, in an instant, from its thumping, blood-red incubator and fall onto the blank page upon the poet's desk.

She is a bird of sorts but as yet she cannot fly because she has no wings: and so the poet dips his pen in his inkpot and pours forth the loveliest words that come into his mind. Every line he creates forms a feather. And when the magical process is over, the little bird flies away and carries those words around the world. We all get to read them because the little bird, gliding onward with her wings outspread, alights upon every blank page she finds. The words are clearly seen because, while the little bird is transparent as air, the words are eternalised in Indian ink.

So the little boy's poem took flight and Poesy rode away on the Wind.

'Where should I take you?' the Wind sighed.

'Take me to the land where the little boy's Papà is held,' said Poesy.

'You must be joking!' the Wind replied. 'They'll take me too and put me to work powering their windmills! No way! It's never going to happen!'

But Poesy begged and begged until the Wind agreed to take her at least as far as the borderlands. So on they went, mile after mile through the pitch-black night until finally they arrived at the frontier and the Wind died down. Poesy alighted, but it was so cold that the poor thing's rhymes were too frozen for it to get off the ground. So she went on foot towards a hedge which marked the boundary line between the two countries.

'Where are you going?' asked an old man with a wick tied to the end of a pole, as he tried in vain to light some stars in the black sky. 'Where are you bound?'

'To the concentration camp,' replied Poesy without stopping.

'Oh dear,' sighed the old man. 'Are they even putting poetry in prison now? What next?'

Poesy scampered on her way and came to the frontier, but no sooner had she passed through the hedge than she was caught up in a net, cast over her from above.

'Aha!' sneered a large man dressed in iron-grey and approaching her with a lantern. 'Where are you off to? Who are you? What's that written on your wings? Are you a spy?'

Poesy explained what she was and where she was going. The man remained suspicious but was convinced enough to put on his glasses and read the lines written on her wings:

Ding dang dong, the little bell
is going to ring tonight...

'No, no, no!' he said. 'Acoustic signalling by night is forbidden in time of war!' And with a brush dipped in Indian ink he deleted a lot of words. Soon he was shaking his head again.

And in the sky one silver star
is going to shine so bright...

'Out of the question! Breach of blackout!' he said. More deletions.

The shepherds will bring gifts of milk
and honey to the Infant King...

'Out of the question! Breach of rationing!' he muttered. And yet more strokes of his brush blacked out the words.

And like a shot the King Magi
onto their camels will spring....

'Out of the question!' he yelled in fury. 'We'll have no kings here! Anyone still talking about kings these days is asking for trouble!' Yet more slashing strokes of his brush.

Then, satisfied, he grabbed a big stamp and stamped Poesy's wings with an official seal of approval, and said she could cross the border, if she still wanted to.

Poesy burst into tears. 'How can I go in like this, with all these crossings-out. I'm not a poem any more...'

'Like it or not at all,' growled the big man showing him a sheet of paper. 'Look here: the regulations are quite clear.'

The regulations did indeed declare, among other things, that in this region everything must be prose; poetry was banned from entering in.

The poor miserable creature turned around. Now, even if she had wanted to, Poesy couldn't fly, as the inky brush strokes had clogged her wings.

'Don't be sad, little one,' said an old man with an enormously long beard, who suddenly appeared, sitting on a rock near the boundary hedge. 'Don't be sad that they haven't let you in. Just imagine, they don't even let *me* in and I have free entry to the most important countries in the world. I've been waiting out here for years.'

'And who are you?' asked Poesy.

'I'm Common Sense,' answered the old man.

The Wind happened by and Poesy implored him, her sticky wings clasped together in supplication: 'Wind, Wind, take me with you! Take me home: my wings have been clipped... I'll pay you a double fare!'

'I cannot,' replied the Wind. 'I have too much on, right now. I have to carry sweet memories and nostalgia to every home in the world. Christmas is the time for memories and it's jolly hard work.'

Poesy walked on through the cold night until she saw someone else appear on the otherwise deserted road. The strange character was moodily mumbling to himself:

What a lovely Christmas
Oh what a lovely Christmas Day!
This song's all wrong
and robs my lungs of air!

What a lovely Christmas
Oh what a lovely Christmas Day!
The roar of war
brings nothing but despair!...

Who was this old mumbler? It was Father Christmas himself, with a long white beard, a sack over his shoulder and a lantern in his hand.

'Hello there!' he exclaimed, stopping to look curiously at Poesy. Then, putting on his glasses, he leaned down to read the few words left on the wings of our poor little bird:

The little bell will ring
One silver star
onto their camels will spring
to the Infant will bring
Geprüft 47...[67]

'Well, look at that,' he exclaimed, 'a hermetic poem!'

The little bird explained that it wasn't hermetic but all that was left of a proper little Christmas poem. This touched Father Christmas's heart to the quick and he said, 'I'll take you home myself. Jump into my sack: it's empty when all's said and done!'

The Poem was amazed. 'Father Christmas's sack ... *empty?*'

'Yes, empty,' sighed the old man.

On this sad earth
who needs toys any more?
All the world's people
work only for war!

Father Christmas shook his head and sighed. 'That's how it is, dear Poesy. My sack is full only of hope. Patience: it'll be full next Christmas. Let's go.'

---

[67] This is all that's left of the little poet's Christmas poem. The fragment ends with the nasty man's *Geprüft* Certification Mark of approval. Father Christmas mistakes the fragment for a hermetic poem. This would have raised a laugh in the hut, with Giovanni politely converted to the hermetic school of poetry by the philosopher Enzo Paci and the hermetic poet Roberto Rebora, who 'speaks a language *incomprehensible.*'

Meanwhile, far away, back at home, Albertino – that's the name of our little poet – was off to bed to hear his granny tell him a story.

Do we want to hear that story too? I'm not sure. We've heard so many fairy tales one more won't harm us. But let's not trespass. Let's wait behind the door.

Look: the child is asleep now, his grandmother has left the bedroom, and silence has spread its black velvet blanket over the entire house.

Listen: after a while there was a tapping at the window. Albertino woke up, got out of bed, and cautiously opened it.

Poesy has returned.

'Well, did you see Papà?'

'No,' the little bird answered and recounted her sad adventure.

So Albertino put on his warm shoes and his hoodie and headed for the door, exclaiming boldly to himself: 'I'll go to my father myself.'

Cautiously, step by step, he crept downstairs. The house was dark and full of mystery.

'My God!' he cried suddenly confronted by two fiery dots piercing the darkness?... Oh, it's the white kitten. What a fright you gave me! Kittie. Now light my way to the garden door.'

And the cat, with his phosphorescent eyes, lit the way for Albertino.

Children's dreams are illuminated by the eyes of kittens, fireflies, stars. It's a very handy kind of lighting because you can see just enough and it doesn't tax the meter.

As he crossed the empty rooms, soft voices could be heard. Now everyone knew what he was about, for when Albertino was telling Poesy his plan, Jiminy Cricket (at home on page 27 of *Pinocchio*) had heard him and escaped the page to spread the great news: 'The boy's going to see his Papà!...'[68]

And so, as Albertino went by, everything spoke to him:

'Tell him I'm counting the minutes until his return!' whispered the clock.

'Tell him I'm devouring the days to make the wait shorter!' whispered the calendar.

'Tell him that without him I can't type a word!' muttered the typewriter.

In the typewriter there was a sheet of paper three-quarters filled: a short story broken off on its final page.

'Tell him, for the love of God, to come back soon,' implored the story. 'Lauretta has been waiting for Giacomino under the clock in the square for eighteen months. You can't leave a poor girl like that, out in all weathers, for years. Tell your Papà to come back and finish the story!...'

Albertino promised to pass all this on. And now, at last, he was in the garden and Flik, the faithful old guard dog, was waiting for him at the door.

'I'm coming to find the master too,' said Flik.

The cat had remained inside. Why should she go off on an adventure on a frozen December night? Just for the pleasure of beholding Papà's face? Cats aren't so sentimental.

It was almost too dark outside to see where Albertino was going, but Flik woke up a firefly hibernating in a crack in the wall. She protested: it's cold, and what's more, so she said, she had no fuel prepared for her taillight.

'But you've got your own generator!' observed Flik.

'Yes, but it's a precious nuisance putting it all together to get up a decent flash rate...'

But the firefly relented in the end and, with her lamp well primed, she set off showing Flik and Albertino the way. They'd barely started out, however, when the gate opened and they found themselves with someone else coming alongside. Someone wrapped up in a long coat and looking like a ghost.

Albertino gave a small fearful cry, but then the firefly lit up the face of this seeming ghost.

'Nonna, it's you!'

'Albertino? Where are you going at this time of night?'

'Well what about you, Granny?'

---

[68] In the fourth chapter of Carlo Collodi's book, the Talking Cricket is a philosopher who attempts to advise Pinocchio, a bit like a conscience.

'I'm going to find my baby,' she replied.

For mothers, their sons are always babies and, if it was up to them, they'd make them sleep in a cot forever. Seeing a metre and a half of leg sticking out of the tiny bed, they wouldn't say, 'My son has grown,' but 'My baby's cot has shrunk.'

Mothers are always doing battle with time and if they sometimes dye their hair when it starts turning grey, it's not from vanity but to convince themselves that time hasn't passed and so their little boy is still a baby.

'You've got a little boy, Granny? Who's that?'

'Your Papà.'

*

Off they went into the night under the feeble gleam of the firefly: Flik, Nonna and Albertino. And what of Albertino's mother? His mother had stayed in bed: she's afraid of the dark and was very cold. Mamma is a bit like the white cat and on a night like this she'd only move if Papà were her baby.

Far-away children must be visited at any cost. With distant husbands it's just a matter of waiting for them. But Papàs travel thousands of kilometres in their dreams just to see the Mammas of their children. Men are sentimental, like Flik. It's not for nothing that man is called a dog's best friend.

*

On and on and on they went until they came to a small isolated station where a locomotive had just taken on a fresh tender of coal and was hooting cheerfully.

'Signora Locomotive,' asked Albertino, 'will you take us to Papà?'

'Impossible,' replied the locomotive. 'Transport crisis, machine-guns firing, shortage of staff...'

'Signora Locomotive,' begged Granny. 'Take me to my little boy. Don't you know what a little boy means to a mother? Don't you have any children?'

'Of course I do,' answered the old steam engine. 'Don't you realise all these carriages are my children? I know just as much as you do what it means to have children far away! If only you knew, old lady, how many of my children are being forced to work over there in the country where your son is!'

'If you know where he is, it means you know my master!' exclaimed Flik. 'In fact, you must know him: he was one of your best customers, he had a season ticket...'

The engine gave a long sigh of black smoke.

'I do know him, but not because of his season ticket. Unfortunately I had to take him there, along with the others. When I remember it, the steam builds up in my cylinder head! Don't make me think about it!'

The steam engine was getting emotional and sighed with all her pistons at once, so Albertino begged her once again and she gave in.

'Get on board, I'll take you as far as I can. You never know what those scoundrels in the mountains might do to you along the way. Into the carriage, ladies and gentlemen, we're off...'

And on they went until, abruptly, the train came to a halt.

'End of the line,' announced the engine. 'The bridge has been blown up. Oh, the wretches! What they get up to! Kids, eh...'

The train backed up and Albertino, Granny, Flik and the firefly found themselves alone in the middle of nowhere.

Which way should they go? Right or left? And how do you tell right from left in the dark? Finally, they espied a little red light moving towards them: it turned out to be the bowl of a big pipe and the pipe was followed closely by an odd old boy with a bushy moustache, a black jacket, striped trousers, and a bowler hat.

'Signore,' implored Albertino, 'please show us the way to my Papà.'

But the oddball replied that he had no idea, he'd seen nothing, he had nothing to do with politics and just minded his own business, and that he was only out and about at this hour because he'd stayed late at a hostelry with his friends. But then, seeing that these were decent, inoffensive people, he took off his moustache, which was false, and revealed that in fact he was a hen.

'I'm a hen from Padua living abroad,' she said, 'and I'm disguised like this so I can come home to lay my egg. I want my egg to be Italian.'[69]

'Stupendous!' exclaimed romantic old Granny, 'Stupendous! You might be a hen from the Risorgimento!'[70]

Then, since the hen was just as romantically inclined, she said, 'Follow this road, count 1,490 paces, then turn right, and go straight on and see where that gets you. *Adios!*'

One, two, three, four, five, six... One thousand four hundred and ninety paces. And when they turned right they found themselves in a wood. And on, on, on they went until they suddenly came out into a pretty clearing lit by big stars hanging from the branches of a tree like fruit made of fire.

It was an airfield: not one of the usual airfields for planes but a landing strip for Angels. Angels of every kind. Single-engined, two-engined, three-engined, four-engined ones were landing and taking off.

War makes a lot of work for the good Lord's air force. Reconnaissance angels overfly battlefields and signal possible concentrations of souls. Transport angels rush to take the souls on board and carry them to Heaven. Hunting angels defend the formations against attacks from black-winged devils. Bomber angels fly over houses, hospitals, and *Lagers* releasing heavy loads of dreams to destroy the damaging effects of despair.

'I'll take you to the concentration camp,' said one of the dream-angels. 'Jump on.'

Here was a beautiful angel with three pairs of wings, a three-enginer, and Albertino, Granny, Flik, and the firefly very soon found themselves high in the sky.

And every so often a little window opened in the black sky and out peeped a star that greeted them by waving a handkerchief. All at once the shutters of a big balcony also opened and the Moon looked out curiously, lighting up the whole night sky.

---

[69] Originating in Padua, Italy, the Padovana is an ancient breed of small crested and bearded chicken.
[70] The period of the political unification of Italy, which established the Kingdom of Italy in 1861.

'Go back inside, you nosy creature!' shouted the angel, but he was too late, a cry was heard and the angel plummeted down with a wing in flames.

The anti-aircraft guns had found them and they'd been hit by flak. Granny, Albertino, Flik and the firefly plunged into the dark abyss.

'Help!' cried Albertino. And the Wind heard him and ran to take the falling travellers on board. He carried them gently down and down, finally leaving them on the soft snow. Then off he went, muttering, 'Blessed dreams! If I hadn't been on the lookout, who knows what would have happened!'

*

Where had our fallen travellers ended up?

In a forest. An immense forest of big trees laden with snow. And snow covered the ground, soft and white as cream. A dark forest full of cold mysteries.

'What do we do now, Nonna?' asked Albertino.

'Have no fear,' his grandmother reassured him. 'We'll always get where we want to go if we ask the way. Look, someone's coming now. Good evening, Signora...'

'Who is it, Granny?'

'It's an ant,' his grandmother explained. 'It's the good ant who works all summer to put stuff aside. And so, when winter comes, the hardworking ant has it easy while the cicada who has wasted the whole summer singing has to beg her for help. And the ant replies, 'You used to sing, now you can dance!' You must always work and save, my boy. Saving...'

'To hell with putting things aside for a rainy day!' yelled the ant. 'A plague and damnation on whoever invented "savings days" and piggy banks and planning ahead! I worked like a slave, saving my pennies, making huge sacrifices for a mite in my old age, and look at the magnificent result! Today, my 50,000 lire is worth the same as 75 lire before the war!... And I have to go and beg from the cicada,[71] who's coining it in after spending her days admiring the view: now, everyone's going to her for descriptions of rosy dawns and fiery sunsets and peaceful mid-days and scented nights from happy times past. Now anyone with a bit of nostalgia in their stockroom is making a packet!... Down with saving! Down with the capitalists! Property is theft!'

And off she went, singing subversive songs.

'This terrible war that undermines so many beautiful fables,' sighed Albertino's grandmother.

'Don't be sad, Signora,' called an Owl, looking out from his little balcony on the trunk of a pine tree. 'Old fables die and new ones are born. Every cloud has a silver lining.'

'Where are we, Signor Owl?' asked Albertino.

And the Owl put on his spectacles and explained.

'On earth there is a Land of Peace and a Land of War. The Land of Peace is all sunshine and blue skies, and its fields are full of golden sheaves, flowers bloom everywhere – on the riverbanks, in the forests, and even on the snowy mountaintops. And its inhabitants work the land, and they all have a little kitchen garden behind their cottage where they lovingly cultivate the big cabbages under which beautiful babies are born in every season.

'The Land of War is entirely the opposite, because there's never any sun and the sky is pitch black, and instead of flowers or wheat, bayonets sprout in the fields, and bombs ripen on the trees. And the men are dressed in iron, and babies aren't born under cabbages but manufactured in machines, and that's why they all have hearts of iron and heads of steel.

'And right on the border between the land of peace and the land of war, there's a crossroads where the road that goes from the countries of the sun to the countries without sun meets the road that goes from

---

[71] Cicadas are a super-family of insects that have featured in myth and folklore as symbols of carefree living and immortality since time immemorial.

the lands where light is born to the lands where light becomes shadow.'

'Signor Owl,' said Flik, 'excuse me, a poor country dog, but I'm finding you a bit *hermetic*.'

'It's simple,' answered the Owl. 'Here the road running South to North crosses the road that runs from East to West. And so, creatures from one country meet those from the other in this forest: the inhabitants of the world of Peace meet those from the world of War. There's nothing to be amazed about. Good night.'

'Signor Owl! Just one more thing, please...'

But the Owl had disappeared into his hole and Albertino, his Granny, Flik, and the firefly were left alone in the forest once more.

They set off among the bushes and on they went until they came upon three Good Mushrooms huddled at the base of a tree stump. They were such good mushrooms that they were deliciously edible, but they hadn't a clue about anything. Very sorry, but they lived a wholly sheltered life and hardly paid attention to politics...

Further on they ran into three red Poisonous Mushrooms with sharply pointed heads like nails, and they asked them too for help, but the mushrooms only shook their stems rudely, muttering '*Weg! Weg!* Be off with you!'

On and on they went until they met a white-haired old man wandering about with a hatchet on his back and a briefcase in his hand. He stopped beside each young tree and examined it branch by branch with a magnifying glass. Then, when he found a rotting branch, he gently cut it off with his hatchet. But first he injected the branch with a local anaesthetic so that it would feel no pain and then he disinfected and bandaged the severed branch.

He pressed his stethoscope against the trunks of the old plants and listened intently. And he massaged the larger knots with camphorated oil, and rubbed pomade onto the exposed roots to protect them from chilblains.

He was the Good Forester who watered the less robust oaks with Proton and put woollen gloves on the ends of the pine branches that had lost their covering of needles.

But, like the good mushrooms, he knew nothing about what was going on. As far as war was concerned, he remembered Garibaldi very well but didn't know whether he'd recovered from the wound he suffered at Aspromonte.[72]

On and on and on they went among the black tree-trunks with the firefly leading the little band. Suddenly they all stopped in fright and ducked down behind a bush. A big man with a red beard was coming towards them barking orders and brandishing a rifle.

'Into position!' he shouted, kicking and punching the trees. 'Into position!'

And all the trees lined up in rows of five, trembling with fear, while the soldier counted and recounted them, and there'd better not be a single one missing!

Then, if a star peeped out from its window in the black sky, he shouted, 'Blackout!' and fired at it. And if a firefly shone its light, the soldier leapt after it and unscrewed its lamp. And he put dark glasses on cats to stop their phosphorescent eyes shining in the regulation darkness.

Mamma mia, what fear! It was definitely not a good idea to ask the Bad Forest Warden for help. Better to stay well hidden.

When the soldier had gone, our firefly re-lit her light and the four travellers set off again.

On and on and on they went until at last they found themselves in a small clearing, where two paths crossed.

'So is this the crossroads we heard about?' asked Albertino's Granny. 'Let's stop here, someone is sure to pass.'

And sure enough, it wasn't long before three Sparrows appeared tramping along the track from the South, each of them with a bundle tied on a stick over their shoulders and a walking stick. And they were singing cheerfully:

---

[72] Giuseppe Garibaldi, a central figure in the unification of Italy.

Here comes the wandering fa-mi-ly:
Mamma, Papà, and the little ba-by:
We're looking for something to eat, you know,
But sadly all we find is snow!

How sad it is to trudge through snows,
No socks or boots to warm our toes!
But never mind: we know good times
are just around the corner!

And at the same moment, from the opposite direction came three Crows in helmets with daggers at their belts, marching ramrod straight. Three black Crows each with a lamp on his chest. Three Crows on night patrol, muttering:

It's ten at night!
Who thinks it's right
to disregard curfew?
Nighthawks and drunks beware,
we're coming for you!

Get your papers in order
or end up in jail.
There's no place for loafers,
they don't get bail.
If you're a layabout you should watch out.
You'll end up in a labour camp
without fail!

'Halt right there! Your papers!' commanded the three Crows rudely: and they wanted to know where the Sparrows were going and what they were doing. And the Sparrows explained that they were going where chance led them, living one day at a time until the good weather returned.

'What kind of life is that?' muttered the Crows. 'Why don't you come with us instead? We'll fill you up with as much millet and barley as you can eat, to put some meat on you...'

'And then?' asked the Sparrows.

'And then we'll stick you on a brand-new skewer – sterilised, rust-proof steel – and we'll cook you over a fire of the finest wood. You'll feel lovely and warm!'

'We'd rather stay in the cold,' the three Sparrows replied.

But the Crows insisted.

'So, roasting doesn't appeal to you? Maybe you'd rather be boiled? We'll cook you in a splendid saucepan of chrome-plated Duralumin. No? Would you prefer to be smoked! See how we look after our friends! If you don't care for smoking we will cook you in a powerful 200-watt electric oven. Or let's say 300: no expense spared with us!'

But the Sparrows still said no. 'Thin but raw!' they shouted.

So the Crows went off indignantly, muttering scornfully, 'Good-for-nothings!' and when they had gone, Albertino asked the Sparrows if they knew which way led to his Papà.

'It's one of these four ways,' advised the Sparrows of the crossroads, 'but which one, who knows? We are poor country sparrows and we don't know anything about compass points. We go by the sun, but there isn't any these days. Perhaps if you wait. Someone is sure to pass by. Goodnight.'

And so they were alone again. The night was cold and dark and the forest was full of mystery. They sat down on the snow at the foot of a broad tree-trunk, snuggling together for warmth. Time went by, but nobody appeared on the path. All they heard was the frozen voice of the forest.

Then suddenly Flik leapt to his feet and pricked up his ears.

'What is it, Flik, what is it?'

A man had come into view, bent under a knapsack he was carrying over his shoulder, and when he was close enough the firefly illuminated his face.

Flik was not mistaken: *it was him*!

Albertino's Papà.

*

Papà had escaped through the wire on Christmas Eve and was now hurrying home. He meant to wander through all the rooms of his old house, at least for this one night, and to appear in the dreams of all the sleepers there.

And so the little boy, the grandmother and the father had met half-way in the forest where, on Christmas Eve, creatures and dreams from two hostile worlds may meet.

'You, here?' asked Granny apprehensively. 'What'll happen to you now? Escaping from a prison camp is no mere sport, you know.'

'But escaping *in a dream* is always good sport, Mamma. It's the only good sport we prisoners have left.'

'Perchance to dream, eh! There are no names, no pack drills in dreams; nor do they have "death zones". In our stinking huts there's no fire in the stove and the air you breathe is like liquefied ice, but the world of dreams is never cold, because all it needs to warm up is the faint glimmer of a star or some delicate moonbeam.

'To dream. How many nights have I walked the road that leads to our little house? And I know that you too, Mamma, have walked the road that leads to the *Lager*. We never meet because it's only on Christmas Eve that dreamers may meet in a dream. It's a miracle that's been happening for centuries: on the Holy Night of Christmas dreamers of the living and spirits of the dead may even take bodily shape and come together...'

Albertino approached his father. 'What's in that knapsack on your shoulders?'

'All my worldly goods, son. Wooden clogs, mess tin, spoon, caddy, your letters... Prisoners never abandon their knapsacks even in their dreams because your knapsack holds the story of your misery. It's got my camp stove in it too. It's a beauty! Let's turn it on.'

'No, don't!' begged his mother. 'You know fires mustn't be lit outdoors after the second roll call!'

'Mamma, how do you know such things? Who told you? Is it in the newspapers?!'

'No, they don't print that stuff in our newspapers. When I come to see you at night, I walk around the huts and I read all the notices. I look at everything: if only you knew how it upsets me to see your vests full of holes... I brought my needle and thread with me once and tried to mend your pullover. But hands in dreams are just made of air.'

Albertino's Papà put down his knapsack and took out his camp stove.

'Oh it is lovely!' exclaimed Albertino, 'like a steam engine... Has it got a whistle too, Papà?'

'We could do with a broom to clear the ground of snow,' his father observed. And no sooner had he spoken than a strange creature flew down from the sky.

'Oh! It's *la Befana*!'[73]

And indeed it was old *Befana*: but instead of her usual broomstick she was riding a sparkling machine.

'I've got myself motorised,' she explained. 'I abandoned the broom and travel by vacuum cleaner – now there should be a power outlet somewhere round here...'

She searched inside the trunk of a great pine tree, found a socket and plugged in. There you go! In a trice a wide circle of snow had been vacuumed clear and the moss beneath was soft and dry as velvet.

'Goodnight!' waved the *Befana* as she took off again.

*

---

[73] In Italian folklore, *la Befana* is a witch who brings good children treats on the morning of the Epiphany, January 6. But if you were bad, look out – you may wake up to a lump of coal.

The stove was lit and its flame rose safely towards the sky, for it was a double-walled stove with adjustable air-flow controlled by a front door opening.

The trees shrugged off the snow from their leafy cloaks and gathered round to warm their numb branches, forming a circle around the small fire. Standing so close to one another they formed a kind of wall that shut out the frosty air, and with their branches stretched out towards the flame they formed a thick roof overhead too.

'We should cook something,' said Papà, 'a Christmas lunch... It would be lovely, being all together like this.'

But there wasn't anything to cook and so Albertino set off with Flik in search of any hazelnuts or berries left on the hedges since autumn.

But what's happening? What's that trumpet call?

It was the tallest of the Poisonous Mushrooms, on guard, sounding the alarm.

'Now's the time!' he shouted excitedly. 'If we get them to pick us and eat us, we will die but they will have horrible stomach ache! What a stupendous rearguard victory!'

All three of them stretched their necks, trying as hard as they could to make the boy notice them. 'Here... here,' they said, 'this is where the best food is!'

Fortunately, the three Good Mushrooms spotted their sneaky manoeuvre.

'We can't let these devils effect their ghastly plan!' they cried. As one they charged against the Poisonous Ones. The battle was long and terrible but in the end the three Bad Mushrooms lay lifeless with their caps squashed down to their feet.

'Now, let us introduce ourselves: they are hungry!' said the three Good Mushrooms generously. And they marched towards the boy with sacrifice on their minds and singing: 'He who dies for his homeland has lived to the full,' like the Bandiera brothers,[74] who – despite everything – were but two and not of course eaten, as the three mushrooms planned to be.

But the noble sacrifice was no longer necessary: Papà had remembered that in his knapsack he had his bread ration still intact.

'Did you eat your Christmas *panettone*?' Papà asked Albertino.

'No, Papà!

'You will have it now.'

'Yes, Papà.'

---

[74] Attilio and Emilio Bandiera were Italian nationalists who led a courageous revolt against Austrian rule in Italy during the Risorgimento.

Christmas 1944

Papà grated the bread with his knife, mixed it with water and made a little *focaccia*.

'How clever!' exclaimed Granny. 'What wonderful things you have learned in prison!'

The mess tin was on the stove. A fir tree gently extended a branch laden with snow and shook it into the can, and soon the water began to simmer. A spark escaped the stove and flew through the forest as it were a star at the mercy of the wind. A bee standing guard on the tree that housed its wild hive saw it. The spark signalled to the bee and the bee sounded the alarm. A swarm of bees quickly filled their tanks, started their engines, and took off – 1,000, 2,000, 10,000 of them. And they flew in perfect wedge formation, three by three, towards the fire zone.

A humming cloud.

When they reached their target, down they swooped, passing over the stove, each bee dropping a spot of honey. A thousand, 2,000, 10,000 spots: and the mess tin was all but full.

Meanwhile, the three Sparrows shook the tops of the trees and rained sweet berries and pine nuts down into the can.

A skylark, with a flood of rapture so divine, pierced the night's black cloak and hovered above the clouds, then up, up among the stars, all the way to the Milky Way, into which it plunged and returned laden with *Candida* whipped cream. Into the pan she shook it, into the sweet, now bubbling, dough.

But the enemy had not been asleep.

From the top of a pine tree, the Crows had followed the sparrows' every move and planned a counter offensive. They threw themselves on a pile of rubbish and began to ingest sharp stones, nails, bits of glass and the heads of matches. They even gobbled up the remains of the three poisonous mushrooms – greedily ingesting them – and they kept on eating until they swelled up like balloons and could barely fly.

Their plan was to copy the bees and, when they reached the stove, to let loose their murderous load into the dough.

Fortunately, the Allied air force was on the alert: 300 fighter bees responded to the alarm and set off to intercept the enemy formation. They piled into the Crows and riddled them with stings.

The Crows plummeted earthwards.

'Bang!'

And burst like fat would-be blisters.

'Splat!'

*

By now the mess tin was bubbling gently and Papà, Albertino, Granny and Flik were warming their hands (and paws) by the fire. Nobody spoke: happiness needs no words. Suddenly, on the Wind, sounded the notes of some distant heart-rending music.

'What's that, Papà?'

'It is *The Song of Melancholy*.[75] One winter evening two eyes looked out through the frosted window at the deserted road, and the frost dissolved into tears at the sentinel's vain waiting. On a white wall inside the room the gaunt shadow of an empty chair fluttered in front of the fire. It was a song that spoke of the pain of all those waiting alone in their sad houses at Christmastime. It was a song which, at the end of a weary day spent waiting, entrusted its notes to the night Wind and reached into all the distant *Lagers*, infusing the men with a desperate melancholy.'

A little later, when the song had disappeared into the night, another approached from the opposite direction: melancholy too, but this time the melancholy was sweet and gentle.

Others waited, too. Those in captivity who, for months and months, had looked at the grey sky that looms over these foreign lands and waited in vain for the sun to break through the dark blanket of cloud and shine once more. But these people do have a secret light

---

[75] The singer comes to the melancholy conclusion that he is not a seeker after truth, only a fool of a poet: *Thus Spoke Zarathustra* (Nietzsche). There is a sense here of the depths of despair into which Giovanni fell in prison.

which brightens those sunless days and starless nights. The living light of love for those in their distant homes. The light of faith. And their song came from the *Lagers* and sailed into the night, reaching the sweet lands of home, bringing words of sweet hope to those who felt that hope had abandoned them.

Now this second song also moved on. All became silent once more.

'Look, Papà!' cried Albertino happily.

The miracle was complete: the sweet dough had swollen into a big scented *panettone*, as soft as cotton wool.

Out of his knapsack Papà took a bowl, the lid of his mess tin, the lid of a box, and a piece of white rag (in which his last food parcel from home, received long ago, had been wrapped). And Granny knelt on the moss and cut the *panettone*.

'Who wants some of this sweet illusion of past happiness?' she asked.

'All of us who have suffered so,' answered Papà. They would have liked to cut the *panettone* into four (so they could take a piece home for Mamma), but Albertino said it'd never work.

'I'll tell Mamma all about her piece,' he assured them.

The slices were cut, Flik had his crumbs, and when Papà lifted his mug he found a letter beneath it.

Post for number 6865! At last! It's four months since No. 6865 received any post and now he's being generously rewarded for the long, painful wait. Because this was an exceptional letter: a letter richly decorated with golden angels, silver stars, and a hen's black footprints:

'Dear Papà, it's Christmas and I'm thinking of you...'

It's a very important letter because they'd all had a part in it: Nonna dictated; Mamma guided Albertino's hand as he wrote it: Grandpa read it out loud, word by word; Flik darted back and forth catching the commas that flew from Albertino's pen like butterflies. And Carlottina, sitting in her high chair, let fly little silvery exclamation marks that fell onto the paper and stuck here and there between the words, to make them even more beautiful.

'Dear Papà, it's Christmas and I am thinking of you...'

Post for number 6865: *Albertino's first Christmas letter.*

Christmas lunch began and the *panettone* tasted of sky and forest. And this wasn't the only miracle, because this was to be a Night of Miracles.

A great fir tree was covered with tiny flaming candles, the eyes of thousands upon thousands of little birds shining in the darkness, reflecting the glow of the fire. So, they even have a Christmas Tree here! And it was the most beautiful one in the world because the star that shone at the top of it was not the usual silver papier-mâché one but a real live star that had slipped down from the sky and become entangled in the branches with its twinkling train.

*

Meanwhile, time passed. On the deserted track, something was approaching from the East. A donkey, led by a stoical old man with a white beard, and on the donkey a beautiful woman with gentle, shining eyes.

The donkey was weary: he'd been walking too long without rest.

Walk on, little donkey: you must find the lonely hut so that the miracle can be renewed once more. So that once again the Son of God can open his eyes to the light of men.

The donkey walked on, escorted by two Angels in the sky holding a big white banner – standard of the God of Peace, on which was written in letters of gold:

'Peace on earth and good will to all men.'

Then, from the opposite direction, along the track that led from the West – from the lands where light becomes shadow – advanced a great, clanging *Carroccio* escorted by a band of warriors five ranks deep, proudly singing one of their hymns:[76]

> *With coat*
> *of armour-plate*
> *with jacket of shining brass*
> *to dazzle all who pass,*
> *with sheet-metal trousers and a cast iron hat,*
> *a soldier's life, what a great life is that!*

> *Our legs beat*
> *down beat*
> *down hard on the ground*
> *a rifle on the shoulder*
> *creating shock and awe,*
> *nothing could be bolder*
> *than making war*
> *for universal peace!*

The clanging *Carroccio* emerged as a tank driven by a man with a helmet on his head, and behind him sat a huge, proud, big-chested woman with hair as blond as straw and *pince-nez* over her wicked little eyes. The cortege was accompanied by two fierce eagles holding a black cloth in their claws with blood-red letters saying:

'War to men of good will.'

And this was the standard of the God of War, the God who will be born tonight (under the orders received by his government) in a castle of steel with a cannon on its roof firing at all the shooting stars and Angels that pass through the sky.

---

[76] A large four-wheeled wagon bearing the city signs around which, in Mediaeval times, Christian soldiers gathered and fought. Generally pulled by oxen, it carried an altar, a bell, the heraldic signs of the city and a mast surmounted by a crucifix.

At the crossroads, the machine met the little donkey: the donkey took the road to the lands of sun, the tank the lands of freezing shadows.

'Peace be with you' greeted the stoical old man with the donkey.

'War be with you,' came the reply of the man with the tank and with '*Gott mit uns*' on his belt buckle.

*

Notte santa, night of miracles. It was late. On the open track another strange procession came into view, three old Kings riding in from the East on their hump-backed camels. A slowly moving star guided them, gently shaking its silvery tail gleaming against the black velvet sky.

Holy Night, night of encounters: on the track from the West a curious trio was also advancing. Three dwarves dressed in red with white beards down to their feet (and noses like potatoes).

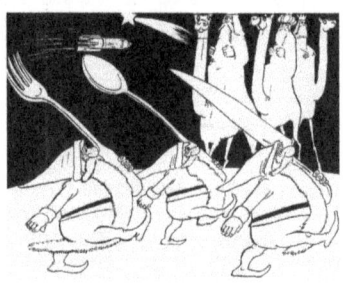

Three dwarves who've apparently escaped from a poster advertising a factory that makes cutlery, given that the first carried a knife on his shoulder like a rifle: the second a spoon, and the third a fork.

They were guided not by a star but by a whistling meteor of dynamite with a fiery tail. They goose-stepped along, walking stiffly, with their chests puffed out.

The old Kings and the Dwarves met at the crossroads.

'God be with you,' said the Magi.

'He already is,' replied the Dwarves haughtily.

'I bring gold to the Son of Mary because he's the good King for men of good will,' said the first of the Magi.

'I bring incense because he's the God of goodness and priest to the God of goodness,' said the second.

'I bring myrrh because he's God, but in his divine goodness he is willing to suffer and die as a man,' said the third.

The Dwarves replied, sneering:

'I bring the knife to our God so that he can slice up the world!'

'I bring the fork to our God so that he can cheerfully gobble it up!'

'I bring the spoon so that he can collect the crumbs and eat them too!'

'Praise be to the God of good,' said the Magi, taking the road to the South.

'Praise to the God of warriors,' replied the Dwarves, taking the road to the North.

*

On their departure the forest was deserted once more. Papà and the boy and Granny were silent, snuggling together in front of the stove. Nothing moved, not even a leaf, because things and men were waiting ... for something.

Midnight...

'He is born!' called a lark on lookout from a cloud.

'Roger!' confirmed the Wind. 'There's a message too. Listen!' And he brought the sweetest of songs from distant places.

The lonely hut was resplendent now: the Baby wailed on the straw in its crib while an ox and the donkey warmed him with their breath.

In the castle of steel, set deep in the shadow of the North, a child was also born and cried (in his armour-plated crib), warmed by the murderous breath of a flamethrower and the exhaust from the armoured chariot. His voice was harsh and his hands already had little claws, because he was the God of War and no one came to bring *him* gifts.

Meanwhile, shepherds and shepherdesses arrived at the hut of the God of Peace carrying lambs and amphorae full of milk. Skimmed milk, I'm afraid, because the sheep had been shorn and the cream had been used to make cloaks of Lanital for the shepherdesses. The shepherds had been upset about this, but now St Joseph smiled: 'Never mind: the fault is not yours, it's the fault of the war.'

After the shepherds, iron-clad warriors came marching in.

'Praise be to God,' they chorus. '*Gott mit uns.*'

Joseph shook his head: 'There must be some mistake. Your God is not our God. He never has been. Your God is the other one, born in the castle made of steel.

'No,' say the warriors. '*This* is our God now.'

'Too late,' replied St Joseph. 'You can keep your God for this year...'

*

One by one the little flaming eyes on the fir tree in the forest had expired and the flames in the stove were merely flickering now too.

It was cold.

The circle of trees around the little group had moved back, and a chill wind was up.

Scattered black crosses attracted silent shadows drifting through the forest. So many crosses and so many shadows...

'What are they, Papà?'

'They are the spirits of the living who have come to look for their dead. They are exploring the crosses that the war has spread all over the world – reading the names engraved on them. When a mother finds her son's grave she sits before it and talks to him about happy times that will never return.'

The Wind meanwhile carried the melancholic song from the *Lagers* back to the homes and the song from the homes back to the *Lagers*.

'Happy Christmas, Mamma; happy Christmas, Albertino,' Papà said. 'Now go back home and may your song go with you.'

'Aren't you coming with us, Papà?'

'Tomorrow, Albertino...'

'Tomorrow or *morgen*?' asks Nonna.

'*Dorgen*, Mamma.'

'Papà, why won't you take me to where you're going?'

'It's not a place for children, even in a dream. Promise me you'll *never* come...'

'I promise, Papà.'

They are gone with their songs, and the forest is silent and now seems deserted.

It is snowing again and a soft new blanket is spreading over the old one, hardened by the wind. The green circle around the fire is white once more. All trace of the paths has disappeared.

'A night for prisoners!' exclaims the chief Sparrow, tucking his head under his wing.

As he moves he dislodges a leaf that falls slowly, twirling to the ground and lands in the middle of the white clearing.

We see that one word only is written on the paper – '*FINE*'.

It is a very small leaf.

Narrow the leaf – wide is my way
Now have your say, I've had mine.
Like it or not, don't wish me bad
I'll tell you one better, next time:
A Christmas fable not so sad.

1945 Dreaming True

Our only privilege is to dream. Dreaming is an essential for us, because real life is outside the barbed-wire enclosure, and we have no way of living it except in our dreams. Only through dreams can we maintain a hold on reality and remember that we are still alive. After futile days, measured by ounces of food and numbers of cigarette butts, dreams offer us the only real activity we know. Dream we must, for in our dreams we recover forgotten values and find new ones we had never known before; we detect the errors of our past and catch a glimpse of the future.

Let us sit outside the hut and project the visions of our desire upon the open sky. Let us dream, with clear heads and open eyes; let us write our own plot and scenario and be directors, actors, cameramen and spectators of our own imaginary story.

I don't know how I came to this place and there is no use my trying to find out, since dreams are not furnished with information bureaux. All I know is that the square where a man in semi-military uniform is walking with a knapsack over his shoulder, is the one in front of the station of my native city, Parma.

But I do know one very important thing, I am that man. I caught a glimpse of myself as I leaned over to catch my reflection in the fountain at the centre of which the statue of the explorer Vittorio Bottego, flanked by two bronze savages, is wondering whether it was really worthwhile to penetrate the upper waters of the Omo and the Juba.[77]

Against the light I see the whole city in profile. Directly ahead, seeming to enfold me in a huge cement embrace, is the great birthday-cake monument to Giuseppe Verdi.[78] The composer takes no notice of me. From the bas-relief of the central altar he continues to look nervously toward the station, as if he were awaiting the arrival of the suitcase in which he packed his suit and hat. Obviously, he is tired of playing the part of an allegorical figure, stark naked and with an uncomfortable broad-brimmed laurel wreath on his head...'

*

---

[77] Vittorio Bottego was one of the first Westerners to explore Jubaland in the Horn of Africa.
[78] This monument was demolished after the Anglo-American occupation. Giuseppe Verdi grew up in Roncole (now Roncole Verdi), where Giovanni lived from 1952.

I enter the still sleeping city and my footsteps on the deserted cobblestones awaken a sign which had been asleep, leaning against a column.

> PEDESTRIANS SHOULD KEEP TO THE SIDEWALKS,
> it grumbles ill-humouredly.

I beseech it to calm down, to let me enjoy the sun. For such a very long time I have dreamed of walking down the middle of a sunlit street. After all, I'm just back from an internment camp.

'Yes, but you've come back on foot and so, as far as I'm concerned, you're a pedestrian and have to obey the regulations!'

*

I am walking between the trolley rails, across the silent, deserted square. As I proceed toward the beginning of the narrow street which leads to the outskirts of the city, someone calls out:

'Giovannino, aren't you even going to say hello to your old café? Pick a wicker chair out of the heap and sit down. Half an hour from now the waiter will be here to open up. Then, later on, you'll see the proprietor, the barmaid, the blond cashier and your friends. Let's have a bit of a talk while you're waiting. If you could have heard half the things your friends have said about you . . .'

'That's quite enough, old café. All I care about is what they've been thinking at home. I was imprisoned for the sake of my family, not that of my friends, and it's for their sake that I have returned.'

*

I go on down the quiet, shaded street, and my footsteps on the deserted cobblestones awaken an echo that was fast asleep beneath an ancient arcade.

'Tap ... tap ... tap... Hello there, Giovannino! I know your step. You've walked for so long on yielding sand that you've forgotten that your footsteps have a distinctive pattern. Now it's exactly the same as it was before, when you used to emerge at dawn from the printers and go home, walking, just as you are now, over the deserted cobblestones. All this time I've kept the sound of your footsteps in a crack in the wall. Tap ... tap ... tap... Do you hear?'

At the edge of the city I come out onto the broad, sunny boulevard.

'Stop, Giovannino,' whispers a horse-chestnut tree. 'You used to lean against me when you were waiting for her, don't you remember?'

'Giovannino, I'm your bench,' murmurs an old stone seat. 'Sit down and tell me about yourself, and about her. And I'll tell about both of you. . . .'

There are still three miles across country before I get home. And so, without stopping, I answer:

'Goodbye, youth, goodbye...'

Here is the dusty, white road, with the telegraph poles all in a row. There is a festive whispering in the air.

'Welcome home, Signor Giovannino!' say the hedge, the trees, the grassy ditch.

All these are good, old-fashioned, country things, which address me respectfully. They speak to me as I pass and try to persuade me to linger. They want to give me something, but they are afraid. They knew me when I was a child; they made me presents of violets, blackberries, and round, flat stones. One day an elm tree gave me a baby bird and a ditch gave me a dragonfly that seemed to be made of glass. But now I am grown up and wear a moustache; they no longer dare offer me a plum or an acacia leaf to make into a whistle under my tongue. Just to show my appreciation, I take a blade of grass to chew.

Chewing the blade of grass, I walk on. Around the next curve I shall suddenly see my own house; when it hears my voice it will wake up abruptly and gaze with astonishment out of all its windows. Just at the curve, there is a wayside shrine, with a bench in front of it,' and someone calls from very far away: 'Giovannino!'

'Old Grandmother Giuseppina, why have you left your peaceful, grass-covered tomb and come so far? I would have come to you, Grandmother Giuseppina, bearing the flower I gathered in that desolate, distant land. I have it right here, pressed in my wallet, Grandmother Giuseppina; I would have brought it to you and told you the whole story.'

'I know, Giovannino, but I didn't have the patience to wait, and so I came to meet you.'

'Have you been waiting so long, Grandmother Giuseppina?'

'Ever since you went away. For months I've been talking about you with this kind Madonna. She knows you just as well as I, from the time when you passed by here day after day, as a schoolboy, with your bag of books over your shoulder. Give her your flower. My grave has flowers of every description growing on it. There's even a red poppy, which I'll give you if you come to see.'

'I'll come, Grandmother Giuseppina.'

I lay my dried flower in the box standing on the shelf in front of the Madonna, and the corolla re-opens and takes on as bright a colour as if it had been picked just a minute ago.

'Goodbye, Giovannino. Don't gulp too much cold water. And better put your cap back on.'

Hobbling along with the aid of her cane, Grandmother goes back across the fields, by the same way she came. Now my house is in sight.

'Don't run, Giovannino,' calls back Grandmother Giuseppina. 'You're too weak to exert yourself.'

In a minute I shall shout something or other, I still don't know what. And my voice will sound like the chorus of La Scala.

*

And so Giovannino has finally come home. But at this very moment he finds himself in a dilemma. The last scene is of capital importance. It would be a complete waste of time to have suffered for months and months, with only sentimental illusions to sustain him, and then to ring down the curtain on a fiasco. The matter requires thought.

His first idea of making a loud noise is quickly discarded. By so doing he would inflict a rude shock upon good people who need to be quietly awakened from the bad dream which has for so long held them in thrall. Making gentleness his aim, Giovannino edges his way to a point just below the bedroom window, and in a faraway, positively dreamlike voice, calls the name of his better half. A moment later a blind goes up, and a sleepy face looks out. There she is!

After a moment of total and utter surprise, her half-shut eyes open as wide as headlights. Her head is withdrawn, and there comes a loud shriek:

'He's here!'

What happens next is something like the French Revolution. The first shriek is answered by a second, and the second by a third, each one farther away than the last. Then comes a shriek from nearby and one from still nearer, inaugurating the Reign of Terror.

Padlocks creak, chains rattle, doors slam: there are dull thuds, meows, barks, ringing bells, crackling words and ear-piercing shouts. Albertino bursts out of bed and, catching his foot in his nightshirt, rolls down two flights of stairs. His dear mother tries to catch him, but slips on a ball, inadvertently grabs the leg of the table holding the goldfish bowl and falls to the floor in a splash of water, while the slimy little fish tumble down the neck of her dressing gown, their tails flailing madly.

The cat is quick to take advantage of this state of affairs and throws herself upon the slimy prey. Giovannino is faced not by his wife, but by a seething mass of hair, fish and catcalls.

Meanwhile his old father, unable to adjust his eyeglasses, is groping his way toward the door. Finding a knob before him, he turns it and stumbles into the china cupboard. The crash of china awakens Giovannino's mother and, because she imagines there must be an earthquake, she calls out that everyone's first thought must be not for her but for the children.

The baby girl, whom all have forgotten, climbs out of her crib and onto the floor. She finds the bell which opens the front door and pushes the button so often that it seems as if all the express trains of Central Europe were arriving together.

'No, no,' sobs Giovannino, before the smoking ruins of his family. 'This will never do!'

Everything is wrong, everything must be done over. He must backtrack, like a moving-picture reel, rewound from the end to the beginning.

The baby girl regains altitude and goes back to bed. The old father emerges from the china cupboard, the fragments of china resume the shape of plates, cups and saucers, and leap up to the shelves. The table leg straightens, the goldfish fly into the bowl, the wife re-conquers the dignity of an upright position, Albertino rolls upstairs and the window closes. Giovannino's words re-enter his mouth, letter by letter, and he falls upon the grass, holding his head between his hands.

'Lord help us! How hard it is to come home!'

'Captain Armistice'

The Captain had first appeared on the horizon of the Sandbostel *Lager*, Bremewörde, in the autumn of '44. He had asthma and it was clear at first glance that he did not believe in secret weapons or in final victory. He was therefore baptised 'Captain Armistice' and, if he hadn't had the unforgivable flaw of being German, he would have merited the epithet, 'a good man'...

When we moved to the Wietzendorf camp in January 1945 [Oflag 83], Captain Armistice came along too and brought his asthma with him.

So it happened that on the morning of 13 April, 1945, cries of joy awakened us:

'The Germans have gone!'

And when we came out of the barracks and saw the German sentries as usual on the watchtowers, our enthusiasm did not diminish and we continued to shout that the Germans were no longer there, partly because the soldiers left to garrison the camp were only six in number and so old and damaged by the war that death could barely be classed as a future event. While, better still, Captain Armistice was their commander – a man of whom it has been said that he was less of 'a captain with asthma' than he was 'an asthma with a captain'.

And asthma knows no particular nationality...

At seventeen thirty on the 16th everyone started shouting 'Here they are! Here they are!' and they threw themselves towards the gate: there were 6,000 French and Italian officers, but I climbed to the top of a fence post and so was able to see the liberating troops. They arrived aboard a black car like a 'Millecento', and all three of them were nice, especially Major Cooley, who had a beautiful ruddy face that recalled the triumphant three-colour-processed advertising pages of Esquire's special Christmas issue (high-proof liquor department). The other two were a Scottish corporal and a Canadian foot-soldier and each carried a machine gun.

The major disarmed the German guard at the gate and handed rifles and men to the French. Then the liberating troops – all three of them – entered the camp and something happened that left the French considerably perplexed. For despite the rigorous Gestapo searches, undertaken with damnable frequency and carried out with such scrupulous meticulousness that they often went beyond the limits of decency, after nineteen months in the *Lager*, cameras appeared by the dozen along with three-by-four-metre Tricolour flags. Not a single cockade surfaced on the French side, however. The fact is that Italians are very good at these matters. Once in Poland, during a transfer from one camp to another, I saw a Sicilian lieutenant come out of the search hut in his shirt (because they had made him undress) and I remember him holding the bundle of his clothes in his arms, and inside the bundle was a large six-tube radio.

Italians know how to 'get by' wonderfully well. It is the one negative quality that harms us the most: but in those days it turned out a positive advantage...

When in January 1945 we were in the process of transportation to this camp near Wietzendorf, all blankets were taken from our beds because, they said, the bomb victims of Hamburg and Bremen were colder than we were. They even took the little scarf I'd made out of a rag of cloth. I left the hut groaning into the freezing cold, surely the least scheming man in the universe, but inside my knapsack I had managed to conceal my house blanket measuring 2.20 by 2.30 metres. Today it keeps Albertino's tender bones warm and whenever

I see it I greet it with a 'Hello, old woman: I haven't forgotten that you saved my life back then.'

I tell no lie: I am an Italian, but in spite of that, I *like* Italians. Every man has his own generic weaknesses!

*

The token liberators greeted the largest of the Tricolour flags, telling us that in the evening or the next morning, a regular garrison would arrive.

A couple of hours later, however, someone noticed that on the watchtower furthest away a sentry remained in position, gun in hand. Nobody had told him anything; for him the war continued, as for the famous old marshal Rodolfo Graziani, the one fascist Marshal of Italy who remained loyal to Mussolini in 1943. When it was explained to the sentry what had happened, the old 'Kraut' nodded that he understood and came down from the watchtower, walked slowly towards the guardhouse and surrendered.

'Get yourself off home!' someone shouted. But the soldier shook his head and continued along his fateful path towards the guardhouse.

He probably didn't trust the Germans overly much.[79]

'International Mess'
APRIL 17, 1945 When we awoke we found a typewritten sheet in which the Italian Command of the camp informed us that we were free, that our sufferings were over, that we were worth reconstructing, and it ended with three lines, all in capital letters:

VIVA L'ITALIA!
LONG LIVE THE ALLIES!
(and LONG LIVE I don't know who else!)

This worried me deeply: clearly, Command had found some paper, a typewriter and a stamp. Who would save us from their agenda now? The good Lord had rescued us from the Germans, but the impossible cannot be counted on, even from the good Lord: a military Command equipped with paper, machine and stamp represents an entity beyond even divine intervention.

---

[79] 'Here They Come! Here They Come!' *Diario clandestino* 1943–1945

'Be on your guard,' I said to Arturo Coppola. 'The whole regime of on-call standby inspections, reports and the yellow envelope for the arrest card are about to bob back up to the surface.'

'Not the yellow envelope! They found the yellow envelopes?'

'It seems so.'

'Well, here we go,' Arturo concluded grimly.

But, as it happened, the good Lord remained on our side. In the afternoon the English major, Major Cooley, returned to confirm that an Allied garrison would arrive for us shortly: and a few minutes after he left, a squad of soldiers armed with machine guns and submachine guns did in fact arrive. Only, instead of being English, they were German.

So it was that we escaped the immediate perils of an Allied military agenda. But our unlikely saviours did give someone a bad time and it was one of their own, a German.

Told in this way, war can seem a joke, but we should not be deceived by appearances. For here, as everywhere else, everything is relative – it is all a question of different points of view. For instance, seen from above, seen from the tree from which he was hung by the neck, it will not have seemed very funny to poor Captain Armistice.

*

Captain Armistice was accused of having failed to resist the English attack, and summarily hanged. He is the only German that I remember without bitterness, because after all he was a good man and I pray to God to forgive him for being born a German, and I recommend him to a quiet corner in Purgatory.

Poor Captain Armistice (now, probably, Captain Last Judgment).

SATURDAY 21 APRIL, 1945 The English major, Major Cooley, failed to show up again, and German soldiers continued to buzz about the camp.

SUNDAY 22 APRIL Then suddenly the order came to pack our knapsacks, abandoning everything that was not strictly necessary. Negotiations had been concluded between the Germans and the English major, and an arms truce had been agreed for a few hours in order to allow French and Italian prisoners to reach the English lines. The Germans had made a present of us to the Allies.

So, without even knowing how, we found ourselves walking on a road skirted by woods scorched by flame-throwers. We passed gutted tanks and crumpled cars, and on the trunks of trees were the marks of machine gun fire.

We walked unescorted, with a Red Cross flag at the head of the column. After five or six kilometres we passed a German guard post with heavy machine guns, then, 500 metres further we came across trucks with the white star.

Many of my companions say that it was such an extraordinary thing that it drove them mad with joy. I don't know – even *I* don't know what I thought. I probably didn't think of anything. What struck me most was that one of the American drivers had a 'Camel' cigarette over his left ear. Before leaving the camp they'd given each of us a one-kilo loaf and an 800-gram can of meat, rations for I don't know how many days, and I remember that, loading my bundle on a truck, I sat down on the earth and ate everything: every last bit of meat and bread.

Everyone thanks Divine Providence as best he can. Then we resumed our journey and eight or ten kilometres further on we suddenly found ourselves in a village so clean and tidy that it seemed newly constructed. It was completely deserted because, two hours earlier, all the inhabitants had had to clear out, taking with them only essentials in a single suitcase.

'Every man for himself,' we were told. 'Avoid fighting over accommodation; there's room for everyone.'

They gave us a village complete with every facility, and many entering the houses found the table set, and the soup still warm on the stove.

For my part, what I remember is throwing open a door and finding myself faced with 600 kilos of sugar...

Here were sacks of flour, rice, sugar, coffee, boxes of canned goods of every description, barrels of salted meat and molasses, closets filled with wool suiting and even un-carded wool, hidden compartments in the walls stuffed with linens, safety pins, soap, neckties and spools of thread. Buried in the gardens vats of bacon, lard, honey, eggs and butter. Up in the attics, underneath the hayricks and woodpiles, jars of marmalade and cans of oil. And barns, barnyards and chicken coops packed with live chickens, geese, pigs, cows and calves. Inspired by the noble urge of self-abasement, Italians had managed to feel inferior even to Germans, those people truly from another world, and now this illusion, in which they had cradled themselves for the four war years, collapsed and fell to the ground. Even in the field of rationing, Italians were no lower than Germans; in fact, they were a cut above them. But if Italians are easily dismayed, they rebound with equal facility. Quite naturally, 'hunger had greater power than sorrow.'

An English patrol was shocked to find an Italian captain sitting on the sidewalk of one of the central streets, plucking a chicken. But we must remember that it was a Nazi chicken and that, while it's easy enough to be a gentleman on a full stomach, it's a very different matter on one that for nineteen months has been empty...

*

Caterina was not the only radio adventure in which I was directly and indirectly involved. There was also Radio B90, made up of an old radio receiver liberated from an empty house by way of war reparations and a loudspeaker that acted as a microphone. With it, I and a group of comrades, organised a kind of radio station, broadcasting a weekly variety programme always preceded by a brief indicative comment.

So one day there was a talk, in earnest serenity, of the North-South divide in Italy; which divide was interpreted by someone from the south in a transversal (viz. polarising) sense rather than the longitudinal (viz. forward-looking) sense which had been our intent. And so, due to misunderstanding, suddenly, among people who for two years had been united by a single fraternal idea against suffering, rhetoric raised its ugly head and the field was immediately divided between northerners and southerners.

A historic manifesto was posted in which the *aut* or *aut*[80] was either make the necessary apologies or stop the broadcasts immediately in order to avoid the armed intervention of popular indignation.

Privately, we were threatened with burning the hut and personal lynching by the Southern mass, who'd been wound up by a couple of popular intellectuals. But I was then attending meetings about progressive democracy so I let it be known that we would not make any apologies, and that the broadcasts would continue regularly. So the night of this broadcast was a really interesting business.

The lawn in front of the broadcasting station was crowded with thousands of good people who had come with the praiseworthy intent of seeing the hut burned down and lynching its cohabitants...

In the very first row, five metres from the hut, 'popular indignation' on duty was on a war footing. People were armed with big clubs – men with high foreheads, one finger and three and even four

---
[80] The 'aut or aut', Latin origin: 'existential choice'.

fumigating nostrils. This was simply on account of the fact that they all belonged without exception to the 110 common criminals (robbers, parricides, amanticides[81] and other gentlemen) who, at the time, had been released from Italian prisons and transferred to the north of Germany, to caves where secret Nazi weapons were being manufactured. Gentlemen who, after being released, had been placed in our group, and with us sent back to Italy where today, probably, together with all the others found in their situation, they pass under the common denomination of veterans and confer an unequivocal tone of elegance and distinction to the most important popular demonstrations that cheer up our town squares.

In that atmosphere I started to tell this story:

Once upon a time there were two horses resting in a meadow. Suddenly one of the two sighed:

'Eh, what a life to be a horse!'

The other horse, which was very sensitive, pricked up its ears:

'Here we go again!' he exclaimed. 'You mean you do everything and I don't do anything.'

The first horse did not mean this but the quarrel began immediately and the two turbulent characters soon came to blows: indeed, to hooves.

'You don't need to get hot under the collar like this," observed a wise owl stationed nearby.

'We can do what we want now,' shouted the two horses. 'We're free!'

The owl grinned:

'And all those straps wrapped around your body? And that bit that you have in your mouth and those ties that you have down your sides and that cart that you have behind you?'

'The two horses were a bit sick to hear this as they'd forgotten they were yoked to a cart. Then they got themselves together and shouted:

'All right! But we no longer have anyone on the wagon to whip us up. Our master tumbled down a ravine. And what's more, we will break these harnesses!'

At that moment a fierce whip lashed the backs of the two horses and when they turned their heads they saw that, in the cart, in place of the old master, was a beautiful woman dressed in red, white and green and with a star on her forehead.

'Forward!' said the beautiful lady. 'Let's move. We have to bring up the bricks to rebuild the house!'

---

[81] Murderers of kith and kin, and lovers.

And the two horses set off once more and concluded with a sigh that it is indeed a bummer being a horse.

That's right: it's tough to be Italian, my friends, and like those horses you're going to have to pull the wagon and take the best route, the shortest and least tiring one. And you don't have to fight to agree on the path to take.

OK, the fairy tale is over: let's hope now that the Horse Union doesn't rise up and accuse me of offending horses by comparing them to Italians.

And the comparison does worry me, because if we start fighting like this while still inside the barbed-wire fences, those horses will be proven right.

*

The meaning of the story was understood and the whole business ended quietly, probably because the Northerners thought: 'Yes, I see, the horse is the North, while the South is a donkey' and the Southerners thought: 'Yes, the horse is the South while the North is a donkey'.

And ultimately they were both right, because, yoked to the chariot of Italy, there are two horses that, too often, behave like two donkeys.

Just to say that, twenty years and six months later, even this fairy tale still retains a certain validity.[82]

And if everything ended well, it was not to my merit, it was thanks to humour, which (albeit of a very modest league as mine may be) had broken the cursed spiral of rhetoric.

*

Homeward bound in cattle wagons we travelled for long days through a foreign land where old men, women and boys scrambled to collect bricks and repair bridges; and it was not clear where we were when we began to meet completely deserted stations, dilapidated houses without a living soul to work around them. And the people of the villages still intact looked at us with indifference or turned their backs on us, and then we understood that we were in Italy.

For a few days they had not given us food, but around ten in the evening, priests availed us of a bowl of soup, a sandwich and an apple, explaining that it was all stuff collected from among our families: and

---

[82] *Signore e Signori* and *Life with Gio* (1995)

this moved us at the time because it meant that our families had not forgotten us.

The next day, in Pescantina, a private charity took us off the cattle wagons and loaded us on a trailer: but first, the Government advanced us 400 lire each, and 500 to those who had to get to Trapani or Calascibetta. And this also moved us because it meant first of all that there *was* a government; secondly that this government did not ignore our existence, and finally that it took into account the different needs of individuals and that it did not consider us a body without a name – so many heads of cattle to be transported from one pasture to another – as the liberators had.

So, with this money we could buy whatever we wanted, and I thought of bringing sweets for my children. But they took me for 200 lire for a packet of cigarettes, twenty lire for a slice of watermelon, 120 lire for a sandwich, twenty-five lire for a glass of wine, and I had only thirty-five lire left, when a pound of candy cost 200. So I said to myself: patience, children...

We traversed cities and towns on the trailer, and the streets were full of people, and outside the cafés it was packed, but no one yelled at us or threw stones at us, yet we had an Italian flag on top of the truck.

Lying on the cylinders, on the engine, there was a deportee who held her soul in her teeth because she was determined not to die on the road, but in her house, on her bed. No one threw an apple core or swore at her. Yet she had such a strange face, with that skin to the bone and with those teeth sticking out of her.

What also moved us was that our homeland was much better than we expected. Now it appeared that stories out of Italy that found their way to the *Lager* were not true – viz that there was no more religion, and that there was no longer human respect, and no government, and that people gutted themselves in the streets, and girls gave themselves up in public in town squares. We looked closely, but we saw neither corpses nor naked girls. In fact they were all well dressed, the girls, and it was nice to find them like that.

The roads of the Po Valley were long and straight as they'd always been, as if the war had not even passed. It was already past midnight, but we continued to meet lonely girls who laughed when we shouted something and some even greeted us. Every now and then some places were crowned in light and people were dancing outdoors.

Again this moved us, because on a sign we read that they were dancing for us.

At two o'clock we reached our city: but there were no longer fifty of us. Along the way, from time to time, someone would jump off, knapsack or box on shoulder, and disappear into the darkness.

I found myself alone, in the big piazza, and I hadn't seen my city for two years, but it seemed to me that it had been two days. I wandered through the deserted streets, stopped to read the signs and writings on the walls, and searched for the memories of my youth. But many were buried under the rubble of bombed houses.

I went to the outskirts and, passing under the portico, I found the nocturnal friend of my twenties. For twenty-four months I had trampled on *Lager* sand which makes no sound, and so my step had lost its voice. Now I found the voice of my step on the porch slabs. Tà, tà, tà: like every night when I left the printing house to go home. It seemed that the echo had been waiting for me hidden in a hole in the wall.

On the road I recognised the bench of my first love and sat down to rest a bit because my knapsack was breaking my back. Someone, lying under the last lamp facing the darkness of the countryside, called me. He was one of the soldiers who had made the journey with me.

'Where are you going, Lieutenant?'

'Home: it's only seven kilometres.'

'You won't make it with that knapsack.'

'I will manage: I have not heard from my parents for a year and I can't wait a moment longer. And you?'

'I am waiting for a lift; I'm farther away than you, Lieutenant, and I don't feel like walking around here at night. They attack people, strip them and then beat them. I saved my skin with the Germans, I don't want to lose my skin with the Italians.'

The soldier rolled up a cigarette and handed it to me.

'Take a toke and pass it back,' he said, lighting a match, then sighed: 'I come home, I call my mother, and maybe my mother is dead.'

'I'm off,' I said, handing back his cigarette. And I walked in the dark and wouldn't stop even if I burst.

Along the way someone came up beside me and we walked a hundred metres together.

'Germany?'

'Germany.'

'They didn't cremate you?'

'No.'

'You're not a politician?'

'No, military.'

'Lucky you. The politicians – they cremated them all.'

He asked me what political party I belonged to and I replied that I hadn't thought about it yet.

When I arrived in front of my house, dawn was breaking and I sat on the edge of the ditch and waited for the sun to rise. Meanwhile, I looked at the shuttered windows and suffered as I had never suffered even in the *Lagers*. Because back then one had a bit of an idea that everything had come to a halt down here, and that only upon our return would life resume its natural course...

Then, all of a sudden, I heard a voice shout something: and it was mine and I was terrified and I waited with wide eyes for the windows to open, and I counted the heads that poked out: one, two, three four.

One was missing, the smallest.

So I left my knapsack on the edge of the ditch and ran inside, and, lost in an enormous bed, I found Signorina Carlotta sleeping. And I said: 'Five!' although the first thing I saw was not a head, but a pink bottom.[83]

---

[83] *Italia provvisoria* Nuova edizione (1947)

Dopoguerra

After war, peace does not come immediately, for between war and peace there is both 'the post-war period' and 'the ante-peace period'. Between war and peace some episodes are negative (as they still belong to the war) and some positive, because they already belong to the peace.

When the negative facts outweigh the positives, this is *post-war*. When the positives outweigh the negatives, this is *ante-peace*.[84]

The war passed, and passed through the towns and cities sowing hatred and land mines. And so in the end the profession of political agitator and de-miner was born, both dangerous because political hatred and mines are suddenly explosive stuff and add to the long list of dead.

The de-miners arrived in that village in *la Bassa* and began to work hard, but, when they had cleared everything except a small field near the provincial road, they didn't finish the job because an urgent need came up to clear a place some way away.

No worries. They planted stakes with barbed wire and signs all around the area still mined and it was a small piece of land of little importance.

Time passed, and one day the owner of the field went to mow the grass. When he got close to the posts he paused to wipe away the sweat, and then gasped. A little boy of five or six was sitting quietly at the foot of a tree in the middle of the minefield and he was playing a game, throwing pebbles.

The man did not scream for fear of frightening the boy. He struck the whetstone on the iron of his scythe and the child raised his eyes and looked at him calmly.

'Stand still and don't move,' said the farmer. 'Still as you are. There are bombs buried. If you move they will explode and you will die.'

The war had passed through heaven, on earth, and in the water: it had crumbled the walls of large buildings of cities and of solitary country churches. It didn't respect anything, and it had even found its way down goats-herd paths into the most forgotten mountain village, killing people and firing houses.

After a war like this one, even children of five or six knew what death is, even if they had never seen a man die, because men were killed a few kilometres from their home and the air was poisoned by

---

[84] Preface to *Italia Provvisoria Nuova* (1947)

hatred all around. In this poisoned air, people age faster, and children no longer have a childhood.

So the boy, when he heard that if he moved, the bombs that kill would explode, turned pale and stood still as a stone, careful to breathe slowly.

The farmer called people together and soon there was a crowd around the field.

The local doctor and parish priest came, then a car was seen in the street, and they all said relieved:

'The Mayor!'

The mayor pulled the car up to the ditch, stopped, jumped out and ran the hundred metres from the road to the field.

The mayor was just like any other man: six months ago no one would have listened to him because six months ago he was just any old foreman. But now he was the Mayor and, when the Mayor arrives at the scene of a disaster, everyone breathes with relief and says:

'Thank goodness, the Mayor has arrived.'

'Whose is that boy?' he asked.

He was a child of the neighbouring hamlet who had come there across the fields. He was still – as still as a stone – in the middle of the minefield. He was paler than ever and breathing hard.

'Mum,' he said almost without moving his lips. He had said it so softly only he heard it .

The Mayor shook his head.

'We have to call the city and have somebody sent out, a specialist with a sonar device. To go in is to risk your skin pointlessly. Both you and the boy will die if the bomb goes off while you go to fetch the child. And if you don't die on the way out, you'll die on the way back.'

'We won't get a specialist until tomorrow morning,' the doctor replied. 'It's not possible to leave the boy there all night. A mine can be the span of a hand away from him. If he falls asleep and lies down, even touches it, that's it.'

They began to think how on earth they could get the boy out of that hell.

A *carabiniere* passed on the road on his bicycle. He saw the car parked near the ditch and went to check the licence plate. Then he looked around, saw the group of people and approached, pushing the bicycle by hand.

He was a *carabiniere* of the commune, but had arrived only recently, and it was soon pretty obvious that he didn't know anyone yet.

'Whose car is that?' he asked, arriving at the scene.

'It's mine,' the mayor said.

The *carabiniere* leaned his bicycle against a mulberry tree and took a notepad and stub of a pencil from his pocket.

'Name, surname, paternity,' he asked the Mayor.

'Why?'

'Irregular registration plate,' explained the *carabiniere*.

The mayor made a gesture of impatience.

'Where do you get your kicks?' he yelled. 'Is now the moment to worry about licence plates! Can't you see what's going on here? '

People began to grumble.

'Go to hell you. And that pig who pays you!' cried a woman.

She was still in 1945 when just to show oneself dressed as a *carabiniere* was an act of heroism.

The *carabiniere* was a man with slow, measured movements and very few words. He turned his head towards the woman, then back at the mayor.

'Can't you see?' shouted the mayor pointing to the minefield.

The *carabiniere* read aloud one of the signs: 'Danger-Mine.' Then he looked at the boy motionless under a bush in the centre of the field. And he looked back at the mayor who angrily explained the situation to him.

'I understand,' the *carabiniere* said. 'Tell the boy to lean back against the stem of the bush and not to move. Everyone else, move off.'

He walked along the barbed wire fence and came to the opposite side: the bush covered the child's back perfectly. The earth, inside the fence there, was bare and bald and the *carabiniere* asked for a bag of street dust. A woman gave him the handkerchief she had on her head and some dust was collected.

With the dust, the *carabiniere* slipped through the barbed wire.

'Give me him a musket,' shouted the mayor.

The *carabiniere* shook his head vigorously, untangled the musket from the barbed wire and passed on in.

Everyone drew back again: maybe it was one of those damned mines that jump up and explode a metre above the ground. You had to be careful.

The boy was in no danger because he had the trunk of the bush behind him, but the others had to be on guard.

The *carabiniere* bent down, sowed some dust in front of him, then took a step. Then he bent down to sow dust and took yet another step, and so on, so that the footprint remained marked on the dust and, if the matter was successful, on the way out, the return was guaranteed.

People followed him with wide eyes and bit their hands.

Nothing happened: he got to the bush, grabbed the boy from behind and lifted him onto his back.

Then he re-traced his footsteps. By now the people were out of breath to hold. The *carabiniere* made it to the barbed-wire fence, passed the boy across, then crossed himself.

And then a scream broke out: people ran and women sobbed.

'You are a hero!' shouted the Mayor as people thronged all around.

The *carabiniere* was a man of slow movements and spare speech, and he was untroubled about what he had done.

He took the notebook and pencil from his pocket.

'Licence plate irregularity,' he repeated to the Mayor. 'Name, surname, paternity.'

The Mayor looked up at the sky, shook his head, then put his hands on his hips.

'Mario Ferretti. Was Luigi, born in Boschetto on 3.5.1901.'

The *carabiniere* wrote slowly, inquiring whether Ferretti carried one 'r' or two.

'Profession?' he asked.

'Sin-da-co,' the Mayor said wryly as people laughed.

'Mayor is not a profession, it is a post,' observed the *carabiniere*. 'What do you do when you're not a mayor?'

'Master builder,' the Mayor said through gritted teeth.

Then he had to give him the documentation. And the *carabiniere* took note slowly, fussily and irritatingly.

'All's fine, thank you Mr Mayor,' he said, touching the peak of his cap. Then he turned to the woman who had shouted at him: 'Go to hell you. And that pig who pays you!' And he asked for her name, surname, paternity, place of birth and profession. The woman put her fists on her hips.

'Now you,' she exclaimed, 'must understand the state of mind of a woman who, seeing a child in that terrible danger, thinks of her own child with anguish. And when she hears someone who, instead of taking an interest in the child, deals with fines...! We women of the people don't have a stone for a heart! '

The *carabiniere* thought about the matter for a few minutes then put the notebook and pencil back in his pocket.

'Given the particular situation,' he said slowly, 'let's overlook it.'

Then he took out the notebook and pencil again.

'Let's overlook the personal offence,' he said. 'But the insult to the government remains. Name, surname, paternity, place of birth. '

He got the data he wanted, mounted his bicycle and pedalled off.

And the people looked at him with hostile eyes.

On the road, however, the boy he had rescued was waiting for him. Motionless and silent he watched the *carabiniere* on his bicycle and smiled just faintly.

But that was enough, because *carabinieri* are satisfied with little.

And so the policeman smiled too.[85]

*

The sun is there, down in the street, twenty metres from my window, and behind those houses over there Spring is waiting for me, lying under the railroad embankment. But it is useless to go down: we might as well stay here and stick words on paper: even down there, as in the keys of the typewriter up here, everything is politics. Politics poisons everything: bread, friendship, painting: perhaps even love (how quickly today's young people age!). Politics even poisons Spring.

Giovanni returned to Italy in 1945 to find the Christian Democracy party, led by sometime Resistance fighter Alcide De Gasperi, ranged against the Communist Party, controlled by Josef Stalin from Party Headquarters in Russia. The monarchy would be democratically deposed by the Italian people the following year.

History defined Giovanni's homeland as a political melting pot. The communist party in Italy (the PCI) had been founded in 1921 and was strong in *la Bassa*. In the same year their sworn enemies, the fascist leaders Benito Mussolini (himself a child of the area) and Dino Grandi and thirty-two other party members, were elected to the Chamber of Deputies, a house of the Italian Parliament. In 1922, a force of fascists marched on Rome and, as I have said, the King summoned Mussolini to be Prime Minister. Every opposition party (including the PCI) was outlawed, including of course the PCI. In that year, as Giovanni recorded in 'Comrade Penèlopo':[86]

Things got pretty hot down in *la Bassa*. The communist co-operatives were in full swing, and they were the Reds' real strength in those days. As you can imagine, it was a situation that was seriously provoking the blackshirts. And once the temperature reached boiling point, the fascists from the city started making sorties into the region with the co-operatives their target. The campaign stirred the fire

---
[85] 'Nome e cognome', *Italia provvisoria Nuova* (1947)
[86] *Don Camillo and Company* (Pilot, 2018).

within as it were the pyre in *Il Trovatore*...[87] And it brought about the complete destruction of the communist co-operatives.

Now, post-war, following the defeat of Germany and the execution of Mussolini, *la Bassa* played host to the new torchbearers for totalitarianism, the communists. More members of the PCI resided there than anywhere else in Italy. Following the liberation of Italy by the Anglo-American alliance on April 25, 1945, the scene was set for bloody communist purges in which fascists, landowners, industrialists and many priests – all declared by communists to be 'enemies of the people' – were murdered.

The earliest Don Camillo stories, with Peppone the communist mayor, would reflect this post-war political landscape, and the fear it engendered, as here in 'L'Étranger':[88]

'Understand. Emilia Romagna very beautiful... Much agriculture... Good food...'

Clearly the little man found something amiss with Emilia but didn't dare say so.

'Speak freely!' exclaimed Peppone. 'What is it you don't like?'

'I like all!' cried the man. 'But I much fear.'

Peppone stopped the truck and turned to him. 'You're afraid? Why's that?'

'Bam! Bam!' replied the Frenchman, imitating the firing of a rifle. '*Les communistes* of Emilia bam bam *tous les prêtres*, all priests, burn churches . . . Much terrible, frighten.'

Peppone turned to Smilzo. 'Hear that?' he growled. 'Hear what people abroad think about us, because of what our reactionary swine are writing in the papers? See how terrified this poor wretch is? He can't wait to get out of here! He thinks he's ended up in a den of murderers.'

---

[87] Manrico's cabaletta from *Il Trovatore – l'orrendo foco di quella pira* (the horrendous fire of that pyre).
[88] *Don Camillo and Company* (Pilot, 2018).

Smilzo spread his arms. 'But what can we do about it, boss? If that's what they think, we can't change it.'

'Oh yes we can!' replied Peppone. 'You watch how I handle this little dope! He'll have a completely different opinion when he goes home!'

Peppone had spoken in rapid dialect, so the Frenchman hadn't understood a word and his eyes were big with apprehension. Peppone turned to him and said, 'See this red thing on the lapel of my jacket? Well, it's the badge of the Communist Party! I communist, my comrade here communist! I boss of all the communists!'

He pulled his Party card out of his wallet and shoved it under the Frenchman's nose. 'Understood?'

The poor little man was terrified. 'Please, sir,' he stammered. 'I get down... much thanks... *Merci bien*... I not offend... I not politic... I no party... I only *travailler*... I two children and wife... please no hurt...'

*

When the first deaths were seen on the streets, a lot of people suddenly discovered that they had suffered severe abuses in the past that cried out for revenge. And since it was as easy as bending down to pick up weapons, and there was no shortage of ammunition either, more bullets flew than flies.

'I know where he is,' the man said to his wife. 'He will certainly not escape me. I've been waiting for this day for years and years–'[89]

The *Dopoguerra* was an excuse for reprisal and revenge, as shown in 'Blood from Romagna', the fictional counterpart of Giovanni's reporting of actual vendetta murders in his column 'Giro d'Italia', the writing of which at this time placed him at serious personal risk[90]

The road divided vast fields of yellow clover and stubble. The sky was still red, but there was no longer a dog around because these were the days of fear. A man pedals along quickly with a child sitting on the crossbar of his bicycle.

After crossing the bridge the man had the feeling that something was wrong and at the next corner he turned his head and saw that 200 metres behind, two cyclists were closing on him at pace.

---

[89] *Italia provvisoria Nuova* (1947)
[90] 'Giovannino's "Libertà": Guareschi's Personal Freedom in Opposition to Power', Professor Alan Perry, Gettysburg College, Pennsylvania (2016)

Spurred by the sudden shock at what he had seen, he began to press harder on the pedals. He let go of the grips and grabbed the handlebars in the middle, towards the steering tube and his big dark, bony hands touched the baby's warm, white little hands.

Like a desperate man, he pedalled bent over the handlebars, his breath lost among the baby's curls, but his pursuers were younger and he could feel them gaining ground.

His house was to the right of the road, to get there you had to go down and through muddy cart track guarded at its entrance by two black ash trees. On one was nailed a notice of the reserved hunt and the man involuntarily thought of his shotgun hanging on a nail in the kitchen. He smelled the smell of home: still three kilometres distant. He pressed harder on the pedals, but by now the two were behind him.

The shot seemed like a cannon shot and he felt a lash on the neck. Then he felt a blow to the back of his neck and stiffened and the last thing he saw was the little white hands of the child clinging to the handlebars, next to his two large dark hands.

The bicycle continued on its way straight ahead for a few metres, then veered to the right, tipping over and overturning onto a pile of gravel.

The two young men stopped. The one with the leather jacket bent over the man lying prone in the dusty grass by the ditch.

'It's not him,' he said, getting up. 'He's the brother.'

The other turned his bicycle.

'Nothing doing,' he muttered. 'Effing pig.'

The child, who had been stunned by the fall into the ditch, got up and began to cry, calling for her father. Then the young man in the jacket pitied the orphaned alone and lost, and standing above her he shot the child in the middle of the head.

They went away. The front wheel of the bicycle, turned upside down in the fall remained running free. But before long it swayed uncertainly shortening its revolutions more and more and soon stopped. And everything was still.

The polarising effects of politics were felt locally not only in the horrific wave of post-war violence, they reached down into the social fabric of life with similar bitterness. With post-war politics increasingly touting the dream of a classless society, rank could not simply be undone in civvy street without a degree of vindictiveness creeping in, as Giovanni soon discovered:

It is appropriate that I speak to you today, in the light of truth, of Comrade Giuseppe Z, otherwise known as Pin. It is appropriate because, over so many years I have gone over the episode again and again and now see it as other than a conversation between two men, rather the conflict between two worlds which resulted from it. The proletariat met in an arena of free discussion with the bourgeois. And the battle was tremendous.

A few days ago I found myself passing through any street of this turbo-slow post-war Milan, completely *donned*; which means that your unhappy parent was wobbling towards his mansion laden with bulky packages, such as a 1.85-metre pine-top for a Christmas tree, three large packages containing various goods, a bag containing seven kilograms of assorted vegetables and fruits, a two-year-old Carlotta (complete with every accessory), loose canned food and sprigs of mistletoe. In tow was a little Albertino, reduced to being very difficult to tow after two years of displacement spent in a wild place where he and his mother lived in the war.

'It's all over!' suddenly someone said. And I gave the comment tacit approval by shaking Carlotta (who was in fact sitting on my head). I found the observation witty at first because I thought I'd come upon an old fellow from the *Lagers* and that he was referring to those days. But I soon had to change my mind.

'Things have come to something when an officer may be seen walking the walk besmirching his cool with candy, while this poor orderly was supposed to be cut out for being the mule and the nanny.'

So, my eyes followed the voice, I turned curiously to Carlotta and found myself at Pin's side.

'Hi, Pin,' I said cheerfully. And he looked at me very antithetically.

He wore a large red handkerchief around his neck.

'If you don't mind, Lieutenant, my name is Giuseppe Z. My friends call me *Comrade* Giuseppe; but you may call me *Mr* Z.'

'Pin's fine by me, Pin,' I replied. 'How's it going?'

'Better than it used to be, Lieutenant. Now the gentlemen officers look after their own baggage and children. And if they want shiny boots they brush them with their own little hands. It's all over, Lieutenant.'

I comprehended that Comrade Giuseppe was the victim of a misunderstanding.

'I think, Pin, you misapprehend how things are – you keep calling me Lieutenant, but if you look carefully under all these bundles, you will see that I am in civilian clothes.'

Comrade Giuseppe replied that this fact was neither here nor there. This was no question of dress: it was a question of mentality, of *social class*.

'You could be dressed up as a dancer, but you will always feel like a lieutenant to me and, to you, I will always be 'that wretched orderly'.

My beloved comrade Giuseppe said 'that wretched orderly' with such inflection of voice that even a deaf person would have understood that they were words in italics and in quotation marks. Moreover, between one word and the next, there was a chasm of sarcasm such that even the least acute would have understood that the author of the quoted sentence was *me*.

And it was so. There was actually a time when speaking of Pin I had indeed said: 'that wretch of an orderly'.

*

Wind back the years to 1936, and your father, after six months of very hard military studies (completed almost completely lying on a beam in the attic of a school in Potenza), entered the barracks in his flaming uniform almost a Second Lieutenant of Artillery.

I was then an aspiring officer, and I continued to be one for three months with a total of ninety-two cappuccinos and ninety-one croissants: which explains why your father, having no assets other than his salary as an aspirant, he had to reduce his evening meal to a latte and pasta and that, one evening – having splashed out on five beers – had to be satisfied with just a latte.

This was how things went until one day my Captain called me aside and had a fatherly word with me.

'I believe, having seen it for myself, that an hour ago you were passing through the main street carrying a large bag of personal linen in your arms. And I say *personal* advisably as that bag contained specifically both a white shirt with a right cuff stained with green, and a pair of long plush underpants, not a matter of induction on my part, as actually most of the two items mentioned dangled outside the bundle. I find the incident scandalous. An officer *cannot* take dirty laundry to the washerwoman.'

I completely ignored this prohibition and promised that from that day on I would endeavour to wash my clothes and underwear myself. It was then that the Captain lost his cool and ordered me to hire a batman. And, since I hesitated, he gave me authority.

'Take Pin.'

I left my Captain with a heart full of anguish.

Rules did not prescribe it, but even the most stingy of officers gave at least thirty lire to his orderly each month; and to charge my expenses with thirty lire would have meant destitution.

I studied the question for a long time, and in the end found a compromise solution: I decided I would give my new batman fifteen lire only, but would never require him to do anything for me. He didn't even have to carry the bag of linen, because I would wash the linen myself.

And so I took Pin as my batman, and a dull fight began between us. For fifteen mornings he showed up at my room, but he never managed to polish my boots because he could see his face in them. So Pin eventually gave up on the undertaking. But first he tried every means not to. He would not show up for five or six days in a row, and then suddenly happened to be in the room at five in the morning to surprise me in my sleep. Yet my boots were always shiny. I cleaned them before going to bed. He cottoned on to the system and came up with a counteroffensive. Returning one evening, I found Pin waiting for me in my room. So I shaved, brushed, said with a wink:

'We are men, dear Pin,' and then left.

I went out and walked around the city until three in the morning.

As I said, Pin finally gave up on polishing my boots, but all was not calm about me because I introduced my bicycle to our little world as I needed one for military service. So it was that one morning, looking out the window of the quartermaster's office, I discovered Pin, armed with brushes and rags, kneeling in front of my bicycle, which I had left leaning against the wall.

I flew into the courtyard.

'Excuse me, Pin, but I have to run to garrison command,' I shouted, jumping on the bicycle and slipping out of his hands.

He looked at me as if I had stolen the machine.

For three months we had a terrible struggle, but every night I polished my bicycle as well as my boots, and so I always won, and Pin never managed to do anything for me. His accomplishment was limited to receiving the fifteen lire that I delivered to him at the end of each month. He tried to refuse it, but I then made a hard voice the winner:

'Pin, obey or I'll have your guts for garters.'

He gritted his teeth and accepted the money.

'Yes, sir.'

After three months, when a second lieutenant's salary would have permitted me to up the fifteen lire to thirty, Pin was discharged for I don't know what ailment, or what decree or what devilry. He left.

I remember that I took him to the front of the station: before entering he glared at my shiny boots and my bicycle that shone in all its nickel plating.

'Bye, Pin.'

'Good morning, lieutenant.'

And his voice was cold.

Later, beloved, you will ask me: why, given that you never needed Pin, did you speak of him and call him 'that wretched orderly'?

You're right to ask. But it's not difficult to explain.

Pin was a very good boy and he loved his father and mother, but so much and so much that he couldn't stay away from them. And so he went home often, forgetting, in a hurry, to obtain the regulation licence to do so.

On these occasions, I, who had to settle the matter, called Pin 'that wretched orderly'.

That is all, my son: and now let us resume our discussion.

*

'Change the dress, but the mentality doesn't change!' said Comrade Giuseppe. 'But the situation has changed and today the lieutenant has to have a discussion with his wretched orderly on equal terms!'

He continued to speak to me as relentlessly as my nemesis might, and his intonation sounded threatening to my middle-class ears:

'It's all over.'

By now we had arrived in front of my house and I told him to come in.

'Are you afraid to, Pin?'

Pin laughed sarcastically:

'For your information, Comrade Giuseppe is not afraid even of the entire body of your staff.'

'This is Pin, my old batman,' I explained to the sweet lady who had come to open the door: and she threw open both doors of the door to let in Comrade Giuseppe, who was carrying the tall Christmas tree in his arms, and the eighty-five packages, bundles, canned goods, and he wore a Carlotta, complete with accessories, on his head.

'He forced the stuff out of my hand as we walked,' I explained to the sweet lady, responding to her stern gaze. 'You know, you can't argue with these extremists.'

Leaning against a wall of the anteroom was my bicycle. Very dirty. And turning around I realised that my companion Giuseppe was looking at her with a strange light in his eyes.

'No, Pin,' I said, planting myself between them. 'That is *no!*'

He didn't even want to have a shot.

'Bye, Pin.'

'Good morning, Lieutenant.'

And his voice was as cold as it had been then.[91]

Meanwhile, coming into view in the post-war workplace was a Trotsky-style dictatorship of the proletariat in open opposition to the pre-war status quo, regarded as 'a dictatorship of the bourgeoisie'.

Luigi Ventritré, a bricklayer, at the foot of the high scaffolding, pulled the rope to send up a large bucket of lime, and the pulley creaked.

'Everyone out!' suddenly shouted the leader, and Luigi Ventritre stopped pulling and stood with the rope in his hand.

'What's up?' he asked, turning around.

'Strike,' the boss explains. 'Put everything down and come away with us. You are in Giacomino's team.'

'Good,' said Luigi Ventritré, and resumed pulling the rope.

The chief, who was leaving, stopped.

'I told you to drop everything and leave!' he exclaimed. And Luigi Ventritré stopped pulling the rope.

'Chief,' he muttered, 'the bucket has already reached the twelfth floor, and I have to send it to the thirteenth. Two more metres and then I'm okay and I can walk away. '

The boss was a one with clear ideas.

'When a strike is declared everyone must stop working. Up to the twelfth floor you are in order: every inch you make after the twelfth floor is a betrayal of the proletariat and you pass into the ranks of strike-breakers. Your work is done on the twelfth floor. Take that bucket down.'

But Luigi Ventitré also had ideas of his own and expressed them with great firmness.

'Boss, everything is fine, but it involves work taking the bucket down: in the interest of logic, you have to choose the lesser of two evils. Since the bucket cannot be left suspended, it is better to raise it two metres than take it fifty down.'

'He's right,' observed someone who had appeared just at that moment.

'We have to see,' muttered the leader. 'Wait until we let you know.'

Luigi Ventritré waited with the rope tightly in his hands and the bucket swinging in the air.

Those from the internal commission were hastily summoned and the case was discussed. One section was with the boss: a decision to raise the bucket would have represented a little victory for the

---

[91] 'Il compagno Pin', *Italia provvisoria Nuova*.

construction company and capitalism in general. Returning the bucket of lime to the ground, on the other hand, made no active contribution to the construction of the house.

On the other hand, pulling the bucket down would be one in the eye the working class, as Luigi Ventitré would have to undertake useless and unpaid work, because it was carried out after the official start of the strike.

There was further great discussion, while Luigi Ventitré waited clinging to the rope and the bucket swayed. There followed a secret vote, but nothing was resolved by this either: eight were for 'yes' and eight 'no'. Even match.

'This is deliberate obstruction!' shouted the leader. 'I'm gonna get violent!'

'Between two quarrelling workers, only capitalism rejoices!' grinned Antonio the unskilled worker, who represented the intellectual element in the commission. And sensibly he proposed a compromise solution.

'You tie the rope to a peg and leave the bucket suspended.'

But the boss was a one-way man.

'Compromise solutions don't solve a fig! Settlements dictated by conscience are strictly *bourgeois*. Revolutions are made or they are not made! And if you decide to make revolution you need but *one* command. I make myself responsible for everything and ask the commission for full powers. But no secret vote. This time everyone must have the courage to take action. Approval by show of hands! *Democracy!*'

All fifteen members of the commission raised their hands. Then the boss with an authoritative gesture made the workers herd towards the fence and plant himself with their legs wide apart in the middle of the construction site.

'Luigi Ventitré labourer,' he shouted in a firm voice. 'Jump!'

Luigi Ventitré let go of the rope and jumped back. Hissing, the bucket full of lime fell from the twelfth floor, splattering on the ground, in a glory mess.

'Well,' they all said, 'the boss is someone who knows what he wants. We'll have to make him a Deputy in the next elections.'[92]

What had disturbed Giovanni about the North-South hostility among Italian prisoners over his Radio B90 broadcast as they were awaiting liberation from Oflag 83, was that it had arisen within the hopelessly bereft prison brotherhood. Essentially it was like a class war but one between the *have-nots* and the

---

[92] 'Decisione', *Italia provvisoria Nuova*.

have-nots – disenfranchised men *in extremis*. Now, in post-war liberated Italy war would be waged between the *haves* and the *have-nots* ever more maliciously:

In Badolino there was a great demonstration against the high cost of living. The people took to the streets, and Bagarotti spoke.

'People of Badolino,' Bagarotti said, 'while the proletariat is suffering and working, the forces of reaction and capitalism are having a great time at the café.'

The only café in Badolino was in the piazza, in the part facing the speaker: then the people did an 'about-turn', threw themselves on the café and smashed everything. Then another 'about-turn' and Bagarotti spoke again.

'People of Badolino,' he said. 'While the proletariat is suffering and working, the landowners and nobility are plotting against it, in their secretive circles and clubs!'

The 'Circle of Reading and Conversation' was in a house in the piazza on the right of the speaker: the people then made a quick 'face-left', invaded the premises of the club, broke everything up and about-turned again towards Bagarotti.

'People of Badolino,' Bagarotti shouted. 'While the people work and suffer from hunger, the vile black marketers speculate on food stolen from storage!'

The only shop of 'Edibles of different kinds' was in the piazza, to the left of the speaker: then the people performed a 'face-right', invaded the shop, broke everything up very quickly and were all ears again.

'People of Badolino,' Bagarotti shouted. 'While the proletariat pays the costs of a war it did not want, the industrialists make millions!'

The people hesitated: in Badolino there were neither industries nor industrialists in the true sense of the word, so the interpretations were two, and the people divided: part of the herd turned towards the left side of the piazza and destroyed the telegraph office, others to the right side and destroyed the cinema. The usual undecided lot, who had remained talking in the middle, reached agreement, went up to the pharmacist's house and slapped his face.

Then everyone about-turned to the speaker.

'People of Badolino,' Bagarotti shouted, 'the exploiters of the proletariat are linked to the American fascist plutocracy...'

The people turned and knocked down the 'Shell' petrol station on the left side of the piazza, in front of the mechanic.

The speaker continued: 'The exploiters of the proletariat are hindering the nationalisation of the electricity industries...'

The people, to a man, 'about-turned', left the square and marched silently up to the bridge. Here Giacomo Cicotta placed a bomb in the transformer cabin, which promptly blew up while the people shouted:

'Long live nationalisation!'

Then the people quickly returned to the piazza losing only the few minutes necessary to destroy the public telephone station, the tobacconist's and the branch of the Savings Bank to protest against *La Stampa*[93] (as the tobacconist also sold newspapers) and to oppose the inflationary manoeuvres of the high flying dealers.

'People of Badolino,' shouted Bagarotti, 'the purulent octopus of reactionary bureaucracy hinders the work of reconstruction! The paperwork lies unanswered in the offices!...'

Bagarotti spoke to the herd from the balcony of the town hall: then the people simply marched side-by-side in platoons, invaded the town hall, destroyed all the files, beat the staff and, since Bagarotti was the Mayor, unfortunately took his trousers and threw them off the balcony at the vibrant cry of:

'Viva la libertà, viva la ricostruzione!'[94]

Then a general strike was declared and an energetic protest was voted against Franco's tyranny and against the enemies of the people in general.[95]

---

[93] Anti-Soviet newspaper at that time.
[94] 'Long live freedom, long live reconstruction!'
[95] 'Alla riscossa', *Italia provvisoria Nuova*.

Christmas 1946: The Birth of Don Camillo

So to the ante-peace, in which such post-war political polarisation would fire Giovanni to write the Don Camillo stories over the next two decades.

We came back from the starvation of the Nazi prison camps to find our country a heap of rubble. But through the ruins in which so many innocent victims had died, a fresh breeze of hope was blowing.[96]

In 1945 Giovanni had straightway been hired by Rizzoli to start up a new weekly satirical magazine. With humour his instrument he made totalitarianism his target. Following his experience of the devastating Nazi one-party totalitarian State during the war and the communist inspired violence of the *Dopoguerra*, he considered totalitarianism – man's dominion over man – the greatest danger for the modern world.

Under his editorship, *Candido* went on to play a pivotal role in the defeat of the Communists by De Gasperi's Christian Democracy party in the 1948 elections, the *Times* reporting that the election was won 'by De Gasperi and Guareschi together'. But his war against communism didn't stop there.

So all-consuming did the Cold War between Russia and America become during the next two decades that there was the constant fear that one side would press the nuclear button and the whole world be reduced to a wasteland. In 1958, Khrushchev became supreme Soviet leader. He had already begun the de-Stalinisation of Russia, condemning the appalling crimes of his predecessor and promising a return to Leninist principles of Party rule. When he made a tour of America in 1959 it looked to some as if the age of détente had arrived. Or was this yet another triumph of Soviet propaganda? In the same year, the Caribbean island of Cuba became a revolutionary socialist State and an ideal launch pad for a Soviet nuclear attack on America. All this would become the political background into which Don Camillo and Peppone were thrust in Giovanni's fourth collection, *Comrade Don Camillo*, mostly written between 1958 and 1960 and much of it set in Russia.

The first Don Camillo story, 'A Sin Confessed',[97] introduces us to the priest and the communist mayor as sworn enemies. It tells of Don Camillo being beaten with a stick while riding out on his bicycle with a bag of seventy eggs hanging from the handlebars, and Peppone admitting to the abuse under the protection of the confessional.

---
[96] Preface to *Don Camillo and Don Chichi* (1963)
[97] 'A Sin Confessed', *The Little World of Don Camillo* (Pilot, 2013).

Amusing, even slapstick, what won him readers was a trademark comic-book satirical element that would not be out of place in René Gascinny's tales of Asterix the Gaul, which would emerge some years later in France, the place where the Don Camillo stories first went viral.

The rollicking movement of the narrative brought his audience in gently on a purely entertaining level. Besides the fun there is plenty of character and a moral undercurrent, but at first nothing too overtly political – it was far from the brutality of the post-war purges by communists in Emilia, which was nevertheless the context of the assault on Don Camillo and which, in the real world, was placing the lives of priests and many others in jeopardy.

The second story to be written dug deeper into the political scene on the street but a lightly humorous touch ensured that one of his greatest characters would not be stillborn.

Published here for the first time in English, 'Peppone' tells the communist mayor's back-story as a young man in pre-war fascist Italy, in the Italian Resistance during the war, and then brings to the fore his involvement in the vengeful violent aftermath of the *Dopoguerra*:

When Peppone turned up at the Osteria della Secchia,[98] any well-to-do or right-thinking patrons would hurriedly down their glass of wine or their coffee, pay and get the hell out of the place.

Peppone was a danger to be avoided at all costs because he was a two-metres tall wild man and scarlet Red even in 1930, when to rant and rage against Mussolini in a public place was extremely ill-advised. Indeed, Peppone was a serious danger even when he wasn't engaged in communist rhetoric, because when he got tired of shouting he'd crash in on someone's table, grab a deck of cards, shuffle them, and say:

'Let's crack open a bottle of cognac.'

It was impossible to refuse a game of Scopa[99] with Peppone: and playing Scopa with him would invariably cost you the bottle of cognac, because Peppone was unbeatable. He had an iron memory and could readily retain and recall cards across three games. Moreover, when he played he was completely changed from being a revolutionary screamer to being silent and impenetrable as a piece of marble.

On the evening when what happened happened, Peppone was cursing enough to make your hair stand on end, whereupon a squad of young men with faces as black as their shirts appeared at the door.

---

[98] A tavern named after a tributary of the Po River.
[99] One of the three major national card games in Italy, Scopa traditionally involves lively and strong-worded banter between hands.

'Tonight someone will be beaten,' muttered the dismayed publican.

An icy silence fell around the room. The fellow who appeared to be the leader of the gang pointed to Peppone to him and asked:

'Is this the guy?'

'Yup.'

The young man came forward, went to sit at a table, began to cut a deck of cards.

'Let's crack open a bottle of cognac,' he said to Peppone, pointing to the chair opposite.

Peppone sat down slowly, threw back his cap and touched the deck. People gathered around the two – speechless, dismayed.

The game took place in the most profound silence, and with frightening speed, and Peppone lost.

'This is how we treat subversives,' said the young man, sneering. Then he drank the brandy, offering it around his companions, and left.

This was a tough one for Peppone to swallow, because no-one had laughed behind their hands at him before. But by the following evening he'd got himself together again and, after having arrived early at the Osteria della Secchia and demolished someone at Scopa, he shouted crazy things at the government and concluded that, he would have knocked the head off that baby octopus with the black shirt.

'But first I want to stick six games of Scopa on him!' he concluded because the matter of defeat had hurt him so. 'Show up if you have the courage!'

Naturally, the following evening, Giacomino (the famous young man himself) swept in like a ghost at the Osteria della Secchia, accompanied by his aforementioned men.

'They told me you wanted a rematch,' said Giacomino to Peppone. 'We'll make the stake the usual bottle of cognac.'

It was a historic evening at the Secchia, because Peppone lost not one but three games of Scopa and, when Giacomino got up, he threw the cards on the table and, as before, exclaimed: '*This* is how we treat subversives.'

Peppone came out of the tavern with a fever, and how people laughed! It took him a week to recover, and when finally he returned to the Secchia and had drunk enough to start off in top gear, he shouted that he'd eat Giacomini in twelve hands as an aperitif, and so, the next evening, Giacomino reappeared and humiliated him in three matches that took everyone's breath away.

Peppone felt poison surge through his veins: Giacomino became an obsession. And he couldn't let it go (so far and wide did the story of his humiliation spread), so the next evening Giacomino appeared at the Secchia again, sat down in front of him and beat him with a 'sweep',[100] before departing as usual with a sarcastic smile, saying: '*This* is how subversives are treated.'

Should he keep *schtum* and avoid further setback? Peppone couldn't do it for two reasons: first of all, because he was 'red' to the bone; secondly, because people would call him out as a coward.

And so it went on for years and Peppone thought more than once of waiting for Giacomino behind a hedge and despatching him once and for all with a bullet.

He changed taverns, but Giacomino had risen in the party, had an ear in every quarter, and turned up wherever Peppone went.

Inevitably, the moment came when Peppone couldn't take it anymore and, one evening full of cognac, he said too much too loud and *le guardie* brought him in.

'You asked for it,' the Inspector explained. 'Five years of confinement wouldn't be too much for you.'

While waiting for the decision of the law, and after kicking everything that can be kicked in a cell, reason took hold of Peppone: after all there was one way, as in any other persecution, to bring an end to it. Almost, *almost* now, he was happy.

That same evening they came to get him, put him in a car, unloaded him, pushed him up some steps, where he found himself in front of a doorway with a sign above it. It was the seat of the fascist party, and Peppone prepared his soul and his ribs for a right going-over.

Thrown inside, he was met by a desk and behind the desk, Giacomino, and behind Giacomino, the aforementioned forbidding faces.

'Let's make the prize the usual bottle of cognac,' said Giacomino, pointing to a chair for Peppone and starting to shuffle a deck of cards.

Peppone lost in the most scandalous fashion, and finally Giacomino sighed:

'If it goes on like this, we'll have to let you play with the table, Signor Peppone. Go ahead. Double or quits the next game...'

When Peppone found himself in the street he picked up a stone and drew a large cross against the wall: then he spat on his hand and stuck the spit on his forehead:

---

[100] A 'sweep' is when you manage to clear all the cards from the table (purpose of the game) in one fell swoop.

'I swear I'll kill him!' he said through gritted teeth.

*

Peppone moved out of the area and, after July 26,[101] was preparing to return, when on September 8 news of the Armistice was announced and he gave himself up to the mountains where he did important things in the Resistance and soon became the head of a Mobile Division. He worked with his men in the vicinity of Trepicchi and the years passed, but his hatred did not diminish: and when he looked out over the valley from the top of his lookout and saw his homeland, he felt his head burst.

One day he couldn't stand it anymore.

'We have to go down to Trepicchi to pick one of those animals up,' he told his men.

'It's dangerous: the Krauts are as thick as flies,' they pointed out.

'I know,' continued Peppone. 'So tonight I'm going alone. '

At the beginning, the whole unit insisted on following him, but in the end he only took two men. It might have been an operation worthy of a book in itself, but Peppone and his two men found themselves in front of the building where he'd been taken apart, facing a patrol of Krauts in what was usually a fairly unpopulated area ,and Peppone had to work miracles just to be able to return to camp with his men.

Foaming with rage, he had to content himself the next day with sending Giacomino a note through a relay: 'Peppone hasn't forgotten: see you soon.'

The end came almost suddenly. One day in April, 1945, after a furious battle, Peppone and his men had the green light they needed and fell upon the village like kites.

First thing, he went to Giacomino's house. He was trapped, hadn't had time to escape. Peppone kicked the door, then piled into it with his shoulder, but realised it had been barricaded from the inside.

'Open up, Giacomino!' Peppone yelled. 'Open the door or I'll destroy the whole place.'

The shutters of a window on the first floor were pushed ajar and Giacomino's voice was heard.

'Peppone, you're making a big mistake! Remember, after July 26, 1943, I retired and haven't been involved since. '

---

[101] The date in 1943 when Prime Minister Badoglio formed a new cabinet and declared martial law.

'Open the door or I'll set the house on fire!' Peppone yelled. 'I have to deal with you for what you did to me *before* July 26! You – open!'

'*You* open it, if you can,' said Giacomino, retreating inside.

Then Peppone got mad and threw hand grenades and set fire to stuff to throw at the door. But the besieged came back at him, making a damn racket with a machine gun and Peppone had to take cover because he was no bad shot. The siege lasted an hour. Finally, Peppone managed to roll a pack of TNT up to the door and it blew to smitherines.

Giacomino defended the staircase as long as he could, but in the end piled in through windows and he had to surrender.

Peppone appeared and pushing the barrel of the machine gun into his stomach made him back up to the wall. Undone, Giacomino went pale and seemed to have aged fifty years.

'It's over!' sneered Peppone. 'The story is over.'

Hatred shot from his eyes and the machine gun trembled in his hand.

Peppone sat down in front of a small table, placed his machine gun on the damask carpet, threw his cap backwards, took a pack of cards out of his pocket and began to shuffle.

'Let's have a rematch,' he chuckled.

Giacomino sat down and, with men armed with machine guns silent spectators, played. He played ... and won again. He won in a perfect, unequivocal, inflexible way. But he didn't say anything. Instead it was Peppone who got up, his face as red as his neckerchief, and angrily threw his cards on the table.

'You're still the same dirty fascist!' he said, walking away, followed by his men.

At the door, he turned.

'But you haven't seen the last of this,' he shouted.

'Okay,' said Giacomino. 'In the meantime, remember to send me the bottle of cognac.'

Peppone sent him a demijohn of it, with a note:

'Drown yourself.'

*

At the Secchia, Peppone yesterday lost the seventy-fourth, post-Liberation Scopa game and, rising gloomily, told Giacomino that, as long as there are reactionaries in Italy, the war will never be at an end.

*

Aptly, Don camillo and Peppone first saw the light of day at Christmastide, 1946, as later Giovanni recalled:

I am perpetually irritated by the virtue of the punctilious pen pushers who have penetrated the most unsuspected places and lie in ambush wherever I go. They favour me with a bored and pitying glance when I rush in at the last minute before the deadline with my typewritten pages and India-ink drawings, 'Poor, Guareschi! Just under the rope, as usual!' they are evidently thinking.

At such times I am full of coffee, nicotine, bicarbonate of soda, and fatigue. My clothes are sticking to me because I haven't taken them off for three days; I have dirty hands and stubble on my chin. My mouth is furry and my head, stomach, heart, and liver are all aching. A lock of unkempt hair is hanging down over my nose and black dots dance before my eyes.

'Why do you always wait until the very last minute?' they ask me. 'Why don't you do your work little by little, while there is still plenty of time?'

But if I had paid attention to the punctilious pen pushers, I wouldn't have got even as far as I am today.

I remember distinctly the day of 23 December 1946 [a Monday]. Because of Christmas, the work had to be in 'ahead of time', as the pen pushers put it. At that time, besides editing the magazine *Candido*, I wrote stories for *Oggi*, another weekly put out by the same publisher. On 23 December, then, I was up to my ears in trouble. When evening came I had done my piece for *Oggi* and it had been set up by the printer, but the last page of *Candido* was still unfinished.

'Closing up *Candido*!' shouted the copy boy.

What was I to do? I lifted the piece out of *Oggi*, had it reset in larger type and put it into my own paper.

'God's will be done!' I exclaimed.

And then, since there was another half hour before the deadline of *Oggi*, I wrote a hasty story to fill the gap.

'God's will be done!' I said again.

And God must have willed exactly what proceeded to happen. For God is no punctilious pen pusher. Because, if I had heeded all the good advice poured into my ear, Don Camillo, Peppone and all the other characters in this book would have perished on the day they were born, that 23 December 1946. For the very first story of the series was written for *Oggi*, and if it had appeared there, it would have gone the way of its predecessors, and no one would have heard of it again.

But after it came out in *Candido*, I received so many letters from my twenty-three readers that I wrote a second story about the big priest and the big Red mayor of a village in the Po River valley. Now, what with one joke following after another, I turned in three hours late, to the disgust of the punctilious pen pushers – the 200th instalment of the adventures of Don Camillo. And an hour later a letter arrived from France to announce the sale of 800,000 copies of my first published volume.

And so I am not in the least bit sorry to have put off until the morrow that which I could perfectly well have done the day or the month before. At times it saddens me to look over the things I have written, but I don't suffer too awfully much because I can honestly say that I did my best not to write them. And I outdid myself in putting them off from day to day.

There, my friends, is the story of how the priest and the mayor of a village in the Po River valley were born. Two hundred times I have pulled the strings and made them do the most extravagant things that anyone can imagine. So extravagant that often they are literally true. Over and over I complain: 'Now that I've brought them into the world, what shall I do about them? Kill them off and call it a day?'[102]

Giovanni took no credit for his fictional characters. He moulded Don Camillo, Peppone, Smilzo, Brusco and the rest, he said, from the currents of life he detected around him in those far-off days:

It is not that I claim to be their 'creator'; all I did was put words into their mouths. The river country of the Little World created them; I crossed their path, linked their arms with mine and made them run through the alphabet, from one end to another. In the last weeks of 1951, when the mighty river overran its banks and flooded the fields of the happy valley, readers from other countries sent me blankets and parcels of clothing marked 'For the people of Don Camillo and

---

[102] Eventually 346 stories would be published.

Peppone'. Then, briefly, I imagined that instead of being an unimportant fool I was an important one.

I gave all due explanation of the river valley and its little world in the preface to the first volume, and today I can subscribe to every word I said there. I don't know what will be the fate of this book of stories and I refuse to worry about it. I know that when I was a little boy I used to sit on the bank of the mighty river and say to myself: 'Who knows? Perhaps when I'm grown up I'll manage to get to the other side.'

My greatest dream was to own a bicycle. Now I am forty-six years old and the bicycle is mine. Often I go to sit on the river bank where I sat as a boy. And as I chew a blade of grass I can't help thinking: 'After all, this side is the better.' I listen to the stories borne down the mighty river, and people say: 'He grows more absurd every year!'

Which isn't true, because I was absurd from the very beginning, thanks be to God.

Giovanni understood the inspirational value of the spirit of place, that every place is a palimpsest, a manuscript on which successive generations have impressed their stories. Even two years earlier in Oflag XB, Bremerwörde, the notion had exercised his imagination and he had written 'A Fistful of Earth':

I pick up a handful of dirt and watch it slip through my fingers. I think of a very ancient city. Of the thousand years of history which have impregnated those walls: for 900 years the shadow has stagnated in that courtyard, for eight centuries the land on which that fortress stands has not seen the blue of the sky. In that old house a prince was stabbed in 1472. There is the thieves' quarter, depopulated by the plague in 1658. Bones of children lie at the bottom of sewers, chained skeletons of women walled up alive within the thickness of enormous pillars. A thousand years of misery and happiness, cries of pain and pleasure, words of love and hate have impregnated those stones, and the air is full of crimes, torments, lost lives; each brick has absorbed a little of the life of men, men's sweat has burnished edges and corners, and their breath coagulated upon the vaults and ceilings. Everything has been greased with the daily dissolution of bodies. Yes, the huge agglomeration of buildings has become something almost human as in the swaddling of a mummy, and therefore also inhuman. A something that has killed nature, a transition stage between thing and man...

In this fistful of earth that I hold between my fingers, there is a bit of the past and a little bit of the future.

I am the present, and my feet walk on my past and my future.[103]

The sense Giovanni had of the spirit of *la Bassa*, the landscape of his birth, often gives the goings on in Don Camillo's village a supernatural dimension:

Things can happen here which don't happen anywhere else, things which are always in tune with the landscape. And the air you breathe there is special, inspiring both the living and the dead; and even the dogs have souls...

In order to understand it one really has to have lived in one of the low houses in the broad valley and to have seen the moon rise like a great red ball over the bank of the Great River. There is no visible movement in the valley and a stranger may have the idea that nothing ever happens along the deserted riverbanks, that nothing could happen in the red and blue houses. Yet more things happen here than up in the mountains or in the big city. For the blazing summer sun gets into people's veins, and that big red moon is utterly unlike the pale satellite they see in other places; it blazes just like the sun, inflaming the imaginations of the living and the bones of the dead. Even in winter, when the valley is filled with cold and fog, the heat stored up during the summer is so great that people's imaginations aren't cooled off sufficiently to see things as they actually are. That is why every now and then a shotgun peeps out of a thicket or a girl does something she oughtn't do...[104]

The Great River, the River Po, flows through *la Bassa*, Italy's widest and most fertile plain and is linked to *il Cristo Crocifisso* on the high altar because every year there is a procession, with Don Camillo carrying the 3-metre-high cross right down to the riverbank for the blessing of the waters. The Great River plays a big role as the symbolic purveyor of the stories 'into the great sea of the history of the world', optimising Giovanni's hope that what he makes work at the micro level of Don Camillo's Little World will one day be made to work universally, the world over:

The river flows placidly and indifferent in the plain. Between her and the villages of *la Bassa*, there is an embankment which prevents the houses being reflected in river conveys them all: funny stories and melancholy stories, and takes them away, into the great sea of the

---

[103] 'A Fistful of Earth' (1944)
[104] 'Shotgun Wedding', *Don Camillo and His Flock* (Pilot, 2015).

history of the world. And, on the way, she tells the stories to those who sit by the water to listen to her chatter...[105]

The story that captures most beautifully a sense of the otherworldliness of Don Camillo's Little World and of the Great River that soaks up the stories of its people is undoubtedly 'In the Land of Melodrama'.[106]

Don Camillo's hens were as usual anticipating the noonday chimes by auditioning for a place in the church choir.

That summer the sun had excelled itself and we would often hear or read about people who, while crossing the piazza or walking down a street, fell like cooked pears splat on the ground, killed by the heat.

Everyone kept as far from the melting asphalt as possible and on the main road only one wretch could be seen, riding astride a battered old motorbike. Half a kilometre from the village its engine stopped humming: it sneezed and came to a halt.

The biker, a man, dismounted and continued on his way on foot, pushing his powerless vehicle. He didn't even bend down to look at the engine, because he knew full well where the fault lay. *Big* breakdown, the biggest: the motorbike was out of petrol. The distributor may as well have been lying on the side of the road, and the rider had no choice but to continue, *calcantibus pedibus*, for he didn't have a penny on him.

Sweating profusely, he proceeded along the deserted road on the lookout for anything that might pass for shade: but there were no plants of any kind lining this road. And had he been able to climb over the roadside ditch into the fields, he would have discovered only burnt stubble there. It was a cursed stretch of road. This and the one further on, where the tree-lined fields began, were bounded not by hedges but by wire fences.

On he went, confusion mounting inside his head. Was it weakness due to the fever he'd suffered for the last two days, or because he'd not eaten for fifteen hours? He was afraid that the sun would any minute hit on his brain. On he trudged, ever more desperately, and when, finally, he succeeded in reaching la Maestà, which stands fifty metres from the first houses you come to in the village, he felt he had escaped miraculously from great danger.

The little shrine afforded the bare minimum of shade and, to enjoy it, he had to press himself tightly against the wall. It occurred to him

---
[105] '*Le Storie del fiume*', written in 1948 and published in *Piccolo Mondo Borghese*.
[106] *Don Camillo Takes the Devil by the Tail* (Pilot, 2020).

that he was like a shipwrecked man clinging to a thin raft. A vertical raft.

Noon was now about to ring and people were beginning to pass by on the street: the man felt that he couldn't stay where he was, could not be seen in that strange situation. Even kindergarten kids had an interest in motorcycle maintenance, and, sure enough, someone would have stopped to ask what the problem was and to give advice and offer help.

He pulled himself out of the shadows, picked up the motorbike and resumed his journey. But now, after a few steps, he realised that, wrecked as he was, he dare not even dream of making it on foot to his home. He lived in the city thirty miles hence. Now it was all about gaining time and, above all, in getting rid of the motorcycle.

He loosened the valve of the front tyre and, when the outer rubber collapsed, he set off walking again. The midday bell was ringing as he arrived in front of Peppone's workshop.

Peppone was hammering away as the man with the motorbike entered the large and airless workshop.

'Please,' he said, 'if I may I'll leave my motorbike here. You might, at your leisure, look at the front tyre. I don't know if it's punctured or if it has a leaky valve. I'll be back in the afternoon, late because I have business in the village.'

He pulled a very ragged leather bag out of the luggage rack and left. It seemed to him that he had made a big step forward:

'For now, until tonight at five or six, I'm okay. The bike is safe, I don't have to look after it, it doesn't embarrass me and I can think quietly about how to get the money together that I need.'

In reality, however, he had only aggravated the situation, because while earlier he had needed money only for petrol, now money had to be found for the mechanic for keeping the motorcycle for half a day and checking the tyre. But hey, this was no big deal. A stranger in a small country stands out, especially when he wanders about just at the moment when everyone is bent on getting something to eat. The important thing, the urgent and necessary thing now, was to escape the curiosity of other people.

He left town and, at the first cart track, turned sharply and sat down in the shade of a hedge. There was a trough still with some water: he washed his hands, dampened a handkerchief and cleaned his face. He then tidied his hair and, pulling out a tuft of grass, dusted off his shoes. He had shaved in the morning with a razor, which he always carried with him inside the motorcycle bag: now he was all set once more and could present himself with dignity wherever he went.

When he'd been dusty, dishevelled, sweaty and had that damn bike to drag along like a cross, he was sure that all his troubles were down to the mess he was in and the obstacle that his machine presented. Now that all was well in regard to both, everything would surely work out well.

But then his spirits fell once more, for he saw that the situation had deteriorated. Who do you sell to at lunchtime? Who was going to buy his shoe polish and soap? Even if he managed to sign up a few orders, who would give him money up front on merchandise when they'd only seen a sample?

The man had been doing the job for four years. The war had taken him out of Civvy Street at twenty-two and when he had returned home after five years absence, he found no-one and nothing as he had left it – not even the family house, which had been reduced to a pile of rubble: everything was either rubble or had been stolen – not even one whole brick had been left.

He'd been given compensation for war damage, and with this and the pittance he'd received after two years imprisonment in Germany he'd bought himself some clothes, some linen and stuff he'd need to make a life in this remodelled world, though God knows how.

The motorcycle did not belong to him; he rented it from time to time, and paid a good price: an astute company had hired him as a rep. He beat the bounds around the city within a radius of some forty kilometres. Up till now he'd been going around offering bad soap and bad shoe polish for four years to people whose shops were almost always full of fine soap and excellent polish. So, in order to sell something, he'd come up with preferential deals, which unfortunately ate up half his commission. In the beginning, when he had but a small supply of goods, this strategy had seemed to make sense.

'If you order this,' he'd say, 'you will receive an invoice for 1,800 lire. It's already a good deal, but, as I want to build a solid clientele, I intend to work only to promote my future and offer you a loss leader.[107] In order to prove what I said, that you would make money even before selling the goods, I will give you 300 lire in cash and when you came to pay, you will have to stump up not 1,800 lire but only one thousand five.'

Now, the very idea of receiving money from the man who is selling to you is, for a certain type of person, rather attractive, and in the beginning the strategy did work. But not for long. Pretty soon, as a direct result, the selling work became ever harder and now, every

---

[107] A loss leader is a pricing strategy to sell a product at a loss to attract future custom.

time he stopped his motorcycle in front of a country shop, the poor man felt his heart fail. And when he turned the handle of a shop door and the bell rang to announce his arrival, he felt an urge to jump on his motorbike and ride away. Even as he was waiting for someone to attend to him, he'd be thinking:

'This time it won't go smoothly. When they know who I am and what I want, they'll kick me out.'

In fact, no-one ever did kick him out: nobody had ever mistreated him. Perhaps because, even though his clothes weren't up to much, he was a handsome man with a handsome man's posture and presentation. Perhaps, also, because shopkeepers were now used to receiving visits from salesmen, and they thought nothing of turning any of them down – indifference born of habit.

But he almost wished they *would* insult him, that they would tell him to eat his lousy soap and the repulsive muck he wanted to put on their shoes. Perhaps then he would have found the strength to awaken and get busy somewhere else. Instead, the routine had continued.

But now something exceptional was happening. In Castelletto, three days earlier, a crazy fever had forced him to stay in bed in the small hotel where he was lodging, and when he got up, the few coins he had in his pocket had barely been enough for him to pay for room and food. The bill was 2,070 lire and he had had only 2,000: but the mistress, on seeing the 2,000 dollar bills, had said that was enough. A miracle. Which, however, had not been repeated when, ten kilometres out of Castelletto, he'd run out of petrol. And so now, there he was, sitting in the shade of the hedge, on the edge of a ditch full of dead water, thinking of how to fill his tank and go home. To go home without a penny and without having *earned* a penny in commission.

Sell something? He had nothing: the bike belonged to the rental company and, even if he pawned it, he'd have to go to jail – a remedy worse than the disease.

He thought back to the days of war and imprisonment: how beautiful life was, then, still full of hope. He looked at the dead water of the ditch; he raised his eyes and remembered something very important: beyond the bank was the river. The river that spread out through the plain seemed immense. He thought of that water and – it seemed to him that he saw it coming – he almost felt a joy. The river, so wide and deep. He got up and his head began to turn towards it. He would walk towards the far bank. But something hooked him in his stomach and held him. *He was hungry.* A desperate hunger. Hunger kept him hooked on life.

'As long as I want to eat, I will never find the strength to throw myself into the river. I *want* to eat, stuff my stomach with food and wine.'

He needed to eat, but above all to drink. Fill your belly with wine! He returned to the road and headed back towards the village. The tavern known as la Frasca stood 200 metres away, an isolated building with a pergola out front.

'Eating and drinking is fine, but paying?'

The thought made him laugh: a man who, in an hour at most, will be dead, must he really worry about such a thing! Does a dying man get upset about who's going to pay for his funeral because he's alone in the world? The very adventure he was undertaking began to amuse him: he had never done such a thing, he had never, through an act of will, put himself in so exciting and dangerous a situation this way. Many people had had a thousand adventures of this kind in life – stepping out from the humdrum into the fray – and were proud of it. Now he too would have his adventure, and he would enjoy going over it in his mind before jumping into the water. He entered the tavern a free agent, full of joy, with an intense interest in knowing how the adventure of the free lunch would end.

He sat down, but didn't take off his jacket. He didn't want to take his foot off the pedal on the last lap.

'I'd like to eat,' he said in a sure voice to the landlord. 'Give me all that you have ready.'

The innkeeper of la Frasca was graceless from beginning to end and a man who had never laughed in his life. He would not have managed it even if he wanted to, so hard and often had he projected his jaw muscles forward in a grump. They called him Ganassa, which is to say 'Jaw'; and his movements were slow and laboured. On occasion, when customers tried it on and he had to look lively, he didn't throw punches like other Christians do: he raised his fist and let it fall like a hammer.

'Soup with lard, salami and omelette with onions,' Ganassa responded grimly.

'All right. Bring some wine straight away.'

The soup arrived and, rather than eating it, the young man infused his body with it as greedily as an inveterate smoker his first cigarette of the day, then threw himself on the omelette and salami. It was hot as hell and the wine was fresh: he drank it like it was lemonade. The hangover headache broke out all at once and for a moment it seemed to the man that his head was splitting in two. Terrified of not being able to move from where he was, he felt his heart gently fail and he fell asleep.

*

'Have you kicked the bucket?' Ganassa's voice woke him rudely.

The man's head was no longer spinning, but his mouth was dry and he downed half a carafe of water.

'What time is it?' he asked the landlord.

'Seven o'clock.'

He thought of the motorcycle without petrol, of the dinner and the wine yet to be paid for... Anguish took hold of him. Ganassa's grim face and huge hands frightened him. Then he thought of the river, of the Great River that waited and, suddenly, he felt calm. It's all OK. He had a large glass of grappa brought and chased it down. And Ganassa watched him.

'I add up your tab,' the man said. Ganassa took a piece of chalk and scribbled something on a tablet. The young man saw his hand moving, his fingers as big as sticks. But what did it matter? Everything would eventually end up in the water of the Great River.

'Six hundred and ten,' Ganassa said finally, pulling his head up to look at his customer. The young man hesitated a moment and then said, 'I'm very sorry.'

Ganassa didn't understand.

'It's a fair price,' he responded in a threatening tone. 'It's the right price. If you want to check it, check it!'

The young man sighed.

'I'm not talking about the price. What I mean is that I am very sorry but I do not have the 610 lire.'

Ganassa approached slowly. Reaching the table, he put his deadly fists on the tablecloth, and leaned towards the young man.

'You don't you have the 610 lire?'

'No.'

'And how much do you have?'

'Nothing,' the young man explained.

The situation seemed too enormous to grasp for Ganassa, who remained stunned for a few moments.

'You mean, without a penny in your pocket you come in here and make me serve all that I gave you!' he roared, as his eyes grew smaller and smaller.

The young man spread his arms.

Ganassa was panting now. 'No-one ever took me for a pup,' he said, pushing away the table between them with a paw.

The young man didn't even get to his feet. Just sat there and waited. Ganassa stepped forward and with his left hand grabbed him by the rags covering his chest, pulling him up. The young man waited for his right hand to make its move out of nowhere but at that moment, a voice rose:

'Ganassa, don't get yourself in trouble for 600 lire.'

The innkeeper loosened his fingers and turned away to reply: 'I gave you food,' he said. 'I'm no man of means. Why, if you didn't have a penny, did you cheat me!'

'I went into the first tavern I came across,' the young man explained, and Ganassa clenched his fists:

'Why when you came in didn't you say that you were hungry and were out of money? I would have given you something anyway.'

'I never asked for charity in my life,' the young man explained. 'And I needed wine, a lot of wine.'

Ganassa had exhausted his repertoire of arguments.

'Enough!' he roared. 'You don't get out of here until you give me something to undo the damage.'

At this, three or four men who had been sitting at a table in a corner of the room playing cards finally stopped playing and waited in anticipation. Ganassa's blood was up and a slaughter would surely follow.

The young man thought of the Great River that awaited him and felt almost an evil pleasure at what was happening to him. As if it was happening to another. He fumbled in his pocket and showed Ganassa the few pieces of junk he had about him.

'There is nothing of value,' he explained. 'Do you want me to leave my jacket!'

'I don't want your rags!' Ganassa grunted.

'I have this bag, my fountain pen...'

'I don't want your stupid rubbish!' Ganassa grunted even more fiercely.

The young man looked at himself then spread his arms:

'I don't know what to give you,' he said. 'I can't even give you a promissory note, because I know I could never pay...'

His eyes fell on one of the inn walls with its typical old country inn prints: Othello about to strangle Desdemona, Rigoletto, with his arm raised, screaming, 'Courtesans vile, damnable rabble...' and so on. It was then that he remembered a story of his own from his POW days, when, to get a pair of wooden clogs from the Germans, he had to sing his own...

He turned to Ganassa: 'Listen,' he said, 'I don't know what to give you. If you want I could sing you a cantata.'

When it occurred to him that suggesting such a thing was tantamount to winding up the innkeeper for his own slaughter, it was too late: Ganassa had already clenched his fists and was advancing upon him.

'You want to pay me with ... a cantata?' Ganassa snarled when he was one step away from him.

'When I was a prisoner of war,' said the man, 'a German gave me a pair of clogs, a slice of bread, and a cigarette for a cantata.'

For a moment Ganassa looked bewildered, then backed away and slipped behind the counter.

'Come on then,' he said.

The young man nodded yes, and cleared his throat. Just then he looked around and saw, hanging above the door, a painting with the rustic face of Peppino, well-known in these parts.[108]

He looked intensely, desperately at the image, searching for Peppino's eyes and finally fixing on them and never letting them go. Two small eyes that sparkled in the shadows like two diamonds.

The young man waited for the nod and when he caught it darting out of the shadows, he attacked a piece from Verdi and kept on singing, never leaving those eyes. And he heard a voice come out of his mouth that didn't even seem to be his and when he couldn't find the breath in his lungs to reach into the higher register he found his way into it with his heart.

Was it the wine? The grappa? The call of the Great River that awaited him?

He sang and when he saw the light in those two gems go out, he realised he had finished singing.

And Ganassa was there, with his elbows on the bar, his head tight between his hairy paws, and he wasn't even breathing. Meanwhile, the three or four men in the little group at the back of the room seemed to be in complete agreement with Ganassa.

The young man made a move for the door because the river was calling him. When he passed in front of the bar, Ganassa roused himself, rose up, opened the till, rummaged around in it and laid 390 lire on the marble deck.

'Signore, here's your change from a thousand lire,' said Ganassa darkly.

The young man turned and was stilled as if enchanted by that extraordinary gesture. Then the atmosphere of the melodrama took him too and he replied, smiling: 'Keep it.'

---

[108] Peppino, not to be confused with Peppone. Peppino was the nickname of the world famous composer, Giuseppe Verdi, son of an innkeeper in the village of Roncole. It is Verdi's spirit that inspires the fantastic virtuoso performance of the young man in the tavern.

'Thank you, sir,' said Ganassa. And a flash of wonder shone in his eyes, because he had never received such a big tip in his life.

Outside, the sun had finished laying waste the fields and was slowly preparing to stage a sunset worthy of the poetry of a sky forged by no less a power than Destiny.

The young man had arrived at the water's edge. But the water refused him. Everything was the same as before, but at the same time *everything* had changed.

'Here is your vehicle.'

The young man turned to see Peppone standing behind him, holding the motorbike by its handlebars. He wanted to say something, but Peppone didn't give him time.

'All done,' he said. 'The tyre and the petrol.'

The young man spread his arms, but Peppone shook his head:

'Take it easy, everything is already paid for: I was at the tavern too.'

They walked down the slope that led to the main road.

'Tell me, how did I sing?' the young man asked.

'I don't know,' replied Peppone. 'It didn't even seem like a voice. I have no idea what the hell it did sound like. There are things that are heard but not understood.'

The young man sighed: 'I was full of wine...'

'What a wine!' muttered Peppone. 'Let's not get silly. I know the sort of singing that comes from drinking wine.'

The young man noticed something in the front fork of the motorcycle and bent down for a closer look.

'I didn't have time to repaint it,' Peppone explained. 'The fork was cracked on both sides and I welded it. If you'd gone another 500 metres, you would have been killed. You ran out of petrol at the right time.'

The young man turned pale and his hands began to tremble.

'It's impossible!' he exclaimed.

'Yes, but today Destiny determines that impossible things can happen,' said Peppone.

Then he was silent for a moment and concluded:

'Young man, say what you will, and politics aside, the Almighty is never less than the Almighty.'

The man jumped on his motorbike and, after only three metres, the engine was already humming.

Peppone stood there listening to the hum of the engine and it sounded to him like a symphonic poem as it slowly melted and vanished into the air.

*

Giovanni was ever the child of *la Bassa*, the palimpsest from which his inimitable characters emerge so vividly. He *was* their environment. In the deepest sense, he shared the spirit of his homeland with them. This is a different way of thinking, involving empathy and imagination rather than the analysis and judgement of politics. And time and again it ensures there *is* divine intervention to the benefit of both Don Camillo and Peppone jointly, and therefore the community – as well, we hope, as universally in the interests of the earth.

Giovanni could always 'belong' in the village of Ponteratto. Before now, the name of Don Camillo's village has not been shared with his English readers. Many may be surprised to learn that it occurs in the very first sentence of the first Don Camillo story, but not in the English translation and not in the Italian text of the Don Camillo stories from which the modern Pilot Productions edition was taken.

Originally, the first sentence of 'A Sin Confessed' read: 'Don Camillo, *l'arciprete di Ponteratto, era un gran brav'uomo.*' Literally, 'Don Camillo, the archpriest of Ponteratto, was a very good man.' Perhaps Giovanni had second thoughts about his earliest judgement of the priest who, while fundamentally good, would soon prove himself unerringly human. More likely, he did not want to suggest he was writing about an actual village any more than he was about actual people:

> The little world of *The Little World* isn't *exactly* here: it is not in any specific place. The village of *The Little World* is a black dot which moves, along with its Peppones and its Smilzos, up and down the river through that chunk of land that stands between the River Po and the Apennines. But its climate is the same, the landscape is the same; and in a village like this one, it is enough to stop on the road and look at a farmhouse, inundated by maize and hemp, and right away a story is born.

Just how real the village was in his imagination is shown by the fact that he couldn't resist introducing his wife and children to it, as if it and his fictional characters *were* real. In 'The Village of Don Camillo', the 'fat man' (Peppone), the 'thin boy' with the bicycle (Smilzo) and the 'huge priest, all in black' (Don Camillo) confront us deliciously in the magical yet paradoxically realistic engine-room of this writer's imagination: Margherita is of course Ennia; the Pasionaria, Carlotta (Albertino's sister).[109]

---

[109] 'The Village of Don Camillo' from *Corrierino delle Famiglie* (1954)

Christmas 1946: The Birth of Don Camillo

We drove for a long time over country roads full of rocks and holes. When we finally got to the village, we parked the car in the piazza.

Mario, a friend who was with us, got out of the car along with Albertino.

'Wait for me here,' he said. 'If this guy's at home, try to get it over with in a quarter of an hour. Meanwhile you can amuse yourselves by looking around you.'

There wasn't much to look at. We were in one of those familiar towns lost in the great plain beside the river: little red, yellow, and blue houses; narrow, winding streets; four little shops under the portico in the piazza.

The usual boredom, the usual sun.

I suggested a beer.

'Fine with me,' said the Pasionaria.

'Not me,' Margherita declared. 'I'd rather stay in the car. I don't trust them here.'

I began to laugh.

'Margherita,' I said, 'this is a civilised place. There aren't any highway robbers here.'

'It's not a question of civilisation or highway robbers, it's a question of politics. This is the reddest town in the plain. In the last elections everyone voted Communist except the priest. I read about it in the paper.'

'So what? Drinking a beer isn't holding an anti-Communist meeting, is it?'

'I'm not afraid of the Communists,' declared the Pasionaria.

'Nor am I,' said Margherita. 'Unless you provoke them, Communists behave just like everybody else.'

'Well, who intends to provoke them?' I asked, rather annoyed,

'It's not the intention that counts, it's your face. Your face is a living provocation. It's a well-known, unmistakable face, and even if they've never seen you in person, they'd know you, and they know what you are.'

'And what am I, according to you?'

'According to me, you're the disgrace of the family.

According to them, you're the fellow who's been heaping insults on them week after week, year after year, making fun of them and drawing nasty cartoons of them.'

'What's that got to do with it? I'm not going to write an article, I'm going to drink a beer.'

'You can't erase the past with a beer! The man who offers an insult writes it in sand, but for the man who receives it it's chiselled in bronze.'

'Do as you like,' I said. 'I am going to have something to drink.'

'Would you really leave two poor women here alone and unprotected? Giovannino, you're very thoughtless.'

'I get it,' grumbled the Pasionaria. 'I'll go, that way there'll only be one woman alone, protected by a moustache.'

Margherita gave a shriek of horror, 'Giovannino, you wouldn't let her go alone!'

'No, Margherita,' I replied, 'I wouldn't let her go alone. The trouble is, she's already gone.'

The Pasionaria was trotting over toward the portico. When she reached it, she turned, stuck her tongue out at me, and disappeared.

'The sins of the fathers!' cried Margherita. 'Oh, Giovannino, if anything happens to that poor little thing, I don't know what I'll do.'

'Neither do I.'

I got my newspaper out of the glove compartment and was soon far from my immediate surroundings.

But not for long.

'Giovannino!' cried Margherita. 'Look!'

I looked, and saw five or six people standing together in the square under one of the arches of the arcade, glancing in our direction and whispering to each other.

'Giovannino,' Margherita groaned, 'they've recognised you!'

'It's not the first time,' I replied calmly, 'that I've gone somewhere and people have recognised me.'

'But it may be the last! Just look, Giovannino, at their expressions!'

The expressions were not, to tell the truth, remarkably cordial. They were, to be somewhat more precise, rather sullen.

'My God!' cried Margherita. 'The child!'

The Pasionaria had come out of the portico with an enormous ice-cream cone in her hand. One of the men called her over as she passed, and pointing to us, asked her a question.

The Pasionaria nodded.

'Now look!' cried Margherita. 'They've asked her if you're you and she's told them you are.'

The one who had asked if I was I stood talking to the Pasionaria. The Pasionaria replied with a shrug of her shoulders. Then she drew away and, still licking that tremendous ice-cream cone, disappeared under the portico.

'She's clever!' cried Margherita. 'She's managed to get away. Let's hope she's smart enough to go to the police... Look!'

The group had now increased somewhat, and the dark looks were still turned in our direction, and the gestures did indeed seem rather menacing.

Then one of the men leapt onto a bicycle and pedalled rapidly away.

'I'm sure of it, Giovannino!' cried Margherita. 'He's gone to get the rest of the gang.'

'Don't be so silly, Margherita. There are about fifteen of them already, and that'd be plenty if they have violence in mind.'

Out of a street at the other end of the square came some men on bicycles, headed by an enormous man with a surly face, and the boy who had bicycled off before.

'Didn't I tell you, Giovannino? There's the gang!'

The huge man and his companions leaned their bicycles against the columns and joined the group under the portico.

'The big man,' said Margherita, 'is the leader of the gang.'

Apparently this time she was right: they were all telling him something, and he was listening attentively, glancing every now and then toward us and nodding his head.

One of the gang had told the big man to look to the left, and there was the Pasionaria, who, having devoured the cone, was now headed directly toward the gang.

The big man stood in front of her and put one of his enormous hands on her shoulder. Then he leaned over and asked her something.

The Pasionaria looked up at him and nodded.

He took his hand off her shoulder, spoke for a moment to the thin boy who had called him, then leaned down to talk to the Pasionaria again.

The boy, meanwhile, had gone to get his bicycle. The big man now put his hands on the Pasionaria's waist, lifted her up, and sat her on the bar of the boy's bicycle.

It all happened so quickly that by the time it was done it was too late. The boy was already pedalling off into the unknown with his prey.

Margherita grabbed my arm.

'Don't move, Giovannino!' she cried. 'They're not going to do anything to her, I can feel it. They only want to get rid of a dangerous witness – an innocent eye!'

The big man muttered something to several members of the gang, then slowly rolled up his shirt sleeves, pulled the brim of his hat down over his forehead, and began a slow march in our direction.

'Quick, Giovannino!' sobbed Margherita. 'Start the car! Let's get out! You can't fight them all!'

The big man was now only a few inches from the car. He looked at me sullenly for a moment, then jerked his hat away and leaned his head in through the open window of the car. Our faces were now but a palm's breadth apart.

He hesitated for a moment or two, then in a deep voice said: 'Diesel?'

'Yes,' I replied. 'Mercedes-Benz.'

'Overhead cam?'

'Yes,' I replied.

The man straightened and looked at the car. Then he leaned in again.

'Can I lift the bonnet?' he asked.

'Certainly,' I replied.

He lifted the bonnet, the whole gang gathered around, and there ensued an animated discussion about the motor.

The discussion went on for quite some time. Then they all gathered around my window, and the big man took the initiative again.

'What do you get out of it?'

'Sixteen kilometres a litre.'

'Cylinder displacement?'

'Thousand-nine.'

'Pickup?'

'Good.'

'Third?'

'Slow.'

'Speed?'

'Hundred and ten.'

'Injectors?'

'Excellent.'

The fat man turned back to the gang, and they had a whispered conference. Then he turned to me again:

'Much noise?'

'Only in low.'

Having made sure the gear was in neutral, I turned on the motor. The gang went back to the raised hood and stood looking at the motor. Then the leader moved to the back of the car and put his huge paw over the exhaust, to see whether or not the motor had a heart murmur. He rejoined his gang and they continued to study the motor for some time. Then he lowered the bonnet.

I turned off the motor. The big man came alongside my open window. He leaned in, his face surlier than ever.

'All right, Signor Guareschi,' he grumbled, putting a finger to his hat.

He left, along with his Chief of State and the rest of the gang. They got on their bicycles and departed. The piazza, once again, was empty and silent.

Margherita sighed with exhaustion. 'The baby...'

The 'baby' was sitting peacefully on the handlebars, demolishing an ice cream cone even larger than the one she had had earlier. A few feet away the boy braked, lowered the Pasionaria to the ground, and left.

All was in order.

'I wanted lemon, and they didn't have any here,' said the Pasionaria quietly as she rejoined us. 'So that monkey gave me a ride to the next town.'

'You might have thanked him,' said Margherita in a low, terribly distant voice.

'Why?' asked the Pasionaria. 'I paid him. A fifty-lire ice cream.'

Margherita, still hardly audible, asked me for a cigarette.

I lit it for her. She took several deep drags, then suddenly pressed my arm as though gripped by fear.

Standing by her window was a huge priest, all in black, with a sullen face.

He leaned in. 'Respectable women don't smoke in public,' he said. His voice sounded deep and threatening.

'She's not respectable,' replied the Pasionaria cheerfully.

The priest, having identified the origin of the voice, drew back in horror, turned his great shoulders, and with a shake of his head started off.

Then he paused. He came back, walked around the car, leaned in my window.

'Diesel?' he asked brusquely.

'Diesel.'

'Overhead cam?'

'Overhead cam.'

He raised the bonnet and studied the motor attentively from both sides, then looked up at me and wiggled the first finger of his right hand. I turned the motor on. He gave it his attention for quite some time, then went around to the back to feel the exhaust.

He came to the front again and held up the palm of a hand as large as a shovel. I turned off the motor. He lowered the bonnet. He pressed down on a mudguard to test the suspension. He kicked one of the tyres.

He put a finger to his hat, turned, and made off. After a few feet, he stopped and turned back.

'The King!' he shouted. 'What's a King?' His face was grim. 'The only King that matters is that one!'

He jerked his head in the direction of the church. The door was ajar. One could see candles flickering at the high altar.

He marched resolutely off toward the door of the presbytery.

The square was silent and empty.

Soon our friend Mario reappeared with Albertino.

'Have you been bored?' Mario asked, as he climbed into the car.

'Not me,' said the Pasionaria.

The car rumbled on, and soon we were on the white road that crossed the great embankment. At the far end were the poplars and the river and – under the wide blue sky – all my stories.

'Diesel?' whispered Margherita.

'Diesel.'

*

In the Don Camillo stories we meet many different sorts of character: relics of Italian nobility, landowning farmers, sharecroppers (tenant farmers of a certain kind), local politicos and servants of the community, multifarious skilled and less skilled workers, traders, vagrants, travellers, wonderfully terrifying women, mothers, fathers, lovers, rebellious youths and children, many of them highly politicised: 'Their passion for politics is so intense that it becomes worrying,' wrote Giovanni.

Don Camillo and Peppone are the characters that allow me to turn what is my polemic [an exhortation to *no* polemic mixed on the palette of his experience in the *lagers*] into a public one. In each tale we have the same event seen from the opposite point of view, along with timely assistance of the Voice of Conscience and common sense that brings the two adversaries to proper reasoning...

The chief *locus* for the political 'dialogue' between his two protagonists is the village square, with Don Camillo's presbytery and church on one side and Mayor Peppone's People's Palace on the opposite side. There is a fine literary tradition to this. A metaphorical *locus* – often a carnivalesque town or village square – in which characters gather and deliver the author's message has been a feature of Western literature since the Agora of Homer's time, on through the Menippean satires, Mediaeval and Renaissance literature and into the work of Giacomo Leopardi, an Italian writer and poet – for many, the greatest Italy has seen since Dante.

In Leopardi's poem, 'Sabato del Villaggio' ('Village Saturday'), the square is located in Recanati, a village in the Province of Macerata, late one Saturday afternoon, in anticipation of the work-free Sunday that will follow. It is a place to which villagers are drawn and where goings-on deliver some truth about the human condition.

With a nod to Leopardi, in the same year as the first Don Camillo story appeared, Giovanni published a mélange of loosely autobiographical stories with the same title as Leopardi's mosaic of thoughts, notes and aphorisms known as *Lo Zibaldone*, its title a concoction of 'zabaglione' with a *la Bassa* style 'zibanda' (coarsely mixed food).[110]

Politics aside, Giovanni insisted that for the most part the people of *la Bassa* 'are pleasant and hospitable and generous, and have a high sense of humour' and it was humour that enabled him to vapourise the pall of nightmare politics in the region.

Looking at the world through a humorist's eyes facilitated his vision. In *Signore e Signori* and *Conferenza a Lugano* he wrote that humour is not merely a literary device to entertain, rather a particular way of broaching and understanding life by reducing facts, episodes and sensations to their *actual* value, as opposed to the value they take on in the context in which they arise. Delimiting their context in this way gave the stories the universal truth-value of parables and led to Giovanni's reputation as 'one of the most prescient and perceptive voices of the twentieth century':[111] 'For me,' wrote Giovanni, 'the humorist is someone who knows how to see today with the eye of tomorrow.'

Beginning in the present he mocked his fellow Italians for their lack of humour, those who 'work, and sleep, and eat, and walk, and love, and listen, and talk, and always hear politically'.

If we had a sense of humour, we would not have put feathers on the hats of our soldiers and we would not have allowed our soldiers to leave for the war with guns made in 1908 or with rayon shirts. Italians, I urge you to humour. Those who cannot smile do not know

---

[110] Giovanni's collection was published in English as *The House that Nino Built*.
[111] Tobias Jones, *The Dark Heart of Italy*.

how to govern. We Italians are serious. We are so serious that we even make people laugh.

In Italy it is forbidden to laugh. Laughing is forbidden as a sincere conviction of the masses that 'whoever laughs is against us'. While, instead, it should be said that whoever laughs at his mistakes is our friend because he allows us not to fall into these mistakes anymore.

Let's get rid of that worst part of ourselves that is lurking inside each of us and awaits a ring, a hymn, a waving of the flag to take off your jacket, roll up your sleeves and make the new history of Italy...

If politicians all possessed a sense of humour! Trouble! Trouble! There would be no more wars in the world!

'Anyone who wrote something like this is a genius,' commented the writer Beppe Severgnin. Giovanni, it seems, was out to transform the DNA of a nation fraught with rhetoric in its political history (the fascist dictator Mussolini being the personification of this, the treaty with Hitler its affirmation), lifting the veil from an entire nation's 'ego-self' and revealing the light of conscience that is 'burning all the time' within.

Humour was the ideal instrument for this purpose. In place of the false logic of political rhetoric that appeals to the worst of our ego-emotions, pride, power, the 'I am right you are wrong' syndrome, his humour pares an issue down and delivers a truth-value good for all times within the form of a story. It may or may not make us laugh. As Giovanni wrote: 'Let's not assume that humour and comedy are two equivalent terms. Comedy is a purely ancillary matter.' The need is for the satire to switch our perceptions out of the main track of our thinking, so to deliver a truth-value (a fresh perception) in a story designed to that end.

... We have been drunk with rhetoric for centuries, and this is because we lack a sense of humour.

... I try with my modest means to break the spiral of rhetoric that threatens to envelop us again.

...Humour forbids rhetoric, and dictatorships are the living negation of humour. A dictatorship does not understand humour and despises it as any of the too many things it cannot understand...

...Humour is the declared enemy of rhetoric because, while rhetoric swells and flares up every story, humour deflates and unadorns it, reducing it with a ruthless criticism to the bone. And here, against the rhetoric that ignites our brains by presenting the war in a glory of flags in the wind, under a sky of allegory with the spirits of heroes riding on white horses, humour presents a war designed not to excite souls, but to incite the brains to reasoning...

His wartime experience convinced him that there was no better methodology:

Do I regret the two lost years of the *Lagers*? Far from it. Because I haven't wasted a single second of those two years. And if today I am what little I am, I owe it to those two years in the *Lagers*!

The Radio B90 broadcast in 1945, when he defused a potentially very ugly conflict on the eve of release from Oflag 83 by telling the story of the two horses, had convinced him that the allegorical context of a fictional story, laced with humour, was the path to take.

There, when I spoke, everything fell into place and nothing happened that day – no lynchings or arson – and the gentlemen who had come to watch the hut being burned down were disappointed. The conflict was defused and everything made safe, but that was not to my merit. It was down to *humour*, which (albeit in a modest way) had broken the cursed spiral of rhetoric. Now, here is the time to grasp the subject by the horns...

It turns out not to have been innocent happenstance that I took you down there among the *Lagers*, into that episode of the two horses, because here, now, exactly two years later, *mutatis mutandis*, we find ourselves in the exact same situation.

An important drunkenness of rhetoric divides the field into two irreconcilable and irrational extremisms.

While it may be reasonable that there is disagreement between the have-nots and those who have too much, it is certainly unreasonable that there is an irreconcilable hatred between the have-nots and the have-nots.

Precisely it is rhetoric (served 'admirably' by demagogy and passionate by its very nature) that leads people to such a state of intoxication as to transform class struggle into partisan hatred and makes us forget that around us, there is still a fence, with sentries watching us from their towers.

Thus is the fable of the two horses still substantially valid. Even if, aboard the cart, the situation has become complicated and the two horses no longer symbolise North and South, they are still two masses of opposite conviction, the horse on the right that paws with the horse on the left. And, on the cart, in place of the lady dressed in the Tricolour, there is a kind of management council dressed in the Tricolour: two or three gentlemen who fight over the reins because each of them says that only he knows the right way along the stony and rugged road. So that in the triple conflict – between horses, drivers, and horses and drivers – the cart makes but three metres forward and four backwards, two to the right and three to the left: all in an epic battle of kicks, neighs, screams, jolts, lashes and squeaks, so as to give the idea that, not content with having lost a war, we Italians are animated by the laudable intention of losing even the post-war.[112]

Had Giovanni locked horns with his fellow Italians that day, however articulate his argument would inevitably have hooked onto the 'I am right you are wrong' ego-emotions to which every polemicist since the beginning of time has been prone. Instead, he made his point by dipping into a satirical tradition as old as the hills, one founded by Menippus of Gadara in the 3rd-century BC. Menippus, a Greek philosopher, was 'a joker about serious things'. Allegory was paramount, as it would be for Giovanni in the Don Camillo stories, where the picaresque (roguish) elements of Menippean satire speak to us through Peppone and his gang. But, crucially, what differentiated Mennipus from those who had gone before was that he took as his target not individuals but attitudes, mind-sets, political ideologies. The only time Giovanni made an individual his quarry, it landed him in prison for a second term.

Readers of the 1950s immediately saw the relationship between the two 'horses', Don Camillo and Peppone, as an allegory of the Cold War. While Peppone is trumpeting the triumphal march of the proletarian communist ideal, Don Camillo is reaching near Swiftian levels of lampoonery by, for example, swapping places with his horse, provocatively named Pèpo, to challenge the Mayor's socialist theories.[113]

And while, in the big wide world, Russia and America are going at each other 'like two scorpions in a bottle, each capable of killing the other but only at the risk of its own life',[114] the two village superpowers are settling their account not for the first time by submitting international politics to a trial of strength at the village fair: 'I am America, and you are Russia; how does that sound, Mr Mayor?'[115]

On the surface we have a rollicking slapstick narrative of fisticuffs and entertaining hi-jinks set in the aftermath of the Second War, while beneath it, the author's serious purpose proceeds. It is altogether a more developed sort of allegory than the one Giovanni rehearsed in *'Favola di Natale', 1944*. We still have a simple story, but now, *il Cristo* (un-blinkered by ideology, un-clouded by prejudice and the context of the present) presides over proceedings from high above the altar of the village church, undermines the stubborn priest's personal prejudices and, even-handedly, often sidies with his adversary, the mayor, so that Giovanni is now in the business of *parable* rather than fable, with conscience its guiding light.

---

[112] *Signore e Signori Italia provvisoria Nuova* (1947)

[113] 'The Way of Good', *Don Camillo Takes the Devil by the Tail* (Pilot, 2020)

[114] J Robert Oppenheimer, one of the 'fathers of the atomic bomb' in 1956.

[115] 'Global Warning', *Don Camillo Takes the Devil by the Tail* (Pilot, 2020).

Christmas 1947

The brutality of the *Dopoguerra* placed the lives of neighbours in jeopardy and the violence forms a singular element in the earliest Don Camillo stories of this child of *la Bassa*. A series of five stands out. 'Fear', '*Carta Canta*', 'The Fear Persists,' 'Thriller and Romance' and 'The Circle is Broken'[116] were written in 1947 and taken together demonstrate well the bitterness and collective sense of fear in the region at this time. They concern the assassination of Pizzi, a farmer. Peppone's lieutenant, Smilzo, has apparently been shot. Pizzi stands accused of the murder by Peppone and his gang because they'd fallen out with Pizzi over a farm workers strike. Pizzi is then shot by way of retribution in front of his wife and son, but it transpires that Smilzo had in fact only been knocked unconscious by an exploding tyre and, to keep a lid on the consequences, Pizzi's murder is covered up as suicide. However, Don Camillo knows that Pizzi has been assassinated and refuses to be part of the cover-up. In '*Carta Canta*' ('There it is in black and white'), Pizzi is given a proper funeral (something not allowed a suicide, who cannot at this time be buried in sacred ground) and Don Camillo is in deep water with the Bishop when he learns what he has done.

Throughout, Giovanni's narrative operates at the level of individual lives caught up in the poisonous aftermath of war. In 'The Circle Is Broken', the final story in the sequence, Spocchia, the communist section boss and barber of Molinetto, takes it upon himself to make ready local party members for the '*seconda ondata*', the second wave of violent purges which, it was feared, would follow the first. Fortunately, somehow, the circle of fear was broken. The second wave never happened and Don Camillo is able to sum up the episode in a few words: 'It is war that has ruined young people. We must not speak of the guilty, but of victims.'

The fourth in this little series of stories is *Thriller and Romance*, an important one as it takes place over Christmas and has much to do with the development of Giovanni's principal theme.

Don Camillo has been playing detective on the Pizzi case and an attempt has been made on his life, a shot narrowly missing him as he applies a paintbrush to the cross above the high altar in the village church in preparation for Christmas, the festival that will never fail to tickle Peppone's conscience.

Now Mayor of Ponteratto, Peppone undergoes a Christmastide awakening every bit as radical as his creator's. Besieged by the violent political chaos of post-war Italy, caught between diktats from Moscow and promptings from his conscience, Peppone is deeply troubled and sees his totalitarian rhetoric for what it is – provocative nonsense dinned into the ears of his people in a bid to

---

[116] 'Carta Canta' is as yet unpublished in English. 'Fear', 'The Fear Persists' and 'Thriller and Romance' appear in *The Little World of Don Camillo*, while 'The Circle is Broken' is included in *Don Camillo and His Flock*.

exercise control over them. Confiding in Don Camillo that he feels a prisoner of his politics, which determine everything he thinks and does, Don Camillo encourages him to set his true self free.

The window through which the shot had been fired at Don Camillo opened onto the little meadow belonging to the church, and he and the Marshal were outside the chapel examining the scene.

'Here's the evidence,' said the Marshal pointing to four holes which stood out against the whitewash, a foot or so under the sill of the now notorious window. He took a little knife out of his pocket and probed one of the holes until something came out.

'It looks straightforward to me,' said the Marshal. 'The gunman was positioned some way off and fired a round from his machine gun at the lighted window. Four bullets ended up here in the wall, but one made a hole in the window and came in.'

Don Camillo shook his head.

'I told you it was a pistol shot, and fired from here. I'm not so senile that I can't tell the difference between a pistol shot and a round from a machine gun! First there was a shot from a pistol, and from here. Then there was a burst of machine gun fire from further away.'

'So the spent cartridge should be somewhere nearby!' returned the Marshal. 'And there isn't one.'

Don Camillo shrugged.

'You'd need the music critic from La Scala to tell by the pitch if a shot came from an automatic weapon or a revolver. If whoever shot at me used a revolver, he'll have taken the cartridge away with him.'

The Marshal started to hunt all around and in the end found something on the trunk of the cherry tree which stood five or six yards from the side of the church.

'One of the bullets scarred the bark,' he said. And that was clearly the case.

He scratched his head in puzzlement.

'Bah,' he said finally, 'let's do a bit of forensic science.'

He took a pole and stuck it in the earth, right against the wall, in front of one of the holes in the plaster; then he started to walk across the meadow, every so often looking back at the trunk of the cherry tree which had been struck by the bullet, and moving to left or right according to whether or not the tree was obscuring the pole against the wall. And so there came a point where he found himself right by the hedge, and on the other side of the hedge there were a ditch and a cart track.

Don Camillo came and joined him, and the two of them started to search the ground, one each side of the hedge. They didn't search for long. After five minutes, Don Camillo said, 'Look here,' and there was a machine gun cartridge. Then they found the other three.

'That proves what I've been saying,' exclaimed the Marshal. 'The fellow fired through the window from here.'

Don Camillo shook his head. 'I don't know anything about machine guns,' he said, 'but I know that other guns don't fire their bullets in curves. Take a look for yourself.'

A *carabiniere* came up and informed the Marshal that all was calm in the village.

'Thanks very much!' commented Don Camillo. 'Nobody was shooting at them! They were shooting at me!'

The Marshal took the *carabiniere*'s musket and, lying on the ground, aimed it at the first pane of the chapel window, close to where he remembered the bullet-hole being.

'If you shoot, where will you hit?' asked Don Camillo.

It was child's play. Starting from there and passing through the chapel window, a bullet would have to have smacked into the first confessional on the right, three yards from the church door.

'Unless it was a very well trained bullet, it couldn't have passed through the altar, not even if you threatened to cut its throat,' concluded the Marshal. 'Which means, Don Camillo, that when you get mixed up in something, it causes enough grief to make us all tear our hair out! Wasn't one gunman enough for you? No, *Signore*, you need two. One to shoot you from under the window, and another to shoot you from behind a hedge 150 yards away.'

'Well, that's the way I am,' said Don Camillo. 'No expense spared.'

The same evening, Peppone gathered all his top brass and most trusted lieutenants from all the Council districts. He looked grim.

'Comrades,' he said, 'a new fact has turned up to complicate the local situation. An unknown gunman shot at our self-styled parish priest, and the forces of reaction are exploiting this incident to raise their heads once again and throw more mud at the Party. The forces of reaction, cowardly as always, don't have the courage to talk openly, but we know they're murmuring in corners and saying we are responsible for the shooting!'

Lungo raised his hand and Peppone gave him the nod.

'First of all,' said Lungo, 'we could tell the forces of *Signora* Reaction to demonstrate that there really was an attempt on the priest's life. Because so far we've only got his word for it. And since there weren't any witnesses, it could well have been the Signor Reverend himself who fired the revolver so he could write slanders against us in his hateful newsletter. Let's see the evidence.'

'Hear hear!' agreed the assembly. 'Lungo's right.'

Peppone addressed them again.

'One moment! What Lungo says is true, but we mustn't rule out the possibility that the incident is a real one. Knowing the personality of Don Camillo, I cannot honestly say he's someone who uses underhand methods . . .'

He was interrupted by Spocchia, the section boss from Molinetto.

'Comrade Peppone, remember that a priest is always a priest. You're letting yourself be conned by sentimentality. If you'd listened to me, his odious newsletter would never have come out, and the Party wouldn't now be damaged by these scurrilous insinuations about Pizzi's suicide. Show no mercy to the enemies of the people! Showing mercy to the enemies of the people is a betrayal of the people!'

Peppone slammed a fist onto the table.

'I don't need lessons in morality from you!' he yelled.

Spocchia was unimpressed.

'And if,' he shouted, 'instead of standing in our way, you'd let us take action while we still could, we wouldn't now have a heap of crooked reactionaries under our feet! I . . .'

Spocchia was a slight young man of twenty-five, with a bush of hair rising in waves and slicked back at the sides, ending in a kind of crest at the back the way it's worn by oafs from the north and roughnecks on the west bank of the Tiber. He had small eyes and thin lips.

Peppone confronted him angrily. 'You are a moron!' he said, looking Spocchia in the eye.

The other man turned pale, but said nothing.

Going back to the table, Peppone said, 'Making use of an incident based purely on the assertion of a priest, the reactionaries are plotting new ways to harm the people. Comrades, we must be determined as never before. To the ignoble insinuations . . .'

At this moment a strange thing happened which had never happened before. Peppone started listening to himself. It seemed that he, Peppone, was down in the audience listening to what Peppone was saying.

(*'. . . the selling of flesh, the enemies of the people recruiting for reaction, the starving farm-workers . . .'*)

Peppone listened and gradually it felt as if he was listening to someone else.

('... *the monarchists ... the treacherous clergy ... the reactionary government ... America ... Plutocracy ...*')

'What does "plutocracy" mean?' thought Peppone. 'Why's he talking about plutocracy when he doesn't even know the meaning of the word?'

He looked around and saw faces he barely recognised. Shifty eyes, and the shiftiest were those of young Spocchia. He thought of Brusco, his most loyal follower, and tried to catch his eye, but Brusco was at the back with his arms folded and his head down.

('... *let our enemies know that in us the spirit of the Resistance has not been weakened ... The weapons we once seized to defend our liberty ...*')

Now Peppone felt as if he was yelling like a madman. Then the applause brought him round.

'That's what we wanted,' Spocchia whispered to him as the meeting broke up. 'You know, Peppone, all you need to do is whistle and the second wave will start. My boys are ready. At an hour's notice.'

'Bravo, bravo!' replied Peppone, slapping him on the back, though he'd rather have cracked his skull. But why?

Only he and Brusco were left, and for a while they said nothing.

'Well?' cried Peppone at last. 'Lost your tongue? Aren't you even going to tell me whether I spoke well or not?'

'You spoke very well,' answered Brusco. 'Very well indeed. Better than ever before.'

Then the curtain of silence fell between them again.

Peppone was doing the accounts in his ledger, when all of a sudden he grabbed a glass paperweight, hurled it onto the floor with great force and yelled a long, complicated and exasperated oath.

Brusco looked at him.

'I made an ink blot,' Peppone explained as he closed the book.

'It's the pens we get from that thief, Barchini,' observed Brusco, carefully not pointing out to Peppone that since he'd been writing in pencil the story of the ink blot didn't add up.

When they were outside in the darkness, Peppone stopped at the crossroads as if there was something he wanted to tell Brusco. Then he abruptly said, 'Well, see you tomorrow.'

'Tomorrow, Boss. Good night.'

'Bye, Brusco.'

*

It was nearly Christmas and high time to get out the Nativity set from its box, clean it up, touch up the paint and mend any chips. Even though it was late, Don Camillo was still at work in the presbytery. He heard a tap on the window and after a bit went to open the door because he saw it was Peppone.

Peppone sat down while Don Camillo went back to work, and the two of them said nothing for quite a while.

All at once Peppone exclaimed angrily, 'God dammit!'

'Have you nowhere but the presbytery to go and blaspheme?' enquired Don Camillo calmly. 'Couldn't you have got your swearing done at the office?'

'You can't even swear in the office,' muttered Peppone. 'Because if you swear, you have to explain why.'

Don Camillo was busy touching up St Joseph's beard with white lead.

'There's no place for a decent citizen to live in this world any more!' exclaimed Peppone after a while.

'And how does that concern you?' asked Don Camillo. 'Have you turned into a decent citizen?'

'I've always been one.'

'Oh wonderful! I'd never have guessed.'

Don Camillo went on painting St Joseph's beard. Then he moved on to his robe.

'Will you be doing that for much longer?' enquired Peppone furiously.

'If you give me a hand we'll get it finished in no time.

Peppone was a mechanic with hands like shovels and enormous fingers that he had trouble bending. But when you had a clock that needed mending, Peppone was the man to go to. Because that's how it is: great big men are ideal for the most delicate jobs. He could paint the trim on the bodywork of a car and the spokes of a wheel as one born to it.

'Can you believe this? I'm painting Nativity figures now!' he muttered. 'You must have mistaken me for the sacristan.'

Don Camillo fished around in the box and pulled out a little pink thing the size of a sparrow, which was the Infant Jesus himself.

Without quite knowing how, Peppone found the little statue in his hand, so he picked up a paintbrush and set delicately to work. He was on one side of the table and Don Camillo on the other, but they couldn't see each other's faces because of the glare of the lamp between them.

'This world is only fit for pigs,' said Peppone. 'You can't trust anyone, if there's something you want to tell them. I don't even trust myself.'

Don Camillo was deeply absorbed in his work: the Madonna's face needed to be completely repainted. Delicate stuff.

'And do you trust me?' he asked casually.

'I don't know.'

'Try telling me something, and you'll see.'

Peppone finished the Infant Jesus's eyes, which was the hardest part. Then he touched up the pink of the little lips. 'I want to jack it all in,' he said. 'But I can't.'

'Who's stopping you?'

'No one's stopping me! I could beat off a regiment with a crowbar.'

'Are you scared?'

'I've never been scared in my life!'

'I have, Peppone. Sometimes I get scared.'

Peppone dipped his brush.

'Well, sometimes I do too,' said Peppone. And that's exactly what he had just been feeling.

Don Camillo sighed.

'The bullet passed four inches from my forehead,' he told Peppone. 'If I hadn't moved my head back at exactly the right moment I'd have been done for. It was a miracle.'

Peppone had now finished the Infant Jesus's face and was refreshing the pink of his body.

'I'm sorry I missed him,' Peppone muttered. 'But he was too far away, and the cherry trees were in the way.'

Don Camillo's brush stopped moving.

'Three nights ago,' Peppone explained, 'Brusco was keeping an eye on Pizzi's house to make sure the gunman didn't get hold of the boy. The boy must have seen who shot his father from the window, and the gunman knows it. Meanwhile I was keeping an eye on your house because I was sure that the man knows you know who shot Pizzi.'

'Who is he?'

'I don't know,' replied Peppone. 'I saw him from a long way off, going towards the window of the chapel. But I couldn't fire until he did something. As soon as he fired, I did too. But I missed.'

'Thank the Lord,' said Don Camillo. 'I know how you shoot, and now I can say there were two miracles.'

'Who is it? You and the boy are the only ones who know.'

Don Camillo slowly said, 'Yes, Peppone, I know, but nothing in the world can make me violate the secret of the confessional.'

Peppone sighed and went back to his painting.

'Something's not right,' he said suddenly. 'It feels as if everyone's looking at me differently, now. Everyone, even Brusco.'

'It'll be the same for Brusco, and for all the others,' replied Don Camillo. 'Everyone's afraid of everyone else, and whenever anyone speaks it's as if they're having to defend themselves.'

'Why's it like this?'

'Let's not get political, Peppone.'

Peppone sighed again.

'I feel like I'm in prison,' he said gloomily.

'There's a way out of every prison on this earth,' answered Don Camillo. 'Prisons are only for the body. And the body doesn't count for much.'

The Infant Jesus was finished now, and with his fresh colour, so pink and bright, he almost shone in the enormous dark hand of Peppone.

Peppone looked at it and seemed to feel warmth from that little body on his palm. And he forgot the prison.

He put the pink Infant Jesus on the table with great care, and Don Camillo put the Madonna near him.

'My little boy is learning the Christmas poem,' announced Peppone proudly. 'Every evening I hear him going through it with his mother at bedtime. He's a phenomenon.'

'I know,' Don Camillo admitted. 'And he learned the poem for the Bishop wonderfully too.'

Peppone froze. 'That was one of your worst skulduggeries!' he exclaimed. 'You still haven't paid for it.'

'Paying and dying always come in their due time,' observed Don Camillo.

Then he put the little figure of the ass next to the Madonna leaning over the Infant Jesus.

'Here's Peppone's son, here's Peppone's wife, and here's Peppone,' said Don Camillo touching the ass last of all.

'And here's Don Camillo!' exclaimed Peppone, taking the figure of the ox and putting it next to the group.

'Huh! Beasts always understand one another,' concluded Don Camillo.

Leaving the presbytery, Peppone found himself in the dark night of the Po valley, but he was completely at ease now because he could still feel the warmth of the pink Infant Jesus in his hand.

Then he heard the words of the poem again, and by now he knew it by heart.

'When he recites it to me on Christmas Eve, it'll be magnificent!' he rejoiced. 'And when the democracy of the proletariat is in charge, we mustn't touch poetry. In fact, we should make it compulsory!'

*

The river flowed slowly and placidly, just two steps away, at the foot of the embankment, and that was a poem too, a poem which began when the world began and is still going on. And it took a thousand years to shape and smooth the smallest of the billions of stones on the riverbed.

And so only after twenty more generations will the water have smoothed a new pebble.

And a thousand years from now people will rush at 3,000 miles an hour in machines with super-atomic rockets . . . to do what? To arrive at the end of the year, open-mouthed in the presence of that same plaster Infant Jesus touched up one evening long ago by comrade Peppone with his paintbrush.

Christmas 1948

Before long Giovanni's polemic developed a satirical reach beyond politics into the social and religious upheavals of the day. He saw the need to escape hegemony, man's dominion over man, in any form. He wanted people to look with a new pair of eyes at all the systems that up until then had controlled their thinking

The history of the Church in Russia under Stalin had been one of violent oppression, and in Italy, the post-war purges by communists had killed many priests, but, as the violence abated, Giovanni became increasingly sensitive to what he called the *democratisation* of Christianity in people's minds, diluting the spiritual message of Christmas – the Incarnation, the infusion of God in the soul of man – with an emphasis instead on socialist principles concerning the alleviation of suffering among the people, common to both the communist manifesto (however hopelessly effected) and many a Christian parable.

1948 was marked by publication in *Candido* of two stories concerning Christmas. In the absurdist 'Comrade Gésu', published here in English for the first time, the communist Cisto hijacks the Nativity for his own propagandist purposes, while Giovanni chases down the heartbeat of the Nativity by showing how ineffectual it would be without the spiritual message that inspires it.

Cabassa is in the north of Emilia, a pig of a region where corn is sown and communists are born.

Since there is a bridge two kilometres from Cabassa, those damned men who dropped bombs on bridges during the war, came along, missed the bridge – it was not even touched – and instead blasted seven houses and the church to crumbs.

As a priority, everyone rattled off money to get the church back on its feet:

'If we don't,' said the Reds, 'what pleasure will we find making the proletarian revolution, if we don't even have a church to destroy?'

Then the revolution never came, but the Reds had grown almost to like it:

'So,' they said, 'the Eternal Father will be more and more fond of the church and, *when* we knock it down, we'll spite him even more.'

Also, having a church, they could fight with the parish priest and this was a very important thing in their lives.

'Even more than *destroying* the churches,' the leader of the Reds always said, 'what matters is to make people move away from Christianity: in short, to be able to convince people of the falsehoods that the Church has kept in circulation for centuries to keep the people down.'

The leader of the Reds of Cabassa was a big player: an intellectual, someone who had studied at school, then in prison, then abroad and finally he had returned to study at home. He could make two-hour speeches without even taking breath: the people of Cabassa wallowed in it and when he was sent by the Federation to give speeches at neighbouring municipalities, a lot of people on bicycles, even if they had to grind through thirty or forty kilometres, would cycle to join him, to hear him speak, and to shout: '*Bravo, Cisto!*' As happens with football teams.

The boss of the Reds of Cabassa had declared war to the bitter end on the Eternal Father: but he was not one of those who dropped bombs on processions or shot priests in the back.

'We are facing an intelligent and very strong enemy,' Cisto always said. 'Therefore, we must fight with cunning. It's no good saying to a Christian: "You don't have to believe anymore" or "You don't have to go to church anymore". You have to say: "Well done, I'm a Christian like you too and we'll go to church together." Then you take him by the arm and, speaking of Saints and Madonnas, you take him along an alternative path. Along *our way*.'

Christmas was approaching and Cisto held an extraordinary meeting. 'Christmas,' he said, 'is a godsend for priests because everyone falls for the story of Bethlehem and even the most indifferent end up in church for Midnight Mass. This year we need to be strong to prevent this filth from happening again.'

Everyone made his proposal: to set fire to the church, to beat up the parish priest and the faithful, and stuff like that. Cisto shook his head and laughed.

'These are the very things that priests are looking for! The idea of flushing out priests, setting fire to churches, breaking the heads of those who go to church is excellent, but it is to be undertaken in due course, later. Now it is a question of undermining the foundations of the Church, then, when the walls are shaky, it will begin to teeter and everything will come down.

'To prevent people from going to Midnight Mass on Christmas Eve, we must take them by the arm and transport them somewhere else. In short: we will *exalt* the Nativity, but in such a way as to attract the interest and curiosity of the people, and in such a way as to *empty* the Nativity of its traditional meaning.

In the meantime, and first of all, we will set up a 'Christian Brotherhood Committee', which will organise an alfresco 'Sacred Representation'.'

'A parody of Christmas, in short,' someone observed.

'Parody my butt!' Cisto shouted. 'Let's stay cool about parodies! This is serious, frighteningly serious. The secret lies precisely in its seriousness: people must be deceived, find themselves snared without knowing it.'

The chief took a handwritten booklet from an envelope.

'The concept is clear: we do a re-enactment of the Nativity just like the priests do. With precisely the same – identical – elements. However, while the priests demonstrate the Incarnation – the thesis of the son of God becoming man, we will be demonstrating the thesis of the son of man who *makes himself God*! Listen carefully, and I will explain.

'A little set is needed: in the square, in front of Giobini's bombed-out house, we set up a large stage a metre and a half from the ground. The rubble is the backdrop, just add some bits of machinery that we can find easily, because it must represent a factory in ruins.

'A flagpole is planted on top, a large pole painted black to blend in with the night. A wire is to be fixed between the top of the flagpole and the roof of Brelli's house, which is one of ours. All the lights are out. Spotlights and sound system we have. And the band for the finale. In short, all the stuff we need exists or we can get together in two days flat.'

Cisto opened the booklet and began to read.

PART ONE
At the appointed time the band strikes up with a sacred, non-political hymn at the top of the main road into the square. People stretch out along each side of the road. When the music stops, the Holy Family appears: two peasants dressed as St Joseph and the Madonna. The Madonna is on a donkey and St Joseph pulls the donkey behind him. Thanks to an agreement with the mayor, all the street lights will be out and a spotlight will illuminate Joseph and Mary. The spot is installed on the soundtrack truck, which will make its way slowly ahead of the Holy Family. The truck is connected with two wires to two microphones: one

fixed on the donkey's head, which serves Joseph. The other fastened to the folds of the Madonna's mantle, close to her mouth, which serves comrade Maria. The action begins: Joseph halts the donkey in front of a house.

JOSEPH: (*shouting in a tired voice*) Ohei! Good people! Will you grant a little rest and a little shelter to a poor suffering mother?'
No one answers and then St Joseph resumes his journey and shortly afterwards stops in front of another house. Again no one listens to him. Our Lady sighs.
MADONNA: (*sighing*) 'It is useless, comrade Joseph, do not worry yourself! They have ears and do not hear, they have eyes and do not see... It is useless to knock on the doors of the rich! Shut up in their lukewarm homes, they happily feast on rare foods and exquisite wines and do not care for the suffering of the people!'
JOSEPH: 'You're right, comrade Maria. But I have not yet lost faith in mankind and I still believe that some doors will open: the rich may be wicked, but there'll be some poor people in this country.'
MADONNA: 'Yes, comrade Joseph, there are poor people all over the world: poor slaves, but they groan in prisons or sleep in horrendous underground cellars and cannot hear our voice!'

PART TWO
Joseph resumes his journey and every now and then he stops and knocks on the doors of the rich, but no one answers. Meanwhile the people, moving around, follow the story with interest. So, all arrive in the square. The square is dark, the spotlight scans across the rubble of the ruined factory. Joseph, Mary and the donkey go up a slope next to the stage and stop in amongst the rubble of the factory. The Madonna painstakingly dismounts.

JOSEPH: 'Comrade Maria, doesn't it seem strange to you that we, the workers of the earth, have found our only shelter in a factory? Doesn't it seem strange to you that we, rooted in Mother Nature, end up here, alienated from the land, in the realm of the machine?'
MADONNA: 'No, comrade Joseph. On the contrary, I see a profound meaning in all this: it is like a divine admonition! Worker and peasant (who relies on the worker for protection) must march together, united in comradeship, along the radiant path of proletarian recovery!'
JOSEPH: 'So true, comrade Maria! Only in this way will the workers be able to redeem themselves from slavery! ...But, alas, I don't see any workers here.'
MADONNA: 'They sleep in hovels or moan in prisons.'

JOSEPH: 'See, everything here falls into disrepair: the cars are beaten up and filthy!'
MADONNA: 'It is the nefarious policy of the tyrant Herod that has led to the ruination of national industry by his throwing the workers out on the street! ...But, comrade Joseph! There is a shiver running through my bones...' (long groan of pain).

For a moment all the lights go out. While the band silently readies itself to break out with another religious hymn, a big red star with a long tail lights up. It hangs from two small pulleys on the wire stretched between the Brelli house and the flagpole above the factory. Slowly, it makes its way towards the factory. Suddenly the lights come up again and the Madonna appears holding the Child Jesus in her arms. A microphone has been affixed to the neck of the Child Jesus, so that Our Lady, skilfully disguising her voice, can speak as if the Child Jesus were speaking.

The red star stops above the factory. The three Magi make their way up the slope: the first is in a car, he is fat and has a tuba on his head and represents Capitalism. The second travels on foot under a canopy carried by four thin and ragged wretches: he is fat, dressed as a high priest, and he represents Clericalism. The third rides in a car disguised as a tank carrying the American star and the initials USA. Militarism is fat and dressed as a general.

Capitalism advances, kneels before the Child and offers him a bag.

CAPITALISM: 'I am Capitalism and I bring you gold to make you rich, oh my God!'
JESUS: 'No thanks, I don't want it! Your gold is tainted with the blood of others! It is stolen from the working people and I cannot be your God!'
(*Clericalism advances and offers a censer.*)
CLERICALISM: 'I am Clericalism and I bring you incense to honour you, oh my God!'
JESUS: 'Take it away: your smoke only serves to cloud the eyes of the people and I cannot be your God!'
(*Militarism advances, kneels and hands a machine gun to Jesus.*)
MILITARISM: 'I am Militarism and I bring you a machine gun so that you can be powerful, oh my God!'
JESUS: 'No, such are the weapons used to tear the flesh of my people and I cannot be your God! Get out! Get out! Away from my presence!'
(*The three so-called Magi go away in shame, and here comes a small group of poor people: women, men, children.*)

WORKER: (*handing his baby to Jesus*) 'Only this have I to offer, comrade Jesus. And I offer him to you!'
WORKER: (*showing his calloused hands*) 'Here is my only wealth, comrade Jesus: my labour. And I offer it to you.
WIDOW OF WAR: 'I have only my pain, comrade: and I offer it to you.'
YOUNG TB PATIENT: 'I have only hope, comrade, and offer it to you!'
POLITICAL PRISONER: 'And I offer you my sufferings and my long years in prison!...'
INTELLECTUAL (*handing Jesus a large book by Karl Marx and one by Lenin*) 'And *I* offer you my study!...'
(*Others follow to make their offerings and eventually the Child Jesus is moved to exclaim.*)
JESUS: 'Yes, comrades! These are the gifts of the heart and I accept them. I accept your sufferings, your hopes, your pains, and I will keep them all here, in the red casket of my heart, and I will think only of your good, oh comrades! Yes, I am and will be your God!'
(*A mighty voice rises, a voice like a hurricane.*)
HURRICANE VOICE: 'Arise, brothers! Arise! The Son of the People is born! The Son of the People was born!'
(*The Holy Family is eclipsed by shadow: slowly, the spotlight rises to illuminate a huge image of Josef Stalin silhouetted against the sky, while the loud cry continues to rise from within the crowd: 'The Son of the People is born!'*)
The band strikes up with the Workers' Anthems, The Internationale and then The Red Flag, while above the tail of the big red star appear two luminous words: 'Read l'Unità![117]

PART THREE
Preceded by the band two workers in blue overalls but with silver wings, holding a large scroll with the inscription: 'Peace to the workers!', lead the procession. Behind them come St Joseph and the Madonna on the donkey with the Child in her arms. Behind them, children, each with a white lily in its hand. And finally the workers carrying flags.

The Boss, when he had finished reading from his booklet, wiped away the sweat from his brow.
 'Well, comrades, what do you think?'
 'Extraordinary!' they shouted, clapping their hands.
 Cisto was satisfied.

---

[117] The official newspaper of the Italian Communist Party.

'Thus is intelligent propaganda enabled,' he explained. 'Take all the elements of your opponent's propaganda and, with slight, almost imperceptible changes, give it a different interpretation. In this case, without altering historical truth even by an inch and without ever falling into irreverence, we have quietly democratised Christmas!'

'There you go! In a nutshell!' the deputy chief exclaimed in admiration.

'That's how to screw the priests!' Cisto concluded.

The next day they went straight to work. They distributed scripts, began to collect the props and to make propaganda. Thirty rehearsals were undertaken in the People's Palace. And so Christmas Eve came and people were dying of curiosity because of all the preparations.

Ten minutes before the parish priest began Midnight Mass, the band played the religious (non-political) anthem and the lights went out. A spotlight flashed and Joseph appeared at the head of the road, followed by Mary on the donkey. It was really a beautiful effect.

When Joseph stopped in front of the first house and his words were heard through the loudspeaker, the people held their breath. Excellent! Success also at the second stop. At the third, when Our Lady observed with pain that it is useless to knock on the houses of the wealthy because the poor can never find anything in the homes of those who are well off, a window of the house in front of which St Joseph had stopped opened and the powerful voice of old Cibacca, the owner of the largest farm in Cabassa, was heard:

'You're right! You are right! In the houses of the gentlemen there are only selfish pigs, but not in all of them! In the Cibacca house there is always a glass of wine and a slice of good grace for all ye merry gentlemen. Mariòla! Francis! Bring fifty bottles of Albana up from the cellar!'[118]

At that time old Cibacca had the only Albana in the whole Municipality! And fifty bottles of it were enough to make an entire province prick up its ears.

'*Bene! Viva Cibacca!*' St Joseph shouted as he hurried into the hallway of Cibacca's residence, followed by his donkey and the Madonna.

Ciro began to scream, but they shut his mouth with a flurry of six glasses of Albana, which they made him swallow one immediately

---

[118] Albana is a white Italian wine grape planted primarily in the Emilia-Romagna region.

after the other. Then they came up with slices of cake that looked just like what he'd want.

Capitalism, Clericalism, Militarism, the proletariat, the victims of the plutocracy, the intellectual with the books of Marx and Lenin, they all forgot everything before the altar of Albana. The Son of the People clung to a piece of cake and never moved.

Then an accordion arrived and the Madonna began to dance with Capitalism.

The donkey, kicked out by old Cibacca, returned home slowly shaking his head. Meanwhile, in the church full of lights and song, people were looking at the other Nativity scene, the un-democratised one, with the usual silver star and the usual angels in white shirts and not in blue overalls.

That is the story of Cabassa.

In the second Christmas story to appear in *Candido* in 1948, 'Appointment at Midnight',[119] we find the same communist antipathy to Christmas as in 'Comrade Gesù', but this time Giovanni transports us to a mind-set that will resolve the conflict by drawing on the one positive note in his experience of the war, so tragically absent in the *Dopoguerra* – that feeling of *belonging* he experienced with his comrades in the *Lagers* after his awakening.

A feeling of at-oneness, deep down beneath the politics and rhetoric, greed, anger and ignorance that had led to war, was experienced also among the many disparate groups brought together in the Italian Resistance by their common purpose to resist the Nazis. And in 'Appointment at Midnight' Giovanni reveals Don Camillo as a wartime member of the Resistance alongside Peppone and Smilzo, 'an honourable past of days of faith, hope, and self-sacrifice', as ever the memory that kept the path to conciliation open between his two main protagonists.

In their mountain hideaways the Italian Resistance had been a potential tinderbox of internecine political rivalries – communists, socialists, liberals, Christian Democrats, Catholics, monarchists, republicans, anarchists, Yugoslavs, Russians, Ukrainians, Dutch, Spaniards, Greeks, Poles, Germans disillusioned with National Socialism, Britons and Americans (ex-prisoners or advisors deployed by the SAS, SOE and OSS)), former officers of the Royal Italian Army, and priests. Their unity cannot have sat well with the Reds' subsequent violent purges in Emilia.

First published in *Candido* on December 26th, the attack mentioned at the start of the story was made, in fact, on Palmiro Togliatti, leader of the PCI (the Italian Communist Party). It almost led to an armed communist insurrection.

---

[119] *Don Camillo Takes the Devil by the Tail* (Pilot, 2020).

The whole thing began one day back in July, 1948, when Peppone and his gang appeared in full force at the presbytery.

'I want a *Te Deum*!' Peppone shouted. 'A public thanksgiving. They shot our Leader!'

Don Camillo feigned concern. 'I do understand,' he said calmly, 'but I don't see why we should hold a service of thanksgiving just because a poor devil has been shot. Say what you like, he was a human being.'

Peppone clenched his fists.

'We want to give thanks because they *failed* to assassinate him! And don't try to be funny, because we're in a state of national emergency. So, here's the plan. You organise the *Te Deum*, complete with music, singing, flowers, curtains, lighting effects, and bells, and announce it by means of a poster with an angel on either side on the church door. Meanwhile we'll print leaflets and put them prominently on display. Then we'll see who shows up. Everyone who fails to show is by definition a filthy reactionary. We'll take down their names and then go from house-to-house and give all of them the Bassa massage.'

'Well said, Boss,' Smilzo solemnly affirmed. 'We must first identify and then punish all those guilty of provocative conduct. The people have had enough!'

Don Camillo looked over at him.

'Are you going to make up a list of names?' he asked.

'Of course,' said Smilzo.

'Then put me at the top of the list for the massage, because I won't be at the service of thanksgiving.'

Peppone pushed his hat back on his head and put his hands on his hips.

'So, you refuse to thank the Almighty publicly for having saved the skin of a victim of a criminal attack, is that it?'

'No. I refuse to hold a religious service that will provide you and your gang of delinquents with a pretext to beat up innocent people. If you really want to thank the Almighty, come with your friends and

I'll celebrate a Mass, just as I did yesterday when Gigino Forcella fell off the roof. Nothing special was done for him.'

Peppone brought his fist down on the table.

'The people want a solemn ceremony, a *Te Deum*, I tell you, not just an everyday Mass. This is not an ordinary episode like what befell Gigino Forcella. This is a significant incident of at least national significance!'

'Every good Christian should rejoice when his neighbour has escaped danger,' said Don Camillo. 'But on your reasoning, if, as you say, your Leader deserves a *Te Deum* for "a significant incident" what should Gigino Forcella's family expect for a wholly insignificant one, poor fellow!'

Peppone's face looked like an advertisement for apoplexy.

'Tagliatti is not Gigino Forcella,' screamed Peppone. 'Gigino doesn't interest anyone outside his own family. Our Leader is of universal importance.'

Don Camillo was not impressed.

'Your leader cares about his family like Gigino Forcella cares about his. The only difference is that Gigino Forcella has a family made up of a few people, while Tagliatti has a family made up of a few million people. It's a big family, but it's a family, not the whole nation. Now, if you, or your leader's family, want me to say a special Mass,' he continued. 'I'd be glad to oblige them. But in view of the threats you made a few minutes ago it will have to be a purely family affair. I don't want to see any of your gang in church and I forbid anyone other than family to enter. I forbid it and I must forbid it because I cannot make myself an accomplice in your damned game of reprisals and violence. People must come to church of their own free will, not because the head of a party orders it, or because he is afraid of reprisals.

'The Church cannot be exploited for political propaganda purposes.'

Smilzo pulled the visor of his cap around to one side, put his hands on his hips and looked up at Don Camillo. 'Look who's talking!' he said with a leer. 'If there happened to be a God, he'd freeze you to the ground for your shamelessness.'

As for Peppone, he was bursting with things to say, but didn't know where to begin.

'You ... Judas!' he shouted. 'You've sold Christ for thirty American dollars!'

'Don't pay him any attention, Boss,' Smilzo begged him. 'Certain people can't be treated any other way.'

He took a notebook out of his pocket, licked the point of his pencil and wrote something down.

'Don Camillo,' he said. 'Exclamation point! Now that you're on my list, not even the Almighty can save you!'

And Peppone added: 'Keep your *Te Deum*s and your Masses as well. The Party has no use for your Madonna and saints. And here's what I'll do to the next Party member that sets foot in your church!'

So saying, he picked up a chair and crushed the backboard of it in his hands, looking straight into Don Camillo's eyes.

'Mind you get it mended now,' Don Camillo said calmly.

Peppone made no reply, but turned on his heels, and left, followed by his gang, who slammed the door behind them. A moment later, Smilzo came back with a defiant look on his face, picked up the chair and bore it away. He held his head high and his chest out, and he strutted as triumphantly as if he represented the inevitable onward march of the proletarian revolution.

*

Don Camillo got his chair back, but he saw no more of Peppone and Peppone's followers and their families in the church again.

Three months later, Bigio had a baby, but as he was a Party member the question of a baptism never came up. Whenever Bigio saw the priest coming he avoided him, but one evening Don Camillo managed to collar him.

'If it's Party orders that stop you coming to church, it'll pass in time. Meanwhile, you have to think about your son's soul. Let him come at least once, to be baptised... Or has he already joined the Party?'

Bigio, who was the most reasonable of the gang, spread his arms.

'Father, the ban applies to the whole family: no-one is allowed to set foot in the church again,' he said. 'If the Boss were to know that I'd had my baby baptised he'd take me apart.'

'Peppone needn't know,' Don Camillo suggested.

That same night the baby was brought to him and was secretly baptised. This was all Don Camillo managed to achieve, but he was not discouraged.

'Lord,' he said to Christ above the high altar, 'I'm waiting for Christmas. In all the years that I've been here they've never missed Midnight Mass. A few years ago, when Giubai was wanted by the police, even he came on Christmas Eve while he was on the run and I saw him there at the back, in the far corner of the church with his coat collar turned up. Lord, trust me!'

'I've always trusted you,' Christ said to him with a smile, 'but can you trust yourself?'

'Well ... to a certain extent. Although I have more faith in you.'

As Christmas approached, Don Camillo tried to find out which way the wind was blowing, and word came back that the ban was a point of disagreement between husbands and wives, with the wives maintaining that on Christmas Eve, party orders had to be disobeyed. As time went on, discussions became more and more heated, until finally the women took a stand:

'We and our children are going to church; you can do what you please.'

A special meeting was held at the People's Palace. Peppone, who, among other things, had received such a kick in the shins from his wife that he was half crippled, recognised that the insurrection had to be taken seriously, and in the end it was decided: the women and children should be allowed to do what they want. As for the men, they would remain firm in their position. They would not set foot in the church ever again. To demonstrate party discipline and prevent any last-minute weakening, all comrades would meet on Christmas Eve at the People's Palace and demonstrate their opposition to the provocative and reactionary Midnight Mass with a democratic Midnight Cell, that is to say a special solemn meeting of the whole Section with readings of classical texts of the Marxist-Leninist religion and selected passages from such great socialists as Stalin and his ilk.

*

When Christmas Eve came, the candlelit church was filled with song, while on the hard benches of the shabby council chamber in the People's Palace, gloomy men listened in silence to Peppone reading stuff none of them understood. Every now and then, during breaks, the night wind blew a few notes from the church organ across the piazza and came to rest on the closed windows of the place.

The Mass was over early because Don Camillo was nervous. It was like he had a nail stuck in his brain, which stirred and irritated him beyond belief. Left alone in the church, he quickly removed his vestments and bolted the church door. He then walked up and down for a few minutes and brought himself to a halt before the crucified Christ.

'Jesus,' he said, 'did you see who came?'

'Yes, I saw,' Christ answered. 'You trusted in your self too much.'

'No, that isn't it,' said Don Camillo. 'I pinned all my faith on you.'
'And so now you have lost your faith in me.'

'Never!' said Don Camillo indignantly. 'I pinned my faith on Divine Providence and failed to do my bit. It's like someone who is hungry and there is a piece of bread on the table and the man says: "I knew that God would not let me starve," and he stands there without moving a finger. Logically, a man knows that if he doesn't reach out and take the bread, God can't be expected to take the bread and put it in his mouth for him. Rationally, he knows that if the bread does not move towards him, it is he who must move towards the bread. In short, trusting in Divine Providence does not mean giving up on reason. Sacred Scripture confirms it: if the mountain will not come to Jesus, then Jesus must go to the mountain.'

Christ smiled. 'Don Camillo, really the phrase is: "If the mountain will not come to Muhammad, then Muhammad must go to the mountain."'[120]

'Forgive me,' said Don Camillo, mortified, 'believe me, I...'

'There is nothing to forgive, Don Camillo: words are not what count, intention is the thing.'

Don Camillo passed his big hand over his forehead and looked up at the Christ. But he thought of Muhammad, and Christ, who knew it, smiled.

*

'Comrades,' Peppone was saying, 'as a fitting close to this meeting at which we have borne witness to our democratic faith, I shall read you a masterly profile of Mao Tse Tung...'

Just then the door opened wide and in came a powerfully built man in a heavy cloak, who made his way like a tank through the benches on which the men were sitting, went up onto the platform, where Peppone was holding forth, and slammed a grey-green box down upon the speaker's table.

The men in the front rows recognised the box immediately. They had seen it many times in the mountains, when Don Camillo risked German bullets to get up there. Automatically, it brought them to their feet.

Don Camillo lifted the lid of the box and revealed his field altar. Meanwhile, Peppone got up and left the platform.

Don Camillo turned around for a moment and grunted. Then Smilzo climbed the platform steps and came to the priest's side, as he

---

[120] A Turkish proverb, retold by Francis Bacon in *Essays*, Chapter 12.

had done so many times in the old days of the Resistance. He helped Don Camillo into his vestments, lit the candles and, when it was time, knelt one side of the altar to serve him.

It was a simple Mass, military style, almost secretive in character. But they had turned off the lights in the chamber, so that the candles on the little altar alone lit the darkness. And then the notes of the church organ, which earlier had come to rest against the closed windows, came alive once more and there was the distant sound of music in the air.

Christmas 1950

In 1949 the Vatican took a hard line on communism. Stalin had shown his measure in the brutal purges of his party between 1937 and '38: the Gulag had consumed millions of lives, but in February 1948 a communist *coup d'état* in Czechoslovakia by various means took control of the Catholic Church (including its finances). Pope Pius XII responded with a Decree Against Communism: Catholics who professed the Soviet ideology would henceforth be excommunicated. More politics, more conflict, which many feared would provoke the much talked-about '*seconda ondata*', with priests yet again in the firing line. It was the antithesis of Giovanni's approach.

'Christmas 1950' appears here, again in English for the first time, to shine a light on Giovanni's deepest fears for the continuity of the Church: 'A ferocious war of men against their God was taking place.'

This is a strange psychological tale that takes place two days before Christmas and seems to delve into the Italian subconscious. Like his Christmas story written in 1944 in Oflag XB, it features a *Carroccio*, a large four-wheeled wagon around which the militia of Mediaeval comunes gathered and fought. Generally pulled by oxen it carried an altar, a bell, the heraldic signs of the city and a mast surmounted by a Christian cross. Priests celebrated Mass at the altar before a battle, and the trumpeters beside them encouraged the fighters to the fray.

Just before Christmas 1950, half a leg of snow had fallen and it was still falling. Don Camillo had taken out the wooden figurines of the crib to retouch them and, at midnight on the 22nd, he was still there with his brush refreshing faces, cloaks and gilding, with the cat keeping him company.

Being a young cat he was jumping around playing with all the small stuff that came within the compass of his paws. So it happened that at some point Don Camillo, curious of what the cat was doing under the table, noticed that the beast was playing with the figurine of the Child Jesus.

Don Camillo yelled and the cat ran away, holding the statuette in his mouth, whereupon Don Camillo pursued him and let fly with a slipper to get him to let go.

The priest had kept the figurine of the Child Jesus till last, the better to work on it: he now pulled down the head of the lamp and, after grumbling a little at the cat, began to focus hard on the fine brushwork his job required.

It was then, suddenly, that the little statue of the Child Jesus slipped from his hand and fell to the ground again. Bending down to pick it up, Don Camillo saw that the cursed cat had caught it as before between his teeth.

But looking closer, he noticed a strange thing: this cat wasn't his. It was larger, with two eyes that looked at him in an odd sort of way. In any case the church cat was usually grey and this one was black. Where had the interloper come from?

'Get out of it!' Don Camillo yelled and the cat jumped towards the door, but it didn't let go of the figurine.

Don Camillo ran after him and the black cat ran into the corridor and, finding the front door ajar, slipped away, tail low. There it was, waiting in the churchyard, totally black against the great white pall of the snow.

'Damn you!' shouted Don Camillo, who was immediately out of the door after it, the black cat on its way with the statue of the Child Jesus between its teeth, Don Camillo following on behind.

The beast took the road to the fields, Don Camillo panting in pursuit because the snow was freshly laid and he sank half a leg into it with every step. The black cat, on the other hand, flew across the snow as if it were a feather, every now and then stopping, turning its nose back over its shoulder, waiting for Don Camillo to come within ten metres, and then resuming its run.

And here's the thing: the black cat got bigger and bigger each time it stopped, and the wooden figurine of the Child Jesus also got bigger and bigger, in proportion.

In the time it took for the black beast to become as big as a buffalo, the figurine was already as large as a real baby.

He was indeed a real child, a baby Jesus of pink and living flesh. A baby Jesus who bled and groaned in the fangs of the monstrous black beast. Don Camillo let out a scream of horror and found himself in front of his table, with the statue of the Child Jesus in one hand and his fine paintbrush in the other.

The cat, the usual grey kitten, was back snoozing before the fireplace. It was already four in the morning and the snow was still falling.

Don Camillo went to take time out in the church.

'Jesus,' he said, kneeling before the Crucified Christ above the main altar, 'I had a strange dream.'

And he told *il Cristo* his dream of the black cat becoming a huge monster and the figurine becoming a real Baby Jesus, bleeding and groaning in the beast's fangs.

'Jesus,' he concluded, 'that dream disturbed me.'

Christ smiled:

'Don Camillo: it is not the dream that troubled you. It is the thought that caused you to dream the dream that disturbed you. A thought that you have within you, a product of your reasoning, the substance of which you explained to yourself in a dream as a sort of allegorical moral fable.'

'Jesus,' Don Camillo exclaimed, 'I understand that dream as an omen, a supernatural warning.'

'It is not an omen, Don Camillo: it is not a warning voiced from outside. It is a voice that comes from within. It is the voice of your fear.'

Don Camillo spread his arms:

'Jesus, I am not afraid!'

'Yes, Don Camillo: you are afraid. But not for yourself. You are afraid for me. You are afraid that men may harm God. One can deny the existence of the sun. One can persecute those who affirm the existence of the sun. It is also possible to make sure that no one sees the sun any more by tearing out the eyes of all creatures, but it will not be possible to extinguish or even just dim the light of the sun. For this reason: men can only harm themselves; they cannot harm God. But I do not reproach you for this fear of yours, because it is nothing but a sign of the immense love you have for me.'

*

Don Camillo went to bed and the little women who came for the morning Mass and found the church door closed, woke him up.

Don Camillo dipped his face into a basin of cold water and ran out to the church.

'It's late, I'm sorry,' he explained to the little women gathered in front of the presbytery door. 'I don't know how this happened to me. The bell ringer didn't come back last night: he got stuck in the city in the snow. '

The grey kitten rubbed against his leg and Don Camillo shivered. He headed for the church, but at that moment there was a crash.

'The roof of the church is falling apart!'

The ridge of the roof had slipped from the horizontal, the ridge had dropped half a metre towards the west end. Some of the beams must have given way, someone said, but Gray, the master builder, came forward and, considering the matter, shook his head.

'Nothing is broken,' he said. 'The main ridge beam rests at one end on the top of the end wall of the church and, at the other, on the collar tie of a truss. The weight of the snow unlatched the struts from the two ends of the collar tie. The struts now rest on the tie, but so long as the rafters of the truss don't come loose from one another, there is no danger.'

It was a complicated way of saying a simple thing: but that being as it may, there was a second crash and the ridge of the roof sank lower still.

'The tie beam broke,' said Brusco. 'Now the weight is all on the vault, the lower third of the truss: if the vault gives way at Mass this morning, the roof goes.'

Don Camillo, who had been watching in dismay, thought of the altar, the Tabernacle, the Crucified Christ.

'Don't be silly!' they shouted at him. But by now he had opened the door of the church and marched in.

But then an imperious voice was heard:

'Stop, Don Camillo!'

And Don Camillo stood at the door for a moment and, just in that instant, the vault gave way and the church was filled with bricks, beams, tiles and snow.

Between where he stood and the altar Don Camillo found a mountain of rubble cemented by snow: but the altar was still there, intact, because the domed ceiling above it had not moved.

He looked up and saw only snow falling from the great rectangle of sky that now stood in place of his church ceiling.

Don Camillo thought of the black cat and could not understand how the black cat in the snow that had made the roof collapse came into it.

The whole countryside, so it seemed, came to see the ruined church; Don Camillo seemed also to be a ruin. For an hour after the fall he was still motionless looking at the pile of rubble in amazement. The snow had piled up on his shoulders and it wasn't possible to be sure whether Don Camillo's face was wet because the snow was melting on his face, or because he was crying.

Suddenly, his gaze, hitherto occupied by the mountain of rubble as a whole, concentrated on a detail of the pile before him.

Then, with a leap, he was on the heap and, grabbing a large beam, shook it and pulled at it until he was able to dig it out of the tangle.

People stepped forward.

'It's the collar tie beam of the truss,' said Bigio. 'Actually, it's half the beam of the collar tie.'

Then he fell silent, perplexed: even a blind eye could have seen that the beam of the collar tie had been sawn half way across and the cut was fresh.

The beam was not sawn through: just three-quarters sawn. The other piece was split.

Don Camillo thought again of the black cat and still felt that his eye was looking at something that he could not fully see.

Then he saw, in the snow mixed with the rubble, the missing link.

And then they all jumped on the heap and started pulling stuff away. After an hour of furious work they found the man who had stained the snow with his blood. Next to him, a saw.

The man lay face down, dead and withered away, his face buried in the rubble. And no one had the courage to turn him over to see who he was, because everyone was afraid that they would know him.

The Marshal of the *carabinieri* did what needed to be done. He also took out the pieces of the beam and studied the cut.

'He'd thought of cutting three-quarters of the tie before leaving, and banked on the increasing weight of the snow doing the rest. He hadn't noticed that the beam had a crack just below the cut, and so everything collapsed before he could get safely out. It was probably a surprise prepared specially for Christmas Day.'

The Marshal didn't say who the guy was that had come down with the roof.

'He's one that we know, one of those who work for peace,' he merely explained.

On the evening of December 23, Don Camillo realised, with immense dismay, that the following evening was Christmas Eve:

'Where will I say Midnight Mass?'

*

And the evening of Christmas Eve came and Don Camillo's people were all locked up in their houses because Fear was howling from the rubble of the church, buried in the darkness of tragedy.

All around the region looked like it was still at war: and a ferocious war of men against their God was indeed in train, while a monstrous black cat was galloping throughout the deserted fields, holding a little statue of the Child Jesus in its fangs.

A horrendous silence fell over the village because it was a wonderful clear night and the immaculately white snow covered the black earth.

Who would break the crystal of that unbearable silence?

Suddenly, the church bells were heard and, shortly after, an unusual light appeared at one end of the long road at the edge of which rows of village houses were aligned.

On a chariot paved with damask, and pulled by eight pairs of white oxen, was an altar, surmounted by the great *Cristo Crocifisso* from the village church. And Don Camillo celebrated Mass in front of the altar.

At the sides of the chariot and behind it was a group of singers, men and women, with flaming torches.

People looked out, left their houses and, as the *Carroccio* advanced, they queued. The *Carroccio* made its way slowly along the long main road, then entered upon the secondary roads and, from every farmyard, people went out and joined the parade.

Then came the return and pause for the Elevation in the crowded village square.

'Brothers and sisters!' said Don Camillo, 'the peaceful army of Christ, tightened around its *Carroccio*, has won the battle against fear tonight. The House of God is the boundless universe, its roof the immense, starry sky. And no one will be able to make that collapse. Do not think about the roof of your church: look at that eternal and infinite sky and sing the praises of the Lord with joy.'

Don Camillo said this and more and serenity returned to the hearts of the people.

People accompanied the *Carroccio* right in front of the church. Here someone shouted that it was time to think about putting everything straight, and placed money on the platform of the great chariot.

And then all passed by the *Carroccio* and gave their offering. Don Camillo had come down and, leaning against the chariot, was looking at the parade with a smile. Among the last to come by, a child, two or three spans tall, couldn't reach to put his money on the platform of the *Carroccio*. And so Don Camillo lifted him up.

It was Peppone's son and Don Camillo looked at him with anguish, thinking of the monstrous black cat that had held the *Bambinello* in its jaws.

He then put the boy down.

Don Camillo had himself brought the Crucified Christ and put it in place.

'Jesus,' he'd said, climbing over the pile of rubble, to the high altar, 'the other night, after I was speaking to you, a man above my head was sawing through the beam supporting the roof of your church. What if you hadn't told me – 'Stop!' I would have been buried alive in all this rubble.'

'Why, Don Camillo, are you still talking about beams and roofs, when you yourself said a little while ago that the real roof of the House of God has no beams and no one can make it collapse?'

Don Camillo looked up. And beheld the great rectangle of starry sky.

Christmas 1952

Following his response to the Vatican's aggressive challenge to communism, Giovanni deemed it time to iterate ever more clearly the beautiful inner self he had uncovered in the *Lagers*. In *Don Camillo and Peppone* (1951) came stories such as 'When the Rains Came' and 'The Right Bell', where Don Camillo is possessed of an inner motion of the spirit – 'a sweet feeling', as he refers to it – that spreads into the hearts of his people, who have fled the flood from the Great River, which threatens the village, but who can still see a light in the presbytery and hear the church bell. And we watch as increasingly this presence is unearthed even in the heart of the declared atheist Peppone, who feels the need to hide from his communist gang members a growing tendency to grasp things in a divine way.

The theme – the extent to which such a spirit may be immanent within, however determined we may be not to let it act upon us – is explored, too, in the dextrously devised 'Soul Trader' (1952), where the fieriest of Peppone's godless gang questions the existence of the soul, but sells his to a believer.

And what we see in 'The Light That Would Not Go Out' and 'Christmas 1952' (excerpted, as one, here)[121] is that this transcendental presence is always there in every person's soul; it is just a matter of lifting the veil on it, while Christmas is the time for its unveiling. In these stories Giovanni emphatically embraces the sense of transcendent mystery which, with St Paul, first gave the Christian Church its impetus:

It was Lungo (who was fresh from a course of political indoctrination in the city), who said: 'Let's get straight to work and start to dismantle the sentimental stranglehold these priests have over the people.'

He then set out his plan.

'The sentimental stranglehold begins with Christmas. When Christmas comes round everyone is happy to give something to the local priest. There's no need to go to church, just make sure that the priests who have invented Christmas eat a little better. At Christmas

---

[121] *Don Camillo's Dilemma* (Pilot, 2019).

even the strongest and hardest of us falls into the emotional trap they lay for us – the kid who recites the poem and puts the letter under the plate, the crib, the greeting cards, the snow, the little angels, the church organ in the night, the memories of childhood... In short, it is all a performance that can make us forget the reality and believe their Christmas story. We must respond and go on the counterattack!'

Peppone spread his arms: 'All right, but we can't hope to be able to force people to change their age-old customs.'

'But we can begin the work by forcing ourselves not to fall into their trap anymore. To drive the poison out of the masses we must first drive it out of ourselves. I've already started.'

Peppone, Bigio, Brusco, Smilzo and the others of the General Staff looked uncertainly at Lungo.

Lungo was Keeper of the People's Palace. He lived with his wife in three small rooms on the first floor of the building and his private life could not be more transparent to those who frequented the place.

'Anyone who has a mind to will be able to check that Christmas at the People's Palace has been abolished this year,' Lungo declared. 'Everything will go on as it would on any other day. If you want to take the idea into your own homes, it'll be the same thing.'

Bigio sighed.

'Difficult to convince the women.'

'No,' said Lungo, who had evidently prepared himself on the subject, 'the difficulty is to convince oneself: once one has succeeded in convincing oneself, it will be only too easy to convince others. Of course, in order to convince oneself one has to have clear ideas.'

Peppone cut in and exclaimed:

'We already have clear ideas and we will pass them on to others. Lungo is right! All begin from this moment the work of persuading our comrades. Work gracefully, without ever forcing your hand. Especially when it comes to those with elderly relatives at home. Our effort to democratise Christmas will be the first step in our breaking the sentimental stranglehold of the priests on the people!'

Peppone was enthusiastic, and the idea grew on him. As soon as he got home he began dismantling the sentimental stranglehold on his wife.

'From this year, Christmas no longer exists,' he said, and his wife asked him if he was drunk with wine or spirits. But Peppone showed her that his head was full of much more toxic fumes than either. The woman spread her arms wide and said:

'Okay, fine, no Christmas. And Easter?'

'Every fruit has its season,' replied Peppone. 'Let's start by abolishing Christmas from the calendar.'

Peppone threw himself into the secularisation programme with gusto. His wife tried a few times to get him to change course, but since it only served to aggravate the situation, she eventually gave up.

On the evening of Christmas Eve itself, the Mayor came home and found everything in the most squalid state of normality – the table with the stained tablecloth, the soup trapped under a layer of lard, and the usual smell of omelette with onions.

When the evening should end had even been planned: 'At eight o'clock everyone to bed,' Peppone commanded. 'And go to sleep without making noise!'

He turned on his younger boy, the seven-year-old:

'Especially *you*!'

Peppone ate his soup in silence and when he had finished made to remove his plate, realising just in time that it concealed evidence of an early betrayal.

He felt the wide-eyed little boy's stare upon him, and clenched his teeth. Putting the plate down again he drank a glass of wine and, throwing his napkin on the table, stood up.

'Don't you want the omelette?' his wife asked him in amazement.

'No!' replied Peppone grimly. 'I'm not hungry anymore. And I have things to do.'

He went out quickly, throwing his cloak around him, striding through the deserted streets.

In the other houses people were about to sit down at table. He thought with pride at the abomination of a dinner table he'd just left. His appointment at the People's Palace was for eight. He arrived a quarter of an hour early and finding the ground floor in darkness he went up to the first floor, where Lungo lived. He found the man, his wife and their boy still at dinner – another sad table, same as any weekday.

'How's it going?' Lungo asked Peppone, pouring him a glass of wine.

'Fine,' replied Peppone. 'My wife played along perfectly ... but there was one slight problem.'

Peppone chuckled and put his mouth to Lungo's ear.

'The little boy managed to slip the letter under my plate.'

'What did you do?'

'I realised he'd done it when I was about to lift up the empty soup plate. I put the omelette down on it, got up and left.'

Lungo laughed.

'I have the one boy and my wife has been able to watch his every move. With great grace I explained how things are. He's a kid who understands things.'

The others were now heard arriving downstairs, and Peppone and Lungo went down.

'Don't wait for me, I'll be late back,' said Lungo to his wife.

'We're off to bed straight away,' the woman replied. 'Even the kid is sleepy.'

They found Smilzo and Bigio on the ground floor.

'I think we should start the tour right away,' said Peppone. 'We'll do a little inspection of all the houses where people agreed to commit themselves to the programme. Let's see who's stepped out of line.'

Brusco lived in a small, isolated house outside the village. When Peppone, Lungo and the other two arrived, there was no light to be seen in any of the windows.

Brusco came to the door half-naked.

'I had a fight with the women,' he confessed very sadly. 'In the end we all went to bed without eating anything. I'm a little sorry for my wife, who is not very well.'

Lungo stepped in:

'Things are done or not done. If you do not do them, then regret nothing.'

'I don't regret anything,' said Brusco. 'But if my wife has a fever, I can hardly be happy about it. However, the important thing is that everything has been done as agreed.'

The inspection continued. Peppone, Lungo, Bigio and Smilzo had to go a-knocking on only ten doors, as the first sentimental detoxification programme had been restricted to a tight circle of the most loyal. Everywhere they found the houses already in darkness, or people accustomed to reading a newspaper at that time of day, sitting doing so in front of the remains of a sad looking dinner.

The last house visited was that of Falchetto. This stood at the end of the village, across the embankment, towards the river: when the bell tolled to call the Catholic faithful to midnight Mass, Peppone and the other three found themselves walking slowly along the embankment road.

'We can truly be satisfied with the result,' said Lungo. 'And it's very important that this little programme was successful because we are now on the way to making the grand plan a reality. When you want to demolish a wall, the important thing is the removal of the first brick.'

They had arrived at the old sewer and sat on the shoulder of the bridge above it.

'It's extraordinary,' said Peppone. 'The simple fact of considering this evening as if it were any other was enough to impress on me the idea that Christmas never existed. It showed me that if you fail to free yourself from sentimentality you will never understand what's true and what's make-believe.'

Smilzo lit a cigarette.

'Of course it's a strange business,' he said. 'One waits for Christmas as it were for the arrival of someone who knows something important. Now, all of a sudden, we realise that Christmas is a day like any other. It does disappoint.'

'Next year you will not experience any disappointment,' said Lungo, 'because now that you can see Christmas for what it is, you will not anticipate it in the way you have this year. The essential in dispelling these sentimental illusions is to *break the chain*.'

They started walking slowly toward the village: it was now close to midnight and the piazza was deserted because those who wanted to attend Mass were already inside the church.

As the People's Palace hove into view, Peppone exclaimed:

'What's up there?'

Everyone looked up and saw a light in one of the windows in the attic. Then it went off, only to light up again shortly afterwards. This was repeated several times.

Lungo looked concerned:

'The key to the top floor is hidden in a place that only I know of. Nobody in my family has ever gone up there.'

They left Bigio to keep watch in the lobby and went up the stairs on tiptoe. The door of the attic was ajar and a shaft of light spilled intermittently onto the floor outside.

Someone was evidently searching for who knows what.

Peppone, Lungo and Smilzo remained in ambush, holding their breath: then, when the nearby bell tower began to beat the first strokes of midnight, they slipped inside the attic room and pressed themselves against the wall, keeping in the shadows.

At the twelfth stroke the light came on and did not go out any more.

It was a small light, a little bulb that lit up the inside of a tiny, shelter or hut sitting on an old chest.

And standing beside it was Lungo's little boy.

The boy stood there mesmerised for about ten minutes and he would still be there if Bigio had not made a noise downstairs, where he was still on guard. At this the boy ran past Peppone and the other two without seeing them and disappeared, whereupon the three men, still well wrapped up against the night, emerged from the shadows and went to stand in front of the hut, each with his hat placed on his chest.

'I wonder whether Don Camillo knows about this,' Peppone muttered. 'A secret nativity scene... Takes one back to the period of the catacombs... Imagine for a moment what a hell of a life it would have been.'

Lungo looked forlorn.

'As children they filled our brains with these tales,' he whispered. 'It is not possible to change the mentality at a stroke... But I would like to know who gave him that stuff.'

Peppone bent to look more closely at the manger scene: 'Nobody,' he explained. 'They are painted earthen figurines. You do them yourself. And they are done well. The boy is not stupid.'

Lungo looked silently down at the little figures in the nativity scene. Then, with a slap of his great paw, swept them all away to fly against the wall.

But the light remained lit over that deserted and devastated scene.

People came out of the church and filled the piazza with happy voices. Peppone goggle-eyed with astonishment at what Lungo had done, which had landed him on the floor, quickly swept past him to reach the door, followed by Smilzo.

Lungo remained where he was, fixated by that light which would not go out.

*

After dashing out of the People's Palace on Christmas Eve without so much as a glance at Bigio, who had been waiting for him at the door, Peppone hurried home, avoiding the main square so as not to run into the crowd returning from Midnight Mass. Smilzo trailed after him in more disciplined style, but got no reward for his pains, because Peppone slammed the front door of his house in his face without so much as a goodnight.

He was dead tired and lost no time in falling into bed.

'Is that you?' asked his wife.

'Sure,' mumbled Peppone. 'Who do you expect it to be?'

'There's no telling,' she retorted. 'With the new directive you've just announced, I wouldn't be surprised if you let some official of your Party into bed with me.'

'Don't be silly,' said Peppone. 'I'm not in a joking mood.'

'Neither am I after this very uninspiring Christmas Eve. You wouldn't even look at the letter your son left under your plate. And before he stood up on a chair to recite the Christmas poem he learned in school you ran away. What have children to do with politics, anyhow?'

'Let me sleep, will you?' shouted Peppone angrily.

His wife stopped talking, but it took Peppone a long time to fall asleep. Even after he finally dozed off, he found no peace, for the most bizarre dreams assailed him, the kind of nightmares that go with indigestion or worry. He woke up while it was still dark, jumped out of bed, and got dressed without putting on the light. And while he dressed he kept thinking about the ham-handed way Lungo had smashed his son's nativity scene against the wall, and the light that would not go out. It seemed that this was all part of a dream he'd just had and yet it was no dream at all.

He went down to the kitchen to heat some milk and found the table set just the way it had been the evening before. The soup bowl was still there and he lifted it up to look for the little boy's letter, but it was gone. He looked at the dirty tablecloth and the leftovers from the omelette, remembering how his wife used to decorate the table on past Christmas Eves. It hurt him to think of Christmases past when he was a boy ... and of his father and mother.

Suddenly a vivid memory came to him of Christmas 1944, which he had spent in the mountains, crouching in a cave in danger of being machine-gunned from one moment to the next. That was a terrible Christmas, indeed, and yet it wasn't anguished as this, because he had thought all day of the good things that went with a peacetime celebration, and the mere thought had warmed his heart.

Now he was in no danger, and his life was going smoothly. His wife and children were there in the next room, and he had only to open the door in order to hear their quiet breathing. But his heart was icy cold at the thought that the festive table would be just as melancholy on Christmas Day as it had been on Christmas Eve.

'And yet that's all there is to Christmas,' he said to himself. 'It's just a matter of shiny glasses, snow-white napkins, roast capons and rich desserts.'

Then he thought again of Lungo's little boy, who had built the secret nativity scene in the attic of the People's Palace, and his directive on Christmas didn't convince him anymore, especially as it was the letter and poem of his own little boy which played on his mind most, and these were in no way reprehensible things compared to the riches of the Christmas table Lungo had decried.

It was starting to grow light as Peppone, swathed in his long black cape, made his way from his house to the People's Palace. Lungo was already up and Peppone was amazed to find him busy sweeping the assembly room.

'Are you at work this early?'

'It's seven o'clock,' Lungo explained. 'On ordinary days I start at eight, but today isn't ordinary.'

Peppone went to his desk and started looking over the mail. There were only a dozen routine letters, and within a few minutes his job was done.

'Nothing important, Boss?' asked Lungo, sticking his head around the door.

'Nothing at all,' said Peppone. 'You can take care of them yourself.'

Lungo picked up the letters and took them away, but came back soon afterwards with one of them in his hands.

'This is important, Boss,' he said. 'It must have escaped your notice.'

Peppone took the letter, looked at it and handed it back.

'Oh, I saw that,' he said; 'there's nothing out of the ordinary about it.'

'But it's a matter of Party membership and you really ought to make an immediate reply.'

'Some other time,' mumbled Peppone. 'This is Christmas.'

Lungo stared at him in a way Peppone didn't like. He got up and stood squarely in front of his subordinate.

'I said it's Christmas, do you not understand?'

'No, I don't,' said Lungo, shaking his head.

'Then I'll explain it to you,' said Peppone, giving him a monumental slap in the face.

Lungo made the mistake of continuing to play dumb, and because he was a strapping fellow, even bigger than Peppone, he gave him back a dose of the same medicine. After which Peppone charged at him like an armoured division, knocking him onto the floor, and proceeded to change the complexion of his hindquarters with a series of swift kicks. When he'd done what he regarded to be a thorough job, he grabbed Lungo by the lapels and asked him:

'Now do you get what I was saying?'

'I get it; today is Christmas,' said Lungo grimly.

'And now go up to the attic and put your boy's nativity scene back in place before anyone sees it. Have you not thought what kind of scary retribution might be in store for us following what happened up there last night?'

'I have thought,' said Lungo, 'and I've already put everything back in place.'

Preceded by Lungo, Peppone went up to the attic to check: and the nativity scene seemed as if it had never been touched. Peppone looked down at it for a few minutes, then mumbled:

'In the end what's wrong if some people choose to believe that a carpenter's son, born 2,000 years ago, went out to preach the equality of all men and to defend the poor against the rich, only to be crucified by the age-old enemies of justice and liberty?'

Lungo nodded his big head.

'Nothing wrong,' he said. 'But people believe that this carpenter's son is actually God. That's the ugly part of it.'

'Ugly?' exclaimed Peppone. 'I think it's beautiful. The fact that God chose a carpenter and not a bourgeois for a father shows that he is democratic.'

Lungo sighed. 'Too bad the priests are mixed up in it,' he said. 'Otherwise it could become something of ours.'

'Exactly! Now you've hit the real point. We must act calmly and keep our heads clear. God is one thing and priests are another. The danger comes not from the existence of God but from the existence of priests. So, we must not eliminate God, but we must eliminate priests. It's the same with wealth and the rich: we must not eliminate wealth, but eliminate the rich and distribute their wealth among the poor.'

Lungo's political indoctrination had not developed his thinking quite that far, and he shook his head in confusion. 'That isn't the basic question. The fact is that God doesn't exist; he's merely an invention of priests. The only things that really exist are those that we can see and touch for ourselves. All the rest is sheer fancy.'

Peppone didn't seem to put much stock by Lungo's thinking, and replied:

'Just because a man is blind does not mean red, green and other colours do not exist in reality. Is it not possible that God exists and you are like the blind man, unable to assert his existence by the sense required to comprehend him?'

This made Lungo even more confused.

'Never mind,' said Peppone abruptly. 'The issue is not one that requires urgent attention. The solution to the problem can be postponed.'

*

Peppone was on his way home when he ran into Don Camillo.

'What can I do for your Éminence Grise?' Peppone enquired gloomily.

'I wanted to offer you my best wishes for Christmas and the New Year,' said Don Camillo politely.

'Me?' Peppone chuckled. 'You send your best wishes to one who has been excommunicated? Well, that's consistent!'

'No more illogical than the care which a doctor gives a sick man. He may quarantine him in order to protect others from his contagious disease, but he continues to look after him. We must hate evil but love the sick.'

'That's a good one!' said Peppone. 'You exclude us and speak of love!'

'No, we'd be very bad physicians of souls if, to destroy the disease, we eliminated those whose souls are affected by it. We treat them lovingly to heal them.'

'Understood: you would like to apply the sort of care you were talking about the other day in the piazza!' replied Peppone.

'I was not speaking about you or people like you,' Don Camillo answered calmly. 'Take typhus by way of a metaphor, the elements to consider in order to eradicate the disease are three: the typhus itself, the infected body lice that carry it, and the suffering patient. In order to eradicate the disease we must treat the patient and eliminate the lice. It would be idiotic to care for the lice and insane to imagine that they could be transformed into something other than a vehicle of contagion. And in this case, Peppone, you are the sick man, not the louse.'

'I'm perfectly well, thank you, Father. You're the sick one, sick in the head.'

'My Christmas wishes come not from my head but from my heart; you can accept them without reservation.'

'No,' said Peppone, 'Heart, brain, spleen or liver, it doesn't matter. That's like saying: "Accept without protest this Navantuno rifle bullet. It's a gift not from the percussion cap but from the barrel."'[122]

Don Camillo spread his arms in dismay.

'God will have mercy on you,' he murmured.

'That may be, but for sure you won't. And come the revolution, no one will save you from hanging from the top of that pole. Do you see it?'

Don Camillo saw it, yes – the flagpole planted on the front of the balcony of the People's Palace. He saw too much of it, because the People's Palace was on the right side of the piazza, and looking through the window of his dining room, Don Camillo never failed to notice that damned flagpole, with its glistening brass

---

[122] A Novantuno is an Italian repeating rifle.

hammer-and-sickle emblem at the top of it standing out against a clear blue sky. It ruined the whole view for him.

'Would I not be a little heavy for your flagpole?' he asked. 'Hadn't you better import some gallows from your Prague friends? Or are those reserved for Party comrades?'[123]

Peppone turned his back and walked away. When he reached his house he called out to his wife, 'I'll be back about one o'clock. Please prepare everything as if it were a normal Christmas.'

'Already done,' she mumbled. 'I was awaiting your countercommand. Stay calm. Be back at midday on the dot.'

Shortly after noon, when he came into the big kitchen, Peppone rediscovered the atmosphere of Christmas past and felt as if he were emerging from a nightmare. The little boy's Christmas letter was under his plate and seemed to him unusually well written. He was ready and eager to hear the Christmas poem, but it did not seem to be quite as forthcoming. Perhaps it would come at the end of the meal, he thought, and continued to eat in happy expectation. But even when dinner was over, the child didn't show the slightest intention of getting up in his chair to declaim some verses in the customary manner.

Peppone looked questioningly at his wife, and the woman shrugged. She whispered something in the little boy's ear and then reported to her husband:

'Nothing doing. He won't say it.'

Peppone had a secret weapon; a box of chocolates which he took from his pocket with the announcement:

'If someone recites a poem, this is his reward!'

The child looked anxiously at the chocolates, but continued to shake his head. His mother parleyed with him again, but brought back the same reply, in the negative. At this point Peppone lost patience.

'If you won't recite the poem, it means you don't know it!' he said angrily.

'I know it, all right,' the child answered, 'but it can't be recited now.'

'Why not?' Peppone shouted.

'Because it's too late. The baby Jesus is already born now, and the poem talks about the child that "must be born tonight".'

---

[123] Reference to the hanging in Prague's Pankrác prison of Rudolf Slánský, one of the leading organisers of Communist rule in Czechoslovakia, at the time (December 1952) that Giovanni was writing this story.

Peppone called for the boy's notebook and found that, sure enough, the poem was all in the future tense. At midnight the stall at Bethlehem would be lit up, the infant would be born and the shepherds would come to greet him.

'But a poem's not like an advertisement in a newspaper,' said Peppone. 'Even if it's a day old it's just as good.'

'No,' the child insisted, 'if baby Jesus was born last night, we cannot talk about him as going to be born tomorrow.'

His mother urged him again, but he would not give in.

'He's stubborn like you,' she finally exclaimed to Peppone.

*

In the afternoon, Peppone took the little boy for a walk and when they were far from the village he made a final attempt to bring him around.

'Now that we're all alone, will you recite the poem?'

'No,' the little boy answered.

'Here, no one will know,' said Peppone.

'But,' the little boy whispered, 'baby Jesus will know.'

And that was the most beautiful poem the little one could have given him. Now Peppone understood and appreciated it with all his heart.[124]

---

[124] From 'The Light that Would Not Go Out' and 'Christmas 1952' *Don Camillo's Dilemma* (1952)

Christmas 1961

In the political arena, disillusion with traditional Christian Democrat values at the ruling party's ideological core had brought it closer to the Socialists, leaving Peppone's Communist party, which had previously been in a block with the Socialists, out in the cold. In 1963 the Christian Democracy Party would form a coalition with the PSI (the Italian Socialist Party), the PSDI (Italian Democratice Socialist Party) and the PRI (Italian Republican Party).

Socialism shares the same stated aim as communism, namely to create an equal society, but unlike the latter's brutal autocratic totalitarian government, it attaches the twin principles of liberty and democracy to its masthead. Don Camillo's anti-socialist stance, revealed in *Don Camillo and Don Chichi* (as well as elsewhere in the stories) at first seems surprising, but in those days of exaggerated revolution he was faced with much that went under the name of socialism that he could not accept, such as that poverty is a virtue akin to authenticity which redeems you from the sin of wealth; that in the party's sacred claims for workers' rights, the employer is always wrong; that those espousing socialism who see it as an ingenious system for not working and making money anyway are within their rights to do so.

What's more, in the Second Ecumenical Council (1962–5), commonly known as Vatican II, he watched the Church making an altogether too desperate appeal to a future generation of churchgoers by taking the same leftwing pathway as the Christian Democrats. The Latin Mass, the standard form since 1570, appeared on the chopping board along with liturgical prayers, east-facing altars, sacred ornamentation, including the huge 3-metre high crucifix of *il Cristo* above the high altar in the village church. In future, the principal focus was to be on pastoral works, with the Good Samaritan as spiritual model.

The dazzling insights of the early Church were becoming muddied by highly developed forms of theology, liturgy and church hierarchy. What of the sense of transcendent mystery? Are not theology, liturgy and pastoral works merely the means and instruments of the Church's striving, rather than what it is striving for? Was the Church losing its heart and soul to community politics?

Don Camillo is an observant Catholic, just as he is a fervent patriot, respectful of the Church's rituals, ceremonies and laws, but against progressiveness for its own sake, especially when it threatens to take the place of God in the soul. For some time there has been pressure from the Bishop for the old reactionary to toe the line and three young, 'bullet-headed', progressive leftwing curates have descended in succession with a mandate to steer Don Camillo into the modern world – Don Camillo digs in.

The first two of these, Don Cesare and Don Guido are introduced in 'The Little Curate' and 'A Work of Art' respectively, both in *Don Camillo and Company*. The third, Don Chichi, a politicised priest who doesn't question his point of view until someone dies because of his near-sightedness and he suffers a breakdown on account of the guilt he feels, is a focus throughout the last collection to be published in Italy in Giovanni's lifetime, *Don Camillo and Don Chichi*. These stories were omitted from publication at the time by the American publisher as being too controversial.

With them, Giovanni looks not only at contemporary change but long into the future, even to the cancel culture of today, in which the so-called free western world is the very breeding ground for domination politics by individuals through social media. Here, in this excerpt from 'The Little Curate', Don Camillo is ill and fancies that everyone is keeping a serious diagnosis a secret.

'If only!' exclaimed Peppone. 'I was merely trying to tell you what everyone in town already knows. You have 'flu, complicated by nervous exhaustion which you inflicted on yourself by rushing around like a madman – pointlessly – during last month's elections.'

Don Camillo shook his head. 'It's not true. If it was, why would they keep me isolated like this, with nobody to talk to?'

'Probably because your condition is more stable when you're silent than when you speak,' stated Peppone.

Don Camillo was suddenly struck by dizziness and his throat felt dry.

'Something to drink, please!' he gasped, letting his head fall back on the pillow.

A moment later, a hand lifted his head, albeit roughly, and another hand brought a glass to his burning lips. He took a long, greedy swallow and immediately felt a surge of heat running from his head to his toes, and the frozen blood in his veins started to thaw. His nerves relaxed and a pleasant confusion numbed his brain.

'What is it?' he asked in a whisper, as his eyes grew heavy.

'A mature rosé. I brought you some in a hipflask. I'll put it here under the bed, beside the little cabinet...'

Don Camillo heard nothing more and plunged into a soft, warm abyss of cotton wool.

*

When he awakened it was already dark. He looked at his alarm clock: after ten. He had slept for twelve hours and it must have been deep because there on the bedside cabinet were the broth and milk for his lunch and dinner.

The house was silent. He pushed his left arm out from the covers and reaching down between the bed and the cabinet, he fished out Peppone's hipflask, hauled it on board and took a long swig.

He found himself standing beside the bed, and his feet supporting him pretty well. His head was no longer spinning either, but there was now a tremendous emptiness in his stomach.

He looked with disgust at the broth and milk, and gritting his teeth he started resolutely to walk. He took his time, and the operation was highly laborious, but he managed to attain his objective without tumbling down the stairs.

In the kitchen, he found bread and cheese on the sideboard, and after thirty days of baby food, he experienced once again the pleasure of chewing. Divine Providence helped him find a bottle of good Lambrusco within reach, and so Don Camillo was triumphantly able to complete the best lunch of his life.

Having placated his stomach, a deep, subtle malaise took control of Don Camillo, and the second glass of Lambrusco served only to make it worse instead of better. So he stood up, threw his cloak over his shoulders, went out of the kitchen and shuffled towards the sacristy door.

*

'Signore,' said Don Camillo to Christ on the high altar, 'I humbly beg your forgiveness for thinking you had forsaken me. Lord, maybe what I have done will hasten my end, but even if it costs me a month or even a year, or ten, of my life, I'll die happy because I have been able to acknowledge my mistake.'

'Do not torment yourself, Don Camillo,' replied the crucified Christ. 'I was expecting you, I knew you would come. Get up and go calmly back whence you came, because you know now that I'll be with you.'

Don Camillo rose up. Weariness weighed on his back and made his legs ache, but before leaving the church, he wanted to go into the little chapel containing the crib which, for the first Christmas in many years, he had not set up with his own hands.

The doctor was clearly right, Don Cesare was a capable young man. He had laid out the crib with care and truly admirable taste. Don Camillo would never have arranged the lights in such an atmospheric way, and even though the landscape had been made from the usual, time-worn elements, it all looked completely new.

Then, suddenly, Don Camillo espied something that made him catch his breath. He thought at first it must be his tired eyes deceiving him, and looked more closely. He had not been mistaken. The two little angels which hovered above the stable roof were the same as every year and were holding the same banner with the same promise of peace to men of good will. But the face and hands of one of them had been painted black.

Black as coal.

'Father!'

Don Camillo started and turned around sharply, to find himself face to face with the curate.

'Why are you here, Father, in this cold? It's madness!'

Don Camillo pointed to the black angel.

'Have you seen this, Don Cesare?' he gasped. 'Who could have done it?'

The curate chuckled. 'I did it, Father,' he explained quietly. 'Christ came to earth for the salvation of all mankind, black people included. Cannot black people enter the Kingdom of Heaven? There is no question of race in the House of God. The Church is with those who suffer and in the world today black people are among those who suffer most. And what about the three Magi who came to adore Jesus? Wasn't one of them black?'

'There is no evidence for that in fact,' answered Don Camillo. 'Saint Matthew simply speaks of "some Magi coming from the East".'

'If, later, the Church felt the need to rule that one of the Magi was black,' replied the curate with some force, 'that surely means it wanted to give a more universal significance to Christianity. Unfortunately, only two angels were available to me. If I had had three, one of them would have been white, one black, and one yellow. It is crazy to ignore China. Seven hundred million souls...'

'Souls are pure spirit and not differentiated by colour,' said Don Camillo.

'Then why do you want the angels to be white?' demanded the curate petulantly.

'White is in fact the presence of all colours across the spectrum, it reflects all colours equally,' replied Don Camillo.

The curate grinned. 'Father, we cannot turn a social question into a technical one. The Church cannot sustain itself with sophistries and quibbles. The Church must break out of its mediaeval lethargy and adapt to present reality. The Church cannot go on walking in the clouds, but along the road where men of good will walk. By which I mean not the exploiters, but the workers...'

The little priest was quite worked up now, leaping about and gesticulating as he spoke, so it was only a matter of time before he lost his balance and ended up on the floor, but two providential hands emerged from the shadows to catch him and get him back on his feet.

'Take my advice, Don Cesare,' said a fatherly voice, 'and go to bed.'

The little priest tottered off and eventually managed to slip away behind the altar.

*

'What are you doing here, at this hour?' asked Don Camillo.

'I came with the curate,' explained Peppone, coming out of the shadows. 'You know how it is. He's young, not used to drinking, and a couple of glasses left him three sheets to the wind.'

'You mean you picked him up in a tavern somewhere!' exclaimed Don Camillo.

'No, Father. He's a very good young man, even if he *is* a priest. He came to have a discussion with us in the mayoral office. He's had an excellent cultural and political education and possesses a fine sense of democracy and solidarity with the working class. It was a very interesting discussion, with positive outcomes.'

'I see,' muttered Don Camillo. 'You managed to get him drunk.'

'A hangover is not a positive outcome,' said Peppone firmly. 'This, however, *is* a positive outcome.'

Don Camillo moved closer to the lamp so that he could read the sheet of paper which Peppone had passed to him, and found it was an application to join the Communist Party signed by Don Cesare. Don Camillo held the paper over a candle flame and set it alight.

'Go ahead, Father,' said Peppone. 'Even if he'd been sober when he signed it, I'd have burned it myself. Priests are less dangerous as enemies than as allies.'

Don Camillo took the little black-painted angel off the roof of the crib.

'Comrade,' he asked Peppone, 'do you think it'll clean up if I put it in bleach?'

'I dare say, Father,' replied Peppone. 'It's your soul that will always be black, even if you boil it in caustic soda. You need to think about that.'

'No need,' exclaimed Don Camillo. 'I'm cured.'

Before returning to bed, Don Camillo gave the little angel an energetic scrub with bleach, and made it white again. Rather too white, for he had to repaint the eyes, mouth, hair, etc.

But that night Don Camillo slept peacefully, and in the morning he was ready for his first Mass.

The story leaves us with the suggestion that Don Camillo might be guilty of racism. There is dialogue concerning 'the facts' of the history of the Nativity and of the science of colour and so on, and before we know it the politics of the scenario have overtaken the celebration of the Nativity, the very nub of Giovanni's 'birth of God in the soul' theology. Notably, Giovanni does not bring the voice of *il Cristo* into play. Don Camillo scrubs the angel clean, goes directly to bed and sleeps soundly. We may suppose that he is going to struggle with some of the changes that are afoot in the post-war world, especially if he goes to bed without signing off with *il Cristo* first.

In 1962–3 Giovanni was invited to make a documentary called *La Rabbia* (*Rage*), with the film director Pier Paolo Pasolini, a passionate Marxist and self-declared atheist, apparently in complete opposition to the Christian humorist, satirist Giovannino Guareschi. They were to take half the film each to address society's ills and to pit their views against one another. It was a challenge to create a documentary film editing snippets of previous news footage about this era of great intellectual ferment and transition, over-dubbing it with their own commentary and music.

Pasolini wrote to Guareschi: 'You will come out the winner of our dispute. But what is victory? Making people clap their hands or making people's hearts beat for you.' Pasolini thought mistakenly that Giovanni would defend the establishment institutions of the Western world, leaving himself in true Marxist fashion to subvert the status quo. But Giovanni turned out to be the master at subversion and in fact had much to say in agreement with Pasolini. For example, both were opposed to modernity – to the materialism of the modern world, to consumerism and to the Americanisation of Italy. For Pasolini, modernity meant the death of beauty (which he attached to Marilyn Monroe); for Giovanni it meant the forfeiture of family values.

But what is most notable about the film is that Pasolini's approach, which is powerfully channelled, Marxist diatribe, does not have the lightness of touch of Guareschi's. With humour as his weapon Guareschi juxtaposes the serious with the satirical, which deepens the appeal of his argument.

As a Marxist, Pasolini identifies the only 'true' and free class of people as those as yet untainted by bourgeois values – he fights for the disaffected sub-proletariat to prevent it being sucked into the lower middle-class; he fights for the African tribesman against imperial exploitation with all the passion of a Rousseau, whose myth of the *bon sauvage* idealised tribal man living in a state of Nature. For Pasolini the tribesman can do no wrong, so cruelly has he been exploited throughout history by the white man. Giovanni provoked Pasolini about this. He wrote: 'When I see a black man cutting a white man's throat, I say "poor white man"; you say, "poor black man".' One is reminded of Giovanni's words, quoted above: 'Humour is not merely a literary device to entertain, rather a particular way of broaching and understanding life by reducing facts, episodes and sensations to their actual value, as opposed to the value they take on in the context in which they arise.'

Again, for Pasolini, the rhythms of tribal dance point to a pure, innocent natural way of life to which the decadent, bourgeois white man is blind. Meanwhile, Giovanni uses music ironically to question this, attaching a sound track of a European-style military march to footage of black warriors performing a frenetic ritual dance. It is an extraordinary moment in the film, for the white man's music fits the black man's dance so truly we cannot believe that they are not meant for one another.

It might have driven Pasolini wild with fury, and others who failed to appreciate that Giovanni, far from laughing at the tribal warriors, was laughing at a tyrannical Marxist dialectic which forbids humour and fears a far-seeing satirical eye.

When the film was released in 1963, it was unaccountably withdrawn after a very short time and Giovanni's half mysteriously disappeared.

It was not until 2008, at the Venice Film Festival, that the film again came before the public eye, but only Pasolini's half. The ensuing controversy, which enveloped Giuseppe Bertolucci, the director of the *La Rabbia* restoration project and head of the committee for the centennial celebrations of Giovanni's birth, only abated when *La Rabbia* was shown to great public acclaim at the Fiuggi Family Festival in 2009, with both parts intact. More recently the film has been made available commercially as a DVD.

In 1964, one year after he had locked horns with Giovannii in *La Rabbia*, and one year after first publication of *Comrade Don Camillo*, in which a group of communist activists see beyond the repressive, politically-correct, virtual world they occupy to embrace their more radical instinct for the spiritual, the hard-line Marxist and self-declared atheist Pasolini suddenly and unaccountably and from deep within also lifted the political veil and created a spiritual masterpiece, *The Gospel According to St Matthew*, which the Vatican declared in 2015 is 'the best film ever made about Jesus Christ'.

Piccolo mondo; Piccolo è bello

It was a great personal disappointment to Giovanni that the films of his Don Camillo stories, made between 1952 and 1965, for all their commercial success, failed to grasp his deeper, satirical purpose to persuade us to let go of the ideas that drag us around with them and wake up to the reality of life beyond politics. A reality of such infinite interconnectedness, interdependence and latent possibility that any single ideological template or '-ism', be it Communism, Capitalism, Socialism, Catholicism or whatever – will, like an ill-fitting gasket in Peppone's workshop, inevitably prove an inadequate interface in the workshop of life.

After Giovanni had dispensed with the communists he began to criticise the Social Democrats and De Gasperi himself. He held no candle to any particular political ideology, he was at war with hegemony and it was an ideologically disinterested war. Certainly, being anti-Communist did not mean that he was pro-Capitalist. Post-war America had emerged as the dominant power, militarily, economically and culturally, and was now exercising its dominion over Europe not by making war but by spreading billions of dollars across it through the Marshall Plan, named after US Secretary of State George Marshall, to ensure a united front in the Cold War against Soviet Russia. In 'Two Robbers Become Three' Giovanni satirised the apparent benefits:

These were prosperous times. It is not known how the thing worked, but it had to be well thought out because people laboured less and less and earned more and more. A sense of well-being brought with it a lot of stuff quite new to us: like night, cabaret, striptease, festivals, Whiskey a Go Go, sexy cinema, rock music, rock fashion, even rock Mass.

The women no longer nursed their babies and instead raised them with tinned feed. They didn't even cook anymore, either because they didn't have the time, or because the modern, beautiful kitchen interiors would have been wasted on it. So they bought everything ready made: canned food, frozen food, hot food from rotisseries, even delicatessens and 'frying tonight' shops.

Comfortable, ready-made living meant that every family had to have special zones in the house for a television, an enormous quantity of household appliances, and the essential car in order to escape from home for the weekend and to spend summer holidays by the sea, in the mountains, or on a cruise.[125]

---
[125] *Don Camillo and Don Chichi* (Pilot, 2021).

New-look kitchens ran with water, both hot and cold. Bright electric lights and heaters replaced carbon-stained gas lamps and coal fires. Gas-powered ovens appeared in place of traditional black, coal-driven ranges. Milk was kept fresh in refrigerators instead of enamel bowls of cold water, and machine washers would soon dispense with the old poss tub and mangle in the back yard. From America came not only fridges, washing machines, cameras, reel-to-reel tape recorders, but always the latest records, which no one in continental Europe had yet heard.

In the twenty years from 1950, per capita income in Italy grew more rapidly than in any other European country. Between 1958 and 1965, the percentage of Italian families owning a television set rose from 12% to 49%, washing machines from 3% to 23%, and fridges from 13% to 55%.

Even the communist mayor of Ponteratto transformed his garage workshop into a large emporium selling such appliances on the never-never, justifying joining the capitalist bandwagon by getting his comrades in the local Communist Section to fund the enterprise on the basis that 'if the working-class people today want a car, a washing machine, a television, a fridge and so on, then it should be their comrades who sell them to them. That way profits will remain with the working people, because the profits of the store will be divided among its shareholders.'

Meanwhile, the attendant mass production methods, advertising, cheap goods and expansionism were instilling in the national psyche a preoccupation with *acquisition*, especially at Christmastide. Soon, in pamphlets and sketches, Giovanni was railing at the growing freneticism of life and the unhappiness which he saw that the newly-minted consumerism would incur as people ran around trying to make more money, get into debt on the never-never, or strike for better wages in order to enjoy an ever higher standard of living. These became regular themes in the Don Camillo stories. The higher the standard of living, the higher the level people would reach for. Dissatisfaction with the present would lead to impatience to want more, and the cost of that to the Earth was already this writer's song:

'Man is behaving as someone who has a beautiful peach, but throws away the pulp to gnaw on the nut,' he wrote. And 'the Devil, when he passes through our streets, no longer stinks of sulphur but of petrol'.[126]

The connection between consumerism, natural resources and the bleak economic and ecological future of the human race was thus made, and Giovanni was not the only person making it. Out of a strikingly similar seedbed arose

---

[126] 'Old Parish Priests Have Strong Bones', *Don Camillo and Don Chichi* (1963)

Ernst Friedrich Schumacher, philosopher, economist and, like Giovanni, a wartime political prisoner who put his time 'away' to good use.

With Hitler's rise to power, Schumacher, born in the city of Bonn in western Germany in 1911, had taken refuge in England, and being German he was interned in a British POW camp, until rescued by the leading economist Maynard Keynes when the latter realised how important were the ideas that Schumacher was developing in captivity. After the war, such was the respect for Schumacher's ideas that Hugh Gaitskell, Minister of Fuel and Power in Clement Attlee's government in Britain, arranged for his appointment as Chief Economic Advisor to the National Coal Board. So began this provocative thinker's important career.

Guareschi and Schumacher never met but shared a vision of a world in which value was no longer calculated in terms of quantity of goods and services, continual growth and the idea that 'bigger was better'. Giovanni died five years before publication of Schumacher's bestselling book, *Small is Beautiful*, his radical challenge to profit-centred, expansionist economics at the heart of the world's social and environmental ills.

Schumacher argued for a people-centred economics, a model that satisfied people's needs, ecologically sound technology, respect for natural energy resources, and was at odds with the call of Western capitalism for globalisation, the process by which businesses seek to operate on an international scale and develop influence internationally, accumulating and using up natural resources and, as is happening today, using natural resources as a weapon to political power.

Giovanni meanwhile was batting on the same wicket, an uncompromising critic of the way things were being planned economically, socially and ecologically beyond Don Camillo's Little World, where in spite of fisticuffs breaking out between rivals, the people of the River Po could claim to be an effective part of a 'living' community in tune with not only the spirit of the place but their own and their neighbours' needs as well as those of the environment on which all depended.

In this section of Giovanni's war against hegemony he saw the psychological manipulation of people to acquire more consumer goods than they need and the preoccupation of Business constantly to grow bigger and bigger, as the ultimate dominating influence on people's lives. He foresaw the whole process alienating us from the realities of life on earth and threatening the very balance of Nature herself.

As early as 1957, he began working on a redefinition of what 'rich' would mean in the Little World of his dreams. 'The Richest Man in the World' appeared in *Candido* in that year and now, for the first time in English, here.[127]

---

[127] Il decimo clandestino (Rizzoli, 1982)

The hired car made it (thank goodness) to within about twenty metres of a shack, which an adjacent petrol station and rusty debris piled up under the porch suggested might be a garage.

As if everything had been organised by the tourist office, as soon as I got out of the car a big man in a mechanic's overalls came out of the shack, looking down the street and so I only had the minimal inconvenience of having to shout, 'Please!'

'French?'

'Italian,' I replied.

'Ah!' muttered the little man with the tone of someone who had derived the tree of knowledge from my one word.

Then he pointed decisively towards the rear of the Oldsmobile and, having opened the flap and removed the fuel cap, checked the petrol with a stick picked up from the side of the road.

That 'Ah!' of his just before all this had bothered me: and now, by connecting it to what the man was doing, I saw reason to be bothered yet more:

Even in Italy, I told him, we know that in order for a car to run you need to put petrol in its tank!

The little man threw away the stick, replaced the cap, closed it tight, then, calmly, explained:

'I fought in Italy, I know Italy. Italian cars can travel forty-five miles with a gallon of petrol; ours do ten or twelve.'

I could have told him that even an Italian dreamer is able to understand how between the 500 displacement of a Topolino and the 5,000 of an Oldsmobile there is a difference of four and a half litres: but I took note of his honest intentions and let it go.

We pushed the big car to the small forecourt in front of the garage and the little man looked into his patient.

'Small piece,' he said as he emerged from the bonnet, showing me a contraption that he had fished out from I don't know where. 'But I have to send to Wolkys for a replacement and I won't get it until tonight.'

I looked around in dismay: the mechanic's hut seemed isolated from the rest of the world and the great asphalt road ran through a desolate, greenish desert.

'Here is high ground and you can't see it,' the big man consoled me, pointing south, 'but Kribby is nearby, only ten miles away. In Kribby you'll find food and a place to sleep. I'll take you there and tomorrow morning, as soon as the car is ready, I'll come and pick you up.

Kribby was a small town like I had seen a hundred others since I'd been travelling America. In a kind of bazaar, which also functioned as a bar and restaurant, I found a clean bed in which to spend the night. But it was nine in the morning, and no matter how much I looked around, I found nothing that could ease me through the day.

It was hot and the mechanic agreed to have a drink with me:

'One glass,' he said, 'because I have a lot of things to do.'

'Blessed are you,' I exclaimed with a sigh. 'Although I don't know how I'll get through the evening.'

The mechanic seemed to comprehend my sad situation and, while he was throwing down his beer, he gave an impression of someone thinking of things that have nothing to do with beer.

'Wolkys,' he said, placing the glass back on the zinc counter. 'At ten, the bus passes by and in an hour drops you off at Wolkys. Wolkys is a big city with one and a half million inhabitants and there you will find a thousand ways to pass the time. Then, tonight at seven, the bus will bring you back here along with the part.'

'Wolkys, dirty town,' exclaimed a nearby drinker as if talking to himself while leaning heavily against the counter.

The mechanic looked at me, then shrugged and walked away without saying anything.

I took a peek at the guy: he was a man of about fifty-five, massive but lean. He was looking at the contents of his glass against the light and that brown, gaunt and sturdy hand looked familiar to me. It had to be the hand of a farmer.

'Wolkys,' the man repeated, still taking an interest in his glass. 'Dirty city. And that's not just my opinion.'

Frankly, I didn't give a damn about Wolkys, and I didn't like the idea of having crossed the ocean in order to be punched by a Michigan farmer. And since this fellow, towards the end of his last proposition, had turned my way, staring at me defiantly, I thought it appropriate to spell out my position:

'I am a foreigner,' I told him, 'and, to me, all cities in the United States are equally respectable.'

The man approved, nodding his head:

'Well said,' he replied. 'If you want, I'll give you a lift. I live in Wolkys.'

He set off and I followed him: the guy's car seemed to have been a sort of hybrid built to order, an estate adapted to a pickup truck with the grace of a tailor who, after cutting off a pair of black tuxedo trousers at the knee, adapted them to a work-wear garment by integrating them with the lower part of a pair of blue canvas breeches.

In the cabin, however, it was comfortable enough and we leapt away at near G-force velocity.

After about ten minutes of absolute silence, the man said to the windshield:

'Wolkys, dirty city, inhabited by 1,777,420 wretches, plus four normal people: me, my wife, my son and my son's son.'

He must have felt that he had not clarified the family situation adequately because he added:

'My son's wife is one of the 1,777,420 wretches who has realised that she can no longer live without the filth.'

He took a hand off the steering wheel and pointed behind him to the window through to the pickup area to the rear. I turned and saw that lying on a bed of straw was a white refrigerator.

'I went this morning to shop in Drybourg. The round trip is 200 miles. But it's worth it.'

'You mean less expensive than staying put and shopping in Wolkys?' I asked.

'No,' he replied. 'You spend a little more, but there is the great advantage of not benefiting some wretch from Wolkys.'

Several kilometres of silence ensued, then the man gave vent to his robust voice once again:

'Wolkys is a dirty town,' he said. 'But *you* will like it. You foreigners come here to see the skyscrapers, the vending machines, the factories, the progress and the other junk.'

'No,' I explained. 'I came here because I'm interested in old America. With all the movies we've seen and the books and magazines we read as kids, old America is, in a sense, part of *our* past, of our life. We are sentimental.'

The man pondered the matter for a long time, then said:

'When my Johnny was still a little boy and my wife couldn't manage the house on her own, we had an Italian here – worked in my house for ten years. His name was Micke and when he had a drink he'd get all nostalgic for home and then he would weep. Probably a bit like you, I guess.'

'I'm afraid it is,' I replied. 'But I don't need the drink to start crying.'

The man shook his head:

'He was a good boy and now I'm sure he'll be fine. When you get back home you should go say hello to him. I'll give you his full name.'

'Where does he come from?'

'I don't know exactly, but it's around Cassino. During the war he went off to fight in Italy and never came back. He's in an American cemetery there. They'll be able to tell you where at the American Embassy. He really wanted to go back to Italy. So he'll be fine there.'

I felt an urge to tell him that in Italy we are all fine, especially when we are dead. But, since I wasn't convinced of it, I kept quiet.

'He had it up to here with those wretched Wolkys people, like so many do,' muttered the man. 'Wolkys was a paradise before those wretches transformed the city into a hell of concrete, asphalt, cars, electric wires, pipes. All they see is dollars. '

'It happens like that all over the world,' I consoled him. 'With us they are not thinking of dollars but of lire, and they're ruining everything, progress kills civilisation. For a little money they would sell their souls, if they had souls.'

'*Fetenti*,' he said in Italian. The man must have learned a lot of important things from Micke.

It suddenly seemed to me as if Wolkys had risen out of the darkest depths of the earth.

'Where do you want me to put you down?' the man inquired.

'Anywhere is fine.'

'What are you interested in seeing? The industrial area?'

'No, no,' I protested. 'I'm interested in seeing the historic quarter first of all.'

The man shook his head.

'Wolkys has no history. Nor has anything historic ever happened to Wolkys. '

'I didn't make myself clear: I meant the old city.'

The man chuckled:

'In that case, we have arrived. The historical part of Wolkys is on the far outskirts.'

He stopped the car and, without listening to my thanks, put me down and drove away.

Indeed, there was a little of old America and, indeed, a whisper of old Europe about the place. Traffic was scarce and only decrepit cars were evident in the quarter's narrow streets.

I found myself in a poor neighbourhood un-gentrified: a half-socks neighbourhood I guess inhabited by people who, in the past, unable to take a seat in the auditorium of life and not feeling like occupying the gallery, would content themselves by standing behind the last row of stalls to give themselves a measure of self-esteem.

A small square with a bench in the shade of an ancient tree reconciled me with Wolkys and with life. And, because the heat was heavy and I was devoured by thirst I also appreciated the presence of a Coca-Cola vending machine in the immediate vicinity of the bench.

The whole world is a country and even in America there are, as in Europe, old gentlemen who, not knowing what else to do, amble around the city in search of people with whom to chat.

They therefore have a particular predilection for places where there are benches: and, when I had drained the bottle of Coca-Cola, unsurprisingly one such old fellow presented himself before me.

Sitting himself down next to me on the bench, he began by telling me that the day was exceptionally hot and, after ten minutes, he knew everything about me, my business and my family.

He was a very nice old man, a retired middle school teacher and, when I asked him why the old quarter of Wolkys was located on the far edge of the city, he gave me a look so full of emotion and gratitude as to warm me to him.

His intention, evidently, would have been to begin at the beginning with Christopher Columbus, but he must have read so much anguish in my gaze as to decide instead to wind forward a few years.

So, after about an hour, I discovered that the inhabitants of Wolkys had soon realised that where the city had originally been built was the worst place to construct it. Apparently, the river that ran through the town, finding porous soil, leaked into the bedrock there and made the houses unsafe and unhealthy. Thus it had developed along the two banks of the river, towards the south-east, towards, that is, the highlands.

At some point, tired of building bridges and walls to direct and regulate the river, the citizens of Wolkys abandoned the northern bank altogether, developing the city only on the southern bank.

His story seemed to me rather banal: something that the old man frankly recognised by the end of his detailed exposition.

'The city,' he said, 'grew to become a very important industrial centre, as has happened to thousands and thousands of other cities in every part of the world. Then in 1906, when the architect, Perkinson, was elected mayor gave Wolkys its own particular story.

'Perkinson was a genius,' explained the old man. He understood that Wolkys's development had to be disciplined, keeping in mind not the needs of the present but those of centuries to come, and he drew up a great *master plan*. Wolkys expanded dramatically and, given the nature of the terrain, tended to lengthen: what was envisaged was not a single city but a series of small self-sufficient cities, each of which would have its own unmistakable characteristic. Once the general plan was approved, the first construction began: the City of the Sun.'

The old man said this in a solemn tone and, getting up, drew a large square on the ground with the tip of his stick.

'The great Perkinson project was later abandoned because personal interests got in the way of it and other self-interested agents took over,' continued the old man. But the City of the Sun is a reality and so beautiful that it has become the centre of Wolkys, the heart of the city.'

The old man completed his drawing by marking out the points of the compass on the edge of the square.

'The City of the Sun stands 1,730 metres long and 1,730 metres wide,' explained the old man, who had resumed work with the tip of his cane. 'Each side is divided into eight parts so as to obtain a lattice of sixty-four squares. At the centre of the large square, there is the city centre public square – you would call it the *Piazza del Sole*, which occupies four squares. Twelve large avenues, each twenty metres wide branch off from it: three to the north, three to the south, three to the east and three to the west. The twelve avenues represent the months of the year: January, February and March are in the North sector; April, May, June in the East sector; July, August and September in the South and October, November and December in the West. Do you understand the concept? '

I believed I did.

'In the centre of the *Piazza del Sole* is the monument to the Sun, with a Rose of the Winds that offers directions to whoever is looking for some place in the City of the Sun. Parallel to the twelve large Avenues of the Months, there are routes which, together with the twelve avenues, divide the city into sixty units.

'By making a single block of the North-East, North-West, South-East, South-West units they total fifty-two. Twelve months, fifty-two weeks!'

But Perkinson didn't stop there.

Each of the fifty-two units was divided by seven roads: four in the North-South direction and three in the East-West direction. Thus, in every normal unit, twenty rectangular blocks of forty-by-fifty metres were obtained: the area required to construct a decent size building. Naturally, in the four triple units, the blocks were larger and used for the construction of rich people's houses. Thus, 365 roads were generated: one for each day of the year. And each of these roads, in fact, bears the name of the day that belongs to it.

The City of the Sun is delimited, but at the same time joined to the wider Wolkys district, by four peripheral avenues, which are called Perimeter North, Perimeter South, Perimeter East and Perimeter West. Do you need to go to 'January 2' street? January is in the North: here is Avenue January, here is the weekly unit and the daily road! Is it not all perfect?'

I took the liberty of raising an objection.

'There are 365 streets: what happens in leap years, when there are 366?'

The old man smiled:

'I was waiting for you to say that! Perkinson knew the calendar. In the last frame of February, there is a small road that splits a block in two. It can be barred with chains and the chains are removed only in leap years. The little street is called February 29.'

The old man was justly proud:

'If you see nothing else, you *must* see the City of the Sun,' he told me. 'The bus stop for the *Piazza del Sole* – is just a stone's throw away.'

I begged to be excused:

'Honestly, I would rather do without it. My mind-set doesn't get along with planned progress and I hate all that is now known as *'rational'*. For me, there is nothing more depressing than a 'model' city or neighbourhood.'

'You must see the City of the Sun because, in the *Piazza del Sole*, there is the most extraordinary monument in all America – perhaps in the world.'

The bus unloaded us in the middle of the *Piazza del Sole* at the foot of a colossal gilded bronze monument, which presented a sparkling allegorical miscellany: the Sun, the Four Seasons, the Cardinal Points and the inevitable Progress that, when lit with a three or four thousand candles, escaped the darkness of Regression.

'Just as I anticipated,' I said less than enthusiastically.

The old man shook his head:

'The monument I was telling you about isn't this one here: it's between Avenue Luglio and Avenue Agosto.'

I had learned my lesson: I turned to the south, aided by the allegory of the Rose of the Winds, yet, between Avenue Luglio and Avenue Agosto, I didn't see a damn thing. As on the other sides of the square the area between Avenue Luglio and Avenue September was full of tall buildings and arcades and wonder shops, but the South-East unit was empty. A gate delimited it and, behind the gate, a high, rustic hedge of green.

'The famous monument I spoke of is *in there*,' the old man explained. 'Behind that hedge.'

We crossed the square and, approaching the gate, I tried to peek through.

'I see only trees, grass and a little homestead,' I said to the old man.

'That's right, the monument is within the homestead. Its owner is Tom Gorth; he is fifty-five years old. His great-grandfather bought this piece of land in 1856 and his life's work was to make it productive. He succeeded and, fifty years later, when they came to discuss selling the whole plot to the Perkinson project as a building area, he chased them away, leaving them in no doubt of his feelings on the matter. The old man died shortly afterwards and, as the city continued to develop damnably, Perkinson's people raised the matter with his son. And then with his son's son, who is this Tom Gorth.

'Tom Gorth's unit is now the only space in the City of the Sun unaligned to the project. And, today, the City of the Sun is the epicentre of Wolkys. They have tried everything to get rid of the Gorths; they brought up the aesthetics of the matter, the public utility, and Tom Gorth replied that the aesthetics of a cornfield are much more valuable than that of a reinforced concrete block and when entrepreneurs get together to build buildings, we cannot speak of public utility because the public is made up of much more than forty or fifty people. Originally, only a hedge separated the unit from the city, but they forced him to install a gate and he did all but slaughter himself over the decision, but in the end gave in and installed one.

'He works as a farmer. There are about five and a half hectares of very fertile land in there. He works it with the help of his son, his wife and his son's wife, he has some fine cattle in the stable, but he is now focusing on vegetables because the councillors are studying ways to prohibit him from keeping cattle in the city centre.

I immediately liked Tom Gorth:

'And is it going well?'

'He's happy,' replied the old man. 'Do you know how much they offered him for his land last year?'

'I have no idea.'

'It's exactly 53,824 square metres at about 460 dollars a metre, that's around twenty-six million dollars.'

I did the count: 'It's impossible!' I stammered.

'That's the truth,' the old man replied. 'And he will refuse even when they offer him 500 and then 600 and then 1,000 dollars a metre. And his son Johnny is made of the same stuff as his father.'

I thanked the old man as it was time to go eat, and we broke up. But I didn't go to a restaurant: instead I walked around the large green square and came again to the entrance gate. It was enough for me to turn the handle to find myself in a normal farm wonderfully tended and with vegetables on display. The farmhouse was in the centre of the farm and, under the porch, stood Tom Gorth… The guy who had brought me to Wolkys in a pickup.

'You forgot to give me your friend's name,' I said to him.

He looked at me suspiciously:

'How did you find me? Wolkys is huge.'

'Yes, but there are few guys like you in it.'

The son and his boy appeared and looked like identikit copies of Tom Gorth.

'This is the fellow I picked up in Kribby,' Tom Gorth explained to his son. 'He wants to go see Micke.'

'That's kind,' muttered the son.

The son's wife came and said it was time for lunch, and it seemed to me that Tom had exaggerated by ranking her among the 1,777,420 wretches of Wolkys just because (I surmised) she had wanted a refrigerator.

Following my thoughts he made me say them aloud:

'Cold was not on the agenda of the people of Wolkys and ice is a genuine need, otherwise the Eternal Father would not have created it.'

Tom looked at me:

'That's fair enough,' he muttered. 'But the Eternal Father doesn't make ice by machine. In any case, come and sit at our table: there is enough for you too.'

'I accept gratefully because the peasants in my area would do the same and I live among peasants.'

At table we talked about land and crops.

'May I ask,' I said at a good moment, 'how much do you make from this farm?'

'Last year it netted me 3,500 dollars.'

I did the math and exclaimed:

'Two million and two hundred and forty thousand lire for seventeen and a half biolche!' Four or five times more than we would. '

'The vegetables are the secret,' Tom Gorth explained. 'It also depends on how the land is worked.'

After dinner, we relaxed in the shade of a plant.

Tom Gorth pointed out the large buildings that besieged the small farm from north, east and west:

'Damned wretches: they choke my farm!' he cursed. 'Is that how things go on with you?'

'They do worse in Italy. With us you even pay taxes on the value of a building area.'

Tom Gorth didn't want to believe it and after explaining to him in detail how things were, I said to him laughing: 'Before you Americans came to teach us about democracy, these things never happened.'

Tom Gorth shook his head for a long time, then muttered:

'The Kingdom of Italy. That's why Micke went home, only to be killed there... Better he doesn't know what you know.'

I stayed at the farm until four in the afternoon. Before leaving, I took out my Rolleiflex and asked Tom Gorth:

'Can I take a photograph of the richest man in the world?'

He let himself be photographed and, before leaving him, I picked a bunch of wildflowers.

'Micke will love it if I bring him these,' I explained.

The wheat was turning golden in a nearby field and I plucked an ear:

'This is for me. I want to take home something really beautiful from America.'

The family accompanied me up to the cart track. When I got to the gate, I turned around and they were still standing there and they looked like the last defenders of a besieged citadel.

All around was the red-hot concrete of Progress and the horrendous neatness of the artificial City of the Sun.[128]

In 1952 Giovanni had moved from the city of Milan back to the land of the Don Camillo stories. He chose Roncole Verdi, a village fifty miles or so west of Fontanelle, where he'd been born forty-four years earlier. He bought some land and built the house he had been dreaming of for years. Over the following two years he 'designed and had the furniture built, was engaged with the garden, and bustled about with nails and tools: these are the most beautiful memories,' his son Alberto remembers. 'Those years were really the only serene years for our parents.'

He died thirteen years later, weakened by imprisonment in Parma's San Francisco jail, serving a sentence for libel after he published photocopies of two wartime letters allegedly written by former Prime Minister Alcide De Gasperi asking the Allies to bomb the outskirts of Rome in order to demoralise German collaborators. After a two-month trial a court found in favour of De Gasperi. Giovanni declined to appeal and was committed to prison:

---

[128] *Little Bourgeois World* (Rizzoli, 1998).

Piccolo mondo; Piccolo è bello

In 1953 I ran into a bigwig and I will spend thirteen months in San Francesco prison in Parma,' he said. 'And, to tell the truth, I will be treated like the most esteemed professional robbers, thieves, rapists, murderers...

In December 1954, in a Christmas letter sent to Ennia, he turned himself into a Christmas tree, dressed in his prison uniform and with the prison slop bucket on his head. Upon his release, he walked straightway into the bathroom at Roncole Verdi and found his other self – his '*Giovannino d'aria*' – waiting for him:

'In the midst of this confusion of photographers and journalists,' my Giovannino of the air explained to me, 'this was the only place I could hope to be alone with you.'

I locked the door because nothing can stop a photographer's march. Then we talked.

'Did my knapsack from the *Lager* work its magic?' he asked me. I still had it on my shoulders and I showed it to him.

'It stinks of mould,' exclaimed the other Giovannino.

'It spent 409 days in the prison warehouse,' I explained. 'They didn't leave it in my cell, because it's not legal...'

He sighed.

'Did you bring any other stuff home?' he inquired.

'Nothing: I only brought back what I had taken with me.'

'Not even a thought, an idea, a hope?' I shook my head.

'In a way it's worse than then,' he exclaimed.

Buon Natale!

'In a way, yes,' I admitted. 'And in the other way too.'

The *Giovannino d'aria* observed me carefully: 'On the other hand, you are fatter than you were in the *Lagers*.'

'Not "fatter": heavier,' I said.

He looked at me suspiciously. 'At our age you don't waste 409 days of your life,' he said. 'Are you going to stand for election?'

'No. And I don't even think about writing *My Prisons*, nor about getting up a film script. Those 409 days have not been discarded: my children have counted them one by one.'

He chuckled: 'And your wife didn't count them?'

'Yes, but in another sense.'

I opened the knapsack and started rummaging inside to find the jar of baking soda.

'How many kilos did you use?' asked *Giovannino d'aria*.

'A bit, and only in the beginning,' I replied, showing him the almost full jar. 'But, now, I have to get my stomach ache back. I miss him.'

The *Giovannino d'aria* bent down, better to follow the manoeuvring of my hands among the junk in the knapsack.

'Isn't that a dream I see in there?' he asked suddenly.

'No, it's the blue goose that Carlotta brought me for Christmas. I have no dreams with me, because, for 409 days, my thoughts belonged to the State administration, and, three times each night, the guards came to the cell on behalf of the State to check on the dreams I dreamed. Now, to gather my thoughts, I need to find my stomach ache.'

Looking back from the vantage point of 1963, after the appalling experience of his second term in prison, he would call an end to his post-war dreams for a new Italy in a preface written for the last collection of Don Camillo stories to be published in his lifetime. However, one paragraph (the first of the two below) was notably absent from the Italian edition on publication, and the whole book was absent from the catalogue of his English-language publishers until 2021:

What a difference there is between the material poverty of 1945 and the spiritual poverty of the newly rich of 1963! The wind that blows among the skyscrapers of the 'economic miracle' stinks of sex and sewerage and death. In the prosperous *dolce-vita* Italy all hope of a better world is dead.

...Nevertheless, in our own Little World, it is still possible to find the sun, the moon, the stars, the wonderful stories held in the stones of the houses, the life that swarms on the bank of a ditch in Spring, the dew that shines at dawn on the green leaves, the sky in which the ship of the imagination sails, the colours of the seasons.

Schumacher claimed the same image, 'As for myself, I may not know how to stir up winds that might propel us, or our ship, towards a better world. But I can hoist the sail, so that when the wind comes up, it will propel us all.'[129]

---

[129] *Osip* – Blog di Paolo Tritto. *Un mondo piccolo e bello.* Vite parallele di Fritz Schumacher e Giovannino Guareschi.